POLLYANNA GAY

POLLYANNA

GAY

JER LONG

ISBN: 978-1-958754-45-0
Library of Congress Control Number: 2023911993

Cover Designed by Michael Hardison
Interior Designed by Sami Langston
Production management by Haley Simpkiss

Printed in the United States of America

Published by
Brandylane Publishers, Inc.
5 S. 1st Street
Richmond, Virginia 23219

Brandylane
Publishers, Inc.
Publishing books since 1985

brandylanepublishers.com

I dedicate this book to each Pollyanna, gay or otherwise, who dares to bravely contest rude realities capable of strangling hope from the tender cry for help. Imagining a life as it should be, better than it often is, they are the future guardians of aspiration.

DISCLAIMER

This is a work of fiction. All characters, organizations, and events portrayed in this novel are either products of the author's imagination or are used fictitiously.

CHAPTER 1

THERE'S NO BUSINESS LIKE SHOWBUSINESS

"Hello!" I called out as I struggled with my overstuffed vinyl Samsonite. One of the suitcase's wheels caught on a buckled porch plank, and I slammed against the screen door.

"Get rid of that," someone inside whispered. A door banged shut, echoing through the cedar log cabin, followed by the sounds of sliding drawers and bare feet pounding the naked wood floor.

I bent over to right my bag and felt the door smack hard against my backside. "Wah!" I belched like a bludgeoned bullfrog.

"August Applegate, I presume." The voice was tenor-pitched, spiced with a snide nasal slide.

Faster than a jittery Jack-in-the-box, I popped to attention. "That's me," I spit out, brushing the seat of my khaki shorts.

"Farley Fairfield." The young man held the door open with his bony foot. He was pale and placid-faced, with a shock of Medusa-wild black hair curling from a parted patch of orange roots. "A bellboy is not included with the price of admission."

I tittered slightly at his joke—if it *was* a joke—but since he didn't crack a smile, I folded mine up for the moment.

Although he was a hair past six feet in height, Farley's excessively thin physique stretched him visually to the lofty height of Gregory Peck. With one hand on his narrow hip, he held a cigarette in the other, Marlene Dietrich-style. A trail of wispy gray smoke snaked from the tip of its ash, circled his buzzard-bent neck, and disappeared into his wide, pulsating nostrils.

I stepped across the threshold, and the mile-long ash of his cigarette immediately broke free and settled on my white bucks. I offered my hand to him, but he only stared at it as if it was Captain Hook's hook.

"You're in the nanny's corner," he said flatly, pointing to the bed at the far end of the room.

The bathroom door squeaked open, and a fair-haired man, square jawed with hallowed cheeks that were reminiscent of Thutmose's bust of Queen Nefertiti, stepped out of the shadowed vestibule. "Hello," he said in a honied baritone. "I'm Pete Pace."

"Peter Pakington Pace," Farley chimed in. "One of the blue-blooded Pakington Paces from Philly's mainline."

Not exactly certain what or where this mainline was, I did what I always did in confusing situations: I smiled confidently. My smile had rescued me from many uncomfortable situations in the past, and judging from Pete's pleasant reaction, it was continuing to serve me well.

I heaved my mega-pound bag on the undressed mattress, and Farley brazenly unzipped it. "My God! It's Grace Kelly on Nation tour!" He peeled my pink cashmere sweater off the top, held it over his concave chest, and peered at his reflection in the mirror. "Too preppy for my coloration," he said, then tossed it on the bed.

"Stick to your basic black and white, Cruella," Pete jested, making the insult sound polite.

I continued unpacking, steering clear of the verbal duel unfolding before the large picture window. *Heavens!* I prayed not everyone at Buck's County Theatre Camp would be as witty or biting as they were. "You guys should be on the Carol Burnett Show."

Farley crinkled his nose. "A regular Fanny Brice."

Catching a glimpse of Pete through the dresser mirror, I blushed at the sight of him staring back at me. I was intimidated before I'd even made my bed. With the intensity of a Cheshire cat charming a mouse, his stare made the hair on my forearms stand on end. "It certainly is beautiful up here," I said, my voice cracking slightly.

"It's not Folsom Prison or Sing-Sing," Farley said, "but as a third-rate internment camp, it's unparalleled."

Pete fiddled with the cord on the wooden blinds. "It's obvious we accept all levels of talent here."

I snapped the tail of the crisp, bleached sheet my mother had pressed, and it bloomed into a dome, stirring up a gentle breeze.

The smell of Mama's lavender laundry soap reminded me of home.

Several of Farley's *Playbill* magazines that had been stacked on the edge of the desk flittered to the floor in the breeze I created. Unaware of its proximity to my foot, I accidently stepped on one. Its slick matte cover shifted beneath my shoe, ripping from its binding.

"Jesus Christ Mary!" Farley screeched, his hazel eyes shooting invisible arrows at my head. "Off! Off!" He reached between my legs, rescuing the photo of Angela Lansbury as I hopped from one foot to the other.

My face burned beet red, and the jugular vein in my neck throbbed with the passion of a Tchaikovsky concerto. I bleated, "I'm so sorry! I'm *so* sorry!"

Pete fired Farley a crippling look, and Farley's seething anger rapidly deflated to a snort.

"Accidents happen," Farley muttered unconvincingly. He pressed the flat of his hand over Ms. Lansbury's deeply creased face.

I gathered the remainder of the *Playbills* off the knotty pine floor and handed them to Farley. He growled and snatched them from my grip. Recognizing the star on the front of one, I enthusiastically gushed, "You saw Mary Martin in *One Touch of Venus*?"

Farley opened a drawer and filed the magazines into the regimented line of their sister editions. "That would make me at least fifty." I heard Pete snicker as Farley crossed to the bathroom, slamming the door behind him.

"Oh dear." I sank onto my freshly dressed bed, its ancient springs whining.

Pete, folded like a giant praying mantis on his too-short bed, stretched his long arms over his head and yawned. "He'll get over it."

"I'd buy him another, but . . . well, where do you find that sort of thing?"

Pete unbuttoned the top of his white linen shirt, stood, and sauntered to the window by my bed. "Drama queens bore me to tears." He opened the window, withdrew a joint from his shorts' pocket, and lit the end with a shiny gold lighter. Inhaling deeply, he closed his eyes and grinned. Smoke rolled over his pearly white teeth when he offered me a puff of his pot, but I declined.

"Farley saves his lunch money and coins he digs out of sofas to buy used theatre memorabilia from some troll rip-off artist who owns a grungy bookstore in the Village." He gestured toward the bathroom door. "It attracts theatre-obsessed queens such as the Baroness of Off-Off Broadway."

"'Baroness'?"

"My nickname for Farley. Of course, he's more burlesque than Broadway, but you get the drift." Pete snuffed the joint out, folded it neatly in wax paper, and shoved it back into his pocket.

Curiously, I was drawn to the lanky blond Peter Pakington Pace, whose splendor matched any of the Greek god statues I'd perused in the art history books in Rockridge High's library.

"What's your nickname?" I asked.

"No one would dare." His smile was intoxicating. Not since my swim coach, Kaiden Kavanaugh, had I met a man so intriguing, so attractive. Fine from any angle, Pete was born lucky. He was leading man material.

However, because I was five-foot-nine, sporting a mass of unruly ginger curls, and battling the stomach bulge that once paralyzed me with self-consciousness, my ascent to any stage would depend on talent. Discipline was the key tool in my arsenal. Willpower determined my fate, and dreams fueled my ambition. The compilation of my charms wielded power. That much I knew. However, I was in constant combat with my formerly chubby self to remain under one hundred and forty pounds.

The bathroom door swung open, and Farley pranced into the room, wearing the most garish cerise speedo I'd ever seen. "Anyone up for a dip in the lake?"

"Bad witches deserve a good dunking," Pete said and dropped onto my bed. He looked Farley up and down. "Won't your mother be furious to discover you've swiped her itsy-bitsy teeny-weeny bikini bottom?"

"According to *After Dark*, this is the hottest color on the Rivera this summer." Farley grabbed a frayed, multi-colored beach towel off a hook and wrapped it around himself, tossing the end over one shoulder with all the flair of a Roman senator. "It ain't Balmain, but it . . .."

"Gets attention." Pete rolled his eyes. "Think I'll pass on a dip

4

with a drip." He turned to me. "What about I give you a tour of the campus?"

"Oh, I don't want to be a bother. They said at registration—"

"Don't be silly," Farley interrupted, jamming his foot into a thick soled, side-buckled shoe. "Pete specializes in tours for virgin campers."

"So says the clown in pilgrim shoes." Pete's tongue darted over his pouty pink lips. "Whatever am I to do with him?" he asked me.

Daring not to react in any manner that might be misconstrued, I remained silent.

"Not everyone has a mother who lavishes them with designer goodies from Bergdorf Goodman!" Farley rummaged through the top drawer of his bureau. "Where in hell are my plugs?"

Pete pointed to Farley's bedside table. "You'd forget your head if it wasn't sewn on, Raggedy Ann."

Farley snatched a pair of ear plugs from the drawer, thumped across the room, and pounded down the front steps as the screen door banged against its frame. We watched him tramp across the lawn through the open window.

My heart sank at the sight of the young man, his arms swinging like two out-of-sync pendulums. "We could catch up with him if we hurry," I said. "I think he's upset."

"She lives for chaos." Pete tapped a cigarette from a pack of Salem Lights on Farley's desk. "Baroness is happiest spinning in a cyclone of controversy. I, for one, steer clear of her rising tides."

I'd heard a male being referred to as a female in derogatory terms, but it always made me uncomfortable. My mother often referred to her hairdresser, Mr. Fly, as Miss Fly when joking with my aunts. Grandma Flora wasn't keen on such musings. She described homosexuals as "fine young men." At sixteen, I wasn't certain how I felt about anything sexual. The rumblings of my gay tendencies were inescapable, but no action had been explored. I was itching to investigate, but hesitant to try. Delving into such fantasies at home with any of my contemporaries was neither prudent nor pragmatic. Either way, my dreams would not be populated by any boy called "Mary" or referred to as "the Baroness."

"Ready for that tour?" Pete pinned a name tag on the pocket of his shirt.

"'Camp counselor'?" I said, reading his title.

"I'm too old to frolic in class with peeps like you." He ran his fingers through his thick, silky blond hair.

"'Peeps'?" I repeated. "I'm hardly a peep!"

"Don't get your panties in a twist." Pete slid his muscular arm around my shoulder, and I nearly gasped. He smelled manly. The warm odor of pot and the stiff scent of cigarettes permeated his zesty vanilla musk. It was invigorating.

"How old are you?" I asked.

"Eighteen. I start Georgetown U come September."

My eyes widened. "I'd be shaking in my shoes." A bead of perspiration trickled down my forehead. At that moment, with Pete's arm around me, I felt like the Push-Me-Pull-You animal in Dr. Doolittle. Part of me longed to linger in his heat, while the other half of me wanted to bolt out the front door.

"I've done this rodeo for five years," he said. "Time to move on."

"I didn't know this type of thing existed. If it hadn't been for my drama coach's recommendation . . ."

"They grow them green where you come from, Pollyanna." Pete chuckled. "Pollyanna. Pollyanna." There was a devilish glee in his eyes as he repeated the name. "Pollyanna. That's the perfect nickname for my new protégé."

"Pollyanna," I muttered. "I don't know. She's a girl."

"Aren't we all at heart?"

Uncertain of my new moniker, I said little as we traversed the well-manicured campus, meticulously landscaped to appear as a natural phenomenon. As Mama says, "Every girl needs a touch of fake to look real."

My stomach flipped at the thought of anybody at Rockridge High discovering Pete's nickname for me. I shook my head to dispel my silly pondering. No one, not even the bully, Chester Chad, could possibly find out. They were hundreds of miles and a world away from this theatre paradise in the Pennsylvania countryside. At least, I *hoped* it was a paradise.

A flock of Canada geese paraded across our path. Pete forged ahead, but I tugged on his sleeve, and he halted in mid-step. "Careful. That fierce warrior is hissing. She knows her ancestors were here long before we were."

Pete tucked a rambling ringlet off my forehead into a cresting wave of bang. "I've never met anyone like you."

"Grandma Flora says I'm an old soul."

"I have a thing for ginger-haired old souls with pretty faces."

Tongue-tied, I automatically batted my lashes as a cool trickle of joy plummeted into the warm pit of my tummy. "This is my first solo trip. I've never traveled alone." I berated myself for betraying my own confidence. Still, I was being honest, and honesty, as my father, Oscar, often proclaimed, was the best policy. "Compared to you and Farley, I'm a hick."

Pete stopped, put his hands on my shoulder, and studied my face. "A hick wouldn't be caught dead in a cashmere sweater and white bucks."

The starched, sunbaked taste of summer was keen in the air, and we lingered on the footbridge for a while. The sound of trickling water in the creek that ran across the expansive green vista reminded me of my secret place by the Shenandoah River at the foot of our hill. Before my father built my Mediterranean-blue playhouse in the apple orchard, that secluded sunny spot of rock jutting out over a rushing waterfall was my great escape when my mother, May, suffered one of her "spells." Our household was ruled by Mama's nervous condition.

"As unpredictable as Mount Vesuvius," my Aunt Tootie had once cogitated. "She'll fry us to ash someday."

"What's your talent?" Pete asked.

The question gave me pause. I searched for his cornflower-blue eyes behind his tortoise-shell Foster Grants, but the shiny black glass, reflecting the noonday sun, made that impossible. "Singing, I suppose, is my first great love."

"Are you good?"

It was a trick question, and I hesitated to answer. Replying with a definitive "yes" would have been egotistical. Pretending to be humble would have been misleading because I knew my voice was big and blessed and pure. So I said coyly, "I suppose you'll have to wait and see." Pete brought out a side of me I hadn't known existed, a playful guardedness.

We circled the main lodge and headed to a large glass pavilion protruding out of the side of a rocky slope. The smooth folds, dramatic dips, and sharp angles of the futuristic structure seemed to be from a galaxy far away. "Interesting," I said as we passed into its atrium, which was populated with exotic plants totally foreign to the soaring oaks, leafy poplars, and blue spruce glaring at them through the glass roof.

"It's a hodge-podge of modern aesthetic, but the theatre itself is a marvel." Pete opened a massive oak door, and I stepped inside. The plush red carpet soaked up the patter of our feet. A welcome, frigid blast of air slapped the back of my head from the vent above. This inner sanctum was an inviting relief from the mid-day heat.

The stage was a marvel to behold. I'd never seen such an extensive light board. The fly loft rose to a dizzy height, and the wings stretched far beyond the proscenium. Both areas could hold enormous set pieces and drops.

"The stage is hydraulic," Pete said proudly, as if he'd invented it.

"Hydraulic?"

"Adjustable." He strutted across the boards. "It can be lowered to the scene shop below and loaded with another set."

"Wow!" I was overwhelmed by its magnificence.

"This is the only decent thing my grandfather ever did."

"This is your grandfather's?"

Pete dragged a stool from the wing and set it center stage. "Besides being a jerk and crook, he did have a soft spot for Broadway . . . or at least, for chorus girls and leading ladies settling a debt."

"A producer?"

"A financier. He'd invest his dirty dough in a show and collect the rewards of others' labor. He was a staunch, conservative Wall Street stockbroker. My father continued the tradition."

"They're dead?"

"Not my old man. Evil never dies." Pete patted the top of the stool. "Show me what you've got."

"Here? Now?" I stuttered. "Me? You want to hear me?" With eyelids fluttering, my mind blasted through a million lame excuses before I spotted the lacquered baby grand. "There's no pianist."

My heart skipped a beat as Pete sat on the piano bench, flexed his fingers, and cracked his knuckles. "I may not be Liberace, but I can pound out a simple show tune."

Reluctantly, I positioned myself on the stool as he tickled the ivories to warm up. "Do you know 'Where Is Love' from *Oliver*?"

"One of my faves." Pete nodded and began the intro. "Whenever you're ready."

"You play beautifully."

"You're hedging, Pollyanna. Sing!"

Closing my eyes, I imagined myself three years old again. The morning sun tanning my rosy cheeks, I held Grandma Flora's hand, and we waded through the ocean of golden wheat. Basking in the warm, blindingly bright light, I was safe. Before starting every performance, or facing one of Mama's explosions head on, I held tight to that memory because it buoyed my confidence. Anything was possible bathed in the yellow light of contentment.

Softly, I eased into the first line of the song. Unlike the brassy belters that showed off the power of my voice, I'd chosen a selection close to my heart. I sang out to the empty auditorium. Though I wished to see Pete's reaction, I dared not look in his direction for fear that he'd see the tear trickling down my cheek. No matter how many times I sang it, the song moved me. Floating on the edge of a whisper, I held the last note for several beats beyond the expected ending.

"Wow, Polly!" He applauded enthusiastically. "That was gorgeous."

"Thanks," I said, brushing the tear away.

"You're so," Pete said, searching for the word as he walked to me, "genuine."

"You liked it?"

He took my face in his hand and looked me in the eyes. "Farley, as Scarlett O'Hara says of India Wilkes, will be pea-green with envy."

My heart caught in my throat. No man had ever touched me with such tenderness. "I look forward to seeing Farley audition. After three summers here, he must be good."

"Even Wendy could fly when she believed in Peter Pan." Ushering me through the side door of the theatre, Pete shuffled across the maple floor to the center of the room beyond and gestured for me to follow. "Our dance studio."

I crossed to him. Standing side by side facing the mirror, we appeared to be two separate species of man. A Picasso cubist statue, I stood in sharp contrast to Michelangelo's *David*.

Pete struck a pose. At least six-four and lean, his long limbs stretched in opposite directions with the poise of a gazelle, he was as elegant as a Leonardo da Vinci line drawing. "Now you," he instructed.

A head shorter, my extension lacked his graceful line of beauty. His every move blossomed into perfection. There was no denying my blooming desire. I was, as my grandmother would say, smitten with Peter Pakington Pace.

"Do you tap?"

I shook my head. "Intro to tap, ballet, and ballroom, but no real training. The nearest dance school is an hour away."

"Where do you live? West Virginia?" he teased.

"Close," I whispered as I blushed crimson. "My mother is from West Virginia."

"Don't worry, Polly," he assured me. "We'll get you out of there."

As eager as I had been to get to camp, as dusk approached, I missed the view of the majestic Blue Ridge Mountain range that encapsulated my childhood. Unaccustomed to being so far from family, the couple acres of earth I claimed as home seemed light-years away from where I stood.

It was nearly six by the time we finished exploring the boat-house by the lake. Keen to settle into the cabin after registration, I'd skipped lunch in lieu of Pete's guided tour. My carping tummy grumbled as we neared the canteen. The succulent aroma of grilled meat and greasy fried potatoes was enticing.

"There's Farley." I pointed to the main lodge's wrap-around veranda.

"Don't wave," Pete muttered under his breath. "I can't bear that gaggle of never-will-bes fawning over the lackluster Baroness de Ruthless."

"He's your friend."

"Nightmares are the curse of unhealthy habits." Pete steered me toward the back of the building. "Why wait in line when we can cut through the kitchen?" He winked as I stepped through the tattered screen door. "The cook has a soft spot for me."

Of course he does. Seemed like everyone he'd introduced me to and the strangers we'd passed by that afternoon melted in Pete's presence. Why wouldn't they have? I did. I melted like a dollop of butter in Grandma Flora's hot iron skillet.

His plate piled to a majestic height, Pete devoured more food in one sitting than I consumed in two days. "If you weren't so nice, I'd hate you," I teased.

"Whatever for?"

I made a funny face. "You're who I dreamed I'd be."

Pete furrowed his brow. "Never idealize me. I'd gladly chuck everything for a talent like yours. If I could sing like you . . . well, it's heaven on earth."

It was the third time he'd made me blush that afternoon.

"You're a phenomenon." He closed his eyes and bowed his head as if he was about to pray. "Much as I want to be an actor, I know my limitations. Backstage is my domain. From the wings, I'm king of the universe."

"No," I blurted out. "Never. You're too young to . . . I mean, you don't know what you don't know. Right?"

"If I learned anything from my family's success, it's that you need to choose early and get on with it. I refuse to delude myself, be a Farley Fairfield, and pretend to be an expert on everything. . . . Farley's a joke on two legs."

I didn't push on. His irritation was apparent. I'd learned the hard way how to maneuver a minefield. In our house, we played by Mama's rules. Dodging bombs had become second nature to me and my sister, April. We escaped to our secret hiding places when the volcano erupted. Dad and Aunt Tootie drank to escape.

"Will you audition for the musical tomorrow?" I asked.

"Camp counselors aren't allowed."

"That's a shame. You're a good dancer."

Pete took a swig of his Dr. Pepper. "I'm designing the set."

"Wow! That's wonderful!"

"The look on your face." Pete chuckled. "As if I'd won a Tony."

I preferred people happy. Aunt Tootie told me I'd bend over backward to put a smile on someone's face. Perhaps she was right. Stuffing the last wedge of hot dog in my mouth, I contemplated tomorrow. "My dance audition is first thing. Nine o'clock."

Pete unwrapped a Snicker's bar and tore it in two. "Whatever you do, don't be late. The choreographer, Mademoiselle Lavish, is a stickler for promptness. If she's nursing a hangover, which she often is, or she's irritable from insomnia, she's la bitch-deluxe."

His tongue darted over his lips, mopping up dribbles of chocolate. "Don't volunteer your lack of dance experience, either. You're a quick learner. Remember, if you go a bit wobbly, stretch up and out. Saves me every time."

Precise as Gene Kelly and as naturally smooth as Tommy Tune, Pete's movements back in the dance studio were athletic and bold. I'd never been required to dance in a show, and so I hadn't any idea what it took to master choreography. My classroom was our rumpus-room at home, and my professors were the lineup of tapping stars from the Golden Age of Hollywood Dad and I watched every Saturday night on *The Late Show*.

"Hey!" Farley called as he stomped down the extensive length of the porch. Following close behind was a uniformed security guard. "There's your culprit!" He pointed his skinny digit at me. "Miss-ter August Applegate."

The sight of the husky officer released an army of butterflies inside my chest. Flipping through every action of my journey from the moment I'd passed through the massive iron gates of the camp to that moment, my temples pulsed to the staccato beat of my jackknifed heart. *What did I do?*

Pete glared at Farley. "What is this?"

The guard's sweaty, pudgy face was framed by a fringe of wet silver hair. Round and robust, the off-season Santa cop narrowed his beady eyes at me through his wire-rimmed glasses. "Call your mother. She's been a pain in the patootie since ten this morning."

A stricken porcupine of panic, I popped out of my seat. "Sorry, sir! I had no idea." I glanced through the canteen window. "A phone. I need a phone."

The officer gripped his thick belt, sending his potbelly jiggling. "By the vending machines."

I dashed through the double doors and made a beeline for the bank of telephones.

Good grief! There was not an empty booth to be had. With every phone occupied, my annoyance flowered with each *tick-tock* of the clock mounted above the kitchen door.

"Gabbing gossip hounds," Farley said, his mouth so close to my ear it tickled when he spoke. He leaned against the wall, his bell-bottom jeans pooling around his clodhoppers like a fishtailed evening dress. He withdrew a cigarette from his pack of Salem

Lights and struck a match. "My parents wouldn't care if I was kidnapped by Charles Manson." He picked the remnant of a string bean from between his teeth with his long fingernail and wiped it on his jeans. "I was an unfortunate accident."

I focused on the center booth, which was occupied by a frizzy-haired young woman twirling a black ringlet around her finger.

Farley sucked a drag off his cigarette and puffed a series of smoke rings in my direction. "You don't remember me, do you?"

"We met a few hours ago," I said, baffled by his question.

"Regional Play Festival last spring." He flicked ash on the floor.

I racked my mind, trying to place this grousing Heathcliff. "I simply don't—Oh, wait a minute! You were in that daring Tennessee Williams play about misplaced—"

"I never appeared on stage." His eyes, ringed with dark circles worthy of a sixty-five-year-old accountant during tax season, narrowed. "Don't put your daughter on the stage, Mrs. Fairfield. Don't put your daughter on the stage.'"

I shrugged my shoulders. He smirked.

"I was the lowly stage manager gushing over your award-winning performance in that cock-a-mamie Ionesco play that I loathe."

"Oh my God!" I said exuberantly. "You made my day!"

"Evidently, I left a lasting impression."

"You did. I told everyone what you said."

"I hate to admit it, but you pulled it off. You won best actor for a ten-minute theatre-of-the-obscure piece no one else would dare to touch."

I enthusiastically defended my school's entry. "*The Leader* is a masterpiece."

"You certainly mastered the piece. A three-minute standing ovation. A star was born."

The door of the middle booth opened, and the frizzy-haired girl stepped out. "My boyfriend can't get enough of me."

"There's no accounting for some people's taste," Farley blurted out.

The girl spun around, her putrid puce prairie skirt brushing Farley's leg. "Nervous about dance auditions tomorrow, Farley Fairfield?" Without waiting for an answer, she skipped across the room to her table.

"My turn," I announced, my hand on the phone booth door.

Farley turned on his heel and marched away. The sound of his flapping bell bottoms smacking against one another punctuated the chorus of conversations rising from the jam-packed canteen.

Closing the door behind me, I sighed. I loved the security of being behind a closed door. Though visible through the glass panels, I was separated from the raucous roar of the excited hopefuls populating the room. "Long distance," I informed the telephone operator on the other end. "Person to person . . . Mrs. May Applegate."

"One moment please," the operator said in a breathy voice worthy of a call girl.

"Mr. March," Mama said between clenched teeth.

"Mama! Sorry. I didn't have a chance to call."

"You promised, Mr. March!" There was an uncomfortable pause as I listened to her accelerated breathing. "How's camp?"

"Everything's fine. I'm in the middle of dinner."

"You were to call the moment you arrived. I was worried sick. You know what that does to me. That was a deliberate act of defiance. I'm so stressed I'll be up all night. Thank God the camp director was so accommodating. Kind and patient. You could learn a lot from a man like that."

"I forgot, Mama. Give me a break."

"Give you a break? Well, that's a fine thank you. Ungrateful. You're as ungrateful as your sister." The sound of her fingernails tapping against the plastic receiver echoed in my ear. "I was nearly apoplectic, and you tell me to give you a break?"

"It's been a long day, Mama." Hundreds of miles from her grip, I felt like an adult for the first time in my life. More than anything, I detested explaining myself. My actions spoke for themselves. My sister, April, and I were teenagers, but Mama continued to treat us like children. At least Dad understood. Good old Dad always understood.

"Selfish. You had people to talk to. I'm all alone here in the dark."

"Alone? Where's Tootie?"

"Off with God-knows-who."

"You know Dad goes fishing with Edgar every Saturday he has free. He'll be back. He never misses dinner."

"Edgar Applegate is an old maid in britches. I don't know why your father bothers."

"I'll call again when I get a moment."

"You'll call me tomorrow, Mr. March, or it's the last time dime you'll get from me."

"I promise. I'll call tomorrow."

I hung up and stared at my reflection in the darkened glass panel of the booth. I knew I was supposed to love and honor Mama, but her obstinacy frustrated the hell out of me.

When she stayed up to catch a Bette Davis or Joan Crawford movie with me or let me tag along to Garfinkel's in DC on one of her and Aunt Jessica's shopping adventures, she was dreamy, the best mother in the world. But when one of her "spells" ignited to flames, life with Mama was hell on earth.

A guy I'd met at registration tapped on the glass, and I snapped to attention. "Sorry. So sorry," I said and slid the door open. "Sorry, Rodney."

Farley was gone when I returned to the table.

"He's off to some lame gathering at the boathouse," Pete said. "The lady's a trap." He snuffed his cigarette on the porch rail and tossed it into the rhododendron bush. "Going to the movie?"

"Movie? What movie?"

"*Funny Girl.*"

"One of my favorites!" I gushed. "Sure. Count me in."

Pete dumped the remainder of his dinner into the nearest garbage receptacle. "They set up a huge screen next to the grove of trees near the lake. Perfect weather for it."

With a few hours to kill before the movie started, Pete showed me around the costume department and scene shop.

"These are my drawings for the *George M!* set," he said, gesturing to the watercolor renderings thumbtacked to the bulletin board.

They were so beautiful I couldn't help but touch them. "These are astonishing. So professional."

"Hopefully you'll be tapping away on them." He sat on a swivel stool next to me, leaving me trapped between his legs. "I've got you now, Pollyanna." He grinned. "Just kidding."

I sat on the stool next to him and studied the detailed designs. "Where did you learn all this?"

"From a set designer I met at the Walnut Street Theatre in

Philly. He taught me everything I know and then some."

Mesmerized by his dashing good looks and brilliance, I couldn't help but stare at Pete as he explained the mechanics of his clever set. For the second time in my life, my attraction for another boy overwhelmed me. Once again, I was reminded of Kaiden, my swim coach, the only other man who'd ever left me feeling so ensnared by my urgings.

Good Lord! I wasn't even certain what two men did together. I'd heard Chester Chad joke about blowjobs. That was the extent of my gay sex knowledge. If it hadn't been for my pal Evangeline Kline, I would have remained in the dark concerning even straight sex; "normal sex," as Chester Chad referred to it.

The last strains of daylight defied the purple band of night gobbling up the heavens as we ambled over the emerald lawn toward the lake. Striating lines of coral and azure streaked the gray edge of evening, reminding me of home. My soul washed with sadness. A baby bird's first flight is the most daring of its life. I saw the security guard locking the front gates and all at once felt vulnerable and small on the extensive acreage of the campus.

Under that same sky, Mama would be washing up after dinner while Dad and Aunt Tootie enjoyed a highball. Aunt Jessica, who'd never learned to cook, would be dining out somewhere in Northwest Washington, perhaps on a date with her airline pilot, or maybe meeting one of her girlfriends for a bite at her favorite Dupont Circle café.

Pete pointed to a rocky incline past the rows of folding chairs being quickly filled with theatre junkies. "This way."

"Pete," I muttered, "where are we going?"

He didn't answer.

"Our own private box seats," he finally announced when we reached the top.

Positioned above the clearing, a flat-topped bolder overtaken with meandering moss offered the ideal respite from the babbling bustle below. Although I savored the energy of a jam-packed theatre, I preferred performing on a proscenium stage. Separation from an audience allowed me space to breathe. *No close-ups, please.*

A giant poplar, shooting out of the rock, stretched at least twenty feet over our heads. The trunk's enormous girth was wide enough for both of us to rest our backs against.

"Straight shot at the screen," Pete said, scooting closer to me. Surrounded by viburnum shrubs, plump with new growth, the precious space was hidden from view.

The gentle scents of honeysuckle and blue spruce wafted under my nose. I was as giddy as a five-year-old romping in Grandma Flora's garden, chasing the fireflies that signaled to each other above the clumps of long grass running along her back fence.

"How many times have you seen this movie?" Pete asked. A slash of light from a lamp post at the edge of the slope lit his bronzed face, highlighting his prominent cheek bones. The milky whites of his eyes glistened.

"Three. My friend, Evangeline Klein, has seen it ten times." I hugged my knees to my chest when the screen burst to life.

As the film progressed, Pete leaned closer to me until our shoulders met. A perplexing zing of vitality surged through every fiber of my being. Thankfully, there was no need to talk during the movie. At that moment, with my heart caught in my throat, I wouldn't have been able to utter a word. My elbow, resting against his, was frozen in place. The heat of his bare forearm against mine titillated my imagination, and thoughts of romance danced in my head. Not even Barbra Streisand, star extraordinaire, possessed the power to lure me from my lustful ponderings.

Part of me wanted to bolt, while the other half of me begged to stay. It was an inexplicable, magical feeling, the likes of which I had never encountered. My head was light, my appetite for exploration keen.

The place broke into riotous applause at the end of the movie. Pete and I sat in the shadows, not clapping.

"She can't hear them." Pete made a funny face, and I laughed too loud and too long. My insides buzzed. Never had I been alone in the dark with a boy—a man. Pete was manly. *Yes. Definitely a man.*

Glancing down, I spotted Farley in the front row. As he stood on a chair, his garish purple-and-florescent-white paisley shirt, unbuttoned to his navel, glowed in the bright flood light.

I sat still next to Pete, unable to move, praying for something, anything, to happen. I didn't know what to do. *What should I do? My mind rummaged through its files of romantic scenes from classic Hollywood movies. What would Audrey Hepburn do? Lauren Bacall wouldn't sit there doing nothing. She'd grab the bull by the horns and kiss him.* But I'd never kissed a man, a real man, and I didn't know how. He was taller. Did I reach up or pull him to me? Hold his gaze as Liz Taylor did before she surrendered in *Raintree County?*

I feared if he didn't kiss me, I'd die on that very spot. My uncontrollable desire to touch him shouted down my Protestant restraint. Clumsily, I stretched and dropped my hand on Pete's bulbous thigh. His quadriceps flexed, but he didn't budge. *Jesus! Have mercy on my soul!* My heart pounded against my ribs, threatening to shatter them into a million pieces.

Sliding his arm around me, Pete pulled me close. My face pressed against his chest, I trembled. "Polly?" he whispered tenderly, then kissed the top of my head.

My chin quivering, I looked up into his eyes, and he ran his fingers through my mass of waves. My inner boiler sputtered and spurted. Thick globs of lava trickled down my throat, and a surge of heat shot to my head. *I'm Superman! I can fly.* Staring at his pouty lips, I took his face in my hands. He bent his head to meet mine.

As if it was a separate instrument, with a mind of its own, my tongue darted over his lips. He plunged his tongue deep inside my mouth, and I pushed him to the ground. Flooded with passion, I was Alexander the Great! Caesar! Queen Elizabeth! We rolled onto the grass, and he straddled me. His grin was as devilishly delicious as Errol Flynn's in *Captain Blood.*

Doubt swept over me. "Am I doing this the right way?" I asked innocuously.

Pete tossed his head back and laughed. "You are adorable, August Applegate."

When he tugged on my belt buckle, I grabbed his hand. "I'm not ready."

Pete rolled off me and sat cross-legged on the grass. His excitement was evident. So was mine. Suddenly, the lush green of the Pennsylvania park evaporated. I was alone in the desert, miles from where he sat. *What's the matter with me? What am I afraid of? Apprehensive to unwrap my privates? His privates? Could I stop if we started?*

I was gay. There was no doubt in my mind. I'd known since Billy Manger kissed me in the supply closet of Mrs. Reynold's first grade class; since the day I'd stood up to Mrs.-Fry at her toy store, demanding she sell me the Barbie she'd insisted would have been more appropriate for my sister. Having sex, however, would confirm Chester Chad's assessment of me. "Fag!" he yelled every day as I pushed through the double doors of the school cafeteria.

"A virgin?" Pete uttered. His tone was flat, lacking honey.

Flooded with shame, my reasoning wavered for a moment. Flashes of fancy, illusions of romance, and my Southern moral propriety surfaced. "I want the first time to be special."

My words crashed against him and tumbled onto the buttercups, yellow and shiny in the grass between his legs. My puritanical roadblock plunged us into silence. Moments ago, the leaves in the poplar had rustled with Mozart. Now, the mockingbird squawked like a hawk. I glanced at the shimmering lake, expecting a falling star to break its surface as one had done the night Grandma Flora passed.

Pete stood and brushed the seat of his madras plaid shorts. "If you're not interested, you're not interested. No big deal, Pollyanna." He mussed my hair the way Dad did when I made a mistake, when I dripped paint on the porch he'd just painted or scratched my nose while I held a piece of wood for him to saw. "Camp counselors shouldn't be fraternizing with the kids anyway."

"'Kids'? I'm a man," I replied, my tone harsher than I wished.

Pete laughed. "It's not the end of the world, Mr. Man."

Perhaps it wasn't the end of the world for him, but the bottom had just dropped out of mine.

When it came to romance, it was impossible for me to make up my mind. Cherry Laney, a senior and head cheerleader at Harrison High, had asked me to the movies the summer we taught tennis together at County Kid's Day Camp. Halfway through *The Aristocats*, she diddled with my fiddle until the lady next to us gave her the hairy eyeball. Afterward, I'd passed on an invitation to her grandmother's dark basement. I walked home alone that night.

Courteously, Pete escorted me back to the cabin. He chattered on about the show and auditions and his set, as if nothing had happened between us. Whip-poor-wills in a grove of sycamores tweeted and trilled their persistent cries for a mate as we passed.

"See you when I see you," Pete said when we neared the cabin.

"You're not coming in?"

Without uttering a word, he continued down the gravel path leading to the main lodge.

•●•

Tucked under my crisp sheets in the "nanny corner" of the room, I surmised there was fifteen feet from Pete's footboard to mine. The space that had seemed too close for comfort just that morning now appeared lightyears away in the splintered shadow of the blinds.

With its yearning cry, the box spring complained at the slightest movement, jostling my homesickness to a new high. That morning, I had been on top of the world. The moonlight was mine for the taking that night, and I thumbed my nose at it. Tears trickled down my sunburned cheeks. What a fool I was. What an exasperating mess I'd made of it all. I removed my watch and noted the time as I set it on the nightstand. In exactly eleven hours, thirty-five minutes, and forty-one seconds, I had managed to isolate Farley, irritate Pete, and agitate Mama.

Reaching up, I opened the slats of the wooden blinds above my bed. Outside, perched on the branch of an ancient sugar maple, sat a bug-eyed owl. First searching right and then left, he turned his flat, wide face to me. *Foolish prig*, he seemed to be saying. "What did I do?" I asked the predatory dinosaur staring at me. I swiftly closed the blinds.

· • ·

As a child, sleeping in Grandma Flora's spare room in the attic on select Saturday nights, I had been taunted by a great horned owl hooting his melancholy melody from the black branch of the locus tree whose skeletal fingers tapped a code on the window by the headboard, making it impossible for me to sleep.

"I'll take care of that annoying bird if you want, Mr. March," Grandad Cleveland had assured me.

I knew his offer could only have meant one thing, so I'd quickly answered, "Please, no." I'd rather have had my dreams tortured by a live bird than haunted by a dead one.

When I was a boy, a weekend at Grandma Flora's was the best medicine for me, a vacation from provocation. In my grandparents' house, I was affectionately called "Mr. March" because I loved the book *Little Women*. My grandmother read aloud to me on countless afternoons, comfortable in her slip-covered wing chair by the kitchen fireplace, my head against her knee.

"You're so Jo March," she'd mused. Since the March girls in the book didn't have a brother, Grandma had invented one; me, Mr. March. I wore the name proudly.

 # CHAPTER 2

WHO AM I ANYWAY?

The glaring morning light, striping my face, teased me awake before the radio alarm buzzed. I peered over at Farley, who was buried beneath a heap of lilac percale sheets. His ratted waves of black and orange hair stood on end, reaching for the sun like a Virginia creeper. Snoring to beat the band, he didn't budge when my box spring cackled unpleasantries from the nanny's corner. Pete's bed sat untouched.

Securing my terrycloth robe around me, I grabbed my dob kit and headed to the men's shower pavilion at the foot of the hill.

At six a.m., the dew on the zoysia grass glistened like a beaded gown in candlelight. An army of lilacs lined the pathway, emitting a stimulating, sweet scent as potent as the ones in Grandma Flora's garden, their flagging leaves heavy with moisture. Mountain coolness rose from the damp earth. A welcome breeze, gentle as a baby's breath, teased the hair on my bare legs, and I shivered as goosebumps spread like a virus over my flesh. Beneath my flip-flops, the worn gravel was a welcome massage to my blistered feet.

"Good morning, sleepyhead!" Pete, wearing nothing but a towel over his shoulder, greeted me when I entered the locker room.

As beautiful as the statue of Hadrian's Greek lover, Antinous, he stood before me brushing his silky blond locks. He was broad-shouldered, and his long, lean torso tapered at the waist and gracefully curved over his dimpled hip and bulbous thigh before tracing his shapely calves. I tried not to look at his member, but it was impossible. Not since Chester Chad flashed me in the men's restroom at Rockridge High had I seen a penis that big.

Until that point, I'd never given the sizes of men's appendages much thought. After sizing up the competition in the school locker room, I'd figured I was slightly larger than average but not in the same league as Chester Chad and left it at that.

Holy Jesus! When I officially came out, would I obsess over the measure of a man's genitalia the way straight guys ogled over women's breasts?

"Hurry up," Pete said, securing his towel around his waist. "Meet you in fifteen."

Farley barreled into the locker room just as I exited the showers, the tattered tail of his maroon flannel robe flapping behind him. "Farley!" I exclaimed.

"Why didn't you wake me?" he screamed.

·•·

"Hey!" Pete, sporting a fresh pair of white tennis shorts and sky-blue Izod shirt, greeted me before I turned the latch of the screen door. "Dress for dance," he commanded. "You won't have time to change before Mademoiselle Lavish's audition." He dug through the drawer of my bureau until he located my dance belt and tights. "Here." He held the dance belt open. "No time to play demure, Melanie Hamilton."

Reluctantly, I shed my robe and stepped into the belt. He handed me my white T-shirt with "Governor's School" plastered on the front in bold black letters. "That's impressive."

"Snobby brats. I'd rather . . ."

"Enjoy it! Show off a bit. Lavish loves awards." Pete grinned and smacked my buttock. "What am I going to do with you? Theatre is a cut-throat business. I'll need to toughen you up."

"You're nice."

"Ulterior motive." He winked and rolled a red bandana for me to use as a sweat band. "The studio gets hotter than Haiti when the crowd heats up." He looked me over. "Mademoiselle Lavish is good, but a demanding bitch. Always be prepared. If she's nursing a hangover, which is generally five days a week, her level of irritation soars to uncharted heights." He laid his hand on my back when I bent over to smooth my tights. His palm was warm and his touch inviting.

"Don't worry, Polly, dear. She'll love you."

I was searching for my tap shoes when Farley bounded through the door. He shook his slick black mane, sprinkling water on Pete's shirt.

"Hey!" Pete yelled.

"I see someone is Fosse-ready and eager to impress," Farley said.

I scoured every inch of storage under my bed and in my wardrobe for my tap shoes, but they were nowhere in sight. "What time does the studio store open?" I asked, frantically unzipping my suitcase. "I can't find my tap shoes."

"You checked your backpack?" Pete asked, concern creasing his brow.

I plunged my hand into the empty bag, then dropped dismally onto my squawking bed. "I can't fake it in white bucks."

Pete stared into space. "What size do you wear?"

"Thanks, Pete, but both my feet would fit into one of your shoes. I'm a size nine."

"Farley," he said, holding one of Farley's scuffed black shoes up by its strings. "Size nine!"

"What is this?" Farley growled and snatched his shoe out of Pete's hand.

"It's an emergency." To Farley's chagrin, Pete gathered his tap shoes and stuffed them in my backpack. "The store doesn't open until one," Pete informed me, "so this is it, kid."

Farley stomped his flip-flop on the floor. "What the hell! They're my shoes."

"And on a respirator, but they're the last ruby slippers in Oz." Pete pinched Farley's cheek. "You owe me."

Farley pushed away and adjusted his purple Barbra Streisand T-shirt. "Okay!" He glared at me. "Your audition is first. Warm them up for me, Ms. Reinking." He turned to Pete. "Happy?"

"Delighted," Pete trilled and grinned mischievously. "You can thank me later."

"Don't hold your breath." Farley clutched his frayed rust-colored gym bag under his arm and kicked the screen door open. "Break a leg, princess!" he cried before exiting.

I glanced at Pete. "I think he meant that."

•●•

The dance studio was a sauna. My forehead beaded with per-spiration the moment we stepped across the threshold.

"Danny." Pete tapped the shoulder of a buff guy with massive thighs. "Danny, this is August. Do me a favor and show him the ropes? This is his first time in the big tent."

With a twinkle in his eye, Danny replied, "You bet."

"Danny's the dance captain," Pete called over his shoulder as he headed for the exit. "He'll take good care of you!"

Flexing at the bar, Danny instructed me on the best way to stretch my hamstrings and adjust my alignment. "So, you're the fla-vor he'll savor for the summer? Enjoy it while it lasts," Danny said and pressed his foot into the small of my back. "Good arch." He had a boyish lisp, which immediately endeared him to me.

My bandana was soaked by the time Mademoiselle Lavish made her grand entrance.

"The white bitch is her assistant, and the Black god is the ap-prentice choreographer," Danny whispered in my ear.

Mademoiselle glided across the floor as though she was sus-pended on wires. According to Danny, her age was a mystery. Some-where between forty-five and sixty, I surmised by the crease in her forearm. Mama swore that was the dead giveaway of a lady's age. Petite and gamine, Mademoiselle's body was as lithe as her face was pulled. Her glossy black hair was slicked into a tightly wound bun at the base of her skull and secured by a turquoise tie-dyed scarf.

Thin as an upright cobra, the assistant followed, her Farrah-Fawcett-feathered coif bouncing with every step. The apprentice choreographer was broad-shouldered and square-jawed, with a wasp waist to rival Grace Kelly's in *Rear Window*. His beautiful dark face was as stoic and regal as a sphinx's.

Danny walked us through the choreography. Watching from the sidelines, Mademoiselle would whisper to her assistant, and she'd record her notes on a yellow pad. *George M!* was a major tap show. The prospect of tapping for a professional, after my limited instruction at Maybelle Moyer's Ballroom, had me quaking in Far-ley's beaten Tic Tap Capezios.

We were expected to master three segments of choreography for the audition. The first was a straightforward ballet bit. Complete with fan-kicks, heel-clicks, leaps, and lunges, the second slice of pie exhibited one's aptitude for rapid-fire tap. The third and final test was left up to the imaginations of us poor schmucks: a freestyle improv.

"Ze freeform," Mademoiselle croaked out like a boozy Bactrian camel. "Impress me vis your mind."

"Evil. Mata Hari is plain evil," Farley murmured, sweat dripping from his narrow chin. "A lot of pressure being *numero uno* on the list." He hissed the 's' in 'list' like a fork-tongued rattlesnake.

"Five. Six. Seven. Eight," Danny counted, and I sprang into action. To be fair, he danced in front of us as we did our best to keep up with him. There was little chance of anyone memorizing Lavish's elaborate choreography after two rushed run-throughs.

The ballet section went swimmingly, much better than I'd anticipated. Pumped by my victory, I sprang into the tap number with vim and vigor. An answered prayer, I shuffled through the mad ordeal with only a few minor slips on my slides.

"Show me what . . . you got," Mademoiselle Lavish demanded, her azure marbled eyes sparkling. She sat watching, expressionless, tapping the beat of the music on the floor with a long, lacquered nail.

Shaking my inhibitions the moment I heard the first note of *Rhapsody in Blue* calling me, I tossed caution to the wind and leapt into the air. I spun, pranced, shuffled, and waltzed fast and furiously across the studio, performing my soggy best.

"My. My. Mister . . . what vous name?" The Farrah-flipped assistant handed her a pair of rhinestone-tipped cat-eye glasses so she could read my name from her list. "Mr. August Appleman."

"Applegate," I corrected her.

The Farrah-flipped assistant glanced quickly at the sphinx, but Mademoiselle grinned, and they relaxed.

"Promising. Mr. Apple . . . whatever," she said, her voice deeper than the Danube. "You show moi promise."

"You showed her Peggy Sawyer," Farley joked afterward, referring to Ruby Keeler's character in *42nd Street*.

I mopped my brow with a hand towel. "I was so nervous. I had no idea what I was doing."

"But you did it, didn't you?" he said, a tinge of nasty in his baritone.

"I thought of Debbie Reynolds in *Singing in the Rain* and cut loose."

"A natural." His ingenuine smile slid into a sneer. "The old battle-ax was impressed. She never says diddly about anybody."

I detested competition but loved a challenge. I looked at Farley jamming his feet into his ballet slippers. *Why should he be jealous?* He'd had three summers at theatre camp. It was all I could do to scrape together the cash for one. Grandma Flora was right. Insecurity breeds hate, and hate has no place in friendship.

Farley was an acquaintance. I hadn't known him long enough to call him a friend. Yet Pete, whom I'd also met just the day before, I felt comfortable calling a friend. Still, when I looked at Farley, dressed in his shabby tights and saturated fuchsia T-shirt, my heart went out to him. He reminded me of the angry, abused dogs I fed at the animal shelter where I volunteered. The ones no one would adopt. Grandma warned me to never judge a book by its cover. So far, the prologue was an analogue of misfortune.

My limited experience had taught me one thing about auditions: It was all about the director's vision. You could be fantastic, but if you weren't physically what they were looking for, then you'd be out on your ear.

What I lacked in the looks and height departments I was determined to make up for in talent and drive; at least, I hoped I could. At the end of the day, I wanted to walk away satisfied that I'd given it my best shot.

Farley held out his hand. "Shoes, dear. I go on after pretentious Phillipa McMartin."

I untied the laces, wiped the shoes clean, and set them on the folding chair between us. "I can't thank you enough. I owe you big time."

"That you do," he said, adjusting his bits and bobs in his too-tight tights. "What the hell. My absent-minded mother must have dried these damn things on high."

"Farley Fairfield!" Danny shouted from the front of the room.

"Hold your horses!" Farley pranced out like a Lipizzaner stallion. Everyone laughed, and he bowed.

I stuffed my belongings into my backpack and was tying my Puma tennis shoes when I heard Danny clap his hands hard to the beat of the music. The ballet suite from *An American in Paris* blared from the speakers.

"Five! Six! Seven! Eight!" Danny yelled.

Unable to keep up with Danny's tempo, Farley flapped and flailed around the room like a wounded pterodactyl. It was difficult to watch his self-flogging and clogging through the second sequence; he never actually tapped a single step. I crossed my fingers and prayed he'd save himself with the free-form portion. Perhaps his quick wit would translate into fast thinking on his feet.

To even the playing field, a different piece of music was chosen randomly for each contestant. The Farrah-flipped assistant dropped the needle on the record, and the stereo speaker blasted Offenbach's *Galop Infernal* can-can music. Bursting out of the gate, Farley galloped into action, jazz-hands waving. Spinning and kicking, sliding and gliding, he bounced like Pooh's friend Tigger from one end of the room to the other. After two adventurous leaps forward followed by three vivacious turns backward, he twirled himself into a cyclone of fluttering limbs as he headed straight for the dynamic trio.

With the dramatic flair of a silent movie queen, Mademoiselle, her matte ruby mouth agape and her charcoal rimmed eyes bulging, grabbed hold of her Farrah-flipped assistant and positioned her as a human shield against Kamakshi Farley. *Bam! Crunch! Clank! Ding!* Farley hit front and center, knocking them both off her chair. If Mademoiselle's verbal intonation sank to the cellar note of E, then her scream screeched a high C. The stoic sphinx crossed his muscular arms in front of his chiseled face.

Stumbling over the wreckage, Farley landed with a splat in his lap. Without hesitation, the god stood, and Farley hit the floor with a clunk.

Springing to her feet, Mademoiselle Lavish adjusted her chartreuse Qiana wrap-skirt, glared at Farley, and pointed to the door. "Out!" Her deep-throated warble peppered with anger was scary enough to fluster a school of hammerheads.

I rushed to Farley and held out my hand, but he refused my help.

"Fuck off!" he screamed before bolting out the door like a jackrabbit in heat.

I grabbed his belongings and shot out the door after him. "Farley! Farley!" I yelled. Sprinting in his tap shoes down the gravel path, he disappeared into a forest of pitch-pines.

•●•

No sooner had I started up the cabin steps, then out dashed Rodney Faber, the guy I'd met at registration. Pretty to the point of ridiculous, he seemed a genuinely nice guy.

"Hey August!" he chirped merrily as he flew past.

"Pollyanna," Pete called out.

"Just dropping Farley's bag off."

"A princess never carries a baroness's handbag." He zipped the fly of his shorts and reached for Farley's *Salem Lights*. "How'd it go?"

"Rodney was in a hurry," I said and sat on the edge of the rattan chair by the window.

Pete sat up and his unbuttoned seersucker shirt parted, exposing his well-defined chest.

Oh my God! What was I thinking last night? He's perfection personified!

"I didn't mean to interrupt," I said, glancing out the window at a band of merrymaking guys singing *There Is Nothing Like a Dame* as they marched down the dandelion-dotted hill to the ravine.

"One song I'll never sing with conviction." Pete crossed his legs at the ankle. "Rodney was running late for his audition." He clicked the lighter and sucked on a cigarette until a string of smoke curled upward from its burning ember. "So?"

"It went well, I think."

"You think?"

"It went well."

"And Farley?"

"I'll let him tell you."

"That bad?"

"I felt sorry for him."

Pete sneered. "If the table was turned, he wouldn't."

"I feel sorry for him," I said, irritated by Pete's lack of sympathy. "He is your friend."

Pete took a long drag from his cigarette and puffed out a series of smoke rings. "Not really. I mean, I've known him for three summers. I know of him, but . . ." His voice trailed off to a whisper.

I untied the wet bandanna and spread it across my lap.

"Polly? Have you ever . . . with a girl?"

My cheeks burned brighter than the cinder of his cigarette. "Once," I said meekly, the word brushing my uvula.

Pete tapped the ash into a golden carnival-glass bowl. "More power to you."

"My friend, Evangeline. Last spring." I regretted my confession the moment it tumbled over my loose lips.

"So, tell me about Evangeline." Pete adjusted the pillow behind his back. Pale blond hair, almost white, covered his chest before tapering to a trickle at his tanned belly button. "Is she pretty?"

"Sure."

"Did you like it?"

"Sure."

"You don't sound convincing." His Cheshire cat smile stretched from ear to ear, and his boutonniere-blue eyes glistened in the light streaming through the picture window.

Pete was beautiful, and there was no denying my attraction to him. I wanted to kiss his pouty pink lips, run my fingers through his hair, touch his chest, and feel his breath against my neck as he held me in his arms. Ridiculous, impossible sexual scenarios coursed through my head, dousing my last ounce of dignity with desire. Uncontrollable, my romantic urges traveled below the waist.

The taste of the previous night's kiss loitered in my mind. I adored kissing. A magic carpet ride, making out, I'd discovered with the few girls I'd cuddled with, was paramount to pleasure.

Pete studied my face. "You liked it?"

Pressed to deliver an answer to his query, I bleated, "I liked it! I liked it."

"Don't get mad at me, Polly. It's more than I've done with a girl."

Abruptly, I stood. "I need to chill out before tonight's audition."

Pete gestured to the nanny corner. "All yours."

Like I'd get any sleep with him fifteen feet away. "I don't want to be here when Farley returns."

Pete snuffed his cigarette out. "Stupid Baroness. She did it again. Screws herself out of another show."

"He's having a bad day."

"She's a heartless bitch. Conniving. Ruthless. Vindictive. And that's her assets. Don't fall into his trap."

"He's . . . I don't know . . . sad. Lost. He tries so hard."

"Dig you, Polly Freud." Pete tossed his hands in the air. "You'll learn."

My heart sank when he said that. What did he honestly think of me?

"Smile, Pollyanna." He caressed my leg.

"I need a swim," I said. Sticky and sweaty, my tights and leotard were glued to my flesh. I took a towel from the fresh supply on the desk and rolled my swim trunks inside it.

"Pool or lake?" Pete asked, drumming his fingers on the nightstand.

"Pool," I said. Kaiden, my former swim coach, popped into my head yet again.

Pete snatched his trunks off his bedpost. "Showtime!"

• • •

There was something transformative—positively curative—about water. That premier plunge into the cold, chlorine-punched pool jolted me awake. Every inch of me tingled with electricity. Pushing off the tiled wall, I glided through myriad shades of blue. Utopia. Under water, I was weightless, suspended between time bands, streaking through heaven on earth. With each stroke, the cobwebs crowding my mind dissolved. *Turn left. Breathe. Turn right. Breathe.* Alone with my thoughts and secrets, I sped past Pete swimming backstroke in the next lane.

Swimming hadn't always been the release it now was for me. For years, I avoided any swimming hole like the plague. I had been traumatized at age four by Chester Chad holding me under water until I turned blue. It was Mama who rescued me from the deep end of the pool and forbade me to return. Wallowing in worry, Mama's fear became my fear, which only multiplied over the years.

"Oh my God!" She clutched her pearls and pleaded any time someone threw a pool party. "Please, Mr. March. Don't even think

31

about it. No swimming. Don't you dare. You can't swim! You'll drown."

Eleven years later, Dad took the bull by the horns. A fine swimmer himself, he was determined to right the wrong. That was my dad. Righting wrongs, defending the defenseless, and searching for the truth. "Truth sets you free," he often said.

"I signed you up for lessons with a young man I met at the IGA. He's home on Christmas break and volunteered to help. Last year, he qualified for the pre-Olympic swim team. He's a Kavanaugh." Being a Kavanaugh in our neck of the woods meant one thing: he was wealthy.

Three feet of snow had blanketed the acreage of the Kavanaugh estate that first afternoon we'd passed through her enormous iron gates. Situated in an improbably beautiful slice of the Blue Ridge Mountains, this was the family's country escape from the hustle and bustle of Washington, DC.

"Jesus," I said when the house came into view. Squat, with a low-slung overhang reminiscent of Frank Lloyd Wright's architecture, the massive stone-chrome-and-glass house shot out of the side of the mountain like a sparkling diamond goiter, complete with an indoor pool.

The housekeeper greeted me at the door, a rotund woman named Berta Bainbridge, bundled and booted, short on stature but tall on attitude. "Kai-dan," she said gruffly in a Southern accent thicker than Louisiana mud. "Kai-dan's down at the poo-all." She pointed to a spiral staircase at the end of the entrance hall. "Down they-ere!"

"Hey!" A chestnut-haired young man appeared, a tad taller than me. His smile, radiant and wide, was enchanting. "Right on time." He extended his hand as he approached in his skimpy white speedo. His grip was firm and his muscular body intimidating.

Having ballooned in junior high, I was embarrassed to disrobe in front of him. That first day, I kept my T-shirt on until I reached the edge of the pool. As I stood on the tile, transfixed on the still water, chills skipped up my backside. Images of Mama and Chester Chad clouded my concentration. However, the sky-blue floor of the pool lying calm in the cool water offered me a secluded space, much as the stage did. As when I was bathed in light center stage, I hoped I'd become one with the pool. "You can do it," I muttered under my breath. "You can do it."

Self-conscious of my fleshy breast (which any adolescent girl would have envied), my double chin, and spare tire, it was a relief to drop into the water. My mortification outweighed my fear.

Within the week, I was swimming laps. By the end of the month, my shame had melted, along with some excess poundage.

Having conquered my two greatest fears, I had a new lease on life. Aunt Jessica was so delighted with the news that she sent a pair of hip-hugger bell bottoms from the exclusive Garfinkel's department store in Washington. Fashion, I soon discovered, was a prescription for success.

Pete was toweling off when I climbed out of the pool. "Ready to slay them tonight?"

Ignoring his enquiry, I pointed to the dark clouds corralled at the peak of the mountain. "Going to be a gully-washer."

Pete patted my dripping curls with his towel. "Ginger. The most exquisite shade of red I've ever seen."

"I wish our school bully felt like you. If Chester Chad isn't yelling 'queer call' at the top of lungs when he spots me, he's joking about my hair. 'I'd rather be dead then red on the head.'"

"A *cou rouge* poet who doesn't know it."

"'Cou rouge'?" I asked.

"French for redneck."

"Cou rouge," I repeated. "That'll be one for Mrs. Bowman's first-year French class."

A remarkably pretty young man called for Pete from the opposite side of the pool.

"That's Henry. He's helping with the set. I'll meet you back at the cabin." Off Pete strutted in his cobalt speedo and black leather sandals.

CHAPTER 3

BEING GOOD ISN'T GOOD ENOUGH

I'd always treasured quiet moments in the afternoon, those precious few hours before evening when work ground to a breaking point. It was a chance to catch one's breath, refuel, reflect, and remember; to contemplate the hours past and dream of the hours ahead. Even when Mama was at her manic worst, smashing dishes or stomping Dad's treasured gardenias to bits in the garden, her psycho-cyclone spun to a halt at teatime.

She crashed in the afternoons. Golden quiet descended on our weary-worn house, and I was free to be me. It became my favorite time of day. Dad called it "teatime," a phrase he'd picked up during World War II when he was an ambulance driver in London.

On a tight time-schedule that afternoon after my dance audition, I used teatime to run vocal scales before Pete and Farley returned. Perhaps it was the moisture in the air or swimming fifty laps that had expanded my lungs, but I was in good voice.

I paced the cabin while I buttoned my periwinkle linen shirt, humming my audition song to loosen my nasal cavity. Too polite to nose through every nook and cranny, as Aunt Tootie would have, I looked but didn't touch my roommates' things as I sang.

As charming and outgoing as Pete was, all his belongings were neatly tucked away and stored out of sight in his sterile corner. A pair of madras plaid shorts hanging on the post of his too-short bed provided the only identifiable clue to his personality.

Centered along the longest wall, Farley's bed was a topsy-turvy three-ring circus. Discarded clothes peeked out from beneath the mattress. Used T-shirts had been flung carelessly over the footboard or draped haphazardly over the rattan rocker. Considering we had occupied the cabin for a little over twenty-four hours, the fact that bedlam brimmed from every fissure of his hazard zone was amazing. However, he'd claimed the only desk in the room for himself before I arrived, and it was as orderly as a nurse's station. Our differences were pronounced, and it was painfully clear that each one of us danced to the beat of a different drum. But devoted believers, we three worshipped the same God: theatre.

Glancing at my reflection in the full-length mirror, I surmised I looked better *in* rather than *out* of clothes. Mama had been the first to point out that I would never be handsome enough to play leading roles, so I didn't expect to ever be offered one. Except for the Regional Play Festival the previous spring, I was never cast as the lead.

"Hone your own style," Mama instructed. "Looks fade, but style lasts a lifetime." She was fortunate to be blessed with both.

I never fooled myself about my looks. I wished I were tall and lanky like Pete. If so, the male lead in any musical would be mine. Dad told me to make the best of the gifts I had. "It is what it is. It's what you do with what you've got that counts." Despite the hell Mama put him through, he remained the most optimistic person I knew.

From the attention I got from girls at school, I figured I was, if not handsome, somewhat attractive. At twelve, I'd suffered through a dreadful period of self-loathing. I hated everything about my swiftly shifting self. Having been hailed as "the most beautiful baby" by Mama and my aunts, morphing from a pretty prepubescent boy to a pudgy, pimple-faced teen was indeed traumatic for me and Mama.

That was about the time Mama stopped touching me. No more kisses. No hugs. No gentle squeezes of affection. I was cut off without explanation. At such a vulnerable period of change, being separated from the one who'd birthed me was intolerable. Like I had been given up for adoption, I would forever wonder why.

When I hit thirteen, Mama demanded I have rhinoplasty to transform my nose, a replica of Dad's, into "something more attractive." So, Dad had cashed a small inheritance he'd received from his Uncle Teddy, which he'd been saving for a rainy day, and the surgery was booked.

When finally relieved of its bandages and splint (with great trepidation on my part), my honker post-surgery had been chiseled to Mama's ideal: her own gracefully sloped nose.

"He couldn't go around with that snout of yours," she scolded Dad.

It was nice enough, but I wished they'd left it alone. I missed the nose my biology teacher, Mrs. Reed, had called "Roman." It sounded so imperial. The choir director, Mr. Schultz, told me I was lucky the aesthetic operation hadn't affected my voice. Perhaps it had already. Even so, no one was about to admit the oversight.

"You're not exactly Frank Sinatra," Mama pointed out the last time she'd heard me, "or Perry Como. Now there's a voice as smooth as silk."

Obviously, she had never cared for my voice. So, I made a point to never sing in the house when she was home. Thank heaven Dad built a playhouse for me. Even if our nosy neighbor, Mrs. Cartwright, had been opposed.

"Do you think it appropriate," she'd questioned Dad, knowing I was within earshot of her annoying, nasal twang, "for a boy?"

Dad had looked her square in the eye and said, "Yes. Yes, I do."

I wasn't certain what or who I was at that point in my life, but I knew whatever that may have been, I'd never doubt it again.

Mama never complimented any of my artistic achievements. She'd look quizzically at my meticulous, blue-ribbon drawings and watercolors and say nothing. Mrs. Campbell, the art instructor who'd nominated me for Governor's School, had asked Mama at the art fair if she was proud of my win.

"He's persistent," Mama had replied.

I was grateful to have Grandma Flora, my aunts, and Dad. They loved everything I did and willingly stroked my bruised ego. However, my injuries from the jabs Mama hurled never quite healed. Poking my sore spots was an art she'd mastered early on.

"Is there anything you can't do?" Aunt Jessica was my biggest fan. She was certain nobody sang, drew, painted, or acted better than I did. Still, it was Mama's approval I craved. It was human nature, I supposed.

Edmond Keen, Rockridge Elementary School's librarian, encouraged my talents. Poring over books on famous artists and performers, or listening to his favorite classical and Broadway albums, we traveled the world without ever leaving the oak-paneled library.

"Reach for the stars, Mr. March," he'd say.

Mr. Keen was a friend of Grandma Flora's. They'd met in the supermarket parking lot. She complimented his choice of radio station, and they'd become fast friends. Affectionately, she referred to him as her "fine young man." Grandma Flora also explained to Mr. Keen that she called me Mr. March because I reminded her of Jo March in *Little Women*.

I would sit before her kitchen hearth, the crackling logs wrapped in red-hot flame, observing her methodically kneading the bread dough as the wind, howling like a hungry wolf, swept the snow into hip-high drifts against her clapboard house. Once the bread was greased with lard and slid into the mouth of the welcoming heat, Grandma Flora would read aloud to me as her loaves browned in the oven. *Little Women*, *The Secret Garden*, *The Wind in the Willows*, *David Copperfield*, and *Pollyanna* were among my favorites. I never bored of hearing them.

Through these fictional characters, I learned that hard work and determination yielded glory. I was naturally disciplined like Dad, and procrastination never appealed to me. Simply being good would never be good enough when working a little harder would deliver the best me possible.

I gazed out the picture window of the cabin. A stiff breeze ruffled the dragon's breath's feathered plumage and rifled through the pink pampas grass consuming the embankment on the gorge. *Better bring an umbrella*, I reminded myself. I tied my pink cashmere cardigan around my shoulders and laced my two-toned saddle oxfords.

Pollyanna. How strange it was that that book happened to be one I had begged Grandma to read and reread. Had the novel influenced me more than I'd realized? Jo March, Mary Lennox, David Copperfield, and Pollyanna were cut from the same cloth. Each was an underdog who, despite their unfortunate situations, faced challenges head-on. With honesty and by their wits, they changed themselves and others for the better. Having been introduced to these characters, I'd been changed for the better. Still, as much as I loved the book, the Disney movie, and Pete's comparing me to such a heroine, I'd never want him to call me Pollyanna in public.

This was who I was. Certainly, other homosexual men like me existed out there somewhere. Pete and Farley wanted the same thing I wanted. Didn't they? To have a home and family and a theatre career was the dream we all dreamed. Wasn't it? We'd never be able to marry, but we could love each other, live together. Once in a relationship, I'd never have to worry again. I'd be quite content sharing my life with that one-and-only. All I needed was to find the perfect guy, that fine young man.

I sat on my bed and brushed my hair. As soothing as a massage, each swipe of the bristles against my scalp dislodged thoughts I'd buried long ago. Grandma Flora calling Mr. Keen her "fine young man"—*Jesus!* I laughed at my own naivety. Mr. Keen was gay.

My cheeks flushed hot, and my mind raced, unearthing memories of Mr. Keen. Kind, attentive, and supportive, he was indeed a fine person.

Perhaps Pete had hit the nail on the head when he'd coined my new moniker. *I am a Pollyanna.* If Pollyanna had been born male, I was certain she'd have been a fine young man too.

CHAPTER 4

ANYTHING YOU CAN DO

My appetite crushed by nerves, I skipped dinner and headed out for a walk before the ominous black clouds reached the camp. Ambling away from the main hub, I strolled down the graveled path through the wooded area thick with blue spruce. The air was potent with the scent of evergreen, and my mind drifted to Christmas days long gone.

My voice coach claimed that any note that could be hummed could be sung. So, I hummed my audition song through the grove of birch trees, swaying in the gathering intensity of the wind. "Here we go," I said aloud when the theatre came into view.

I eased into a plump, velvet seat at the back of the auditorium. Most of the others had gathered down front. I preferred isolating before a performance. Centering myself physically and mentally prepared me for the limelight. Closing my eyes, I imagined I was walking across the golden wheat field with Grandma Flora.

All chatter halted when the director, Crocker Philpot, and the music coach sauntered down the main aisle to their seats. Acid splashed against the wall of my stomach, and I wished I'd brought a hunk of white bread to quiet the roiling ocean.

A crack of thunder and a flash of lightning, visible through the giant glass windows of the auditorium, warned of the storm seconds away. *Flash! Crack! Bang!* Another round of admonitions summoned the ruckus closer. Mighty oaks stood their ground, their clawed branches swiping at the gathering wind. The hula skirts of the weeping willows flapped and bowed to the fierce force of nature.

"August Applegate!" the pianist yelled from behind the baby grand.

The moment I heard my name, calm washed over me, and I glided to the stage.

I handed the pianist the music and crossed to the spotlight center stage. I planted my feet firmly on the creaky pine floor, raised my chin, and stood tall. The light on my face, as bright as the noonday sun, was a warm welcome. I was home. Real life felt like playacting compared to life on the stage. On the stage, there was no denial. Once onstage, I turned on. Unlocking my emotions, connecting intensely with another being was walking a tight rope. Anything could happen. Each moment was alive!

I nodded to the pianist, and she began the intro to *She Touched Me*. Evangeline called it my "show-off song." The first verse was soft and mellow; the second verse built to a booming belt, an ideal fit for my tenor.

Mesmerized by the particles of fine dust floating in the swath of light pooling around me, I opened my mouth and flattened my tongue, and the first word slid over my lips with ease. Pitch perfect, I sailed through the first verse.

Concentrating on the sincerity of the lyrics in the second verse, my mind wandered back to Pete's tender kiss. "'He touched me. He put his hand near mine, and then he touched me.'" Gently, I climbed the scale an octave and belted, "'And suddenly, nothing is the same!'" The last words of the song I tapered to a whisper. "'Nothing! Nothing! Nothing is the same.'"

Then, the most unusual thing happened. Something that never happens at auditions. The audience burst into applause. Even the directors joined in. Flabbergasted, I bowed politely. Though slightly embarrassed, I adored the gratification.

"Wow," the pianist whispered, handing me my music. "You have some pipes."

As I descended the stairs to the seats, I glanced out the massive windows of the auditorium and noticed a fuchsia blur streaking past the hedges lining the walkway. No sooner had I plopped down in the first empty seat in the front row then the auditorium doors banged open.

His sopping black hair plastered to the side of his sharp, angular face, Farley bounded up the steps to the stage, his shoes squeaking like a dolphin and his soaked bellbottoms slapping together like a clapping seal. He pulled the sheet music from its protective plastic and arranged it on the piano ledge, to the pianist's chagrin. His polyester fuchsia plaid shirt clung to his boney ribcage, a second skin that expanded with every breath.

He bent over to wring the water out of his elephant bells. Then, raking his fingers through his hair, he stepped into the spotlight. Though it was a difficult selection for the most seasoned soprano, he chose Eliza Doolittle's "I Could Have Danced All Night" from *My Fair Lady*.

"Are you sure?" the pianist asked in a stage whisper. Farley shot her a fierce look, and she pounded the keyboard in retaliation.

Farley missed his cue at the first go round. Determined, he straightened his posture, but jumped in a measure too soon during the second intro. "'Bed! Bed!'" he wavered in a stringy vibrato. "'I couldn't go to bed.'"

The pianist hit the chords hard, attempting to aid Farley in his quest to reach the moon.

"'My head's too light to try to set it down.'" He scraped the sharp edge of a withering top note.

Someone gasped. I glanced back at the directors, who were clutching the backs of the seats in front of them, their eyes bulging.

When Farley started dancing on his tip-toes around the stage as if he was about to take flight, Mr. Crocker Philpot snapped out of his trance and bellowed, "Thank you very much!"

The pianist halted abruptly, and Farley, teetering dangerously near the lip of the stage, froze in mid-turn.

His cheeks ablaze, Farley clomped across the stage, snatched his music from under the pianist's nose, and thumped his way down the steps. Out of breath, he sank into a seat at the far end of the first row. Catching my eye, he glared at me. I was puzzled by his contempt.

I waited until the end of the auditions to leave the theatre, not wanting to cross his path. But when I stood to go, I realized he was already gone. Uncertain as to when he'd departed, I was nonetheless relieved by his absence. Pete, standing near the front doors, flagged me down before I walked past the indoor tropical garden, where I spotted Farley perched on an iron architectural beam.

"You were amazing," Pete said, squeezing my arm. "What did I tell you?"

"You weren't even there."

"I snuck into the balcony," he said. "Didn't think I'd miss your debut?"

"What about Farley?" I asked, hoping Pete had skipped out before Farley had stolen the spotlight.

Pete shook his head and looked at Farley straddling the beam. "Pathetic."

"Do you think he knows?" I wondered aloud.

"That he lacks talent?"

"People see what they want to see. He must be . . ." I glanced at Pete, but he was looking up through the atrium's glass roof at the sky, which was beginning to clear. "My heart goes out to him. Can you imagine what he's going through?"

"He should never have come back." Pete guided me around the crowd to the side entrance. "He needs to stop."

"Maybe he can't."

We walked out into the cool night. Every evergreen, bloom, and vine that had survived the downpour glistened in the fractured light of the building's floodlights. Pools of still water rippled whenever a drop trickled from the foliage above.

"What do you mean he can't?" Pete asked at last.

"Desire is a powerful influencer."

"Tell me about it." Pete started down the path to the boathouse. "There's no comparing an orange to a rotten apple. Sorry, Michael Jackson, but one bad apple can spoil the whole bunch, girl."

We walked on in silence for a while. The air was thick with fragrant plant life and the rich smell of wet earth. "I love this smell," I said. "It reminds me of my grandma's farm."

"I love to go riding after a storm. Or early in the morning when everything is fresh," Pete said.

"You have a horse?"

"We stable our horses at Haycock, not far from here."

"What's your horse's name?" I asked.

"David. David Copperfield," Pete replied. "It's one of my favorite books."

"Mine too."

The boathouse was deserted. I'd been told that most everyone hung out at the main lodge during the evenings to gab, dance, play games, or eat. I was glad to be alone with Pete. Although he frightened me a tad, I found him good company.

We sat in a dry boat under the hanging enclosure. "Feels like a waterbed," I joked when Pete sat opposite. "Dad goes fishing in his friend Harold's dinghy. I've been once or twice, but Mama has a fit if I'm anywhere near water."

Pete reached over and removed a tiny twig from my hair. "I'll never tell." He dug into his pocket and withdrew a joint. Clicking his monogrammed gold lighter, he lit the miraculous wand.

I'd smoked pot at Evangeline's Halloween party last fall, but nothing had happened. I hadn't felt the magic. However, when Pete offered me a drag, I eagerly partook in the hopes it might quiet the raging war of wits inside me. In silence, we puffed the joint down to a nub. "It's chilly." I untied the sweater around my shoulders and slipped it on.

Our legs were touching. Pete rested his elbows on his knees and gently rubbed my calves. "Warmer?"

My head suddenly felt light and heavy at the same time. Though neither of us uttered a word, I laughed. When I felt his warm palms grip my arms, I placed my hand on his hand. A rush of heat exploded in my chest, and I stared into his eyes. I stiffened immediately. "I don't know what to do."

"What did you do with Evangeline?"

"She made the first move."

Taking my face in his hands, Pete pulled me close and kissed my eyelids. His peppermint-laced breath tickled my ear. Wrapping his arms around me, he hugged me tight. "You smell delicious," he whispered. "You're a high school dream."

I wasn't certain what he meant, but at that moment, I didn't care. I squeezed him tight and kissed his chin. I explored the nape of his neck with my tongue. When he gasped, I figured I was on the right track. My back arched when he tugged my shirttail free. Reaching under my shirt, his hands explored my tingling flesh. His fingers glided over my pecs, and I shivered when they touched my nipple. This was far different than my rendezvous with Evangeline.

•●•

Evangeline had been naked when I came out of her bubble-gum-pink-striped bathroom that Wednesday after school. She'd gestured for me to join her on the bed. Without bothering to unlace them, I pulled my shoes off and sat on the edge of the mattress.

She'd spread her legs wide. "Get naked, Augie," she said and laughed.

I'd stood, stiff and nervous, at the end of the four-poster.

"My parents will be gone for hours," she'd said as I stretched out next to her. Her hand on the back of my head, she pulled me close and kissed me. "Time you learned what all the fuss is about." Then, taking my hand, she guided me to where she wanted me to be. She pushed my face against her thigh, but I didn't venture further. Her belly smelled of lavender soap and her vagina like sourdough bread.

When I didn't respond to her command, she sighed and guided me on top of her. Once I was inside her, instinct had kicked into automatic drive.

"Slow down, Augie," she'd whispered. "It's not the Kentucky Derby."

• • •

The taste of Pete's flesh tickled my senses. A kaleidoscope of butterflies flapped their iridescent wings in my rib cage, fanning my yearning. Tucked under his arm, I felt small and protected. He reached behind a stack of life jackets, pulled out a plaid picnic blanket, and wrapped it around us. The boat rocked gently as I pressed my head against his chest. I wondered when or if he'd planted the blanket with the hope of luring a conquest into his lair. However, my mind was focused on one thing. Besides, knowing so little about him, it was impossible to reason why and how he did the things he did.

A human puzzle, the curves, valleys, dips, and hills of our bodies interlocked perfectly. He leaned back, stretched his long limbs the length of the dinghy, and opened his legs. I didn't wait for instruction. I eased myself on top of him and he wrapped his legs around my hips. Pulling his polo shirt off, I ran my hand over his chest, taut, muscular, and butter-soft as kid gloves. My head foggy from the pot and my morals tossed to the wind, my imagination ran wild. Over every inch of his chest, neck, and face my hands investigated the enchanted minefield of pleasure, and I tested my not-yet-mastered skills on his map of flesh.

"Oh August," he whispered in that deep, honeyed baritone that plucked my heartstrings.

Up and down his chest, I kissed and licked each feature as if it was newly discovered gold. All of a sudden it hit me: *Is my way the right way?* Evangeline and I had never bothered with foreplay. Mechanically linked, we'd simply gone at it.

I paused, and he opened his eyes to my dumfounded expression, his questioning brow crinkled and his nostrils wide. "Don't stop now, August." We laughed, and he hugged me tightly. "You are too cute, Pollyanna." His smile flattened suddenly, and a seriousness washed over us, but his change in attitude was not penetratingly crippling, as with Mama when she was about to explode.

Pete took my hand and pressed it against his erection. Then, cupping mine in his hand, he kissed me passionately, pressing so hard I feared my lips would split against my teeth.

Afterward, we sat holding one another beneath the blanket. Not even on stage had I ever felt so satisfied, content, and grounded. That nagging restlessness I'd rumbled with since puberty snored peacefully in my soul. There was no turning back. I'd crossed the river Jordan, singing, "Hallelujah." I was complete. I was gay. No if, ands, or buts; I was, as Chester Chad had so colorfully described me, "Queer as a two-dollar bill!" I was utterly a homosexual and thrilled to be one. All was right with the world. Strong and virile, every muscle in my body pulsed with a maleness unknown to me. Born in the bloom of romance, I was truly a man.

"You know you're still a virgin with a man. . . technically?" Pete informed me.

I laughed, but he looked at me earnestly, and I stopped. "But we . . ."

"Only anal sex truly counts," he said, grinning.

We snuck into the cabin and headed for our separate beds. His musky scent of vanilla, pot, and a smidge of bacon lingered in my nostrils. My skin, tattooed by his touch, ached for a repeat performance. Confined to the nanny's corner, I found it difficult to sleep in the same room. However, with Farley just north of me, I dared not tip-toe across the rough pine boards in the middle of the night and slip under Pete's covers. That would be the final straw for Farley. He'd report our behavior to the powers that be, and we'd be tossed out on our ear faster than I could say, "The rain in Spain is mainly on the plain." Well, at least, *I* would be tossed out. Since Pete's family owned the land, I doubted they'd shuffle him off to Buffalo. I resorted to yearning from a few yards east of where my buffed and beautiful lover—if I dared call Pete that—had bedded down for the night.

Farley, hidden under his *The Unsinkable Molly Brown* comforter that featured the one and only Debbie Reynolds in quilted comfort, rhythmically snored and farted in a round robin I wished I could have ignored. Although he was in La-La Land, it was the first time I'd seen him since the audition. I prayed he'd land a role in the show. Hopefully, a change of luck was on the menu for Farley.

On my way back from a midnight bathroom trip, I checked to see how my Prince Charming was sleeping. From the smile on his face, I surmised his dreams were pleasant. I peered down at his, as Aunt Jessica would say, "perfect Protestant face" and wondered if I was featured in any of them.

• • •

I was exiting the shower pavilion the next morning when Farley marched by, bumping my shoulder in a forcefully rough way.

"Farley!" I yapped, rubbing my shoulder.

He continued as if he hadn't noticed me.

"August!" Pete called as he approached. As instinctively as Pavlov's dogs, I salivated with desire. "Coming or going?"

"Going." I gestured toward the showers. "But Farley—"

"Go," he commanded. "I'll deal with Farley Fairfield."

"But . . ."

"You don't know him like I do."

"It's just that . . ."

"No!" Pete squinted his eyes, and I withered. "Pollyanna, your job is done here." He touched his hand to my cheek. "So cute. My ginger gentleman."

I scanned the room quickly for probing eyes.

Pete kissed my forehead. "Nobody cares here."

• • •

Neither Pete nor Farley had returned by the time I'd dressed. Having skipped dinner the night before, and drunk on the after- glow of our titillating tryst, my appetite had increased three-fold. Strapping on the Gucci watch Aunt Jessica had given me for my sixteenth birthday, off I trudged to the lodge for breakfast.

I was splurging, drizzling maple syrup on my stack of pan- cakes when Danny, the dance captain, flirtatiously bumped his hip to my mine. "How's it hanging?"

Sparsely populated, the dining hall sat relatively subdued.

"This poor building must sigh with relief when it's locked up for the night." I sat by the window overlooking the flower garden.

I was glad Dad was into gardening. Although he was a self- taught novice, I'd learned so much under his tutelage. Besides his nightly cocktails and fishing, gardening was a relaxing pastime for him. Together, we'd created raised garden beds bursting with an- nual flowers he'd purchased at the local hardware store and grown from clippings from Grandma Flora's garden.

I gazed at the garden beyond the lodge window, exploding with pride. Sweet Williams, calendula, foxglove, and pansies grew in abundance to the point where it was impossible to discern which stem or leaf belonged to what plant. I preferred a crowd of flowers over a crowd of people any day. Toss a puppy into the mix, and I would be in heaven.

Although there was plenty of room on the opposite side of the table, Danny slid into my side of the booth and winked. I never could abide a winker, but it was different with Danny; there was something genuine about his wink, as natural as dotting an "i." "Pete's the best, don't you think?"

"His set designs are amazing." I stuffed a dripping wedge of pancake into my mouth.

Danny laughed and nudged me. "You are too cute, Pollyanna."

My cheeks burned.

"Don't worry, love; your secret's safe with me."

My appetite melted with the butter swimming in the sun- soaked moat of syrup surrounding my flapjacks. "Safe with you?"

"Pete tells me everything, doll. Once you've been one of his boys, you're in the club."

"Club?" *Betrayed. Double-crossed and betrayed. Pete was no better than Mama when she'd dress me in drag and laugh at me, not with me.*

He reached under the table and pinched my thigh. "I was the chosen one two summers ago. Farley, believe it or not, was three years ago, and—"

"Farley Fairfield?"

"The one and only." Danny slathered mayonnaise on his egg and cheese sandwich, then, catching the sight of my stunned expression, said, "Oh honey, he looked nothing like the freak he is today. Kind of preppy and not so skinny. Cleaned up and with his natural hair color, he's not half bad. If you ask me, he's never gotten over Pete. The way he dresses . . . that hair . . . screaming for attention." He wiped a dab of mayo off his chin. "Get a life, that's what I say." He speared a wedge of hash brown on my plate and popped it in his mouth. "Tragic, really. I'd never judge anyone on their sex life, but he . . . he sucks anyone willing to drop their pants. Believe me, girlfriend, he's not picky." He crinkled his nose as if he'd gotten a good whiff of donkey dung. "Mexican gardeners. Busboys. The postman last summer. Can you imagine? Low lives. It's bad enough we get all that Jersey trash in Philly." He dug a sesame seed from between his incisors. 'Trash. If there's one thing I can't stand, it's *cou rouge.*" Although I'd never seen him in the buff, I speculated Danny was one of those people who was stunning in or out of clothes. "If Pete hadn't saved Farley's lizard-hide last summer . . . well. He was nearly kicked out when he was caught in the boathouse with that hunky security guard. Idiots! Both of them! The hot Italian was fired, and a letter was sent to Farley's parents. Now I ask you, who would be dumb enough to get fucked in broad daylight?"

Flabbergasted, I stared at the clematis leaves fluttering in the crisp morning breeze. I wish I hadn't run into Danny. An unwanted cloud on a sunny day, he had rained on my parade. In a matter of minutes, he'd managed to deflate my utopia and wallop my positive attitude. I wanted to yell at him to shut up. *Just shut up!* I could have punched him square on his puss, right after I kicked Pete's prized buns.

Pete had shared precious details of our romantic evening with someone I barely knew. I'd thought I was special. *Am I simply another notch in Pete's belt?* "Excuse me." I gestured for Danny to let me out of the booth.

"But darling, you've barely touched your pancakes—or hotcakes, as you Southerners say." He didn't budge, so I dropped back into my warm seat. "Besides, you should be ordering champagne!"

"Because of Peter Pakington Pace?" I was livid, but uncomfortable wallowing in cynicism. I needed to escape, run against the wind until I'd sweated out the rage engulfing me.

Danny cocked his head and grinned. "Silly Sally. Did you see the cast list I posted by the front door?" He patted my leg, dangerously close to my privates. "You'll be the cutest George M. ever."

He could have knocked me over with a feather. I was instantly lightheaded, and the entire room spun faster than the agitator on Mama's miracle Maytag washing machine. "But I'm first year. You must have misread the sign."

Danny put his hands on his hips, and his thick brown lashes fluttered as coyly as Carol Channing's in *Thoroughly Modern Millie*. "I should know. I typed the bitch myself."

# CHAPTER 5

ANOTHER OPENING, ANOTHER SHOW

I welcomed the six weeks of intense rehearsal. Truly, I needed every second of it to master the demanding challenge of being the lead. The character I was playing, George M. Cohen, was from Providence, Rhode Island, so any trace of my Southern accent had to be quelled. As I'd been imitating stars such as Marilyn Monroe, Cary Grant, Roz Russell, and a million other Hollywood celebrities since I was a boy, accents came easily to me.

"You've got the ear for it," Aunt Tootie would say before begging me to repeat my Fred Gwynne as Herman Munster: "Oh Lilly!" It had her in stitches every time.

The *George M!* score fit my tenor to a T. Dancing was my biggest challenge, but contrary to negative gossip circling the theatre tribe about Mademoiselle Lavish, I found her patient, polite, and positive.

"To bad vous so old to dance ze ballet, August Apple-turn. I could have made you ze star." She pressed my shoulders. "Nose to the floor, Mr. Apple-cart."

I left the cabin early every day to avoid Pete and Farley. I hadn't the time or energy to waste on overreaching sneers and underhanded jabs. At night, I was sound asleep before either one stumbled to their squeaky twin mattresses in the wee hours of the morning.

Unavoidably, I still dealt with Farley daily. Miracle of miracles, he'd been cast in the show. We had a few scenes together, and I was pleasantly surprised by our on-stage chemistry.

During the final dress rehearsal, I flagged him down backstage to tell him how proud I was of his performance. "You're really good."

He looked down his nose at me. "Do I look like I need an amateur's approval?"

There was nothing I could say that he didn't take the wrong way.

Although I longed for Pete, I avoided him like the plague. Perhaps I was to blame. *Am I being too sensitive? So what if he talked to a friend about me?* On the other hand, they might have had a good laugh at my expense.

"Polly paranoia!" Danny jabbed when I eventually asked.

I'd followed Pete's lead in the boathouse and somehow still screwed it up. *What don't I know about gay lovemaking?* I needed answers. I'd have settle for a clue.

Occasionally, Pete would saunter into rehearsals with Rodney shadowing his every step. He'd make a big show of being overly affectionate with him, but he didn't fool me. I caught him countless times staring at me as Rodney hung on his every word. *Games.* I was barely out of the closet and "already jaded," according to Danny. The games humans played were mind-boggling. *Dogs are more honest! They sniff, bark, growl, wag their tail, and move on.*

Pete was my first real crush. My heart was breaking, but I wasn't in love. I wasn't exactly certain what love was, but I knew it wasn't what I felt for Pete. That was something else altogether: lust; a scorching fire-red pining, potent enough to peel the skin off my common sense.

Danny proved to be a better friend than I'd expected. "Don't mind me, girl, I'm just South Philly trash. Babble. Babble. Babble. You know how I am." He'd run on about some guy we knew, or he'd rail against my "Pollyanna prudery," but in the end, I reckoned he saved me.

Without his private tutelage, I never would have learned so much dance in such a short time. Six weeks of rehearsal conquering unfamiliar territory was an uphill battle I needed to win. By dissecting one segment at a time, I was able to decipher the mechanics of the choreography and how each piece interlocked with the next.

"You're an instinctual dancer. You feel the measure," Danny said. "I'm the opposite. I count every beat."

Since Danny's roommates were shacking up with their girlfriends, I ended up staying at his cabin most nights. Located yards away from the theatre, crashing there allowed me an extra twenty minutes of golden slumber. Only once did I consider fleeing from my safehouse.

Having fallen asleep the moment my head hit the pillow around midnight, I was startled awake at half past two by Danny's enthusiastic kisses. The moment his hand crept under the waistband of my tidy-whities, I bounded out of bed. "Danny!"

He sat on the edge of the bed casually. "Can't blame a girl for trying."

He was so astoundingly handsome, I felt I could have fallen for him if he were a different sort—but then, he wouldn't be Danny.

Nothing about being gay added up. I'd speculated that gay relationships might be easier because I'd be dealing with a same-sex mate who should understand precisely what I needed, wished for, and desired. *Wrong!* I was unequivocally wrong.

I tried not to judge the actions of others because I didn't want others judging me. Yet, I did judge. I knew I did. *To each his own*, I thought, but my soul wasn't designed for hand jobs under the table, as I witnessed Sandy Silverstein perform on Mr. Philpott at one of his Saturday night soirees. I saw things that summer I'd never dreamed of. Heaven knows I could never have been brazen enough to strip to my all-together in a room full of strangers, as Carson Gilroy did at every pool party. It was sleazy, and I wasn't comfortable being drenched in seedy. *Does promiscuity go hand-in-hand with being gay? Christ!* What was the answer?

I couldn't do what Farley did. I was covetous of his daring appetite for adventure and disgusted by his rumored triumphs. None of these incidents were beautiful, joyous, or romantic. I'd had one chance at coming out, and I'd blown it. If only I'd had access to H.G. Wells's time machine. I would have dialed it back to 1963, back to the simplicity of being a boy.

"Oh, Augie," Mr. Philpott said one evening when he cornered me in his bathroom. "You're missing all the fun." He squeezed my thigh and planted his fish lips on mine. A great sloppy kisser, I scrubbed my mouth with toothpaste for five minutes after he left and wondered, *Where are the gays like me? Where do I fit into the world of sexual chance?*

Thank heaven for theatre. It sustained me to the finish line: *opening night!*

· • ·

Mama insisted on coming to the opening, so I secured seats in the center of the fifth row for her, Dad, and my aunts. I was beyond thrilled. Except for Julie Andrews and Judy Garland, Mama disliked musical theatre stars more than she detested musicals. Begrudgingly, she'd attended our junior high production of *Oklahoma* and Rockridge High's *Annie Get Your Gun*.

"Your father was on the edge of his seat whenever you were on stage," she'd said, opening and then snapping the brass clasp of her handbag. "I missed your big solo. The ladies' room is a mile away."

The only show she'd sat through entirely was Mrs. Reynold's first grade class's nonmusical production of *Three Billy Goats Gruff*. It hadn't been me nor my fellow classmates that captivated her attention that Friday afternoon in the stuffy auditorium of Rockridge Elementary. It was my pink bunny costume, which she'd fashioned from a *Butterick* pajama pattern, that everyone was cooing over.

As Aunt Tootie whispered in my ear afterward in the back seat of Dad's burgundy Thunderbird, "That's showbiz for ya."

· • ·

The morning before opening night, I bolted out of bed at five a.m. Enthused, I was in the dance studio by five-fifteen going over the tough bits of choreography one last time.

"It's six o'clock in the morning," said Danny when he arrived in his short, poplin pajama bottoms, rubbing his eyes. "Get a grip, girl!" Throwing in the towel when I wouldn't budge, he joined in, running me through my paces.

We were headed toward the canteen for breakfast when Pete spotted us.

"August!" He jumped over the veranda railing with the athletic aplomb of Donald O'Conner. "This came for you." He handed me a folded piece of yellow paper.

Call home is all it said. "Who gave you this?"

"A security guard," he said, smiled broadly, and touched my arm. "Knock them dead!"

I made a beeline for the bank of telephones. "What is it, Mama? I thought you guys would be on the road by now. Don't forget to check into the inn before you come here."

She interrupted me, her voice stern and flat. "We're not coming."

In the blink of an eye, my entire being melted into a puddle of despair, froze crystal cold, and cracked down the middle. My heart lay stranded on a block of ice plunging over Niagara Falls. Mama's felony of abuse crippled me. I was the cub with his paw caught in her trap. My esophagus burned from the geyser of stomach acid bubbling up. My jaw monetarily locked and my scalp tightened. My head was light, and my heart hung heavy. "Not coming?" I muttered. "Why? I reserved great seats, fifth row center."

"I can't."

Rinsed in a chill, my sweaty body trembled in the heat. "What about Dad and Aunt Tootie?"

"I need them here."

"The whole run is sold out, Mama."

"There'll be other openings of other shows." Gruff and low, the dragon's fiery breath scorched my ear. "You understand how it is."

"I do," I said, meek as a lamb cornered by a rabid wolf. "There will be other shows." My mind fizzed with blankness. "I've got to go, Mama. Hope you feel better." I dropped the receiver in its cradle and stared at the graffiti-infested wall of the phone booth. "She wins. She always wins."

• • •

Standing backstage, behind the curtain, saturated in the splendor of an overture was a gift from the gods. Every fiber of my being was ignited. I knew if I made it through the first scene, it would be clear sailing. As the overture rose to its brassy conclusion, I closed my eyes and thought of Grandma Flora's golden wheatfield. She was with me, and I was calm.

The show ran swimmingly well. Surprising ourselves, we triumphed over hurdles we'd previously stumbled over. By the time the *Yankee Doodle Dandy* scene opened, I was eager to tap.

"Thanks," I whispered to the dressers frantically changing my costume backstage. I reached for my cane on the props table. "My cane! My cane!" I whispered in a panic. It was imperative that I had it.

The stage manager and the costume assistants scoured the backstage but returned empty- handed. Anxiety scaled my spine with the agility of a black widow spider. Sweaty and hot from the lights and the dancing, I furiously dabbed at my face and neck with the towel I kept in the wings. That's when I noticed Max, a chorus member on stage, holding a walking stick. It wasn't as long as the cane and lacked a handy hook to grip, but it would have to do.

Hearing my cue line, I vaulted onto the stage with the cocky self-assurance George M. was famous for. When the intro music rose from the orchestra pit, I did a bit of improv with Max, and, taking the hint, he handed me his walking stick.

At the conclusion of the number, the audience sprang to their feet. *A standing ovation! For me! Oh Mama, you don't know what you missed.* Perspiring like a Protestant peasant before Bloody Mary, I took my bow. I'd never enjoyed bows before, but that night, with so much at stake for me personally, I embraced the glory of the moment.

• • •

The remaining two weeks of the run were sheer pleasure. Acting workshops and classes in costuming and set construction filled my days. In the afternoons, I'd have my daily run, relax by the lake, then nap in the cool of Danny's cabin. I felt as glamorous as an MGM star.

After the evening performance, Danny would gather a gang of his favorite flavors of the day for a party by the pool. A relaxing swim at midnight, and I'd sleep like baby till ten. Free of restraints other than my own, I rode high on a self-indulgent safari through an amazing adventure and enjoyed the hell out of every blessed second of playing grown-up at sixteen.

We never found the missing cane, but Danny was convinced Farley had nabbed it. "Girl," he said, "that little twat needs to grow up. Sure as I'm standing here, she pinched it." He cocked his head back and yelled at the heavens, "Grow some cahoonas, you ba-boonas!"

•●•

The faculty arranged a farewell party the last night of camp. A stage was erected by the lake. Mountains of food from the lodge kitchen filled a ten-foot-long table, and all was devoured entirely before the open mic cabaret began.

"That bitch just poured ketchup on a napkin and swallowed whole," Danny said, pointing to Farley.

"Sorry bitches, this is the last slice," a drunken Farley spit out—and then he stuffed the entire triangle of pizza in his mouth.

Someone in the crowd yelled my name after Ruth Russell wrapped up her energetic version of *I'm Just A Girl Who Can't Say No*. People began clapping and catcalling for me to take the stage.

"What should I sing?" I asked the audience.

"*She Touched Me!*" Pete yelled louder than the competition requesting songs from *George M!*

I looked at Pete a few yards away. Freckles of regret peppered my heart. Breathtakingly beautiful in the glowing maize light from the Chinese lantern hanging above his head, he stood smiling broadly in that sea of dark silhouettes.

I turned to the piano player and asked, "Do you know it?" She nodded.

It being a cool evening, the warm spotlight on my face was inviting. Tossing caution to the wind, I switched pronouns; I sang "he" instead of "she." I was officially out.

Moved by the night, the moment, and the man, I sang the song from my heart. I was in tears before the first verse was completed. "He touched me!" I belted. "He touched me! And suddenly . . . nothing is the same!" Blurry-eyed by incessant tears, I took my final bow at Buck's County Theatre Camp to thunderous applause.

"I'm going to miss you, girl," Danny said, and then he kissed me passionately. "Well," he said when I came up for air, "you can't blame a girl for trying." He hugged me tightly. "He's out there somewhere. Don't you want to say goodbye?"

I was hugged and kissed out by the time I'd swam through the ocean of well-wishers. "See you next year!" they'd say.

I smiled and replied, "Next year!" knowing I'd never be able to afford another summer in paradise. I knew I'd miss that world where an army of misfits were the stars in the spotlight, not the jocks, the crude party boys, and the cheerleaders. I would never look at Rockridge High the same way again; I dreaded returning to the bullies and the closet I would be relegated to.

"Have you seen Pete?" I asked Rodney, skunk drunk and hanging all over Sam Edelman, who'd arrived at camp with his girlfriend on his arm. Seemed I wasn't the only freshman homo on the lot. They both pointed to the boathouse.

A single porch light lit the path to the entrance of the gray clapboard boathouse. It appeared deserted, but when I heard Pete's voice inside, I swung the door open. I could barely see my feet as I maneuvered my way through the stacks of storage boxes and towers of life vests in the near dark cavern.

"Pete," I whispered. "Pete." He was standing with his back to me when I spotted him. "Pete! Pete!"

His eyes as big as saucers, he jerked around so fast he knocked a huge spool of rope off a wooden crate. Hitting the floor with a thump, it rolled across the bare planks and banged against the corrugated metal barrier.

"August!" he said, zipping his fly.

I stepped closer but froze when I saw Farley kneeling before him.

"August!" Pete said, stumbling over a box of racing flags.

I shot out the door and down the path.

"August! August!" I heard him shout.

CHAPTER 6

IT'S ONLY A PAPER MOON

Due to the limited bus schedule to and from Buck's County Theatre Camp, Farley and I ended up on the same Greyhound bound for DC. The bus driver had barely cracked the door open before Farley Fairfield pushed his way in. "My bag's outside. Please store it in the luggage compartment," he demanded and headed to the back of the bus. I assisted the driver with our luggage.

"Thank you, Mr. Applegate," he said. "Nice to know there's at least one gentleman in this younger generation."

By the time we reached Philadelphia, I was out like a light and didn't stir from my snoozing until I heard the hissing and sighing of the bus's brake pads rubbing against the rotor in Baltimore.

A man probably in his thirties boarded the bus. Although there were plenty of empty seats that Saturday morning, the moment we made eye contact, he made a beeline for me.

"Is this seat taken?" he asked politely, his baritone as smooth as a milkshake. "Rupert Siegal."

Mesmerized by his glistening indigo eyes, I couldn't speak. Taking my silence as a sign of approval, he dropped into the seat next to me.

I offered my hand, and he grasped it for a few beats past normal. A smidge shorter than I, he was muscular, dark, and handsome. He scanned me like a land surveyor perusing the boundaries of a plot of prime real estate. His form-fitting khaki shorts and white T-shirt left little to the imagination. His cologne, a touch excessive, introduced itself before he did, a pleasantly masculine combination of cedar, sage, and geranium. Neatly trimmed, his sideburns contrasted his thick black mane of hair. The long, defiant waves, brushed high off his forehead, hung loosely over his prominent features.

Nearly nose to nose, Rupert looked me straight in the eye when I spoke as if everything I said was of national importance. Occasionally, his hairy knee would brush against my bare leg, and I had to fight the excitement stirring in my groin. Although brief, my spirited romance with Pete had unleashed a sexual proclivity that reared its head at the most inopportune times. He asked me if I was familiar with certain bars and restaurants in DC, but I wasn't. When I told him I would be a junior in high school, he sat back in his seat, and his leg never again "accidently" ventured toward mine.

Talking with Rupert, the remaining hours of the trip flew by. The tales of his New York trips and all the Broadway shows he'd seen made me daydream about a possible future on the Great White Way.

"There's my aunt," I said, waving at Aunt Jessica from the window as the bus pulled into the DC station.

Rupert peeked out the window. "Evidently, beauty runs in the family."

We stepped off the bus, and Aunt Jessica, in her immaculate white mini wrap skirt and hot pink fitted tee, opened her arms to me.

"You must be Aunt Jessica," Rupert said and offered his hand. "I'm Rupert Siegal."

Perplexed, Aunt Jessica slid her oversized square-framed Ray Bans on top of her slicked-back hair. Her eyes darted from him to me and back to him as she shook his hand.

"Your nephew was kind enough to share his theatre camp adventures with me." Before she could respond, Rupert patted me on the shoulder and excused himself.

"Take care, August Applegate," he said, handed me his card, and walked away. *Rupert Siegal, Vice President of Visual, Wallis & Fitch Haden Department Store*, it read.

"That's my favorite store," Aunt Jessica said when I showed her the card. "We have a week together before Oscar picks you up next Saturday. Perhaps I'll treat you to lunch at Wallis & Fitch Haden's Azalea Room."

Someone slammed the trunk of a car, and we snapped our heads in that direction. A mile-long Chrysler New Yorker, parked illegally on the sidewalk, was blocking a frustrated cabbie, who laid on his horn, eager for his next fare.

A husky, dark-haired man gnashed his teeth and grumbled as he dragged Farley by the scruff of his neck around the Chrysler New Yorker and tossed him into the back seat like a discarded blanket. I gasped.

"What a brute," Aunt Jessica whispered.

One of Farley's shoes popped off in the scuffle and slid under the car. When the car screeched into traffic, his pilgrim shoe still lay flattened and dead on the sidewalk, tire tracks framing the scene of the crime.

•●•

A week later I was back home, and the circle of life continued under Mama's rule. During those blissful periods when Mama was incapacitated, Dad steered the ship into calm waters. As horrible as it sounds, I was glad—or rather, relieved—when she crashed. The house drowning in delightful quiet was sheer heaven. Worry and fear were put on hold during those halcyon days we knew would soon disappear.

"You've changed, Mr. March," Mama complained whenever I didn't complete a requested task to her ridiculously high standards. "Ever since that theatre camp . . . well, you're impossible!"

In all honesty, she hit the nail on the head. I had changed, and I preferred the difference. Having succeeded beyond my wildest dreams in *George M!*, I had the confidence to stretch my wings. I was convinced that anything was possible if I set my mind to it. *I may not always succeed, but I'm damn well going to try.*

No longer did I wish to beat myself up over trivial miscalculations. I attempted to accept life as it came. Every day would not deliver a grand triumph, but each one presented the prospect of discovering something new. As Mama's favorite actress, Bette Davis, remarked in *Now Voyager*, "Don't let's ask for the moon. We have the stars."

After years of fearing the many moods of Mama, I was determined to cease living in her shadow. I didn't want to end up like my sister, April, frazzled by and furious at Mama's lack of affection, so I stopped waiting for the magical transformation I knew would never come. Five years my senior and a tad tightly wound herself, April was a thorn in Mama's side. She'd gotten married her freshman year at the University of Virginia, and I was certain it was because she couldn't bear the thought of returning home to Mama.

Mama's new best friend, Valium, prescribed in 1975, had made her far more manageable. At last, Dad could enjoy a cocktail or a beer without her flying into a rage. Thankfully, she was a teetotaler. I trembled at the thought of how fierce she would have been lit.

We knew the quiet days were but a temporary reprieve from Mama's fury, and a paper moon lit our midnights. Still, for the next two years, we soaked in contentment for the duration of every cease fire.

•●•

At age four, I had realized that whatever illness Mama suffered, she wasn't equipped to handle it. Grandma Flora was the only one capable of coaxing her off the ledge during "one of her spells." Dad did his best to protect us from the worst of her wrath. Facing Mama, shrieking like a banshee, he willingly sacrificed himself without complaint for April's and my sakes.

When we were small, April and I fled when Mama's typically ladylike demeanor crumbled. We slithered over windowsills with the dexterity of jewel thieves and sprinted across the field, where a dense populous of bluebells bloomed come spring, in our mad rush to our secret cave beneath a rocky overhang by the Shenandoah River. April kept her favorite doll in close proximity at all times, just in case. In a space between two limestone rocks, I hid my own lifeline: a cigar box stocked with colored pencils, a tiny watercolor kit, and scraps of paper on which to draw.

After Dad built the playhouse, we would lock ourselves inside and sit quiet as mice when Mama banged on the door. Holding our breath, we would watch her shadow climb the yellow walls to the ceiling. I'm not certain how we knew, but instinctually, we always did: when to run, and when to return.

Occasionally, though, we were caught off guard. One of the most traumatic incidents unfolded the morning of my sixth birthday. Rising early, Dad surprised us with crispy-edged hotcakes, sizzling on the griddle. Topped with a healthy dollop of butter and dripping in maple syrup, his griddlecakes were just the way we liked them. Engrossed in the pleasure of the sweet sensation, neither April nor I noticed Mama creeping down the back stairs.

The minute she spotted the splattered batter on the counter, she went ballistic, grabbed a paring knife from the dishrack, and plunged it into Dad's calf. Then, seeing the blood gushing from the wound, she collapsed into a chair.

April sprang out of her seat and bolted out the door, leaving her treasured doll, Agnes, face-down on the tile. I rushed to Dad.

"Quick, Augie. A dishtowel," he whispered so as not to rile the wayward beast. He ripped the dishtowel in two and wrapped it tightly around his leg as I mopped up the mess on the floor. Steady and calm, he bent before Mama and kissed her cheek. Then, taking her in his arms, he hugged her close. Gentle as a summer breeze, he sang their song from the war years, *Swinging on a Star*. They slow-danced until her head bobbed on his shoulder. Lifting her in his arms, he carried her upstairs to bed.

Ali McGraw says on her deathbed in *Love Story*, "Love means never having to say you're sorry." She was wrong.

• • •

Senior prom was the last rite of passage before Rockridge High's graduation. Weighed down by expectation, such events often expanded to mythic proportions. There was no denying their importance, and I threw myself into it wholeheartedly. But after the exuberance of my success at Buck's County Theatre Camp, school lacked the glamor I craved. Minute or grand, I was determined to enjoy the last bits of high school life, but I could never shake my longing for Buck's County Theatre Camp. I was now too old to attend, even if I could have squeezed the money from my parents' bank account.

The theme of our senior prom was Springtime in Russia. Why the committee chose an unrelatable theme so foreign to our tiny hamlet in the Shenandoah Valley, I hadn't a clue. However, with a little help from volunteers, it turned out to be surprisingly lovely.

Peggy Carhart roped me into painting the backdrop and constructing paper mâché stars to suspend from the overhang above the dance floor. The shop teacher fashioned a fountain out of a plastic baby pool that Dad disguised with sandstone rocks.

Evangeline convinced her mother, who owned Sally's Florist, to donate the bulbed flowers to fill the raised garden boxes. Mama, subdued by Valium, made chintz tablecloths with Aunt Tootie to mask the crude folding tables. Gratefully, the home economics instructor sewed yards of fake grass together to cover the molded chicken-wire landscape surrounding the room. Once the place was flooded with cherry trees and festooned with paper blossoms, it resembled a garden party at Montpelier. Somehow, the Russian theme got us where we needed to be: back to Ole Virginie.

Evangeline surprised me by accepting my nemesis's invitation to the prom. The source of my public humiliation, Chester Chad, football quarterback and lead bully—I decided he must be dealt with. I couldn't leave high school without standing up to the halfwit who, despite my popularity, had managed to reduce me to the lonely, fat kid on the playground I once was every time he zapped me with one of his choice zingers. Among his favorites was "Queer call, faggot, and half-breed!" to which I always responded, "Yeah, just like Cher!" That annoyed him to no end, but it hadn't stopped him from repeating it a million times, even though my joke always scored the laugh. "Cocksucker," he reserved for those intimate moments in the locker room or men's lavatory.

Evangeline discoed down in the sherbet-orange organza halter gown that I'd selected for her, line-dancing the night away with her terror in a tux. Astoundingly, we sat at the same table.

"What's up?" I asked Evangeline when C. Chad trotted off to the can. "He's almost human."

"Be nice," she said, clicking her glass against mine. "He's hung like a horse."

It wasn't until the prom afterparty at Lana Lane's house that I found the chance to have a word with him. I was Lana's date. She'd asked me during our run in the spring musical, *Music Man*. She'd played Marion, the librarian, to my Harold Hill. Perhaps it was the passionate kiss on the footbridge in the third act that had piqued the head cheerleader's interest in a theatre nerd. I don't know. However, slow dancing with her under the cardboard stars, I decided she would be the end of my foray into females, literally and figuratively.

In spite of our differences, or because of our differences, we had a rip-roaring good time. My John Travolta impersonation on the dance floor got the biggest laugh of the evening.

Before the afterparty, we rushed back to Lana's house to change. The sooner I could ditch my rented cream-colored tux and lavender ruffled shirt that matched her backless lavender dress, the better. I had no sooner stepped out of Lana's lavender-tiled bathroom onto the lavender shag carpet of her bedroom—when she pounced.

"Come on, Augie," she said, tugging on my belt buckle. "Rumor has it you're a tiger." I was startled by her aggression when she pushed me on the bed. *My God!* She was a lioness, sexually concentrated and dedicated to her amusement. *Damn Evangeline!* She must have gotten high during one of their slumber parties and blabbed. She never could keep a secret. She even told her mother the first time we checked out the difference between little boys and girls when we were five.

"Loosen up." Lana unbuttoned my striped button-down and licked my chest. I couldn't breathe. She pulled her tie-dyed T-shirt over her head, took my hands, and placed them on her breasts.

The contrast between Pete and Lana's lovemaking was light-years apart. In both situations, I was cast as the submissive one. "Damn it," I muttered and flipped her over on her back.

"Sock it to me," she joked, quoting Goldie Haan from *Laugh In.*

"I thought you were a fag," she said afterward. She ran a brush through her feathered locks and spritzed them with Aqua Net. "I'll be around this summer."

By the time I bopped down the stairs, the place was jam-packed.

"Hey!" Jeff Jenkins, three sheets to the wind, hollered in my ear. "I used a hairpin on the lock of her old man's bar." He swirled the caramel-colored liquid in his glass. "Rum! I think."

Unlike my family's cramped Cape Cod, the Lanes' house was expansive. I wandered from room to room, more interested in the décor than talking to drunk schoolmates or strangers I'd never see again. As I unlatched the French doors in Mr. Lane's study, a bracing breeze slapped my hot cheeks. The sweet smell of lilac along with damp earth and boxwood wafted under my nose. The aroma of spring was unyielding, cajoling me out into the dark. Buttoning my nubby cotton cardigan, I crossed the cobblestone terrace to the jade green lawn. I noted that wealthy people's grass felt like carpet beneath my feet; Kaiden's parents' garden had been the same.

A mass of sugar maples, their budded green branches bobbing, lined the walkway leading to a small stable that once housed Lana's and her brother's ponies. The door to the stable was open. The moonlight over my shoulder, I sauntered in.

No longer stuffed with bales of hay, the stable sat scrubbed and scoured, Borax clean. Folded lawn and iron patio furniture was stacked high in the first stall, and the second one was packed tight with cardboard boxes. The third one had been converted into a workshop. Several Chippendale dining chairs in various states of repair sat outside.

I brushed the sawdust off the sturdiest looking one, dragged it into the stall, and sat down. Glancing at my watch, I noted the time, 3:35. Soon it would be morning. Since Lana's parents were conveniently at their beach house for the weekend, they had asked the housekeeper to arrange a buffet breakfast for their darling lavender-loving princess and her chums. There was no way I was staying to watch the herd of stoned water buffalo stumble from their beanbags to the trough.

What had started out as lovely, fun evening had ended tainted by acts of desperation. I couldn't say sex with Lana hadn't been exciting (she'd taught me things I hadn't known were possible), but it hadn't been satisfying. Any sexual situation reminded me of Pete, which made me sad and regretful. It all boiled down to the fact the romp with Lana had been ugly. Nothing felt intimate. She hadn't even bothered to dim the lights until I'd complained about their blinding brightness.

Pete was right. I was a Pollyanna, a gay Pollyanna. I was living in a parallel world. There I was at the prom, marveling at the beauty we'd created with our bare hands, beauty that few noticed and fewer appreciated. I was a conundrum to myself, an extroverted introvert. Out of some great desire I didn't understand, I molded my popularity. The most sought-after dance partner on the floor, I was everyone's witty best friend and the nicest guy anyone had ever met. Though it was rewarding for my ego, the role left me lonely and depressed. I was caught in the loop and found it difficult to stop. I'd be no one if I didn't play the game. I wanted to rush back into Lana Lane's packed house and scream, "I'm a homosexual! I love men!"

I dropped my head and gazed at the floor. Its bricks, worn by horse hooves, were striped by the moonlight cutting through the slatted walls. A prisoner of my creation, I prayed for a new start come fall. At college, away from what bound me, I would have the opportunity to unearth the true August Applegate. *My days and nights must be mine,* I decided. The heavy cloud of remorse lightened, and a tear of relief trickled down my cheek.

Just then, a shifting amoeba-shaped shadow fell across the moonlit floor. A pair of Converse All Stars stood before me.

"Chester Chad," I said, standing.

He said nothing. Looking me square in the eyes, he came toward me.

I blocked him with a chair, but he shoved it aside. "Go ahead!" I said boldly. "Hit me. You can beat the crap out of me, but I'll tell you one thing . . . I'll tell you one thing, Chester Chad, I'm hitting back!" My fists were positioned to box.

Smiling, Chad took my hands in his. His palms were soft and warm. Was this the calm before the storm? He reeked of whisky. A tad precarious on his feet, he was obviously snockered.

I attempted to step around him, but he blocked me with his bulky body.

"Move," I said with authority. "Move."

Chad didn't budge. Instead, he wrapped his big bear arms around me, hugged me uncomfortably tight, and kissed me. A Rudolf-Valentino-potent kiss. Passionate, robust, yet gentle, it was dynamite. I nearly passed out from the intensity. It was beautiful. Chester Chad gave me the most beautiful minutes of the night.

His head resting on mine, he held me in his arms a while longer. The sound of crickets in the field beyond the gate beckoned the dawn. Embraced by the muscular mountain, I gazed at the fading stars in the dusty purple sky, their twinkle barely visible. Then he kissed the top of my head, turned, and walked out of the stable with his head held high. I said nothing. Grandma had warned against waking sleepwalkers.

• • •

Our graduation ceremony was held at dusk. A few stars, as sparkling as champagne bubbles, dotted the cerise-streaked amethyst sky. Standing center stage during my solo, *The Way We Were*, I had an ideal view of my class. His big white face like a lighthouse in a harbor of black robes, Chester Chad sat staring straight at me, tears streaming down his cheeks.

CHAPTER 7

GLITTER AND BE GAY

My junior year of college, I transferred from the University of Virginia to a small liberal arts college to attain more practical experience in all aspects of theatre. Although it was a prestigious school, I found the opportunities available to undergrads at UVa lacking. Between battling for an increase in federal funding and attempting to launch community art programs, the faculty was stretched thin. To salt the wound, most leads went to grad students. So, despite the excellent class instruction and workshop assignments I devoted my heart to, I was lost in the crowd.

It was Evangeline who suggested I give William Hedgerow College a go. She raved about their drama department. "Top notch productions!" she said. Although she longed to work with theatre offerings, she was a music major juggling a plethora of opera and recital performances. Besides her impressive talent at the piano, she was blessed with a soaring operatic soprano.

Lodgings, however, were a problem at Hedgerow. As a state school on the verge of becoming a university, it was busting at the seams with applicants, most of them fellow Virginians. Greedy for status and the cold, hard cash students' parents were willing to cough up, the school turned away few, which in turn created a housing shortage. Half-constructed dorms littered the campus. Unfortunately, I needed to find a place pronto.

"I'd be out on my patootie if they found you here," Evangeline whispered, as if anyone could hear her through the thick plaster walls of her dorm room. "I was lucky to get this place. Truth is Daddy gave an impressive donation." She cracked the window and fanned the pot fumes outside. "But who cares! I'm in!" Her life was a bowl of cherries. Seeing the look on my face, she added, "Don't be discouraged, pet; something will turn up. Heavens, darling! It simply must." Ever since her mother had sent her to charm school in Richmond, she really put on the dog.

Dad had always advised against resting on my laurels. I tried to never take anything for granted. When my big break came, I wanted to be ready.

Off to the student center we scampered. Evangeline explained that they had a huge announcement board in Dorchester Hall where rooms for rent and houses to share were posted daily. The line wrapped around the main lounge and out the door by the time we got there.

"Oh, Augie," Evangeline said after several minutes. "Maybe we shouldn't have stopped for coffee."

She was right, but I said nothing. After all the help she'd offered, I would have been an ungrateful ass to complain.

"Here, look: '315 West Benevolent Street, male roommate preferred,'" I read aloud, unpinning the postcard from the corkboard once we finally reached it. "Know where that is?"

"A few blocks from my dorm," she replied. "It's a lovely, tree-lined street."

It was the last of the five listings we checked out that day. The first three had been rented out before we knocked on the doors. The fourth was a room in a tastefully furnished Victorian east of the main quad. Evidently, it had once been the college president's house before they'd built an elegant Edwardian replacement on campus.

"It's yours for the taking," Mr. Prescott Wolcott said, his fox-red toupee drifting cockeyed over his right eye.

I conferred with Evangeline on the front porch. "It's a magnificent house."

"It is."

"I've always dreamed of living in a place like this, descending the grand staircase in the morning."

"Sleeping with a truncheon behind a triple padlocked door," she said sarcastically. She lit a cigarette and tossed her lighter in her blue suede shoulder bag, its fringe banging against her leg.

"The price is right. Way under budget."

"Oh, you'll pay the difference," Evangeline said as she sat on the balustrade. "Augie!" She snapped her fingers in my face. "You're such a Pollyanna!"

My eyes nearly bulged out of my head. "Pollyanna?!"

She grabbed my arm and pulled me down the front steps. "You have so much to learn about men. He's a salacious swine!"

Number 315 West Benevolent Street, with its neglected English garden and tattered veranda, sat in the middle of one of the loveliest blocks in town. Lined with interlocking silver maples, the street boasted a variety of sturdy, post-war housing.

An inviting clapboard monstrosity, 315, the singular Victorian remaining on the block, rose three stories from the rich, dark earth it had been planted in decades before. Meandering wings, topped with turrets, ran north and south of the front door. The entrance, framed by a dilapidated trellis, hung heavy with shedding yellow roses.

Peering at it from its front gate, I fell hopelessly in love.

Evangeline marched up the front steps and studied the three doorbells. "Which one?"

"Number one," I read from the card.

She rang the bell. The sound of a slammed door echoed inside.

"Hold your horses!" a male voice grumbled, his slippers scuffing the floor behind the paneled door.

"Hi!" Evangeline said before the door was completely open. The guy's face, shadowed by the door, was difficult to see from where I was standing. "I'm Evangeline Kline," she said and stepped aside. "This is my friend—"

"August Applegate!" Farley bellowed.

"Farley Fairfield?" I couldn't believe my eyes. All thought screeched to a halt. My mind buckled, unable to process the impossible view before me. The fickle finger of fate had pointed to my last hope of housing and that just happened to be the residence of one ex-nemesis deluxe.

Every moment from Buck's County Theatre Camp flooded my head. Bobbing in the murky memories, both sunny and bleak, were Pete and Farley. Neither high school nor my two years at the University of Virginia had dulled the javelin jabbing my melancholy heart. *Have they given me a second thought since they returned to their fascinating lives in cities far more exciting than my minute hamlet? Most likely not. Why would they?* I'd left one seething and the other one frustrated.

"So, you two know each other?" Evangeline's eyes darted back and forth in their thickly mascaraed sockets.

"'Know each other'?" Farley said and swept his flaming orange hair out of his face. "We lived together!" He chuckled charmingly and swung the door open. Quickly shimmying out of the thread-bare maroon flannel I recalled vividly from years before, he tucked the tail of his black T-shirt into his hip-hugging jeans. "Certainly, August has told you about his madcap season of frolic and fear."

"Fear?" Evangeline said and stepped over the threshold.

"Opening night jitters." Farley smiled and winked at me as if he and I shared a great secret. "Our dear lad here was the star attraction that special summer. Not even Joel Grey could compare to the marvel that is August Applegate."

"I missed it. I was kibitzing on a kibbutz in Israel that year." Evangeline crossed the dark paneled hall to a set of pocket doors. "What's in here?"

"'Why, the parlor,' said the spider to the fly." Farley gestured like a game show hostess at the doors before pushing them open.

Christ! He must be desperate for a roommate. No wonder his advertisement was one of the last ones pinned to the Student Union board. Farley Fairfield was desperate and needed me as much as I needed him.

"It's spacious," Evangeline said and peered out the bay window facing the front garden. "Must have been a queen of a house in her day."

"And now it's a house fit for a queen," Farley tittered. "Or queens."

Gracious to the point of unbelievable, he gave us a tour of the downstairs apartment. The light-filled, six-room flat—with access to a generous backyard and the veranda that wrapped around three-fourths of the house—felt familiar, as if I'd lived there in a previous life.

"It's cheap, and he's desperate," Evangeline whispered when Farley excused himself to answer the phone in the hallway.

"But it's Farley Fairfield!"

"Look at it this way, Augie. You've seen the best and the worst of him. You're one step ahead of the rest of we poor suckers waiting to discover the axe in our roommate's closet."

"He despised me."

"Is he the one you surrendered to?"

"God, no!" I shook my head. "Never!"

"Those furry eyebrows could use a good pluck and his chest is in dire need of a mower, but he's not that bad." We peeped around the corner at Farley, his hand cupped around the telephone receiver, buzzing in an undecipherable whisper. "Darling," Evangeline said, imitating Liza Minelli's Sally Bowls, "this is it."

"The only game in town," I said. A bit shabby, and terribly furnished, I knew then and there that 315 West Benevolent would be my new home.

"Settle in," Evangeline said. "Glitter and be gay!"

Farley's distinctive braying echoed down the hall, and we both pricked up our ears.

"It's either the princess or moving back to Floyd's flop house, and I burned my last caftan with your Maidenform bras after that women's march on the state capitol last year," we overheard him say.

Evangeline slid her arm around my shoulder. "I'm a few blocks away."

Queasy, light-headed, and more than a bit apprehensive about my future roommate, I'd reached the end of the line. "The last station stop." I moaned. Grandma Flora's voice reverberated in my head: "You're the captain of your own ship."

I scoped the details of the handsome Greek key relief on the baseboard. *Beautiful.* The once-elegant parlor, washed in the noon sun, glowed with promise. My decorator's mind ran wild with possibilities. I loved the seasoned smell of the rooms well-lived-in. The melancholy notes of cedar logs in the hearth, the nutty hint of cigar smoke, the bitter-sweet aroma of perked coffee and fried sausage lingered in its plaster. The hall floor creaked a welcoming melody under our feet as we followed Farley to the kitchen. The names Jane and Leo had been etched into the dining room window. *Precious.* I was falling in love, and there was no turning back.

"All right. All right!" I waved to Farley, still yacking away on the phone. "I'll take it." He grinned and shook his head, but his eyes sat stoic in their sockets.

"As Jane Russel tells Marilyn Monroe in *Gentlemen Prefer Blondes*," Evangeline said, crinkling her nose the way she had as a contented five-year-old, "'You can't fight it honey. You just can't fight it.'"

• • •

With my mustard vinyl Samsonite parked by the front door, I added the freshly pressed key to 315 West Benevolent Street to the others dangling from the brass ring, merrily pinging against one another. Then, closing my eyes, I uttered a hasty prayer, "Forgive us our trespasses as we forgive those who trespass against us. Lead us not into temptation but deliver us from evil. Please deliver me from evil."

"Hello!" I called out as I stepped into the house. No reply. "Farley!" No reply. I exhaled with relief, and my frazzled nerves settled to a Hindu hum. I was glad he wasn't there to greet me. Just as when Mama collapsed after days on the warpath, I welcomed the silence. I could hear myself breathe.

Farley must have been as reluctant as I was to enter a game of chance. One roll of the dice could yield exorbitant profits or plummet one into ruin. Tomorrow was as unpredictable as a circuitous storm cloud threatening rain.

In the book *Pollyanna*, orphaned Pollyanna, expecting to be greeted with open arms by her Aunt Polly, arrives to an empty house. Obviously disappointed, she decides to follow her much-cherished parents' advice to focus on the positive of the situation. "'If you look for the bad, expecting it,'" she says, "'you will find it. When you know you will find good, you will get that.'" I was keen to unearth the encouraging treasures of my new home with or without my new roomie.

No longer confined to the nanny corner, my room was the largest of the three bed chambers. Two sets of double sashed windows facing south and east meant I would have brilliant light from sunrise to sunset. Being a creature who thrived in the light, I was delighted that Farley occupied the north-facing room down the hall. From what I could tell from the outside, he never bothered to open the shutters, which hosted a convention of spiders.

On my way to the kitchen, I noticed a piece of notebook paper taped to the brass arm of the dining room chandelier. It was flapping like a nightgown on a clothesline in the stiff breeze rushing through the open window. Written in red ink, Farley's chicken scratch was difficult to decipher.

> *A.A.,*
>> *I won't be in until late. The fridge is divided into two distinct sides. Yours is the right. Make sure you lock the back door if you go out. Squirrels, as you will soon realize, are the enemy and will destroy anything they get their greedy paws on. Last year two of them chewed through two of my After Dark magazines. Collector's editions!*
>> *My room is locked at all times and completely off-limits!!!!*
>> *F.Y.I. I sleep late. So, no banging pots and pans in the morning. No radio, TV, or stereo until I am out of the house. If you make a mess, you clean it up. I assigned you the task of dragging the trash cans to the curb on Mondays. I pulled a muscle while water skiing in July, and the doctor claims it will be months, if not the entire year, before I can lift anything heavy.*
> *Later,*
> *F.F.*
> *P.S. Welcome.*

•●•

Since our schedules were completely reversed, Farley and I rarely saw one another. Farley did indeed sleep late, rose at noon, and dashed off to afternoon classes. An early riser, I was out the door before seven a.m. and returned for my afternoon run around one p.m.

"Not that we spend any time together," I shared with Evangeline, "but I think he's different." I told her about the incident at the DC Greyhound station, when Aunt Jessica and I had witnessed his father tossing him into the back seat of his car like a duffle bag of laundry but swore her to secrecy.

"That's dreadful," she said and grimaced. "And I thought my dad was bad."

A few weeks after I moved in, Farley went to New York to catch the smash hit musical *Ain't Misbehavin'*. Taking advantage of his absence, I invited my parents and Aunt Tootie for the weekend. They arrived with tools, a sewing machine, bolts of fabric, rugs, spackle, paint, and Aunt Jessica!

Aunt Tootie's skill with a Singer sewing machine was unmatched. In one day, she produced a chintz slipcover for the threadbare sofa (whose compressed springs Dad repaired); toile drapes for the living room, dining room, and my bedroom; as well as gingham curtains for the kitchen.

Mama rearranged the kitchen cabinets and scoured the dingy bathroom tile to a gleaming white. "I don't think this place has been cleaned since John Kennedy was president."

Dad and I patched holes in the thick-plastered walls and painted them a soft cream that reflected the sun's luminous yellow glow. Broken appliance handles were replaced, and jammed windows were jimmied open, their mechanisms oiled for an easy slide.

Aunt Jessica had framed prints of Impressionist paintings from the Smithsonian. Together, we arranged them over the credenza we'd found at a flea market that Saturday afternoon.

Exhausted and hungry, I plowed through Sunday brunch.

"Leave the silverware, for heaven's sake," Mama said, grinning.

She was beautiful when she smiled, serene and pleasant; you'd never dream of the horror lurking inside, horror that she smothered with medications and fought tooth and nail to conquer. That day, her high cheekbones delicately rouged to perfection, her coral lips at ease, and her thick, auburn hair swept into a French twist, she was the mother I wanted: the caring, jovial, patient Mama of my dreams.

Dad, once the handsomest fella in the room, sat with his small paunch hanging over his belt, enjoying the hush of the quiet minutes ticking by. *Will I look like him as I age?* I wondered. Thinning hair, dark rings under his eyes, and slightly stooped; *Will that be me?* Still, nothing could kill that sparkle in his eyes.

Aunt Tootie was a carnival door prize. Over-processed, packed into her colorful clam-diggers and striped sleeveless blouse, with her swinging plastic earbobs noting the seconds, she was, at heart, a rich scoop of red clay, molded by an unfortunate life.

Classy, lithe, and slender, Aunt Jessica was the cream of the crop, the sister who got away. Her skills served her well in the DC law office she worked in. Soft spoken, with a manufactured English lilt in her pronunciation, she was our very own Jackie Kennedy. How I'd loved playing in her walk-in closet as a boy in the sixties.

"Never have too many clothes," she'd often lectured me. "The best you can afford."

Her orderly closet contained but a few tailored suits, with matching pillbox hats on a shelf above and coordinating pumps on the floor below. A strapless crème silk evening dress hung in a clear plastic zip bag in a prime spot and a princess-cut, iridescent midnight-blue cocktail dress on the back of the door. She was perfection. She was a goddess. She was what I longed to be.

By the time they'd piled back into Mama's green-paneled Ford Country Squire station wagon after Sunday brunch, every room except for Farley's dismal den had been transformed from frayed and fractured to cottage chic.

I sat on the porch, waving to them until they disappeared around the corner of Pious Street. These people, my clan—they were a part of me. We belonged to one another, and that thrilled and frightened the bejesus out of me. *What unknown curse lies ahead for me?* I'd rather have died than be burdened with Mama's plight. I loved my dad, but I didn't wish to play second fiddle in my own show. Certainly, if I kept dieting and working out, I wouldn't end up overweight and alone like Aunt Tootie.

Unlike most of my friends, I had been born into a family of humble means. Our family tree boasted such honorable professions as insurance salesman, part-time receptionist, legal secretary, and cashier at Woolworth's.

April was the first to attend college and I the second. What people assumed and the reality of our situation was a world apart from the doctors, lawyers, and corporate execs the stork had delivered my friends to.

With my tummy full and the crisp autumn breeze caressing the windowsill, I curled up on the slipcovered sofa. Wrapped in Grandma Flora's quilt, with the cool air licking the back of the sheer curtain panels hung behind the drapes, I drifted to sleep.

· • ·

I was stirred awake by the sound of Farley unlocking the front door. "Hey," I said, rubbing the sleep from my eyes. It was almost dark outside. I'd slept the afternoon away. "What time is it?"

I clicked the lamp on, and he pointed to the mantle clock that read 7:15.

In a trance, Farley walked around the living room, soaking up all the new additions, but said nothing. After checking the remaining fruits of our labor, he carried his duffle bag into his room and slammed the door.

An hour later, he poked his head into the living room, where I was sketching costumes for a production of an original student musical the department head had requested I design after seeing my portfolio from UVa. "Off to the Pube," he said, grinning. He'd rebranded the local watering hole, Jake's Pub. "Want to come?"

I begged off, and he skipped out the door as if everything was peachy-keen. My gut told me otherwise. Like with Mama, it was what he didn't say that was most disturbing.

• • •

"He said nothing?" Evangeline asked the next day at lunch. I shrugged.

The chill in the air, unusual on a sunny Virginia day in September, offered a preview of coming attractions. I preferred the cool weather, autumnal colors, fires in the hearth, and cuddly warm sweaters over the crowded beaches and sticky heat of summers.

Evangeline and I bagged our cafeteria lunches and dashed to the quad before the best spots were snatched up. A tranquil escape from the hustle and bustle of the busy campus, the quad was landscaped with a plethora of evergreen, camellia bushes, and holly trees that provided intimate bowers of seclusion.

"The first couple of days were rocky," I said, referring to life with Farley, "considering our past and all. But now, we've settled into a nice, congenial relationship." I speared a cube of cucumber with my plastic fork.

"What do you talk about?"

"Theatre department, mainly," I said, then paused. "He *has* changed."

"Still wear those hideous shoes you told me about?"

"No." The thought of his dead shoe on the sidewalk outside the Greyhound station flashed in my head. "But last week he started wearing bracelets."

Evangeline force-swallowed her bite of corned beef on rye. "What kind of bracelets? Leather? Chain-linked?"

"Horse-bits."

"Horse-bits?!" She made a face. "Horse bits?"

"From the wrist to near the elbow . . . like Kayan neck rings . . . on his forearm."

"That's nuts." She took swig of her Diet Sprite.

"Makes a big to-do out of it. Marches into the living room, where he keeps them in a bowl on the mantel. One by one." I held up my arm and demonstrated. "*Clank. Clank! Clank! Clink! Ching!*"

"The apartment looks great, like a real home," Evangeline interjected. "He's a total dick if he doesn't like it!"

•●•

I was stuck in the costume shop all afternoon, so it was dark by the time I arrived home. The moment I noticed the toile drape hanging cockeyed off its rod in the front window, my heart sank. *My God! Have we been burgled?* I unlocked the door, tossed my bag on the hall bench, held my breath, and slid open the mahogany pocket doors to the living room.

My eyes bulging and my heart racing, I stepped onto the faded Oriental that used to be in my parents' living room. Like a Titanic stateroom after the iceberg, everything was at sixes and sevens, a topsy-turvy nightmare tipped on its ear.

The prints Aunt Jessica had framed where tossed willy-nilly about the room. All the furniture, which we had arranged cozily around the fireplace, had been smashed against the walls. Aunt Tootie's chintz slipcover was draped over the arm of the sofa as if it had been shot by a firing squad, its unfastened zipper a gaping wound.

A folded piece of paper had been taped to the mantle mirror with my name printed on the front in Farley's childish scrawl in red magic marker. My jacket still on, I slumped into Grandma Flora's ancient wing chair, the one that had sat by her kitchen fireplace, the one she'd sat in to read wonderful tales of my childhood heroes to me. With trepidation, I unfolded the note.

Princess Pollyanna,

How dare you! Just because you wear a Gucci watch, designer jeans, and cashmere sweaters does not make you an authority on good taste. Who gave you the right to repair MY SOFA? I DETEST the ugly slipcover! I could barf on the dreadful drapes cluttering my windows. I can't find anything in my kitchen! I'd rather gauge my eyes out than stare at those HIDEOUS impressionistic paintings! It looks like a VICTORIAN SEDUCTION ROOM! I HATE IT!!!! YOU'RE ARROGANT! CONCEITED! A BITCH! I HATE YOU!!!!

Sincerely,
THE VICTIM

Oh my God! I'd thought he'd be grateful. I'd thought he'd appreciate the hard work we'd put into improving our home. I'd thought my presence would be more palatable if I demonstrated how much I cared for 315 Benevolent Street, Apartment Number 1. I'd been wrong. Appallingly, I had miscalculated the situation.

Within seconds, my humiliation turned to anger. Outrage rose to the boiling point. I had to get out. I had to think, and I couldn't do it there in the aftermath of an assassination. I wadded the note and tossed it on the cold log in the fireplace, then dashed into my room and changed into my jogging suit and Adidas running shoes.

・●・

The beads of sweat on my forehead tingled in the chilly air rushing over my face. Pumping my arms and legs high and hard, I sprinted up the steep incline of Bryce Hill, which overlooked the town. It was evening, and families, students, and professors were returning home after a long day. Like lighting a Christmas tree one candle at a time, the windows of houses lining the avenues slowly sparkled to life. Cars, their headlights beaming, scoured blocks in circles until they claimed that precious parking space nearest to home. The town sat cradled between two mountain ridges, as handsome as the model city Dad and I once built for my matchbox cars.

Zipping the turtleneck of my tracksuit, I sat on the damp ground, catching my breath, watching life move on. That was when it hit me. I'd made a huge mistake. In my desire to beautify 315 Benevolent Street, I had, as Grandma Flora would have said, "tossed the baby out with the bathwater." Consumed by my desire to please and improve, I had completely forgotten that I wasn't the only person my decorating would affect.

I stood, shaking my limbs loose, and charged across the flat top of the hill, picking up speed. Pacing my stride as I descended the other slope, I slipped on a slick patch of wet leaves. I caught myself before I hit the ground.

In the distance, the brightly lit copula of Sedley Hall was a lighthouse in the darkening sky, guiding me in the right direction. Even so, I ended up lost in a spiderweb of streets and alleys, finding myself farther from my destination with every turn. So when I spotted the train tracks that I knew ran in a straight line toward campus, I darted across a busy intersection to reach them.

It was pitch-black along the tracks. I struggled to keep my footing on the rail ties. However, when the student center came into view, I sped up, eager for familiar territory.

A four-wheeler appeared as if from nowhere, blinding me with its high beams as it whizzed past in the opposite direction down the road that ran parallel to the tracks. Disoriented for a moment, I missed a tie. A fishplate caught the toe of my Adidas, and I tumbled toward the graveled ditch. Flapping my arms as wildly as a mad goose, I grabbed hold of the first object before me, a Norway Spruce, to break my fall. The brittle branch snapped under my weight, and I plunged face-first into its prickly, fury foliage. In the shuffle, a forked finger on a branch poked my eye, scratching my cornea.

"Jesus H. Christ!" I yelled.

My ankle twisted, my eye throbbing, and my ego bruised, I hopped along the side of the tracks to the student clinic.

The intern at the clinic cleaned my wounds, removed the gravel embedded in my knee, and bandaged the wound. A bit zealous, the student nurse made an eye patch that covered half my face. After the intern wrapped my sprained ankle, the nurse adjusted a pair of crutches for me and walked me around the waiting room for a test drive.

"Best call someone to help you home," the intern insisted.

I phoned Evangeline numerous times, but she never picked up. After ringing several other people, I finally rang the apartment. "Farley," I said, "I need your help."

Half an hour later, he escorted me back to Benevolent Street. As he swung his arms, the exposed bracelets sticking out from beneath his jacket sleeve *clank*ed and *ding*ed and *ting*ed like the bells on Grandma Flora's Christmas wreath. Annoying though the bracelets were, I resisted the urge to rip them off his arm.

"Farley," I said the moment we entered the front door. "I'm sorry if I upset you, but I thought—"

"That's just it," he said flatly. "You didn't think. This is my house too. As a matter of fact, it's been my home for the past two years."

I dropped onto the hall bench. "You're right. I was so eager to surprise you, I didn't stop to ask your opinion." I took his hand. "I'm sorry. Truly I am."

"Me too," he said, jerking his hand free. "I . . ." he hemmed and hawed, "was a touch melodramatic."

"You?" I raised an eyebrow. We both laughed. It had been a long day, and I was tired. "A truce?"

We shook on it.

"How did you manage all this in one weekend?" he asked as he removed his jacket, freeing the Carillon Tower of bracelets to *cling*, *clang*, and *ding* at full volume.

"My family chipped in. They're a marvel in action."

"How nice," he said, his subtle smile sliding into a frown. "Never my family. Not in a million years."

I thought of the hairy beast of a man tossing him into the back seat of the Chrysler New Yorker, and my heart ached for him. He sat down beside me to remove his boots, and I wrapped my arm around him. He was uncomfortable, but it was the right thing to do.

"We could order pizza," he said, grinning.

I didn't complain about my diet; I simply agreed. "Oh my God, that would hit the spot."

CHAPTER 8

LAZY AFTERNOON

By our second semester of co-habitation, Farley and I were, if not best pals, at least friendly. By coincidence, we signed up for the same time slot for three of our required department courses. Having avoided morning schedules for two and half years, he assigned me with the undesirable pleasure of waking him before I left for my eight o'clock dance class.

"You must, Pollyanna. I don't care if you have to fire a cannon. I'll never make it to a nine o'clock without your help. Besides, you owe me."

"Owe you?"

"You nabbed the lead in *She Loves Me!*"

"And?"

"And! I've been here for years, busting my buns, volunteering on set crews that I deplore, sucking up to every troglodyte casting a show, kissing the asses of the perfect, popular persons everyone swoons over, and you, Little Miss Sunshine, waltz into the department in your smart YSL to steal a lead right out from under me."

Ignoring his insulting flutter of frustration, I cut the conversation short. "Remember, you asked for it."

• • •

The daily chore of coaxing the Baroness from her slumber was akin to raising Lazarus from the dead, an unfeasible task that required skills beyond my pay grade. However, five days a week, I gave it my best shot. "Farley!" I'd say, rapping lightly on his door. When that didn't work, I resorted to banging a few of his bracelets together, but he was so accustomed to their clanking that he didn't stir.

"The best way to woo a swine is through his tummy," Aunt Tootie suggested.

A beastly burden, I often fired up the black iron skillet and fried up a country breakfast. The aroma of sizzling bacon and crispy-edged eggs popping in the inch-high lard was almost always the charm that lured the zombie into the land of the living.

Summer, winter, snow, or the sweltering heat of July, Farley greeted the day in a foggy haze. His door would creak open, and he'd scuff down the hall in his fleece-lined slippers. Crossing the kitchen, he'd strike a pose and peer out the French doors at the morning. His ragged plaid flannel robe roped tightly around his miniscule waist, he'd gaze into the garden and deliver his favorite Jane Fonda line from the movie *Julia*: "I think it's going to snow, Dash." Each time I laughed as if I were hearing it for the first time. He was that funny. And yet, played for a joke, he was so sincere in his delivery that I wanted to hug him.

Once he trusted I wasn't out to get whatever it was he thought I was out to get from him, Farley bloomed into the gracious Baroness of Benevolent Street. He'd find interesting articles in *After Dark* and *American Theatre* magazines—or his bible, *Playbill*—to share with me. Once, he even brought me a lovely still of Lucile Ball as a nineteen-forties glamor queen back from New York. "It was there. So, I bought it. Happy birthday, Princess Polly."

He refused outright to commit to house chores. "I lived in filth before you got here, and I didn't contract dysentery. It's a college rental, not a permanent home, for Christ's sake, Polly!"

Perhaps not for him, but for me, it was my first real home since my tiny playhouse, and I loved it. It was grand to open the front door of what must have once been an impressive entrance hall. The staircase that led to the top floors had been walled off, but the exquisitely carved mahogany archway that once framed its opening was still intact. As I crossed the threshold, I liked to imagine the elegant Edwardian mistress of the house, resplendent in her satins and laces, descending to her guests waiting in the oak paneled hall below.

I hadn't grown up in the luxury I imagined Peter Pakington Pace had, or even Farley. From the pictures Farley shared of his parents' historic townhouse in Alexandria, Virginia, I surmised money had never been an issue for the Fairfield family. The only thing that didn't add up was Farley's wardrobe. His family was nicely dressed in the photos atop his bureau, but he seemed to revel in his slobbery. *Oh well—to each his own.*

My family wasn't in the same league. Our house was tastefully furnished. Though our closets were light, the clothing we did have was expertly tailored and constructed from the finest fabrics we could afford. Farley was correct. I didn't dress like anyone else. My fellow theatre students' T-shirts, frayed jeans, athletic shoes, and parkas simply didn't work for me. After I came out, I came to see myself as a stylish young man. I dressed more as my father had in his youth, but that's who I was: always a bit out-of-step with the modern world, off-kilter with seventies society. Always in style, my clothes were nonetheless unique.

"You're an original," Aunt Jessica once told me. "As with most of the gay men I've met, you're a peacock among the chickens."

Guilt about not coming out to my parents haunted me. Every time I drummed up the courage, something got in the way. It was easy with Aunt Jessica and Aunt Tootie.

"Honey, when you came home with that Barbie doll, pleased as punch, when you were a little thing, I knew." Aunt Tootie squeezed my shoulder. "Your parents weren't born yesterday."

"But it has to come from you," Aunt Jessica insisted.

She was right. I knew she was right, but when and how I would come out to my parents, I wasn't sure. In my heart, I hoped they would love me no matter what, but it was still a scary bridge to cross, because I could never truly know how they'd react. Eventually, I decided our school's Parents' Weekend would be the ideal time to spring the news.

•●•

Farley's parents arrived before mine. His mother, Virginia, was a dormouse in head-to-toe beige; a neater, drabber version of her son. His bear of a father, Francis, a personal injury lawyer, resembled Mr. Potato Head, his face full as a ripe pumpkin. His corn-kernel teeth were visible through his fish gill of a mouth when he smiled ambiguously. Even on that clear, sunny morning, a dark cloud accompanied them.

Virginia faded into the woodwork against the cream-painted living room wall. Selecting the most uncomfortable straight-back chair by the pocket doors, she was positioned to slip into a crack in the cushions at the slightest hint of conflict. Farley's older brother, Frank Jr., was a wall-hugging, thinner version of his father who had evidently inherited his mother's dismal disposition and dead gray eyes. A guardian gargoyle, he hovered within arms-length of his mother. Their appendages interlocked, they appeared to be a single alien species.

"Hot as Haiti in here, boy!" Francis hollered from the wing-back chair that barely contained his girth. "A cold beer."

Farley, minus his bangle bracelets, stared dumbfounded at his father.

"You did buy beer?"

Farley shook his head.

I hated to dash out and leave the panic-stricken Farley alone with the inhuman monster-mash, but I volunteered to run to the nearby 7-Eleven. "I need to get ginger ale for Mama anyway," I lied. Frances Fairfield, I decided, may be easier to digest if he was pleasantly buzzed.

•●•

Carrying a six-pack of beer in one hand and a bag with several bottles of ginger ale in the other, I noticed Dad's burgundy Thunderbird when I turned the corner of Pious Street. "Hey!" I called out, trotting down the sidewalk.

Farley's and my family had assembled on the front porch, a Picasso version of Norman Rockwell's *Saying Grace*. Mama in her taupe tweed pantsuit, Chanel-inspired ropes of pearls and chains dangling from her neck, sat at the far end of a bench from Francis, smoking her Kool Super Light. Dad was diddling in the garden, attempting to separate the tangle of ivy from the climbing roses. Aunt Tootie, decked out in a one-piece jumpsuit that Mama complained made her look like an airplane mechanic, sat unnervingly close to Farley's mother, who perched sidesaddle on the edge of the rickety wicker settee in an effort to distance herself from accidental human touch. A satellite docked to the mothership, Frank Jr. sat shoulder to shoulder with his mother. Farley sat alone on the wide balustrade, yards away from either clan.

In a good humor, Mama was doing her best to engage all and sundry in small talk.

"Well," she said, "how about we walk over to that charming little bakery for a quick bite to tide us over until lunch?"

Francis narrowed his beady eyes. "Not until I have at least one beer."

So, we waited until Farley's father downed two. He offered one to Dad, but Mama shot him a sharp look, and he politely declined.

Half an hour and three beers later, we set off for a tour of the campus. Dad and Aunt Tootie, coils of cigarette smoke trailing behind them, serious looks on their faces, were in conference as they meandered down the sidewalk behind us. Was Aunt Tootie preparing Dad for my announcement? After all, she'd known for over a year. When she caught me sneaking a peek of the centerfold of her *Playgirl Magazine*, the cat was out of the bag.

I knew my parents. Neither of them were religious, but Christian doctrine had been ingrained in them by ancestors long departed. Although Dad was a committed Eisenhower Republican and Mama a staunch Democrat, they shared liberal viewpoints on social justice. *Heaven, help me*, I needed justice. Coming out to my parents, no matter how liberal their viewpoints concerning others, would be stressful. I was their only son, the last Applegate of my generation, and I was petrified that when it came to their own flesh and blood, they may not be so understanding. It was not going to be easy, and I had one chance to get it right. After reading and hearing horror stories about parents disowning their children when they came out to them, the situation seemed precarious. If only they had been as bold as Aunt Jessica, who'd asked me outright, "Are you gay?" the day she'd treated me to lunch at Wallis & Fitch Haden's Azalea Room, then this tempestuous chore would have been dealt with already.

I was walking a tightrope without a net. I scolded myself for not doing it sooner and getting it out of the way years ago. Instead, I had passed on so many ideal opportunities that I was now left with little choice but to manufacture the perfect moment.

It was the honest and proper thing to do. Until I confessed my truth, peace would elude me.

As we toured the backstage of the Walton Theatre, our performing arts center, I explained to Virginia and Frank Jr. the process of making up one's face in the dressing room in an attempt to engage them. I might as well have chatted with two coat hangers. They weren't the least bit interested. I passed them off to a volunteer student guide, then scurried off to relieve myself.

I dashed into the men's restroom and hurried to the long wall of urinals. Facing the mirrored wall, I quickly glanced around the room. Until I heard the unlatching of a stall door, I thought I was alone.

My eyes nearly popped out of my head when I saw Farley, his back bent and his head down, shuffle across the tile and out the door.

The stall door stood ajar, with a clear view of Francis Fairfield zipping up his pants. A javelin of pain pierced my chest, and my brain burned with unfathomable thoughts. Thank heaven he was woozy and slow. I rushed out without even washing my hands.

••

Sitting across the table from Francis Fairfield at the restaurant, I barely touched my lunch. I couldn't look at the disgusting pig. I knew I was rushing judgement, but the situation had looked like Pete and Farley in the boathouse. No matter how I tried to focus on something else, the images of Farley skulking out and Francis zipping his trousers repeatedly played in my head. I couldn't comprehend it. I couldn't imagine Dad, in million years, putting me in that kind of situation. I kept balling my fist under the table. I wanted to punch Francis Fairfield square in the kisser. He sat there nonchalantly, stuffing his ginormous face with a sticky bear claw, sugary syrup coating his triple chin.

I wanted to tell Dad or Mom or Aunt Tootie, but I didn't wish to spoil their day. How would I broach the subject? *Oh, by the way, I saw something interesting in stall number one in the men's restroom.* It was a preposterous position to be in, and yet there I was, stuck between most likely and absolute.

Farley was blank and silent as we toured the College President's residence and the garden behind the library. His silence was not golden. His pain was palpable. He was Munch's *The Scream*, a victim of his father's perversion. Though I couldn't understand the dismal dance between them, the entire affair made me queasy. I wanted nothing more than to lace my Adidas running shoes and pound the pavement or dive into the deep end of the blue tiled pool in Huffman Hall to erase the memory, at least momentarily, from my muddled mind.

Bored and lethargic from his second lunch at Wendy's and the remaining three beers in our fridge, Francis insisted they leave early to miss the Northern Virginia traffic on Jefferson Davis Highway. "Here!" he barked, and tossed the ring of keys at Frank Jr., missing and hitting his wife on the forehead. "Drive!"

Francis Fairfield flopped into the back seat of his Chrysler New Yorker and was snoozing before Frank Jr. turned the key in the ignition.

•●•

Farley's metamorphosis was swift after his family disappeared in a puff of smoke from the backfiring Chrysler. Shedding his oppressive chrysalis, he made a beeline to the bowl on the mantle where his bangles sat quietly waiting to be animated. Stacking his trademark bracelets on his arm, he *clink*ed and *ding*ed his way back to life. A shaman cleansing the house, with each clank of his vociferous artillery, Farley dispelled a little more of his father's curse.

"Come, Mrs. Applegate!" Farley took Mama's arm. "I'm anxious for that honey fried chicken you promised." Off they tarried to the back of the house. Occasional laughter echoed down the hall from the kitchen, where Mama was preparing dinner.

"I declare," Aunt Tootie said, "Chip and Dale. Cleopatra and her eunuch." A paisley scarf lassoing her poodle perm, her head resembled a nineteen-twenties flapper. "A pair of misfit toys, those two."

Dad packed his pipe with tobacco and stepped out onto the side veranda. Tootie winked and pointed to the French door. "Go on!" she whispered. "What are you waiting for? Charlton Heston

88

to part the Red Sea?" Turning on her cork-soled wedges, she headed to the bathroom.

Dad looked up when he heard the porch planks creak beneath my feet. "Tootie's quite the chatterbox today." He sat on a wrought iron chair, looking out at the untidy garden. He changed the subject before I could reply. "All this yard needs is a little love. Shame it's been neglected." As he puffed the tobacco to a steady glow, its blend of fragrant, herbaceous notes, spiced with eucalyptus and sweetened with cherry blossoms, encircled my head. This was Dad's scent. "Calendulas and pansies," he said, pointing to the picket fence. "A hedge of purple cabbages and rust mums along there." He was doing what I did when I saw a neglected something in need of restoration. We looked at catastrophe and imagined it as it could be, as it should be and not as it was.

I had talked to my dad a million times about a million things, but never about sex. Though not usually a procrastinator, he had delayed the birds and bees talk until it was inaptly late. Taking a deep breath, I opened my mouth to start.

"Augie," he said calmly, "it's alright. I've known since the day we bought your first Barbie doll."

My breath caught in my throat. *My God! He knows! He's always known!* My cheeks were on fire. My heart leapt into a tarantella, and the chains binding my soul broke and burst into a billion particles of redemptive light.

Seemingly unfazed, Dad adjusted his plaid silk pocket square. "You know, fellas teased your Uncle Edgar when we were growing up. I never questioned him. Perhaps I should have, but I didn't. I wasn't going to be another smug bully accusing him of being something he may not be. After twenty-six years, he and Phyllis seem happy enough, but . . . what I'm trying to say is, it doesn't matter to me. I don't care if you are or not because love isn't that way. I can't say I understand it, but that's neither here nor there. Warts and all, you must take people as they are. Plenty of people question me about your mother. They never try to understand, see what I see. I'm a simple man. Uneducated, I follow my heart and my instinct. You see, Augie, maybe I should have done better by you and your sister, but . . . but she's my wife and your mother. Even a part-time mother is better than none at all." A shapeshifting tail of smoke rose from the chamber of his pipe. "My parents had a fit first time they witnessed one of her spells." He ran his hand along the ivy overtaking the balustrade. Touching green fed his soul. "I could never put her away, even for a rest. The embarrassment would kill her. She's quite sensitive, you know. She doesn't mean . . . she can't help the things she does."

"She's better on Valium."

"She's trying. She was a sweet, innocent lamb when I met her. To my mother's displeasure, I broke up with my fiancé two days after I met your mom. I just knew. I hadn't even asked her out, but I knew." Reaching over the railing, he freed a single yellow rosebud being chocked by a tangled rope of ivy. "I pray you'll be safe. It's an unkind world out there, full of unkind people who are full of hate. Some people hate anything different from them." He checked the tobacco in the bowl of his pipe. "You'll never come home again—to live, I mean. I don't blame you. There's not enough there to keep a bright young man like you content. Besides, homosexuals do better in cities."

I did what I could never do to Mama: I hugged my dad.

· • ·

When the oven died on Mama, we ordered Chinese carry-out from the Hunan restaurant.

"Needs an element. Easy enough to repair," Dad said as he yanked the dead coil out.

Fascinated and a smidge jealous, I watched the easy rapport between Mama and Farley. However, it was difficult to hold fast to jealousy after what I'd seen that afternoon in the men's restroom. So, I resigned myself to be happy for him.

Sitting at the kitchen table, chatting about the old movies and stars of the silver screen Mama adored, Farley was at his charming best. His face and body had filled out a bit, and three years of intense dance training with the theatre department's movement specialist had done wonders for his posture.

The month before, he'd even begged for my sartorial help. "No if, ands, or buts! We're going shopping. Wave your magic wand, Pollyanna. Time to turn the frog into a prince."

So, off we'd tarried downtown to Reginald Reed's Department Store. Catering to the fashion-minded, the men's shop carried a section of better labels. With the money he'd saved from his work-study job doing secretarial work for our department head, Farley had purchased jeans and a pair of lightweight cords that fit. The minute we got home, I'd threatened to incinerate his baggy-butt pants that hung like a loaded baby diaper.

The gods were looking out for Farley Fairfield that afternoon. "Look!" I'd said, holding up a blue-and-gray herringbone blazer on the sale rack. "My treat, but only if you promise I can cut your motheaten corduroy jacket into ribbons." Though I'd been saving my measly checks from my job in the costume shop toward a new stereo, I'd shelled out the cash for Farley's sake. There was something to that Christian teaching: it's better to give than to receive. It was marvelous to witness his transformation. A simple act of kindness, a tad-bit of magic, and a touch of tweed turned Cinderfella into a baroness *du jour*.

"Next stop: A salon to tame that wild hedge of autumnal orange," I'd said before ushering him into Daryl's Design Studio.

An hour later, Daryl had spun Farley around in the chair to face the mirror. Farley had stared at his reflection as if he was gazing at a stranger. His bangles clapping their approval, he'd run his fingers through his newly disciplined locks. "I don't know what to say," he'd said, his eyes glistening. "Thank you, August. Except for my autographed Streisand album, this is the nicest gift ever."

"My pleasure," I said. His smile had seemed sincere, and for the first time since we met, I'd thought he looked handsome. My heart had swelled with pride. "Payback for creasing Angela Lansbury's face years ago," I'd joked.

Aunt Tootie had brought a tin of her famous coconut macaroons for dessert, and Dad made coffee with a scoop of cocoa, as he preferred it. Their tummies pleasantly full, Dad, Tootie, and Farley comfortably camped out in front of the crackling logs in the living room fireplace, drifting off to sleep. I gazed at the grinning Farley, pleasantly snoring, as I slid the pocket doors closed. The missing square of a quilt, he easily fit into our eccentric clan.

I cleared the remainder of the dishes from the dining room table and carried them to Mama. Rubber-gloved and elbow-deep in bubbles, she scrubbed the last of Grandma Flora's every-day blue willow.

I took a deep breath. It was now or never.

Standing in the doorway, my heart pounding and hands shaking, I cleared my throat. "Mama," I blurted out before I'd collected my thoughts. "Do you . . . do you know why I . . . I never have a girlfriend?"

My words hung in the air like a skywritten message of smoke. Exasperating, the moments ticked by at a snail's pace.

Without turning around, Mama wiped her hands on a towel and untied Grandma Flora's pinny. "Yes, Mr. March," she said with the authority of Agatha Christy's Miss Marple, "because you're gay."

I gasped. A tsunami of mixed emotions slapped me hard, and I felt faint. I collapsed into a vinyl chair and attempted to calm the explosion inside me. "How did you know?"

"A mother always knows." She slumped into a chair, removed a shoe, and rubbed her foot. "Eight hours in heels is a day's work."

"When did you know?"

"The day the nurse put you in my arms." She yawned and stretched her legs under the table. "Remember when I dressed you like a girl? You never complained. You mastered high heels faster than I did." She tapped a cigarette out of its pack and struck a match. "People thought you were beautiful as Betsy Ross in first grade." She massaged the back of her neck and grinned. "It was the cosmetic department thing that kind of threw me. I thought you'd be thrilled when I took you shopping with me. What gay boy could resist all that glamorous boxed bounty of scent and skin care?"

"Scary! Those painted Kabuki mavens slathering, dabbing, and spritzing . . . yuck!"

"Your sister's worse than you." She took a long drag off her cigarette. "Do you think April's a lesbian? She's so athletic and . . ."

"Stereotyping."

"I always assumed."

"Mama, why didn't you come to Buck's County Theatre Camp that summer?" I don't know what made me ask her. She was relaxed and calm, and I shouldn't have upset the apple cart. But regrettably, I did.

A fire-breathing dragon, she opened her mouth and smoke rolled out. "That was eons ago."

"It was important to me."

"It was a play. I figured there'd be others. There's always others." She puffed harder on her Kool Super Light, the smoke encircling our heads in a wispy wreath of gray.

"Never again. That moment is gone forever." I felt the heat rising in my chest. My mouth was dry as the sandy Sahara. Knowing that Mama's paybacks were hell, I never picked a fight with her. Instead, I followed Dad's example. I coddled her when she was down and walked on eggshells when she spiraled out of control.

Only this time, we weren't at her table in her house. I paid the rent for 315 Benevolent Street. Sitting barefoot at my table with her hair down at the end of a long day, she was vulnerable.

"Farley told me you're the lead in the next musical," she said, her face as stoic as a monk in solitary confinement. "Why now?" Her voice dropped an octave. "Except for Judy Garland and Julie Andrews, I don't like musicals!"

"If you would only—I'm somebody else. I—I . . . it's magical in the spotlight."

"As sentimental as your father. He couldn't get enough of that boring June Alison when we were dating. Do you know how many times he dragged me to—"

"I don't care about June Alison!"

"Shush!" she said, putting her finger to her lips. "You'll wake the others."

I stared out the window at the abandoned vegetable garden. Like a giant's ancient palm, the sparse brown earth lay stripped of its beauty. Evening's shadow frolicked along the boxwood hedge and settled under the weeping willow. "Do you know how terrifying you were?"

Puzzled, Mama stared at me as if I was speaking gibberish. "Afraid of your own mama? How absurd."

I pushed back from the table, the chair scraping the floor. "You remember. Don't sit there and pretend you don't. You do. You know you do!"

"Just like your sister. April has a chip on her shoulder the size of Afton Mountain," Mama said, her jaw tightening. "I'm terrifying? You're scaring me. What in hell's gotten into you? You were the best kid; an angel, my ginger-haired angel." She searched for her shoes under the table and jammed her feet into them. "I didn't make you gay. You were born that way."

"What's that supposed to mean?" I gripped the edge of the table. "I know I'm gay. I like being gay!" I'd never raised my voice to Mama. I had never stood up to her, questioned her motives, or challenged her. I bore the weight and the scars of her atrocities. She knew. I knew she remembered. She was simply too stubborn and proud to admit her shortcomings.

"It's easy to blame the mother. Always the mother. When something goes wrong, blame it on Mama." She wound her auburn hair into a French twist and jabbed bobby-pins into the graceful swoop. "I remember when you were no more than three. You'd put your little hand at the back of my head, and I'd wrap my hair around it. At four, you pinned it for me. Your little hand was the perfect size." She looked tired. Even through coverup, the dark circles under her eyes were evident.

Mama's iron blockade, mellowed by Valium, shaved into ribbons of steel, fell like Pick-Up Sticks on the cold linoleum. She was finished for the day. "Oscar! Oscar!" she yelled. "Time to hit the road!" The sound of her heels clicking over the parquet floor echoed through the apartment. She pushed the living room's pocket doors open but didn't cross the threshold. "Oscar! Tootie! It's late!"

Dad scrambled to his feet. Aunt Tootie, sluggish as a sloth cradled in a cecropia tree, slowly came to life. Mama marched out the door without saying a word.

"Well, we're off," Dad said and squeezed my arm.

"Someone's dishing attitude," Tootie whispered in my ear when she hugged me. "We're in for a pleasant ride over the mountain."

My soul bruised and my ego battered, I sat on the front steps to wave goodbye.

What had been a lovely, lazy afternoon had ended in poignant regret. I'd ruined the day. Just when everything had been going well, I opened my big mouth and stuffed my foot in. Instead of graciously counting my blessings and being happy with my lot, I'd destroyed what should have been a beautiful memory.

I looked up when Farley sauntered onto the porch, the sight of his half-zipped fly reminding me—Oh, the dreadful sight of his father zipping his pants . . . I wanted to scrub my mind clean, erase the incident. The tips of my ears were on fire.

Setting the bowl of untouched fortune cookies and two sodas between us, he sat on the steps. The overhead pendent above our heads struck the cut facets of the bowl, washing the vanilla cookies in a rainbow of light.

"Your mother's a hoot!" His bracelets clanked against the glass. "Ahh. The last RC Cola." He popped its top and chugged down half the bottle. "She promised to take us shopping." He snapped a fortune cookie in two and pulled the tiny piece of paper out. "'A feather in the hand is better than a bird in the air.'" He curled his nose. "Only if the feather is attached to a boa!" Closing his eyes, he selected a fortune cookie for me. "Next!"

The cookie broke easily, and the paper fell into my lap. I unfolded the fortune. "'A beautiful, smart, and loving person will be coming into your life.'"

"But I'm already here!" he squealed, then popped the cookie in his mouth. He couldn't stop grinning.

It was the happiest I'd seen him in . . . well, the happiest I'd ever seen him. I was thrilled that he and Mama had hit it off. Still, jealousy nibbled on my wits because I'd seen Mama being so tactile with him. Why did Farley garner such affection? *Oh!* Wondering and reasoning were frustrating affairs. *Why torture myself over a mother who doesn't care? Okay, Mama! I get it. Now I understand.* I utterly understood that she didn't love me.

CHAPTER 9

LADY IN THE DARK

When all else failed for Elinor H. Porter's Pollyanna, she turned to "the Glad Game" to lift her spirits. The point of the Glad Game was to find something about everything to be glad about. It was up to me to find the silver lining in even the darkest cloud. I spent my childhood searching for the emerald in a box of green glass. The hunt, Aunt Jessica promised, was the most exciting part. It was the one thing we disagreed on.

I was used to juggling several projects in addition to my classwork semester after semester, but with the extended weeks of rehearsals for *She Loves Me* running past eleven nearly every night, I was left with little time for late-night reading for class. Two pages in, and I would be dead to the world. I was grateful that Evangeline had finished the same class the previous semester and had Dr. Grose's syllabus, which evidently hadn't varied in the past decade. I planned to devote Christmas break to American lit.

Though Mama hadn't gone to college, she was an avid reader and was excited about my American literature class because her favorite author was F. Scott Fitzgerald, and *The Great Gatsby* was on the required reading list.

The summer before, when the Robert Redford/Mia Farrow movie version had been released, Mama had dragged me to see it seven times. Like a child, she'd sat there, doe-eyed in the dark, powdered and perfumed like a film star, sipping her Diet Sprite. For her, every viewing was the first time. Each time Gatsby was shot, she dug her nails into my arm.

Two weeks before Thanksgiving, Mama came to town for

a regional Democratic Party meeting and treated me to lunch at Woolworth's, a favorite of mine since I was a kid. I was tucked up in a warm booth overlooking Courthouse Square, sipping on my strawberry milkshake between bites of my grilled hotdog, comforted by Mama's fragrant White Shoulders perfume. The world was a delightful place where nothing bad could touch me. I was halfway through my hotdog when Mama grounded my magic carpet ride.

"He's the nicest man," she said and nibbled on a French fry. "I want you to meet Lloyd."

"Who's Lloyd?"

"Well," she whispered, rolling her eyes coquettishly. "My friend. My special friend."

I stared out the window at the passing traffic, unable to look her in the eye. She was forcing me into the role of Nick Caraway, Gatsby's chosen confidant and messenger.

"Your Aunt Jessica knows, but for God's sake, don't tell Tootie, the mouth of the South. She can't keep a secret. Your father would be crushed if he found out."

What nerve! Crushed? He'd be broken-hearted. Her animated reflection in the glass said it all. She was in love and busting at the seams. Spring had sprung that autumn. Mama was radiant, and I wanted to kill her.

She'd lost ten pounds, her cheekbones were rouged with the artistic touch of a Reynold's portrait—she was beautiful. A permanent smile was plastered on her face; she was literally tickled pink! My mind, however, turned to murderous thoughts. I daydreamed of her in her mile-high heels being chased by rabid wolves. Better yet, tossed into a pit of cobras. No way, no how would I meet Lloyd. Lloyd could drop dead as far as I was concerned. *Screw Llyod! And screw you, Mama!*

She rattled on about how she'd met him volunteering at a Democratic fundraiser six months before. All I could think of was Dad. Dad, who'd stuck with the vixen through more rough patches than Napoléon at Waterloo. Another husband would have let the authorities lock her up and flush the key down the toilet. *Thanks for nothing, Mama!*

I wanted to poke her violet-shadowed eyes out! I didn't care if she loved me, because I hated her. I despised her casual attitude about her clandestine meetings with her lover. . . . *Oh, God help me!* My imagination ran wild. *Jesus H. Christ!* I wanted to scream. Dealing with my own sexuality was bad enough without knowing that Mama was doing it with some strange man in some seedy hotel room.

The minute the waiter brought the bill, I grabbed my coat off the back of my chair and headed for the door.

"Where are you going?" Mama called after me from the cashier's stand.

"I'm late for class!"

••

It turned cold early that November. No sooner had Halloween been packed away than the temperature plummeted twenty degrees. A foot of snow was forecasted, and I prayed it wouldn't ruin opening night for *She Loves Me*. Plus, it would provide Mama with a convenient excuse to skip the performance. *Why should I even care?* I wondered. She certainly didn't.

Mama had sworn me to secrecy, and though I was wracked with guilt on many levels, I had to talk to someone. Evangeline was the only person who had known me, my family, and Mama long enough to understand what I was going through.

"Well, beat me with a spoon!" She fell back on the overstuffed pillows piled high on her platform waterbed. "Your poor dad. Poor you!" She squeezed my hand, and I stretched out next to her. Evangeline was petite but well-proportioned. Whatever she wore, she belted it to show off her tiny waist. She was the only girl I'd known in high school who wore high heels to class. She often said, "My personality is too big for flats!"

I hadn't realized Evangeline was Jewish until college. Her father, our town doctor, had set up shop smack-dab in the middle of Protestant country. In order to blend in, they joined our Episcopalian church. The only thing I knew about Jewish people was Barbra Streisand, Archie Bunker's rants about them in *All in The Family*, and my TV heroine, Rhoda Morgenstern.

"Think she'll leave your dad?" Evangeline asked, screwing up her face in that irritating pity-pouty expression that ignited my ire until I noticed her welling up.

"Remember, you're not the parent, Augie."

"I know."

"No, you don't. I know you. You feel responsible."

"I won't be able to look at Dad. He'll know."

"Acting. You're a good actor," she said.

"Never in real life. I'd jinx my gift. I hate lying. I'm a terrible liar."

Evangeline dragged my unruly bangs out of my eye. "Think of your dad. Do it for him."

"Mama wants me to meet him. Lloyd. *Lloyd*. A hideous name."

"No way!" She rolled her eyes. "Holy Sodom and Gomorrah. Your mother has balls."

We laid there on her bed, staring at the brightly colored Christmas bubble lights stapled to the ceiling as the citrine-hued sunlight faded to a cool lavender.

"Your hair looks auburn in this light," Evangeline said. "Like your mom's."

I ran my fingers through my curls and yanked on a tendril. "Never. I hate her hair. I need a haircut."

Perhaps I should have checked with the director or waited until after the play had wrapped, but on a whim during Christmas break, I marched into my hairdresser's salon with a ginger head of waves and exited a platinum blond. When I walked through my parents' kitchen door, Mama looked as though I had speared her in the chest.

"Your beautiful hair," she whined. "It's your one asset."

I wore a stocking cap to rehearsal the first evening back, waiting to unveil my transformation until the director called me to the stage.

"I'll dye it back if you—"

"No," Dr. Fisher said as he ascended the stairs to the stage. "It's nice. Of course, it won't match the publicity photos, but what the heck, every show needs an element of surprise." He held my chin in his hand and studied my profile. "The play is set in the 1930s. It'll be slicked back anyway." He grinned and winked. I blushed.

"Your mother's up to something," Aunt Tootie noted the week before opening night. She worked for Woolworth's and had driven in for a regional meeting. "I've known her since she was a kid. Just because she reads more books than me, she thinks I'm dumb. But honey, I'll tell you one thing, I'm no Sherlock Holmes, but I know a sinner when I spot one. I should know: it takes one to know one."

I wanted to confess everything I knew then and there, get it off my chest, but I couldn't. It would be deceitful. If I broke my promise, I'd be no better than Mama. What was she thinking? My entire life, she'd looked down her nose at "trashy wenches," as she referred to cheaters. "They know better," she'd say, holding her imperial head high.

•●•

Despite the snowstorm, or perhaps because everyone was trapped on campus, the theatre was packed on opening night. The only empty seats in the house were the ones in box number one, which had been reserved for the Applegate family. "There's nothing you can do," I said to Dad when he called. "Chains or no chains, I wouldn't want you to risk it." I asked to speak to Mama, but he said she wasn't home.

"She's stuck at Wilma Walker's house," he said. "I told her to sit tight until the roads clear."

My heart fizzled in my chest. I was glad that everyone was safe. Thankfully, Dad was in the dark about Mama's dalliance. I was livid with her forcing him into such an unfortunate position. She knew better. She had taught me better. *Please!* I wanted to be spared the sordid truth of her crass *liaisons dangereuses*.

There was a mystery gift waiting in the dressing room at intermission. Someone had hooked a stuffed Christmas ornament on my mirror. It was a primary yellow star with button eyes and a vibrant red smile stitched below its embossed rose-tinted nose. The note pinned to it read, "A star for the brightest star in the galaxy." I asked everyone I ran into if they'd seen anyone in the dressing room, but either nobody had or else wouldn't fess up.

Aside from the carousel set locking at one point, delaying the action momentarily, the show ran smoothly. When the second act curtain rose, I was primed and ready for action. The cast was tight and the chemistry sparkling. Grateful to the theatre gods, I was glad the show was set. Now I could relax and enjoy the remainder of the run.

Farley brought the house down as the waiter in the restaurant scene. That character was the comic highlight of the show, and he milked every second for laughs.

"I do wish your mother had seen me tonight," he said on the way to the cast party at Jake's Pub.

For some cockamamie reason that escaped me, he'd insisted that we wear the matching sweaters Mama had bought us for my birthday. "Oh, Princess Polly," he'd trilled. "It'll be hysterical!" Somehow, he'd officially added "princess" to Pete's nickname for me. I'd given up complaining about it. By second semester of my junior year, nearly everyone in the theatre department was calling me Polly, princess, or a combination thereof. A few people had insisted on calling me something other than August but didn't prefer Princess Polly, so I'd allowed them to call me "Mr. March."

"Just two little girls from Little Rock," Farley belted like a foghorn as we high-stepped through the two feet of frozen white.

Swathed in snow, the sturdy iron railing and overhang at the main entrance to the bar, with its twist of dead vines and naked trellis, looked like an unfinished crocheted sweater. The unplowed sidewalk along Merchant Street had been whittled down to a jagged path, its snow trampled by a multitude of marching boots.

"After you, Princess," Farley said, reaching for the door handle.

Before he could, the door unexpectedly swung open and out tumbled Cindy Pritchard, a costume assistant who had only hours before declared her undying love for me. She slammed into both of us, knocking Farley and me against the railing. The crocheted canopy of snow crumbled, blanketing us all in ivory powder.

Farley flew into a rage. Like a drenched dog, he shook the snow off, scooped a handful up, and smashed it into her face. "Up yours, Cindy Pritchard!" He tramped into the bar.

"Come on, Cindy," I said and offered my hand. She was so drunk, I don't think she'd even noticed Farley. I dusted her off and led her back into the warmth of the sweaty-windowed pub.

"She's lit," I said, handing Cindy over to her roommate, Susan Halevy. By the time I squeezed through the crowd of fans, Farley was on his second gin and tonic, holding court at the center table. "You wouldn't believe what I go through on a daily basis," he howled over the noise. "It's not easy living with Polly Purebred!"

The table roared with laughter until I stepped into the clearing.

"Princess!" Farley clutched his imaginary pearls and squealed. "Look everyone! My twin!"

"All yours," purred Dilbert Dobbs, the beautiful Black music major from my French class, as he patted the seat of the empty chair next to him. Dilbert was one of those men who oozed pheromones as easily as a snake sheds its skin, and I was highly susceptible to his charms. The week before Christmas break, we'd been alone in the French lab, studying how to turn a singular noun into a plural. I'd nearly had a triple when we made out in booth number three.

"August," Dilbert said, his hazel eyes sparkling with sin, "just what the doctor ordered."

Farley shot a panicked look to one of his friends, who shrugged. Evidently this small gesture eased Farley's worry, because he bounced back with another funny retort about Susan Halevy, far from the torch's flame. "Don't put your daughter on the stage, Mrs. Halevy! Don't put your daughter on the stage." I'd lost count of the number of times he quoted that tired Noel Coward line, each rendition with a different name inserted in the blank.

I had really started to think Farley had changed for good, that he'd hung up his court jester hat and the snarky persona he'd perfected at Buck's County Theatre Camp and turned over a new leaf. A royal misjudgment. Farley Fairfield, I now realized, was about as trustworthy as Mama. No wonder they'd hit it off. *Two peas in a pod!* Thank God I never blabbed about my personal life in front of him or said anything about anyone that I wouldn't say to their face.

Glancing around the table, I marveled at Farley's appeal. Somehow, someway, he'd mastered the art of being popular. As we rarely went out socially together, I wasn't part of the Baroness's court. Planting himself like a bloated bullfrog on a Lilypad, his sticky tongue eager for gossip, he'd pry the lid off a vacuum-sealed drum.

But I'd trained in the best of bad situations. During Mama's spells, I'd learned how to disappear, make myself small, and tiptoe out the back door. Hiding in plain sight, I kept my secrets to myself.

Farley often poked and prodded me about my sex life. I may have been a Pollyanna, but when it came to the delicate dance of dating, I certainly didn't need Farley barking in the town square. From all accounts, his sex life was a promiscuous parade of one-night stands, midnight playdates in the park, and shuffling services behind stall doors.

My occasional rendezvous were playful and romantic and genuine, and even if I was not in love with the person, they were at least a friend. In all honesty, I'd never been in love and hadn't the slightest idea what it felt like. I just knew that when it did happen, it wouldn't be sleezy or anything like Mama and Farley's sordid trysts. I knew they were damaged people, but just then I hated them both.

"You were incredible," Dilbert whispered, distracting me by resting his hand on my thigh. "Let me buy you a drink."

He ordered me a scotch, neat, and we reminisced about our frolic in the French lab. If his hands were tied behind his back, I think he'd be speechless, because Dilbert's hands were in constant motion when he spoke. He was tactile to the point of distraction; I thought if he accidently brushed an erogenous zone, I'd explode.

"Thanks for the star on my dressing room mirror." I put my hand on his. He looked puzzled, and I thought he was playing dumb. "No. Really. I loved it."

He pulled his hand free. "Not me. Must be another admirer."

Suddenly, a pair of hands cupped my eyes. "Guess who," someone said. The mellow baritone voice reverberated in my ear. I was instantly aroused by his masculine tone and appealing musk.

My Adam's apple pulsed when I touched my hands to the stranger's long, slender fingers. "Your voice is so . . ."

"Ta-da!" Pete said and swept me into his arms. "You were amazing!"

My eyes bugged out of their sockets like Wile E Coyote's when the Road Runner pulled another fast one on him. "Why? Who?" I glanced over at the grinning Farley and put two and two together. "You came."

"And you're blond!" he said. We laughed.

"No longer the lady in the dark," Farley shouted across the table.

I shot Farley a mock angry look. "I can't believe you're here." I said to Pete, then gestured to Dilbert. "This is my friend Dilbert. Dilbert, this is Peter Pakington Pace from Philadelphia, Newport, and . . ."

"And Embassy Row in DC." Pete pulled an empty chair up to our table. He winked at Farley, and Farley made a funny face. Had Farley invited Pete here for me? *Oh crap! Jeez. Maybe he's not the bitch I took him for.*

Dilbert looked Pete up and down and pulled a face that only I saw. Pete did the same when Dilbert turned to talk to whoever was on his left. There I was, stuck between the two most stunning men in the room and feeling "as plain as a mud turtle," as Aunt Tootie would say. I never understood what hunky men, such as they were, saw in me. I was neither handsome nor pretty. I'd cultivated a clever and cute demeanor, which for me was a triumph extraordinaire. Still, no matter how successful a mountaineer I had become, by the time I reached the highest peak, I always discovered there was yet another higher.

I never liked competing with anyone but myself. In a situation where several suitors were vying for my attention, I usually excused myself. Nine times out of ten, they ended up together, which was often a relief because I figured that was the way it was meant to be. Was I realistic or the world's biggest coward?

"Where are you staying?" I asked Pete.

"With you, silly," he said. "My things are in that tiny little room off the dining room."

"There's no bed in there."

"I brought a sleeping bag. I'll be fine. I'm just stopping in on my way down to Miami. Family vacation," he added, grimacing, before I could ask. Then he shook his head and smiled. "Polly, you look great. I didn't think it possible, but you're better than a high school dream."

Although I didn't always get Pete's assessments of my worth, I enjoyed the romantic chord he plucked. I tried to engage Dilbert in our conversation, but he soon tired of being the third wheel and begged off.

"Nice to meet you, Pete," he said insincerely, then kissed my cheek. "Call me," he whispered in my ear.

Farley poked his head between me and Pete. "Honey, when it

rains, it pours!" He clinked his glass against ours, and I noticed his jingle was missing.

"Where's your bracelets?"

"Time to hang up the Wonder Woman bit. Besides, the enemy hears me coming a mile away!"

By closing time, I was three sheets to the wind and feeling no pain. Too much booze without dinner had left me stumbling out into the snow, much as Cindy Pritchard had earlier that evening.

By the time we turned the corner onto Pious Street, I was numb to the cold and too smashed to reason with the silly side of my brain that insisted I tap dance on a patch of bare blacktop. Springing into action with the vim and vigor of Ann Miller in *On the Town*, I arched my back and leapt onto the solid sheet of black ice. My derriere hit the ground as my boots rocketed past my ears.

Stunned from the tumble, I heard Farley shout, "Come on, boys!" His gang of five hoisted me into the air. Egyptian fashion, they carried me home and laid me on the living room sofa. Too gone to complain, I allowed Pete to fuss over me. He lit a fire and wrapped me in Grandma Flora's quilt. Cocooned on the down-filled cushions, I didn't care to budge.

"Pete," I whispered. "Sleep in my bed. It's already made." Minutes later, he held my head over a bucket while I tossed my cookies.

Pete washed my face, tucked me in on the couch, and kissed me gently on the cheek. "August Applegate," he said in that honey-toned baritone that had melted my resistance at Bucks County Theatre Camp. "I . . . oh well, you know."

• • •

The next morning, I miraculously woke without a hangover. It was a brilliantly sunny day. The room was flooded with sharp white light reflecting off the fresh layer of snow beyond the bay window. A heap of ashes sat cold in the hearth. Stretching and yawning, I stacked fresh kindling and struck a match.

After brushing my teeth, I eased my bedroom door open and peeked inside. Pete was a study in magnificence, bathed in sunshine, his artic blond hair framing his pale, sculpted face, and his long legs hanging off the end of the bed. I longed to caress his porcelain skin, pure as polished marble and soft as silk.

Careful not to wake him, I stretched out beside him. His breath against my chin, the warmth of his flesh centimeters from mine, I studied every inch of the human masterpiece. I pulled the cover over myself when I stiffened. He rolled onto his back and settled his head into the curve of my neck, his lustrous locks lax against my cheek until he finally began to stir.

"August." He raised his head.

"Yes?" I let my head fall forward, my lips against his forehead. His musk excited me, and I kissed each of his eyelids, the bridge of his nose, an earlobe, and gentle as a tickle, his lips. I dragged my tongue, warm and wet, along his jaw line, then plunged it into his ear as he unbuttoned my pajama top. His nude body, curled under the crisp drape of ivory linen, aligned to mine.

"Wait," I whispered, "Farley!"

"He got lucky last night with your friend."

"No!"

"Not as lucky as me."

I ran my hand over the dips and bulges of his muscular torso. "You must have been cold last night."

"You're hot," he said, tracing my chest with his finger. I took his hands and pressed his palms against my chest. A spark of electricity shot through me, and I gasped.

Pete grinned. "Ha! Now you're mine."

Wrapping his arms around me, he hugged me so tight I could barely breathe. But I didn't care. I was dreaming and didn't wish to wake. He stiffened against my stomach and moaned, low and soft like an accordion expelling air.

"Is this sex?" I asked.

"Augie." Pete kissed me passionately. "You're adorable." He mussed my hair and took my face in his hands. "May I?"

"You'll be my first." I was willing to, wanted to, and I promised myself that this time, I would go the distance.

•●•

Flushed radiant, Pete cradled me to contentment. Afterward, we cuddled beneath the covers. "It's official." He kissed the tip of my nose. Though I had bucked his advances at first, I soon relaxed into a rollercoaster of pleasure unlike any I had experienced before.

"I could stay right here all weekend," Pete said, rubbing his eyes. "I know. I know. The show must go on."

"I can't believe you drove here in this mess." I sat up in the bed.

"My little MG went where no man dared to go."

I'd never showered intimately with anyone before, but I melted to the erotic pleasure of wet flesh against wet flesh.

"Our honeymoon," Pete jested afterward when he brought a breakfast tray into the living room. The crackling fire toasty and the coffee steaming, we snuggled on the sofa wrapped in a plaid Pendleton blanket as howling gusts of wind slapped the corners of the house.

"Now I know," I said, "the majesty of the moment every baby bird feels during his first flight."

CHAPTER 10

MAD ABOUT THE BOY

"You should go to Miami with Pete," Evangeline said on the other end of the line later that afternoon. "I'm off to Fort Lauderdale. Bubbe bought a place on the beach." She cleared her throat and imitated her grandmother, "'A real bargain. How could I resist?'"

"Pete hasn't asked me."

"Ask him!"

"I can't afford to pay my own way, let alone his."

"His parents are millionaires with houses everywhere, and you're worried about—what? Afraid you might have a good time?"

"I don't know." I pulled my robe closed. The hallway was drafty, and the last thing I needed was a cold. "I'm freezing!"

"He's nuts about you. I can tell. I'm astute about these things."

"Yeah? I don't know why he would be. Just a little hick from Timbuktu."

"Dickhead! You're soooo insecure!" She sighed. "Come with me, then. All you'll need is airfare. Bubbe's fridge is well-stocked and my allowance generous."

"It's tempting," I said, fantasizing about baking on a hot sandy beach. "I really should stay and work on the costumes before the festival."

"Martyr! Are you sure you're not Jewish? Okay. Have it your way . . . coward."

Although I wasn't certain what the complete list may have contained, the truth was that I feared Pete cared for me for all the wrong reasons. Just like at Buck's County Theatre Camp, whenever

108

I was with him, I went deaf, dumb, and blind. But alone, hundreds of miles away from him, I knew I'd be tormented by uncertainty.

Mama was right. Style was my beauty mark. Physically, I was plain next to Pete. His perfection only exacerbated my insecurities. Guilt plagued me. It was vain to obsesses over my appearance. Indulging my ambiguities was a sin I wallowed in. It helped to be in a show; I felt attractive on stage, but I couldn't live on stage.

"Who called?" Pete said as he stepped into the hall, pulling his striped sweater on. It fastened on one shoulder, so I secured the toggle buttons for him, leaving two undone to expose the sexy line of his clavicle.

"Evangeline really likes you," I said by way of an answer.

"I like her." Pete stepped into his brushed navy cords and tightened his belt. "What's up?"

"She invited me to Lauderdale for spring break."

The tips of his ears burned scarlet. He stared into the mirror as he brushed his towel dried hair.

"That's nice. Going to go?"

"I've never been. Isn't that close to Miami?"

"Not that close."

"Evangeline said they sometimes drive to the Eden Rock for dinner. She said it's next to the Fountain Blue, where you're staying."

"Evangeline. Evangeline. Is she a tour guide? She seems to know everything about everything," Pete scoffed.

"Sorry," I said, taken back by his sudden change of attitude. "I just thought . . ."

"I can't, Augie. I'll be with my family, and I wouldn't wish them on my worst enemy." He tossed the brush into his bag. "Ask Farley if you don't believe me."

Farley! I didn't respond because my ire was up. I couldn't believe he had invited Farley to meet his parents but wouldn't even entertain the idea of introducing me to them. "I need to work on my costumes if I'm going to have a chance at the grand prize," I said, dropping the subject to avoid a bout with him.

"Probably a good idea," Pete said, sounding much relieved. "I know what a perfectionist my Polly is."

Well! Talk about turning on a dime! I felt used, foolish, and confused. The hangover I'd avoided hours before hit square between my eyes. I sat on the edge of the bed, watching Pete clean his boots. I detested feeling jealous. It was uncomfortable to say the least. I was glad I'd clapped my trap before I made an utter fool of myself.

"I've always been and will probably always be in love with you," he said.

"Probably"! I'd had it up to here with probably. According to Mama, I'd probably look better with a nose job. I'd probably be more sophisticated if I could afford a grand tour of Europe. Probably, I'd be able to understand romantic entanglements if I'd had more experience with them. I wished I could have afforded psychotherapy. There was so much I didn't understand. Farley and his dreadful father, Mama and her affair, Pete running hot and cold. Pete baffled me.

The bedroom felt as cold as the ice rimming the window looked. So I dressed hurriedly, popped some Tylenol, and joined Pete in the living room. The only room with a working fireplace, it was the coziest spot to be on a snowy day below freezing.

Less dependable was the oil-fueled furnace. Antiquated, it could never pump enough warmth to counter the frigid drafts seeping through the cracks under the doors, in the floor, and around the windowpanes. The windows rattled during windstorms, crying for mercy. Askew on their hinges, the doors grumbled when the cold rushed them. An elderly patient, the house complained of its every luminous pain.

Cuddled together, Pete and I sat silently, watching the flames waltz atop the crackling log. A corner of the log broke away and fell into a pile of ash. Outside, though the temperature held steady at twenty-seven degrees, the bright sun beat on the snow and melted its surface. Trickling down the spouts, water rinsed the copper duct work clean as it rushed to its destination.

"This is it," Pete said. "Makes me almost believe in God."

Despite my frustration concerning Florida, it felt true to be tucked up under his arm.

"All I've ever wanted," I said and wrapped my arms around his torso.

"Oh Polly. My Polly."

Pete rested his hand on my thigh, and I pressed my ear to his chest. Continuous and calm, the rhythm of his heartbeat matched mine. *Slow and steady wins the race.* Was this love? Having never been in love before, I had no idea what it felt like. I'd had plenty of crushes on boys at UVa, but none of those inklings had matched the baffling potency of my feelings for Peter Pakington Pace.

I'd once thought I was in love with Stephen Porter. He was an architecture student, and we had oodles in common. He loved theatre, and I often went to hear him play saxophone at a little jazz dive on Saturday nights. We both felt as though we were displaced from the roaring twenties, and our arrangement flourished until he confessed to being a swinger.

"But I'm a square," I'd said.

Jamie Jenkins was in the closet, but I'd come to adore him as well. I'd pined for him when I hadn't seen him for a day, ached for him when he couldn't spend the night, and fretted over my appearance before every date. It had only taken one weekend at his parents' house to open my eyes to my unquenchable appetite for him. Sleeping in separate rooms under the Reverend Jasper Jenkin's roof had been a painful endeavor.

I hadn't cared for the boring side of Jamie, though. His lengthy dissertations on mankind's future and his predictions that we'd soon be living in a Star Trek world—calculated, planned, controlled by computers and devices—had left me cold. Wrestling with my desire for a boy I had so little in common with had forced me to come to grips with my true sexual nature. I'd wanted sex with Jamie Jenkins at least three times a day. I certainly hadn't been coy about it. Once a guy had seen me naked, I shed my inhibitions.

Still, according to Pete, we'd never really had sex because there'd been no anal intercourse. In my mind, if two people were naked together, touching one another's bits and bobs, ending with a sizzling hot grand finale, then they'd done the deed.

Content in Pete's arms, I lingered in his warmth until I noticed something odd. At first glance, I thought it was a delusion. Framed by a fading tan, Pete's ring finger boasted a noticeable white band. I turned his hand palm-up and inspected it.

"What are you doing?" he said and jerked his hand away. He laughed and mussed my hair to make light of the situation, as he always had, but I held fast to my suspicion.

"Where's your wedding band?" I asked.

Pete sat bolt upright. "It's not what you think," he said, his voice shrill and his stare sharp.

"I don't understand, Pete." My heart skipped a beat, a sure sign that I'd accidentally tapped the lid of Pandora's box.

Leaning forward, he dropped his head in his hands. "Don't make me go there, Augie. I can't. . . . Please. I can't."

I stood abruptly, crossed to the bay window, and peered out. A cold draft from the French door licked my bare ankles. The trampled path along the street, which had frozen overnight, was now melting into a steady stream rushing for the gurgling drains along the sidewalks. The trickling sound of water from the thawing roof dripped rhythmically onto the porch. Shielding my face from the blinding sun, I watched a chipper cardinal, brash and bold, hopping nimbly from one branch to another in the red cedar.

"When cardinals appear, an angel is near," Grandma Flora would say.

I prayed the angel was her. She'd been patient and supportive of me, and I missed her down-to-earth wisdom. Somehow, she always managed to right my upturned boat and cast me out on the quiet sea. *Please. Please! Tell me what to do. Oh, Grandma, please tell me what to do.*

A wounded elephant, Pete sat in the middle of the room, uncertain of where he'd been and where he was headed. Having sex with him had only complicated matters. I'd been too wasted the night before to see clearly, but there was no excuse today in the brazen light of day. It was up to me to do the right thing. My head was spinning. *Do not unto others as you would have them do to you.*

Pete was twenty-two years old. Four years had passed without a single word from him. As Pete was a sticky wicket between us, neither Farley nor I had broached the subject of our mutual friend during our time at 315 Benevolent Street.

A smaller, less flamboyant cardinal swooped down from somewhere high, flapped her wings seductively, and landed beside her dandy prince, unable to fight her nature. A bird of a different feather, I stood in the bay window, caged behind its glass panes, as flummoxed by my mate as she was hers.

Like a Fellini movie, Pete's entire wedding played in my head. *The gorgeous groom and his stunning bride. What color was her hair? Ginger like mine? Platinum highlights? Jet-black like Farley's dyed locks? Floating down the aisle in a satin cloud, her face shielded in Belgium lace, her tiara shimmering in candlelight as she made her way to her beloved. . . . No! No! I can't! I won't!*

I won't!

"Why?" I asked him, emotion pinching my vocal cords. "You don't like women."

"I said I never tried."

Unable to breathe, I crossed to the pocket doors. I couldn't think because I was drowning in a tide of retribution. I felt somehow responsible for his deceit—his deceit to me. "I can't do this."

Like a grasshopper on a dead fly, Pete pounced. "No! No, August Applegate!" Hugging me close, he kissed my forehead, neck, chin.

Vulnerable to his touch, I fought the urge to surrender. *Grandma! Angel! God give me strength!* Gripping my shoulders tightly with his meaty mitts, he shook me the way April used to shake her Raggedy Ann doll when she was frustrated with Mama.

"You're hurting me!" I winced.

Embracing me tenderly, Pete rocked us back and forth. My face pressed against his chest; the fine hairs of his thick worsted-wool sweater tickled my nose. His chest rose and fell as he wept, his teardrops on the top of my head. I wanted to scream. Trapped. He was powerful and a head taller than myself; I shrank to a boy in his clutches. I was thirteen again; seven; five. I was disappearing in plain sight. *No! No!* I couldn't. Perhaps I'd used the last of the magic corn or forgotten the proper incantation, but try though I might, I couldn't vanish.

That's when it kicked in, that survival instinct honed in my youth. When pushed to the wall, I stood tall. Pete was a loose cannon, and I wasn't certain what might light his fuse. Besides all the mess I had to handle with him I had a matinee performance at three. "Pete," I whispered, my voice stripped of emotion so as not to rile the beast.

"You owe me nothing," he said.

I took his hand, sweaty and warm, and held it to my cheek. Was this the comfort that welded Farley's brother, Frank Jr., to his mother? Unyieldingly painful though it was for me, I was determined to bear it because of the connection between us. Sticking together through thick and thin—was this the connection everyone dreamed of finding? Had Dad dreamed of such a connection?

Was that connection the reason he'd broken the engagement to his fiancé to pursue Mama? Though I presented a calm façade, every organ in my body hummed with remorse for what I had and hadn't done. Was it love? "You've given me two great gifts. Being my first . . . you will forever be . . . my first."

"I want more!" Pete's faced tensed, and I brushed a tear from his cheek.

When faced with emotional people, I tended to go numb, blank. I floated somewhere outside my body. Free of judgement, I observed the mechanics beneath the surface. An actor must be both inside and outside himself simultaneously. He must be capable of directing his actions at the same time he releases his emotions. Genuine. It had to be a genuine connection.

Should I slam the door in his face? Kick, scream, and yell? I deserved to. He deserved it. However, I could see that my friend Pete was in a terrible quandary. He desperately needed help. I feared for his state of mind. *Mother frigger!* Here I was again, typecast in the same role as the supportive, understanding, reliable . . . Pollyanna. For better or worse, I was her.

"Whatever happens," I said, "I'm here for you."

"Oh Polly . . . I didn't mean to . . . I swear." Pete dropped into a bucket chair, taking me with him.

"Not deliberate, I hope." I stood. "Oh course, now I'm the other . . . whatever." I knelt before the fire, reduced to a hovering blue flame begging to be fed another log. So, I arranged two splits of wood on the ashy embers still smoldering in the hearth and prodded the kindling until a red-hot flame leapt into its irritated dance. "Do you love her?"

Silence. I turned to look at him.

Pete shook his head. "I'd lose my legacy and my allowance. There was little I could do."

"Oh, to be poor and free of the ties that bind."

"You sounded like Farley just then," he said.

"Funny. I feel a bit like Farley today." *His twin. He called me his twin.*

The sounds of boots stomping across the front porch and Farley's braying laugh echoing down the long veranda startled me.

"Is he alone?" Pete said, wiping his wet face with the sleeve of his sweater.

"He's not with Dilbert." I recognized the other laugh. "It's Evangeline."

As Pete collected himself, I quickly plumped the sofa cushions. It's what I did when I was nervous. Their voices grew louder as they entered the hallway. I chose the wingback by the fire, and Pete sat in the straight-backed Chippendale armchair opposite me.

Slowly, the pocket doors rolled open. "Mamie!" Farley bellowed. "You look awful." His quoting Vera Charles's line from *Mame* proved he was in a good mood. I laughed as I always did when he delivered it. Twenty minutes before, I'd been dreading his return. I now welcomed it with open arms.

"Augie!" Evangeline squealed. "Look who I caught walking home in shame."

"Put the blame on Mame, girl." Farley said and pointed to me. "Put the blame on Mame."

I couldn't decide which was more terrifying, Farley fearful or Farley fun. Sex was his Valium, and I prayed that his rolls in the hay would be everlasting.

"Everybody got laid but me!" Evangeline unwound her absurdly long purple cashmere scarf and draped it over the back of the sofa. Decked out in a red turtleneck, beige ski pants, and multi-colored striped socks, she plopped down on the sofa and kicked her feet up on the coffee table. "The only offer I got was from Mary Quince, and her mustache is thicker than anything you guys could grow."

Pete excused himself. "I need to pack. I have a long drive ahead on bad roads. Route-1 to National Airport is a bitch in the best of weather.

"So who fractured this fairy tale?" Evangeline said the minute he was out of earshot. "Honey, your prince has been zapped into a bullfrog."

Farley pushed Evangeline's feet off the coffee table and sat on it between us. With the flare of a magician about to reveal the surprise in the box, he shrugged, smacked his lips, and whispered, "A-R-A-B-E-L-L-A."

"Arabella," Evangeline said. "Drag? Woman? Transexual? You?"

Farley smirked. "Wife."

Heavens! Just what I didn't want: a name. The bride had a name. That made her real.

Evangeline sat bolt upright. "He has a wife? A real, honest-to-goodness woman?"

Farley patted me on the knee. "Certainly, you knew. Did I not tell you?"

"You didn't even tell me he was coming."

"Don't get your knickers in a twist." Farley put his finger to his lips. "Shush. It's a horrible situation."

Evangeline scoffed. "I should say."

"I was there," Farley said. "I witnessed the one-act farce."

Evangeline sat on the arm of my chair and hugged me. "Oh, Augie. Just when you catch the big fish, you have to throw it back in the river."

"He doesn't love her," Farley assured me.

"Please," Evangeline said. "No bawling brats, I hope."

Farley shook his head. "No, but she keeps ovulating, and they keep trying. She's as unrelenting as Anne Boleyn."

"Young man." Evangeline kissed the top of my head. "You are coming to Florida with me. Forget Bubbe in Lauderdale. We'll book a room at the Fontainebleau. I want to get a gander of Frankenstein's bride."

"No way," I said. "'Enough is enough is enough.'"

She waved her finger in the air. "Forget it, Donna Summer."

Farley glowered. "Streisand! Please!"

"I've got costumes to construct," I said. "Dr. Midge has been great, and everyone's pitched in extra hours—volunteered hours. I can't take off when so much is at stake. You realize if I was lucky enough to win the competition, I'd have a chance to intern with a Broadway professional?"

"You can stitch costumes on the beach. The queens would love it!" Evangeline dropped another piece of yellow oak on the burning stack in the hearth. "Kill two birds with one stone."

I thought of the happy cardinals when she said that and wondered if they were nesting somewhere in the nearby forest. The thought of them brought me to tears.

"Lamb," Evangeline said as she knelt before me. "What is it?"

I couldn't speak.

"Girl, the mistress always gets the best end of the stick—or something that rhymes with it." Farley only aggravated my angst. I didn't want to be a mistress. I didn't know her, but I would never knowingly hurt Arabella.

"Augie's built to be a bride." Evangeline rested her chin on my knee.

The sound of the bedroom door opening echoed down the hall, and Farley gasped. "Get a grip girl," he whispered as he sank into the cushion of the sofa.

The sight of Pete, his ecru Brooks Brother's scarf snaking around his neck and his Burberry beanie pulled down over his ears, tugged at my heart. *Going! Going! He's going!*

"Pete." I stood abruptly, accidently knocking Evangeline against the rolled arm of the sofa. "Pete."

Evangeline and Farley quickly shuffled out of the room, two Geishas exiting the stage on tip-toe.

Pete slid the pocket doors closed and got down on one knee as if he were about to propose to me. Instead of a velvet box, he held out a beautiful, intricately carved wooden pencil case. "We can't, but if we could, would you marry me?"

It was a sincere but empty gesture, a romantic, compelling impossibility for two queers in love to dream. Audaciously, Pete had dreamed the dream I'd once dreamed.

I pulled him to his feet. "My grandmother said that once you love someone, they're yours for life."

"I would, you know."

"You have a wife." Words, comforting or otherwise, eluded me. Only blank verse surfaced from the depths of my despair. Outside, feathery snowflakes flittered down from the gray heavens God had forsaken during the storm. God was hope, and hope had vanished the moment Arabella had trounced on our fairytale.

"Snow," Pete uttered like a zombie weatherman. His head lowered, he collected his bags from the hallway and headed for the front door.

"Pete!" I yelped and sprang across the living room. "Pete!" *What to say? What to say?* I wanted to shout *I love you! I'll marry you!* and linger in the dream a few moments longer, but I buttoned his coat instead. "You'll catch your death out there." The draft from the crack in the doorframe flooded the warm space between us, and I shivered.

"I love you." His simple declaration bounced off the walls and circled the hallway; a hawk eager to soar; a hawk soon to be grounded the moment Pete opened the door. "Pollyanna," he whispered, pressing the pencil case into my hands, and kissed my forehead. "My Pollyanna, I . . . I . . ." He shook his head. "You don't understand."

No truer words had been spoken the entire weekend. I didn't get it. I hadn't the slightest idea what he was attempting to tell me with his proclamation. What did he expect? I couldn't say what I think he wanted me to say because . . . because he was *married*, and the moment I'd heard Arabella's name spoken aloud, my heart had frozen. Complicated and confusing, paranoia plunged a stake into my heart.

What did I know of love? My parents loved each other, but that love hadn't saved them from the pits of hell.

April couldn't breathe without her husband's approval. That couldn't be love. It simply couldn't. Dependence wasn't love. Control wasn't love. Blind devotion wasn't love. And if it were these things, then I'd rather not fall into it.

Perplexing. Pete's marriage was perplexing. Did he love this Arabella? Was it possible to love two people at the same time? Is sacrifice love or the selfish means that benefits the taker?

The only thing that I was certain of, as I stood in the frigid draft, was that I had no idea what love was. Desire haunted me day and night. I understood longing, but love? What the hell was it anyway?

The shawl collar of my cardigan flapped in the gust of cold air as I held the door open to the elements. Whistling through the gaps in the fascia along the roof line, the wind rushed the veranda, snatching Pete's beanie off his head. Not that he'd have been able to anyway, but he didn't chase after it as it cartwheeled over the caps of ice. Instead of tracing Evangeline and Farley's path from the street to our front door, Pete stomped his own path through the snow to his car.

My face beet red and my feet frozen in my slippers, I stood on the porch, watching him shovel his MG sportscar out. I called to him, but he didn't bother acknowledging me. My chest tightened with regret. I'd screwed up again.

Eventually, two husky guys from the frat house on the corner rushed to his rescue. While they pushed against the trunk, Pete revved the engine, and the car rocked forward and backward until its tires found traction on the plowed blacktop.

He didn't beep or wave. He didn't look back but cranked the volume of the radio to ear-splitting and sputtered and spun around the corner to Pious Street. *Going. Going. Gone.*

I slumped against the window casing and burst into tears.

CHAPTER 11

REVIEWING THE SITUATION

Pete left messages for me at the costume shop, with Farley, even at the counseling center where our newly formed gay support group met. The few times I bothered to return his calls, Arabella answered, and I, coward that I was, hung up.

"It's not like she knows you shagged her husband," Dilbert said. "You could be a client." Though he was from Little Rock, Arkansas, ever since he'd studied a year abroad in Britain, Dilbert had begun peppering his conversations with English slang. *Oh well, what the hell.* Affected maybe, but charming on him.

When I looked at Dilbert, I felt like kicking myself for letting him slip through my fingers. He was gorgeous and kind, and now . . . Farley's boyfriend.

"Do it now," Evangeline said, pointing to the phone on the counselor's desk.

I glanced around the packed office and shook my head. "Not in front of everyone," I whispered.

The therapist, Sofia, tapped her finger on the receiver, a sure sign she disagreed. "August, what do you want to do? I'll support you either way." She curled her lip softly into a cock-eyed smile, which translated into "foolish child."

"What should I do, Sofia?"

"You can't run forever. When you're ready, you'll take care of business."

If Sofia hadn't come backstage to tell me how much she'd enjoyed my performance in *She Loves Me*, I never would have met her. It was providence. We'd hit it off immediately. After several conversations over cups of tea in her office, we concluded that what our school was in desperate need of was a gay support group. Although straight, she had a soft spot for our dilemma and volunteered to be our faculty sponsor. By word of mouth, a month later, we'd gathered a small army of supporters to the cause.

"So," Farley said, "what's the verdict on our name? What shall we call this merry band of renegades?"

Sofia sat her teacup on her desk and sighed. "When the dean refused us permission, I went to Dr. Stickler, and . . ."

"You did it!" Evangeline clapped her hands. "You're the tiger's meow!" Dr. Stickler was our college president.

"No. No. Before you order stationary, let's get the facts straight." Sofia folded her hands in her lap. "Under no circumstance will he allow 'gay,' 'lesbian,' 'transgender,' or 'queer' to be in our title."

"Bloody hell!" Dilbert said. Farley took his hand and kissed it.

"However" —Sofia's voice climbed an octave— "my clever husband has come up with an idea that may solve our problem." She paused for dramatic effect. "'Alternate Lifestyles.'"

The room fell silent for a few moments as we test-drove the label in our heads.

"Alternate Lifestyles. Alternate Lifestyles," I said. "It doesn't carry the punch of 'Gay Alliance' or 'Queer Discussion,' and I'm not crazy about the word 'alternate.' But I like the provocative inuendo of it."

"I can see it now. We'll be swamped with bi swingers looking for fun," Farley protested.

Dilbert tugged thoughtfully on his ear, a habit when he addressed the group. "We're a queer political discussion group who dares not mention the two words that define us, 'queer' and 'political.'"

"But we'll officially be a group," Evangeline said.

"I say we go for it," I suggested. "We have to start somewhere."

A sea of hands shot into the air. "Twenty-three to seven," I counted aloud. "We're officially Alternate Lifestyles."

"I don't care if we're called the G-Spot!" Evangeline said. "Our goal is to join the gay rights march on Washington on October fourteenth."

"Let's do it for Harvey Milk," I said. "He was trying to get us there."

"1979 is the tenth anniversary of Stonewall too," Farley interjected.

Dilbert pumped his fist in the air. "Brilliant!"

• • •

Come September, we had one hundred and ten people signed up to join us in DC. Sofia contacted Joyce Hunter at the national office in New York and officially registered us in the march.

Mama, who had marched with Aunt Jessica for women's rights a few years before, was surprisingly none too pleased about my participation. "You have no idea the crazies that'll be out there."

"That didn't stop you and Aunt Jessica."

"We were scorned, but you're despised," she replied.

"What do you think, Dad?" I asked my father, who was puffing away on his pipe. A cloud of smoke scented with cherries, cinnamon, and patchouli hung in the air, as calming as the green damp-earth smell after a storm. He never smoked during Mama's dark episodes, but the minute she collapsed, his pipe was lit. The smell of his tobacco signaled freedom.

"You must do what you think is best," Dad said as he stared out the window at his garden, which was settling in for a long winter's nap. "Until I faced the front lines in the war and picked up scraps of human life out of the rubble during the Blitz, I took our liberties for granted." He tapped the last ash from the bowl of his pipe. "I fear for your safety, but part of being a man is accepting responsibility for the risks you take."

If Mama hadn't been there, I would have hugged him. Ever since she'd confessed her romantic fling, I found that everything she did irritated me. We had been inseparable during my high school years, but ever since the fall open house, we'd been butting heads on almost everything. "I'm going," I said firmly.

• • •

By the eve of the march, our promised one hundred and ten marchers had dwindled to five. "I had no idea 'Alternate Lifestyle' meant gay!" Suzy Sterling said as she crossed her name off the list. "I'm not getting myself killed over a pack of fags."

"Packs, gaggles, tribes, herds," I said. "What are we, water buffalo?"

"It's easier to hate a faceless mob." Evangeline sneered. "Take it from a closeted Jew from Hick Town, USA."

Her comment sent cold chills down my back. At that moment, it struck me how remote and rural my upbringing had been. "I must have been the talk of the town when I bought my first Barbie doll."

"Without a doubt," Evangeline said. "To my mother's chagrin, I was determined to be your friend."

"A curse and a blessing, you see what you want to see, Pollyanna," Farley chimed in. "Northern Virginia is thick with Republicans like my father. All they care about is winning. They don't give a shit about humanity. Equal rights belong to monied white men, and Phyllis Schlafly is the ideal Americana Mama. If it's that challenging in Alexandria, I can just imagine what it's like in your hamlet."

"Why do you think this Jew joined the Episcopalians?" Evangeline made a funny face, and we tittered.

"'Fags will roast in hell,' my faultfinding father proclaims," said Farley, adding to the list of reasons I detested Frank Fairfield.

"Talk about denial," I blurted out without thinking.

Farley had a puzzled look on his face. "I deny nothing. There are many secrets in the Fairfield House of Horror, but my being gay isn't one of them."

My face burned. "I was . . . I meant—" I stumbled.

"He meant generally," Evangeline jumped in.

"My father thinks all we do is bugger each other," Dilbert said. "Don't I wish."

We all laughed.

• • •

"Here." Farley pitched his bag in the back of Evangeline's hand-me-down '76 Mercedes station wagon her dad had given her when he upgraded to a '79 model.

"Everybody in?" Evangeline pulled away from 315 Benevolent Street without waiting for an answer. I looked back as we turned the corner; the house, with her upper shutters hanging askew on their rusty hinges, looked sad and lifeless without us.

At five a.m. on Saturday, the highway was nearly empty. Since I wasn't driving, I dropped off to sleep before we'd passed the first exit and didn't stir until I heard Farley say, "Pee break, Sleeping Beauty."

Unfortunately, Dilbert had fallen asleep on my shoulder and slobbered on the collar of my jacket. Farley nudged him awake. Farley was no better. Gazing at the passenger door, I noted a fair amount of drool dripping from its leather-padded handle. They'd redefined bed-wetting.

• • •

"Should we tell him?" I heard Evangeline ask Farley as I sauntered out of the restroom, much revived after an hour-long nap.

"Shush!" Dilbert said when he saw me come around the corner of the station. Evangeline and Farley snuffed out their cigarettes on the side of the building. "Feel better, love?"

"Much," I said.

They headed to the car, me a few steps behind. What were they hiding? Except for birthdays and Christmas morning, I detested surprises. Evangeline of all people should have known I don't take kindly to being left in the dark. I had a sneaking suspicion it had to do with Pete, whom I hadn't seen since January. I'd refused to take any of his calls and left his letters unopened on the hall table. He'd given me little choice but to accept the extravagant box of roses he'd sent after that fateful weekend, so I'd arranged them in vase from the props department and set them in the green room of the theatre for everyone to enjoy.

"Buckle up, boys!" Evangeline said, sliding behind the wheel. Buckles clicked in unison.

Sitting directly behind Evangeline, I had a clear shot of her through the rearview mirror. I raised an eyebrow when our eyes met. Ignoring me, she perched her Ray Ban Wayfarers on her nose and cranked up the sound on the cassette player. Donna Summers's *Bad Girls* blasted from the speakers.

Long stretches of Interstate 66 were blanketed with acres of harvested fields, divided by patches of forest that reminded me of the hectares on Grandma Flora's farm. The trees were thick with autumn foliage, saturated in dusky rust, apple-yellow, and crimson. Beautiful as they were, it saddened me to think of the dying leaves. Though they were clinging to their branches, they'd soon be ripped from their mother tree by the next storm. The cycle of life.

As a boy, I'd discovered what a difference a daily dose of nature did to lift my spirits. To run my hand over the peeling bark of a birch, touch the silky petals of a Meiland tea rose, or feel a cool carpet of grass beneath my bare feet was heaven. Like Dad, I needed that connection to the earth. It settled the restless buzzing inside. Fall was a challenging season because it was no longer life but death I was stroking.

"Hey!" I tapped the back of Evangeline's seat when she veered right of the Lincoln Memorial. "You missed Constitution Avenue!"

"I'm parking in Kalorama. We'll take the train to Metro Center. It'll be a madhouse around the Mall."

The arrangements surprised only me. I stared out the window at the city's loblolly pines, red maples, and chestnut oaks. I regarded trees as individuals, as varied in personality as my fellow humans. Plain and simple, I was a tree hugger. Trees spoke to me.

When I was younger, depressed and lethargic post Mama's spells, I'd walk through the apple orchard. The trees' blossoms showering me in petals; it was as uplifting as a ticker tape parade. Climbing high in the sugar maple outside my bedroom window, I'd shelter behind its foliage and stretch across its sturdy, crisscrossed branches. Cradled in its arms, I'd stare at the sky and dream of a life far, far from the maddening muddle we called home.

Energetic joggers and determined cyclists raced along the narrow trail in Rock Creek Park, so close to the winding road at certain points that I clutched the door handle whenever a car zipped around a bend.

Evangeline exited onto Massachusetts Avenue and headed up the hill on California Street. The houses and condo buildings lining the street were classic Edwardian and early-twentieth-century designs. The manicured front gardens and grand arched entrances of each one signaled wealth. Spotlessly swept clean of city debris,

Embassy Row was an American dream town worthy of an MGM back lot.

Without hesitation, Evangeline steered the car into the parking lot adjoining a seven-story Beaux Arts building. The intricate moldings and reliefs, ideally shadowed, blossomed into an elaborate decoration reminiscent of the buttercream icing atop a wedding cake. A long hunter-green canopy, fitted between a double set of stone Athenian columns, stretched from the iron and glass French door that opened onto the street.

"We're here!" Evangeline announced and unbuckled her seatbelt.

Speechless, I climbed out the car. It was simply one of those intimidating neighborhoods where I imagined everyone spoke in proper Miss Porter's School-speak, as breathy and elite as Jackie Onassis. Correctness was the order of the day.

"Welcome!" a familiar voice called out from the raised front porch. From our angle, his face was hidden by the downward slope of the canopy. However, from the shape, length, and bulge of the thighs beneath his jeans, I knew at once it was Pete.

I pinched Evangeline's arm as we crossed the blacktop. "Thanks for the warning."

"Ouch!" she complained, rubbing the fleshy part of her arm.

"Seems you know where you're headed." I slowed my pace, drifting behind the others.

Spotting me, Pete bounded down the steps to the sidewalk. "Hey guys!' he said, rushing past the others without as much as a nod. "Pollyanna! You came!"

"Hey Pete. How's it going?" I attempted to play it cool and failed miserably when my voice cracked.

"Mr. Pace." The doorman nodded as he held the door open for our entourage.

We crossed the vestibule and entered a two-story lobby reminiscent of a Venetian palace. Paneled in gray-and-white marble, it boasted a series of classical columns reaching twenty feet to the convoluted molded plaster, framed by a coffered ceiling. This was a step up from Aunt Jessica's simple, post-war apartment building near Dupont Circle.

Holding hands, Farley and Dilbert chatted Pete up, going on about the latest Broadway theatre they'd caught during their summer trip to the Big Apple. Evangeline, sliding her hand into the crook of Pete's arm, pushed the elevator button in a manner too familiar not to note. *Ding!* The door parted, and we filed in. The car was a small, mirrored jewel box. Any which way you looked, you made eye contact with someone else's reflection. Nowhere to hide. Nowhere to run. Pete squeezed me into a corner and slid his hand around my waist. Like a missing puzzle piece, I fit snuggly into his arm.

Pete unlocked the door to his seventh-floor unit and gestured for us to enter a black-and-white marble-tiled entrance hall as big as my parents' dining room. A series of doors ran along the corridor, whose walls were papered in an elaborate nineteenth century mural depicting Washington at its Regency best. A sweeping carved wooden archway framed the entrance to the main salon, a cream-and-beige affair decorated in an eclectic mix of modern and antique pieces. I was breathless. Gazing at the sophisticated marvel of Pete's home, I felt small, insignificant, and poor.

"Can I get you anything?" Pete asked the group. In his black crewneck sweater and brown tweed blazer, he was, as Dilbert would say, "to the manner born." If anyone answered him, I didn't hear. Glimpsing at myself in the huge, quilted mirror between the set of French doors leading to the terrace, I wanted to cry. Why hadn't I gotten a haircut? I was giving Little Orphan Annie a run for her money with my untrimmed shrub. My khakis needed pressing, and the toe of my shoe was scuffed from when Farley accidently stepped on my foot getting into the car that morning. My corduroy blazer, creased from my back seat slumber, hung limp from my shoulders. Unkempt, unstrung, and uninformed, I balked at my stature in Pete's elegant unit.

"Give me a hand?" Pete said, snapping me out of my thoughts. On our way to the kitchen, we passed through a moss-green dining room. Tucked beneath a spotless glass-top table, lustrously polished Chippendale chairs glowed in the shimmering light of a crystal chandelier. The room was as intimidating as Hillwood Estate, Marjorie Merriweather Post's house in upper Northwest DC.

No sooner had he dragged me through the pantry doors than he was lifting me off my feet and kissing me. I was too stunned to fight back if I'd wanted to. The fact was, I didn't want to. I wanted to rip his perfectly pressed clothes off and dash into the nearest bedroom for a midmorning delight.

Playfully, he pressed me against the glass door of a dish cabinet, sending a teapot into a rocking dance. "Oh Polly, you're here. Augie. August Applegate is here."

I should have yelled "Arabella" at the top of my lungs and bolted out the front door. I should have kneed him in the groin, but I didn't. I prayed for God to show me the way. *Send me a sign! Please Lord! I'm desperate!* Whether one believed in the Almighty or not, it was human nature to cry out to him in emergency situations, and this was one of those times.

When I felt Pete stiffen against my abdomen, I pushed away. "Pete. Pete. What about Arabella?"

A pinched expression on his face, he dropped into a wooden side chair. "No, Augie. Not today. She's in New York. At her parents'."

"Does she know about the march?"

He took my hands and pulled me onto his lap. "She knows, Augie. I told her. She insisted I go."

"Why?"

He kissed my ear. "I love those little lobes."

"Pete. Please. You're killing me."

"She's working on her PhD in psychology at George Washington. She's no fool."

"And she's okay with you being gay?"

"Bi. She insists I'm bisexual." He blushed. "She says no gay man can fake it that well."

"Bisexual," I said, grimacing from the bitter taste of the word on my tongue.

"I fake it because I have to," he said. "I can't say I like it." He took my chin in his hand and looked me in the eye. "I can't fake it with you. I've never faked it with you. It's the real thing with you."

I wrapped my arms around his neck. He was so brawny, I felt like a child in his embrace. Trouble was, I wanted to be his child, his baby, his boytoy. I knew it was wrong, but my thoughts were my thoughts, and I couldn't change them.

"I don't know what to say." I looked up at the gold-rimmed China behind the glass, glimmering under the spotlights. "I thought I was sophisticated until I walked in here." I closed my eyes and sighed. "I'm a rube, a hick, a hayseed. I'd embarrass you at my first soiree. Soiree. Like your wife would ever allow her bisexual husband to have . . . a what? A mistress? A man-whore? What would I be, Pete?"

"As soon as she has a son for my father, I'm divorcing her. I won't live my entire life in the closet. No how! No way!"

"Where does your father live? The House of Tudor?"

"He's lobbed a few heads off in his day."

"We'd never see each other. I'm such a faithful Joe," I said. "I could never sleep around if I was with you. I'm not made that way. Faithful as a sheepherder's collie."

"I wouldn't like it, but I give you permission to do what you need to do. Double standard. I can't exactly forbid you when I'm having sex with Arabella."

"Oh, to be a bit of boy on the side; that's depressing."

I rolled off his lap and out of his arms, then stood facing the door to the kitchen. "I don't need your permission. You're not my knight in shining armor. I'm not a damsel in distress." I glanced back at the door to the dining room. "Do you eat in the formal dining room every day?"

"What an odd thing to ask." He patted my hip. "You're a silly willy, Pollyanna."

I pushed through the kitchen door. Blinding sunlight bounced off every gleaming glass-fronted cupboard, metal-trimmed white appliance, and Formica countertop. Cheerful poppy-printed wallpaper covered every surface above the wainscoting, and the wooden floors were buffed to a high gloss. "This is where I would eat." I pointed to the beaten oak table positioned in the far corner. "Right here."

"You fit in everywhere?"

"But not in your back pocket." There was a prolonged silence.

"You don't get it," Pete said at last. "Why is it you never get it?" His hands on his hips, he paced back and forth. "You're not dense. You're not an idiot. You're plenty good at pointing others in the right direction. Why can't you, for once . . . just once . . . do something for yourself? Do something for me? Jesus, Augie! I love you. Love. It doesn't come along every day. Do you know how special it is?"

Suddenly, I was five years old in Mama's kitchen. Trapped.

Trapped! I glanced quickly around the room, searching for an escape route. I backed against the door to the service porch. The knob poked the small of my back, and I reached behind me and clicked it open. Pete stomped across the room and pushed it closed. I shielded my face with my hands, fearful he might strike me.

"Augie, what are you doing?" His face was pain stricken. "You're not afraid of me, are you? That's preposterous."

Preposterous. That's what Mama told me in the kitchen of 315 Benevolent Street. "I don't know. Maybe," I whispered, a lump growing in my throat. "Yes. You frighten me when you get like this."

Embracing me, he kissed my neck. "I could never hurt you."

I wanted to believe I was safe, but I went numb when others were feeling too much. I simply wasn't sure. When his roving hand wondered downward, I took his face in my hands and kissed his pouty lips.

CHAPTER 12

DON'T RAIN ON MY PARADE

Fearful of separation, the five of us held hands as we maneuvered our way through the crowd for a better view of the stage. Theatrically intense, the atmosphere whirred with life. There was so much to see, so many nationalities and types of people I'd never met face to face. I had so much to learn. My heart raced. My insides were as chatty as a flock of geese, but outside, I was too dazed to speak.

Pre-performance jitters jostled the roughly one hundred and twenty-five thousand gathered on the Mall. Wide-eyed, anxious, and vigilant of the present danger lurking on the fringes of the fenced-off area, I peered at every holly tree, stone wall, and spruce we passed.

Pilgrims. We were pilgrims setting sail for a new world, the First National March on Washington for Lesbian and Gay Rights. It was imperative that our demonstration run smoothly to prove to the world and ourselves that we deserved a place at the political table.

Paddy O'Brian, the only other member of our Alternate Lifestyles group who attended, waved from across the green when he recognized us. He'd driven up the day before to visit his family, who had a house in Woodley Park, a few blocks from the National Zoo. He was all fumbling hands and gooey-eyed over a raven-haired boy in a "PHILLY-FAGS" T-shirt.

"There she blows," Farley said. "Never meets a stranger."

Everyone loved Paddy, a jolly soul. I'd told him once, "You remind me of my dad." Although he'd never met Dad, he was flattered by the comparison.

Recognizing Paddy's friend, Farley waved, his bangles tinkling like Disney's Tinkerbell. "That's Boyd Lloyd, a Buck's County alum from before your time, Polly. A simple pair, the two of them. In their case, two heads are better than one."

"Nasty queen." Evangeline whacked the bill of Farley's baseball cap, knocking it to the ground between a woman's feet.

"Sorry, ladies." Dilbert snatched it up before the woman noticed, brushed it off, and handed it back to Farley. "Here, love. The first and hopefully last time I reach between the pins of a dyke." The woman apparently overheard his comment and shot Dilbert a withering look, but thankfully moved on. The chains crisscrossing her ample bosom appeared capable of much destruction.

Holding Pete's hand in public for the world to see, I felt like the empowered gay man I wished to be someday. "I so wish Aunt Jessica hadn't gone to my parents' for the weekend. I wanted to share the experience with her."

"I'd like to meet her. Maybe another weekend," Pete said.

"Yeah," I replied, but I wondered if there would be another weekend. Caught in the rising tide of people bobbing up and down, back and forth, and from side to side, we plodded through the thick of it, scampering across the brief clearings like a chorus of concubines late for their entrance.

"We're living history today," I said. "Funny: I used to think Stonewall was so long ago, but . . ."

"Ten years is a drop in the bucket in history," Pete interjected. "Our lives will be but a blip on the timeline."

"I'm so glad we came," Evangeline said and kissed my cheek.

Farley sneered at Paddy, who was laughing it up with a drag queen dressed as—well, I wasn't certain who. "Drags are talentless, wish-to-be stars; so depressing. And Paddy . . ."

"He's a lamb," I interjected.

Farley leaned close, his bangles tinging and dinging when he raised his hand to whisper in my ear, "Bitch better keep her sweaty paws off my baby if she knows what's good for her. She's a bit too familiar, if you know what I mean."

I did.

Farley's transformation from psycho-nerd deluxe to university chic was mind-bending. I was glad to have played a minute part in it. Surprisingly, with instruction, he had decent taste. Perhaps Aunt

Tootie's perspective was keen when it came to our relationship. "He'll never get noticed with you in the room," she'd said the last time I was home. Of course, in this crowd, jam-packed with characters worthy of a Luis Bunuel movie, he needed, as Mama often advised, "A little faux glamor." That's where the bracelets entered his mind—and reentered the picture.

Two young women with short-cropped hair squeezed through the crowd, handing out buttons. I accepted the offering. Printed on the front was "National Gay March" and the date surrounding a silhouette of Lady Liberty. However, it was the Harvey Milk quote at the bottom that tugged at my heart. "Rights are not won on paper: They are won only by those who make their voices heard." I wore it with great pride.

"Harvey was our chance to have a voice in Congress," Evangeline said, reading my button. "God damn that crackpot closet case. Dan White deserves to be hung and quartered."

"Then we'd be no better than them," I said.

"'Them'?" Farley said. "The likes of them . . . assholes like my father and the rest of my troglodyte family. Honey, I'd sell them on the corner for a ham sandwich."

I kept my trap shut. The mere thought of his father made me queasy. I couldn't imagine the hell Farley had been through. He was lucky to be normal; whatever that means.

A wave of exhilaration traveled through the throngs as the first speakers claimed the stage. Several people spoke briefly about the march and how it would serve to nationalize our movement, which had previously focused on our struggles and not our expectations for an inclusive government of, by, and for all people.

Allen Young summed it up best in the final paragraph of his welcome message, which was printed in the event programs.

"Today in the capitol [sic] of America, we are all here, the almost liberated and the slightly repressed; the butch, the femme and everything in-between; the androgynous; the monogamous and the promiscuous; the masturbators and the fellators and the tribadists; men in dresses and women in neckties; those who bite and those who cuddle; celebates [sic] and pederasts; diesel dykes and nelly queens; amazons and size queens, Yellow, Black, Brown, White, and Red; the shorthaired and the long, the fat and the thin; the nude and the prude; the beauties and the beasts; the studs and duds; the communes, the couples, and the singles; pubescents and the octogenarians. Yes, we are all here! We are everywhere! Welcome to the March on Washington for Lesbian and Gay Rights!"

We, the thousands, exploded into thunderous applause. I cheered, whistled, and raised my fist in solidarity with my fellow inmates of a justice system askew. In those opening minutes, I could feel my chemistry sputter to a boil. Shifting, realigning, transferring, reshaping, my brain transmitted new waves in uncharted territories in its quest to reprogram the core of who I was. My communicative tools sharpened, my batteries recharged, and my direction refocused, I shouted loudly, proudly, "I am here! I am queer!"

· • ·

"I've been circling this bar for twenty minutes!" Evangeline complained.

"Didn't you hear?" Farley piped up from the back seat. "There was a little gay march today."

She stuck her tongue out at him.

"Darling, you best keep that tool locked away for tonight," Farley said. "For dykes, that's the equivalent of wagging your wang in front of—"

"You!" Dilbert joked, and we burst into laughter.

"There's one!" Pete jumped out of the car. He waved a carload of drag queens away to clear the space. "Sorry girls! We were a split second faster."

A drag queen, her platinum hair scraping the roof of the car, rolled her window down. "Baby," she yelled and licked her florescent fuchsia lips, "if you weren't so damn scrumptious, I'd accessorize your manly backside with tire tracks."

Several minutes later, when she spotted us in the line to enter the bar, the same drag queen said, "Come on baby, light my fire." Hooking her finger into Pete's belt, she tugged. "This way, sugar. I know people."

"I'm sure you do." Farley grabbed hold of her elbow.

"Sweetie, you ruin my Bill Blass and I'll cut your fingers to the quick." She walked off, and Pete—cock-sure in his disarming charms—went after her, beckoning the rest of us along. We followed our Pied Piper down a filthy, rat-infested alleyway that reeked of piss and pot, which ran between the bar and an abandoned building humming with muffled moans of pleasure.

"Baby, if this alleyway could talk," the fringe-flapping siren said as she approached the bar's back door. Careful not to break her four-inch-long sequined nails, she banged on the door with her wrist. Then, turning to Evangeline, she stated flatly, "You owe me twenty-five dollars, bitch."

"What for?" Evangeline shrank a foot in her six-inch heels before the painted mountain staring her down.

"You've got to pay the man, or they'll slash your tires, baby. Them's the rules."

Smirking, Evangeline dug in her pocket for cash, but Pete beat her to it.

"Here," he said, handing the drag queen a wad of money. "Keep the change."

She counted the bills faster than a bank teller and stuffed the cash in her bra. "Thank the Lord! My babies can eat!" Puckering her glistening lips, she kissed Pete on the mouth.

Just then, the door swung open, and a husky man stepped out in an orange suede vest that had seen better days. "You!"

The drag queen mussed the balding man's ring of hair. "Hush, Mr. President," she said, imitating Marilyn Monroe. "You know you love me, Ernie."

"I'll love your boney ass, Lenard, when you pay your rent on time." Then, soaking in the glory of Pete, he grinned. "You can sit on my face any day." And he stood aside to let us all file in.

I honestly didn't know what to make of Pier Nine Disco in Southwest DC any more than I knew how to take Lenard and Ernie. All three were gritty, seedy, cheap, and fabulous. As with the march, everything and everyone was deliriously, delightfully exaggerated. The energy of the crowd seemed unsustainable. Frivolity flourished in every dark corner and freckle of light from the spinning mirrored disco ball. This was the wild flipside of our revolution. My innocence was being peeled back one layer at a time.

As soon as our wrists were stamped as legit customers, I headed for the men's room. The revolting smell of putrid urine slapped me before I even opened the door. The faucets were busted, so water trickled from every basin in the row of sinks, their drains plugged with sopping wet paper towels. Several empty bottles of poppers and a capless tube of KY lay discarded in a corner. Lenard came in to touch up her inch-thick makeup while I was washing my hands. Even though I was apprehensive about approaching the only drag queen I'd seen in the actual flesh, I sidled up to her and asked, "Enjoying your evening, Lenard?"

No sooner had the words darted out of my mouth than her baseball-mitt-sized hands were clutching my throat. Slamming me against the mirror, she stuck her face centimeters from mine. Up close, the garish, clownish paint, her snarling mouth, and the spittle spritzing my face made for a living nightmare. "When I'm dressed as Jean Harlow, I'm Jean Harlow! Got it, fag?"

I coughed and dropped onto the counter when he released me. "Sorry . . . Jean," I said, struggling to catch my breath. "Sorry, Miss Harlow."

Like a searchlight on a convict, she looked me up and down. "What does that prime slab of man see in a twink like you? You're not even pretty."

I exited the bathroom quickly, grabbed Pete's hand, and pushed through the traffic jam heading to the dance floor. It was my first city disco. I was determined that Jean Harlow would not spoil my premier dive into the deep end of delinquency. Beauty opened doors in the world, and as soon as the divas pounding the dance floor got a glimpse of Pete, the crowd parted like the Red Sea for Moses.

Basking in the glow of his ethereal light and the mirrored ball spinning above our heads, I surrendered to the gritty glamor of the nightclub.

When I glanced at the gyrating gaggles colonizing the floor, I spotted Farley and Dilbert bobbing up and down in the crashing wave of the strobe-lit sea. Paddy had his arms wrapped around the neck of a large bear wearing a T-shirt that read "Proud! Loud! And Queer!" Evangeline was sandwiched between a stunning blonde vixen and a woman more butch than our high school wrestling coach. Bumping, grinding, kissing, and rubbing, their smoldering sexuality pulsated to the disco beat.

By the time Donna Summer's *Last Dance* blasted from the speakers, Pete was eager to assemble our ensemble for a swift exit. To no avail, we scoured the joint for any sign of our cohorts-inslime before giving up and heading for the door. Outside, we hustled down the street to the car, only to discover, like our friends, it had been abducted by aliens. Pete hailed a cab and off we trekked to DC's most exclusive zip code, 20008.

Every south-facing window of Pete's co-op offered a postcard view of the capital city. The architectural reliefs, highlighted by spotlights, gave the White House the appearance of a detailed block print. The iconic Lincoln and Jefferson Memorials stood smug against the horizon as the first sliver of dawn washed their white marble edifices in an encouraging carrot yellow. Even the roof of Aunt Jessica's building was visible from Pete's perch on the Hill.

Perhaps it was the after-school special I'd watched long ago on the birth of our nation, or my dad's recollections of a post-World War II US, ripe with prose and opportunity, that gave me faith in our government, but I was certain that once the powers that be understood our campaign for equality, they would never let us down. America's power was in its diversity, and in the past it had welcomed the destitute, the brave, and the honest. Certainly, people would welcome us gay people once they saw how like them we were. I was convinced that the truth would set us free. We just needed the courage to come out and be proud of who we were. Marching with my fellow Americans in the streets of Washington, feeling the immense power of numbers and remembering the welcoming handshakes and sincere smiles offered that day, I'd connected with a part of myself I hadn't been previously aware of.

Oh, I had inklings of the activist taking root in my soul. I remembered sitting in the third row of the Grand Movie Theatre with Evangeline and marveling at Barbra Streisand's character, Katie, in *The Way We Were*, as she stood strong against fascism. Every time I'd stepped between Chester Chad and one of his carefully chosen victims, a call to duty ignited in my gut.

Compared to the crowd that day on the National Mall, compared to the population of the planet, I was but a small cog in the wheel. However, lives can be altered by one tiny voice in the forest, and my contribution to the choir would add volume to our message. If it hadn't been for the Lovings, the interracial couple who stood up for their right to marry, the Supreme Court would never have ruled it legal. One voice combined with more can become a million voices. I prayed I'd live to see that relay race to the Supreme Court in my lifetime.

In the White House's Lincoln bedroom, there's a copy of the Emancipation Proclamation, which Honest Abe signed in that very room on New Year's Day 1863. One idea born in the head of one man changed the world for the better. Hokey as it would have sounded to many of my friends and acquaintances, I was proud to be an American.

"A penny for your thoughts," Pete said.

"Millions are flashing in my head."

•••

After we'd made love, I lay staring at the intricate pattern of the plastered ceiling. Pete was peacefully snoring away beside me, oblivious to the ramblings racing in a continuous loop in my head. Politics. School. Theatre. Friends. Family. Lovers. Politics. School. Theatre. Friends. Family. Usually, sex smothered all the other obstinate matters vying for my attention. But as I cozied up with Pete, the many facets of my life refused to retreat to the shadows when the brilliant sunshine burst through the part in the silk drapes. A lion I didn't know existed roared inside this lamb, awakening the brave six-year-old in me—that boy bold enough to buy a Barbie of his very own.

Like the captivating thrill that gave me goosebumps the moment I walked onto a stage, the march had sparked an eternal flame in me. As we'd paraded past the White House, waving our flags, bearing our banners with dignity, and holding our placards high for the world to see, my heart had swollen to bursting.

Thank heavens Pete was a sound sleeper. He didn't stir when I tip-toed across the creaking parquet floor to the bathroom.

The last strains of the disco beat thumping in my head melted away under the hot water pelting my pale flesh red. I stood in Pete's shower in his and Arabella's home in a city hundreds of miles from my bedroom in 315 Benevolent Street. As I massaged shampoo into my hair, the expanding volume of lather engulfed my curls, broke free, and slid down my nose to my chin. Sacrilegiously, I scrubbed Pete's touch from my skin. Was this the end of Pete and me? Had our relationship, with its bumps and grinds, run its course?

Securing a terry robe around my waist, I padded down the hall toward the kitchen, but paused when I noticed a bedroom door ajar. Curiosity may have killed the cat, but a lion survives on knowledge. I peeked inside.

It was her room. I had no doubt about it. Scented with woman, its confident decor had a female ambiance.

Plush as a mohair sweater, the cream silk carpet felt soft and luxurious to my beaten feet. *Rich.* The room reeked of wealth and privilege. As sumptuous as the Mayflower restaurant where Aunt Jessica had taken me to tea once, Arabella's Paris-inspired bedroom was a study in shades of white, a monochromatic tomb of calm. Ivory damask silk hung from a gold-leafed crown mounted to the wall behind the Louis XVI headboard. Two bergère chairs flanked the marble mantled fireplace. Sleek brass-and-glass tables accented the room, a chic modern contrast to the stylish antiques.

Competition? Arabella wasn't competition. She was spouse, mortgagee, and perhaps soon to be mother. She'd bagged the grand prize. With a ring on her finger, she held the lofty position that I, as a gay man, could never hope to claim with Pete: a legitimate marriage.

•••

"Coffee?" I asked as I hoisted a silver tray onto Pete's nightstand.

"Augie," he said, yawning. "What time is it?"

"Nearly ten." I filled a cup and handed it to him.

Pete patted the feather mattress. "I can't kiss you way over there."

I removed the cover from the plate of sausage and scrambled eggs. "I made breakfast."

Pete perked up. "That delicious smell. I thought I was dreaming."

I secured the legs of the bed tray and climbed onto the king mattress next to him. "I'm famished."

Pete kissed my forehead, speared a sausage with his fork, and popped it in his mouth. "Delish."

"Your paper, Mr. Pace," I teased, handing it to him.

Downing his glass of orange juice, he unrolled the Sunday

edition of *The Washington Post*. Pictures of the march were splattered across the front. He dropped his fork. It clanged against the plate. His eyes bulging, he shoved the paper in my face. "There! Right there!"

"What? I don't see . . ." But then he tapped his finger against a small photo at the bottom, and I saw the point of interest. The picture was a tad smudged. "Oh," I said, locating the two of us after a moment's straining. His arms wrapped around me, we looked every inch the ideal gay couple out for a day of politics and protest. "No one will notice. It's such a small picture. Your parents are in Philadelphia, and your—your wife is in New York."

Tossing the comforter off, he shot across the room, his naked body as graceful as an Olympic ice skater's. "For Christ's sake, Augie, my parents get *The Washington Post*! Her parents subscribe to *The Post*!" He dropped into a slipper chair by the window and stared straight ahead. "There's no getting around this one. No denying I'm a big fag. I'm fucked!"

I scurried across the floor to my backpack, pulled a fresh pair of jeans and a clean tee out, and quickly dressed as he ranted and raged over his ruined life. "Well, maybe if you were honest with one another, you wouldn't be in this mess," I finally said. "One lie begets another and another and another."

"Jesus! We look more in love in that photo than any of the hundred shots of Arabella and me at our wedding!"

Like a boomerang hitting an unexpected iron rod in the fog, his comment struck me right between the eyes. "Peter Pakington Pace," I said boldly, "go to hell!" I grabbed my bag, tore out of the bedroom, and strode down the hall to the coat closet. I jerked my jacket off the hanger hard. The hanger banged against the wall. "Screw it!" I mumbled to myself as I wrestled my hand into the jacket sleeve. I tightened the latch on my backpack, hoisted it over my shoulder, and hurried to the door.

"Augie!" Pete yelled, securing his robe as he rushed after me. "Augie!" He grabbed hold of my bag, and my hand slipped off the front door handle. "No!"

Yanked down to the floor, I hit the Aubusson carpet with a muffled *thud*. The flap of my overstuffed bag snapped open, spilling the contents onto the golden wool rug. Yesterday's jeans splashed against my ankle. "Why did I ever trust you?" I burst.

"I'm an idiot! Foolish! I should have stayed home and read the recap in *Time Magazine*."

Pete attempted to help me collect my things, but I pushed him away. I'd never been so angry, and it frightened me. *God have mercy*, I prayed. *Save me from Mama's fate. Please! Please!*

"I'm sorry," Pete said. "I was out of my head. Shocked. It was the shock of the picture and the thought of my parents and her parents and her." Despite all the chairs in the hallway, he sat on the floor next to me.

"Arabella," I said. "You never say her name. It's always 'she' or 'her' or sometimes 'my wife,' but never her name. She's a human being too. She's not your baby machine any more than I'm your mistress."

Pete gripped my arms. "Nobody cares as long as I'm discreet."

He embraced me tightly, but I pushed back. "Off," I said, as calm as Grandma Flora's pond on a windless summer day. "Let go."

He loosened his grip, and I fell backward from him. "Well." I fiddled with the strap of my bag. "I'll be at Kramerbooks. Evangeline can pick me up there."

Pete, the six-foot-four Adonis, crumpled. "Don't leave me, Augie."

"Christ, Pete. You don't want this. You hate drama."

"Yet, here I am, drowning in the middle of one."

"Of your own making."

"This double life . . . double standard, secret life . . . gay, straight, bi life is not for me. I crave sunlight and spotlights. Skulking in the mist, waiting for Brigadoon to appear again . . . our Brigadoon."

I sat on the floor beside him. "Would you have me put my life on hold?" I asked. He traced the pattern of the French rug with his finger. "Please don't ask me to do this, because I don't think I could resist you, and you . . . you know it's wrong. I'd be loyal, and where would that get me?"

Pete bowed his head, and I raked my fingers through his hair. He was right. I'd never felt this with anyone and might never again.

"It's not good for you to straddle the line," I said. "Make a commitment to Arabella and see it through. I don't want a married man, Pete. I want a husband of my own. I know, I'm dreaming the

141

impossible. I'll never marry a man because the law denies me the right. Someday maybe, but not in my lifetime. I can't imagine."

He said nothing as his finger traced the pattern in the rug.

· • ·

I wasn't looking forward to the three-hour ride home. My head whirling with thoughts of Pete, I was in no mood to lift everyone's spirits, and yet I knew I must. Staying positive in the face of adversity was my crutch to bear. Dad claimed that a person could cheer themselves up just by smiling. It was worth a try.

The atmosphere in Evangeline's reliable Mercedes was oppressive. Her mind reeling from hours of feminine indulgence the night before, Evangeline was on the verge of a revelation. Farley sat opposite me in the back seat, and Dilbert had claimed the passenger seat up front. The elation of the march that had originally united us had now forsaken us. We were each riding solo in a pack. Not one word did we utter until we pulled into a gas station to refuel and relieve our overburdened bladders.

Farley pressed a button, and the vending machine regurgitated a Pepsi.

I popped the tab on my Fresca. "What happened last night?" I said, eyeing the caramel-creams in the Snack-Shack corner of Buddy's CITGO service station.

Farley pointed to the dark circles under his eyes. "Bette Davis at a four-a.m. call."

"And your bracelets?" His arms were bare again. "Where's your bangles, babbles, and beads?"

"Lost to the ages. I think I accidently dropped them in the Georgetown canal."

I took a swig of soda. "We looked everywhere for you guys. I can't believe you left us high and dry."

"You?" he said, his face as exaggerated as Elmer Fudd's when Bugs Bunny outsmarts him yet again. "Evangeline ditched us for the Isle of Lesbos."

"Where did you sleep?"

"Under Whitehurst Freeway." Farley stretched his back. "It was *that* glamorous."

I was tangled in a knot Houdini couldn't escape. I knew that by the end of the day, each one of my traveling companions would corner me, demanding my attention. If I refused to listen to their grievances, guilt would plague me. This was a pattern I'd fallen into long ago with Mama. Rooted in my youth, starring in the role of "doormat" had become second nature to me. No matter how hard I tried to resist the urge to help, whenever Mama called, I jumped. For hours, I'd listen to her moan and groan about her dismal exitance. Solving her dilemmas before she spun out of control benefited everyone.

"She's a bitter pill to swallow," April had often complained. "I'd help, but you know how it is between us."

Unlike April, who found it easy to sneer and walk away when Mama threated suicide or some other dramatic act of revenge, I sat with the responsibility required . . . yes, *expected* of a good son. Faking it or not, she was crying for help. Mental or physical, her pain was real. That much I knew. How could I have abandoned her? Her demons were eating her alive. They were eating all of us alive. I bore it for the family, knowing perhaps if I listened, she wouldn't go off on Dad, or Tootie, or April.

"Since Mother died, you're the only one I can talk to," she'd whisper through the crack in her bedroom door.

Listening was the only ace in my deck. My good ear was vital to my friendships. Nice, kind, and pleasant, I was August Applegate, the kid with the golden ear, the guy you could trust with your darkest secrets, the young man offering up surprisingly sound advice you might expect from a parent. *Parent.* That's what I was. A twenty-year-old parent of a burgeoning family.

I glanced over at Evangeline, who had a can of root beer wedged between her thighs, one hand on the wheel, and the other stuffing barbeque potato chips in her mouth. At least I had someone to turn to. She gave as good as she got. With a needy mother such as hers, she appreciated my survival skills. I patted her shoulder and mouthed in the rear-view mirror, "Love you." We were two lions trapped in a badger cage.

"Life gives you what you need when you need it," Dad often said. He would have known. How else had he survived decades with Mama?

CHAPTER 13

WHEREVER HE AIN'T

"Why not?" I mumbled to myself. "Surprise him."

Farley's door stood ajar. Nearly two years we'd lived together, and I had never set foot in his room, his purple den of iniquity. A sliver of purple wall was all I knew of his "chamber of chills," as Dilbert referred to it. Farley had declared it off-limits to me that first day. So, out of respect, I'd never darkened his threshold. It was odd, but about a month before, he'd stopped locking his door every time he left the house. *My. Oh, my. What treasure awaits on Gilligan's Island?*

"What are you hiding in there, Mrs. Danvers?" I once teased. "Is that Rebecca's room?"

Oh well, what the hell? I've vacuumed the entire apartment. What's one more room?

Between the deep eggplant walls and the black-out shades, I could barely see my hand in front of me as I felt for the light switch. When I clicked it on, the ceiling light's low-wattage incandescent bulb splashed the room in a golden hue.

Twice as big as mine, Farley's room had formerly been a parlor. It featured a raised vestibule, and the intricate woodwork framing the entrance and mantle was in dire need of a fresh coat of paint. I ran my hand over the fluid lines of carved cherubs holding aloft an ornate Della Robbia garland and imagined Edwardian ladies gathering around a tea table, chattering like a flock of sparrows as an orange-tipped blue flame skipped across an ashy log in the hearth. *How lovely.*

I raised the blinds and cracked the window. The afternoon sun, low in the periwinkle sky, washed the room in a sepia tone reminiscent of vintage photos. I plugged the Hoover in and clicked the "on" button. But faced with the possibility of ruining any shred of rubbish in the stacks of books, magazines, and albums, I soon gave up. It was a senseless waste of time. The best I could do was vacuum the inch-thick layer of dust bunnies circling the perimeter of the parquet floor. I tugged the cord out of the socket, and it leapt up like a dancing cobra, hitting the side of a hat box wedged precariously between a stack of books and a tan bag festooned with Cheetos-yellow fingerprints.

A plethora of holiday cards and unopened mail slid onto the floor, exposing a ratty, moth-eaten peach velvet chair. *Oh Jesus!* Down on my hands and knees, I scooped a few dozen envelopes into my arms and sat them on top of the heap of *After Dark* magazines piled on a side table. Two or three of them slid off again, one landing on the top of my shoe.

What's this? Boldly addressed in my handwriting was my application for the MidAtlantic Regional Theatre Festival. Sputtering, my mind spun like a casino roulette wheel. Farley had promised to mail it for me months ago. I broke out in a cold sweat as I ripped the envelope open. *No! No! Please. No!*

I unfolded the enclosed application, my chest tightening. *I knew it. I knew something was wrong. No wonder I never heard back from the committee.* My entry form and portfolio of pictures from our spring production rested in my icy palms. The deadline for the costume competition had long passed. It was too late to reapply. I tucked the envelope under my arm and rolled the Hoover toward the exit.

"Fuck!" I screamed when I bumped into another ominous stack of papers, which shuffled across my path like a deck of cards. Without bothering to pick up the mess, I rolled the vacuum over the pile. The unlevel stack crumbled further into a flat mountain on the floor, exposing another treasure that had previously been well buried.

My lost cane from George M! I kicked Farley's precious memorabilia to the side and fished my cane out of the rubble.

It was dark by the time Farley arrived home from his French literature class with Madame Snow. I watched through the part in the drapes as he bounded up the front steps of the veranda. A smile on his face and a bounce in his step, he sang "I Whistle a Happy Tune" from *The King and I* as he unlocked the door.

"'Whenever I feel afraid,'" he crooned and clicked on a single sconce in the alcove, "'I hold my head erect and whistle a happy tune. So no one will suspect I'm afraid.'" He hung his jacket on the coatrack and dropped his bag on the hall table. Twirling left and then right, he waltzed across the living room, sashayed around the coffee table, then reached under the shade of the lamp by my chair. I clicked the switch on before his skinny fingers could touch it.

"Oh my God!" Farley shrieked, his eyes bulging and his chest heaving as he slung himself onto the sofa. "Want to give a girl a stroke?"

"No such luck," I replied.

"Jesus, Polly!" He dug in his pocket for his cigarettes. "Sitting alone in the dark like Dracula. Not still mooning over Mr. Pakington Pace, are you?"

I tossed the envelope on the table.

"A letter from Pete?" He lit his cigarette and inhaled. Smoke curled out of his nostrils and rode the crest of the air pumping from the register above. "Is this a guessing game? I'm in no mood for games, Pollyanna, glad or otherwise. After the day I've had . . ."

I reached behind my chair, grabbed the cane, and ceremoniously laid it on top of the crumpled letter. His gaze fixed on the objects. I could see the wheels turning in his head.

Eyes darting from me to the objects, from the objects to me, he smacked his lips and swallowed like an iguana gobbling up a grasshopper. "What were you doing on my room?" he said, his voice hot with contempt.

"From now on, wherever you are, I ain't." I leaned forward, inches away from his face, close enough to tweak his nose or poke his eye. "What was I doing in your room? What was I doing in your room?" I balled my fist. "Don't you dare. Don't you dare play the victim with me, Farley Fairfield."

Farley sat bolt upright, a panicked prairie dog evaluating the situation. He glanced at the French doors and then at the set of half-closed pocket doors.

I dramatically sniffed the air around him. "A pile of shit. You. Are. A. Pile. Of. Shit."

His head jerked, and his hand trembled when he gestured. "Princess darling, I can explain."

"I'm all ears." I drummed my fingers on the arm of his chair.

Farley's eye twitched. Even though he'd lost his bangles during an orgy in DC, I could hear the clanking, clinking, dinging as he squirmed on the cushion. "A joke. It was meant as a joke."

"A joke?"

"I forgot!" Farley stood, knocking the cane to the carpet. He took a step, but I grabbed hold of his sweater, and he toppled over the coffee table. His back on the carpet, he shielded his face with his arms and kicked at the air until he hit my shin.

"You ass!" I grumbled, rubbing my leg. Farley tried kicking me again, but I grabbed hold of his shoelace. Wriggling and writhing, the imprisoned feline hissed. The more he squirmed, the tighter I held on until the cordovan leather saddle shoe I'd given him popped off in my hand. He scampered to his feet, then pushed, pulled, and pounded on the disobliging pocket doors. One was stuck, and the other wouldn't budge.

Winding up for the pitch, I hurled his shoe at his head, but he ducked, and it smacked hard against the door.

Mumbling animal sounds, grunts and snorts, Farley barreled toward the French door, but I blocked his exit. A quick glance at the locked windows, and he darted back across the room, throwing his weight against the pocket door. *Bang! Bang! Kerplunk!* The door jumped its track. Like a cockroach flatting his exoskeleton, Farley squeezed his skinny self through the opening and beat feet down the hall. I followed in hot pursuit.

No more Mr. Nice Guy! No more cutting him slack because his father abused him. Mama abused everyone in our household, and we didn't wear our hearts on our sleeves. We got on with it. We didn't wear our shame as a badge of honor. We smiled through the hurt and the pain. No one saw past our cheery façade. It was vulgar to plead for pity. I'd held my head high through the worst of Mama's tirades. I could have turned bitter. I could have used promiscuity and pot to self-medicate. I could have played games with others' lives.

Racing past Farley, I threw myself against the back door. "No!" I yelled so loud his chin quivered. He raised his paws and scratched and clawed at my shirt. With the flat of his palm, he pummeled my cheek and chin. Swinging left, right, and center, I punched him in the abdomen and smacked him square in the eye.

Farley dashed into the kitchen, shielding himself behind the refrigerator door.

"Ha!" I pressed my weight against the door, trapping him against the counter.

"Second-rate Cinderfella!" Farley screamed. "Fractured fairy!" His cheeks burned fire-engine-red. Gripping the edge of the linoleum countertop for leverage, he butted the door with his hip, sending me stumbling backward onto the cabinet. A wild, bucking colt, he hammered me, wedged against the carcass of the fridge, with the heavy door.

"You spoiled everything for me!" Bearing his sharp fangs, he snarled. "Summer camp! Pete! Dilbert! You stole my men, the roles that should have been mine, and . . . you strolled in here . . . grander than Glenda Jackson as Queen Elizabeth I. All grins, charm, and grace, just as you did at the Regional Play Festival! I hate you! I hate you! I hate you!"

Bracing myself, I took a deep breath and shoved the door. Farley pushed back, but I refused to relinquish power to such a troglodyte. "Ahhhh!" Throwing my weight behind it, I shoved the door against him. *Bump! Bump! Thud!* Farley fell, his boney butt hitting the hard linoleum. The refrigerator door banged against the cabinet. The vibration from the impact knocked a ketchup bottle off the shelf, but I caught it before it hit the floor.

I stared at the bottle. The voice of evil shouting in my ear drowned out the voice of reason. Faster than a sped-up Buster Keaton silent, I shook the bottle and unscrewed the cap. A colossal blob of Heinz ketchup landed with a *plop* on top of Farley's orange head. Down the side of his face it ran, a red tributary headed south. It pooled in the nape of his neck and saturated the white collar of the striped rugby shirt I'd given him the Christmas before.

A deranged marionette, Farley sprang to his feet, snatched two eggs from the carton, and smashed them on the sides of my face.

I retrieved a two-liter plastic bottle of Pepsi from the counter, shook it fast and furiously, and hosed Farley up one side and down the other.

Farley gasped. "Backstabbing Jezebel! After all I did for you!"

"Made my life a living hell!" I popped the lid on his yellow Tupperware container and dumped half a family-sized can's worth of pork-n-beans on his head. "Evil under the sun! Murderer! Traitor! Lying, conniving thief!"

"Pete was mine before you pranced into our lives," he said scathingly. "I loved Buck's County until you ruined everything!"

I smashed a glazed donut in his face. "I would have stayed at UVa had I known Beelzebub lived at 315 Benevolent Street. What a joke! Benevolent Street. The Baroness of Benevolent Street is a BITCH!"

He beat a box of Quaker Oats against my shoulder until the box split at the seams. My face was wet from the eggs, so he plastered me with raw oats. "I hate and despise you!" he shrieked. "You no-talent, loathsome creature from the black lagoon. Pretty boys won't be in style forever." He grabbed my face with his hand and slammed my head against a cabinet door.

I kicked him in the groin.

"Mother fucker!" Cupping his privates, he fell into a chair.

"Father fu—" I yelled, catching myself before I totally crossed the line.

Balling his fist, he hit me square on the nose. Blood gushed from my nostrils and trickled down my throat, pungent and tangy on my tongue. Incensed, I grabbed him by his shirt collar and threw him against the stove.

Farley reached behind his back, grabbed a greasy spatula, and swatted my face with it. I grabbed his wrists and pinned him to the top of the stove. Oatmeal was trickling down my nose and over my upper lip, so I wiped my face against the front of his shirt. He spit in my mouth.

"Yuck!" I yelled and stuck my head in the sink. As soon as the warm tap water rinsed the spoils of war off my hands, I splashed my face clean. Farley mopped his face with the tea towel. I reached for a hand towel, but he took hold of my ears.

At first, I thought he was still trying to fight, but instead—he kissed me. It was intense, curiously sloppy, and bewilderingly engaging, but completely one-sided since I was too stunned to respond.

After an eternity of moments, we broke away for air. Exhausted and exhilarated at the same time, we dropped into the pink vinyl padded chrome chairs Mama had rescued from her neighbor, Mrs. Wilson's, garbage.

Dazed and confused, we stared at one another. Then, in unison, we both said, "No."

CHAPTER 14

I REMEMBER IT WELL

To say the least, it was difficult to forgive Farley for betraying me. According to him, Theodora Redfern, a graduate student and the assistant costume designer, was the brains behind the scheme—or "joke," as they termed it. The joke had certainly been lost in translation.

A joke is one thing, but to purposely fiddle with my future was an act of cruelty. Stealing my cane during *George M!* I could forgive because . . . because . . . well, we were kids. But as a grown man in college—*Farley* . . . *oh hell! It's infantile! It's demonic! It's . . . unforgivable! Okay!* I wasn't there yet. Perhaps I'd never reach that angelic plateau where forgiveness is not a four-letter word. He'd treaded on me hard!

I swear to God, I tried. I really tried. I'd bent over backward for him because the situation with his father was repulsive and because for some unknown reason, I wanted him to like me. I worshipped his cleverness. I understood why his minions gathered around him. Witty, snide, and disarmingly charming in a shockingly crude manner, everything I detested about him I admired as well. What kind of fool did that make me? *A grandiose one!* I shuddered at the thought.

Mama and Farley had a great deal in common. It was no wonder they'd bonded quicker than hot glue to cardboard. Both could turn wicked on a dime. Their anger zoomed from zero to sixty in a split second. Their egos were grand, and the entire world revolved around them.

I was so like my dad, at least most of the time. It took a lot to anger me, but when I reached a breaking point, I was Mama, a bat out of hell. Farley and I, two gladiators tossed into the center ring, teased with trinkets by the theatre department and tempted by fame in the minute pond we splashed about in, were bound to trip over one another's feet on the climb up the ladder. We lived together, worked together, played together, and fought each other with the same passion we reserved for our shared religion, theatre.

My parents' marriage suffered from too much togetherness. A bit of distance provided perspective. For as much as Mama's unrelenting grip trapped my dad, I believe Dad's enabling her outrageous behavior caged the wild beast.

Would Farley's and my friendship last past graduation day? Did I care? Did he care?

I'd had it up to here with being screwed over. The ugly realization that no one cared was evident. Yet, every time I hit rock bottom, I bounced right back up again. Somehow, someway, my Pollyanna stumbled onto that sliver of silver lining shimmering in the misty aftermath of controversy. Part of me despised Polly's glowing optimism, but to snuff it out would have been equal to killing part of me; the very heart of me; the Grandma Flora in me.

Why did I bother with people determined to dismiss me? Was it the challenge that intrigued me or the determination to change the small part of the universe within my grip? If I could win the hearts and admiration of those inclined to push me away, belittle, or badger me, would that make the victory a greater triumph?

Accepting the unchangeable aspects of the people in my life was a tremendous task. Attempting to be the perfect friend, lover, son, and brother often had me tied in knots trying to please everyone. Was I buying into my own publicity?

"What will you do?" Evangeline asked as we sprawled across her waterbed, staring up at the Christmas lights that would soon be dismantled. "I'll miss the lights, this room . . . you."

I couldn't look at her. I knew if I did, I'd blubber worse than Lucy Ricardo when she was separated from Ethel Mertz. "Can't afford grad school. New York is outrageously expensive."

"Your moving to New York is only a matter of time if you want to be an actor." She blew an enormous bubble from her gum until it popped, sticking to her brow and lashes. "Yikes!"

"Nasty habit," I commented. "Gum is not allowed in Mama's house."

Evangeline cleaned her face, rolled the wad of gum up, and

tossed it in the trashcan a few feet away. "Farley's moving to New York."

"Two years is enough co-habitation," I said. "Besides, he'd be a constant reminder of what I don't have. What I missed out on."

"Augie," she said and rolled over on her tummy. "Let it go. It wasn't meant to be."

"Your future is mapped out. Not a worry in the world." I scooped up a handful of popcorn and shoved it in my mouth.

"There's always a price to pay." She nibbled popcorn from my cupped hand.

"Free tuition to Georgetown. I'd say your dad's pretty generous."

"But I wanted Columbia!"

"Jeez. You and Pete in the same town. You're moving there just as my Aunt Jessica is moving in with Mom and Dad."

"Why? How could she leave the city after all these years?" Evangeline slurped her icy Dr. Pepper. "Something's up."

I shrugged, then changed the subject. "I got a letter today."

"Pete?"

"No. Arena Stage."

Evangeline sat up. "Arena Stage? You got cast. I knew you would. I could feel it in my bones."

I sat up and inspected a tiny hole in my argyle sock. "A summer internship doing hair for the costume designer. May lead to a full-time job. No promises."

"You're great with hair. All those period wigs you did for *Tartuffe* were faboo. Everyone raved about them." She raked the last bit of bubblegum out of her bangs.

"It pays crap."

"I'll be living in that girls-only boarding house, or—"

"Are you a lesbian?"

"Jesus Christ, Augie!" She pinched my cheek.

"Hey!" I rubbed my throbbing flesh. "You went home with two lesbians that night after the march. I don't think you rolled each other's hair and talked about boys."

She stretched her legs in front of her and leaned back on her elbows. "It was . . . well, I don't know. It was hot, but something was missing. Maybe it was them or me, but no fireworks with either of them."

"What about a lipstick lesbian?"

"You know, Augie," she said, looking me in the eye. "I'd make a damn good lesbian if I was so inclined. If I . . ."

"What?"

"If I wasn't gaga over P.E.N.I.S!"

• • •

"Congratulations on Arena Stage," Farley said, adjusting his tie. "A week from now, I'll be living in the Big Apple." He brushed his hair against the flow of his cowlick, but it stubbornly bounced back. "I was lucky Danny needed a roommate. It's in the Village. Close to everything. Bars right outside my front door."

"That's great, I guess," I said. "I mean, for you. I don't know if I'd like that or not." *Christ. Lucky bitch. Why hasn't Danny called me?*

Farley slid his arms into his black acetate graduation gown and checked himself out in my full-length mirror. "In this caftan, I look like Liz Taylor in *The Blue Bird.*"

I opened my robe. "And I look like . . ."

"Robert Redford in *The Sting*," Farley interjected. "Damn you! You'd look chic in a Shelly Winter's tent dress."

Underneath my robe, I was wearing white linen and the spiffy gold silk tie Dad had bought for me. My two-toned oxfords had been a graduation gift from Aunt Jessica.

"From your favorite DC department store, Garfinkles!" she'd said. However, she'd phoned early to say that her allergies were plaguing her, so she wouldn't be attending. "Oh, Mr. March, enjoy your day. I'll be with you in spirit."

Was I disappointed? I was heartbroken that she wasn't there, but what could I do? She'd contributed to my education as much as my professors had. Where else would I have learned all the niceties of dining in a fine restaurant or the particulars of being well dressed, and a million other things I'll never forget?

"Oscar promised to take a ton of pictures with his new Nikon," she added.

• • •

"I need the can!" Aunt Tootie announced, barreling down the hall to the bathroom.

"You can't take her anywhere," Mama groused as she crossed the threshold of 315 Benevolent Street. She was decked from head to toe in tasteful cream; her full-skirted jersey Halston wrap dress, accessorized with a protuberant gold pendant necklace and pearl button earrings, made her appear as angelic as June Cleaver from *Leave It to Beaver.*

When Dad opened the screen door and paraded in wearing his gray sharkskin suit and the same yellow tie as mine, I nearly burst into tears.

"Farley!" Mama called out from the hallway outside his door. "Are you coming with us?"

The sound of his heavy-soled lace-ups clonked across the wooden floor, echoing from his chamber. The door swung open, and he leaned against the frame. "Oh, Mrs. Applegate," he said. "I wish I could, but well . . . you met my father. He'll be bent out of shape if I'm not with my kin."

Mama pinched a pleat into the knot of his tie. "Such a gentleman today, Mr. Fairfield." She kissed his cheek.

I blushed when she kissed him because I was embarrassed for myself. Embarrassed and a bit bitter. Once I'd turned seven, Mama had cut off all physical displays of affection toward me. Touching or kissing her was completely off the table.

"Farley!" Mr. Fairfield yelled through the screen door, apparently unaware of our presence inside. "Get the lead out!" He banged the door open and waddled into the house. "Farley!"

"Father," Farley said, "you remember August's parents and his aunt."

Beet red, Mr. Fairfield squared his shoulders. "Sorry to interrupt, but my wife and son are waiting on the sidewalk. Shall we all walk to campus together?"

Farley's face said it all. A combination of panic, disgust, and defiance, he stood straight and tall, surrounded by my family. "Go ahead, Father. We'll catch up with you." He didn't shake, stutter, or cower to Mr. Fairfield as he had in the past. As Farley smiled at my dad, the hate I had for him dissipated with as much gusto as it had arrived. I was proud to be a small part of his transformation. The new and improved model was equipped to take on the world. Now, if he didn't screw it up with Danny in his Village digs as he had with me, Farley, I hoped while damning him, was headed for success.

"Where's April?" I asked Aunt Tootie as we strolled down the sidewalk behind the gaggle of mixed blessings.

"Tied up with the boys. You know how she is. More reclusive with every passing year. Like the Loch Ness monster, she appears when and where she wishes, and that's not very often. She hasn't been to the house since Christmas."

I fiddled with the tassel on my mortarboard cap. "She's a scrappy gal."

"She's a mess."

"Why can't she grin and bear it? We do."

"Farley's strangely quiet," Aunt Tootie whispered and shook her wrist. "No noise!"

"Lost his bangles in DC."

"A gift from God, if you ask me." She stabbed her hot-pink Lee nails into her frosted poodle perm. Brightly attired in a rose-colored double-polyester pant suit and rope-soled wedges, she was the outrageously tacky aunt I could depend on. "Where's little Evangeline?"

"She met her parents for breakfast at The Elms."

"That's where we're going for lunch," she said, licking her lips. "I'm famished."

Glancing at Mr. Fairfield and Farley, I grimaced.

"If you ask me," Aunt Tootie said, "something's strange there. Old man Fairfield gives me the willies."

I took her hand, and we quickened our pace to catch up with the others.

CHAPTER 15

I'M CALM

"August Applegate?" asked a gray-eyed, mousy young woman with gigantic wire-rimmed glasses parked on the bridge of her pointed nose. "You're two minutes late. Christine is waiting for you. By the way, my name is Regina Ruggles. You can call me Ruggles. Everyone else does. However, Christine must always be addressed as Miss Cadeau. Respect, you know? Get it? Cadeau. You know."

I smiled. It was the most I could muster. Disoriented by my harried commute, the unfamiliar surroundings of my new workstation, an overcrowded storage room, and now the yapping caricature of a human named Regina Ruggles, my head spun in a cyclone of doubt. Where once I'd been confident of my talents and secure in my ability to manage them, I stood stupefied before Miss Cadeau's right-hand maiden. "S-s-sorry," I mumbled, "for being late. I'm not accustomed to the Metro, and when I switched trains at Metro Center—"

"You took the Metro? Where are you living? Tardiness is forbidden."

Her shrill soprano voice sent shivers up my spine. *What the hell have I done? I never should have accepted this job sight unseen.*

"She fired three outstanding assistants last summer for tardiness. Punctuality, proficiency, and precision with one's tasks produce quality theatre. We're a well-strung Stradivarius. I've worked with Miss Cadeau in every major city from coast to coast. She's top-drawer, cream of the crop, and a woman of substance. Not only is she the classiest fashionista I've ever met, but she's the best costumer out there. She's a Tony winner in waiting. What Christine demands, I deliver." Inhaling deeply, Regina—*Ruggles*—paused in front of a prop mirror to adjust the barrettes strapping her thin whisps of hair in place. "You attended Hedgerow?"

Jesus H. Christ! I wanted to push past her and barrel through the door. *Prison.* I'd tumbled down Alice's rabbit hole and awaken in a not so wonderful *Never-Never Land!*

"Hedgerow's a university now. Christine's mother went there back in the Dark Ages. She was impressed by your resumé and your flexibility. Most actors would think it beneath them to work backstage. Too high and mighty. Once upon a time, I longed for the spotlight and glory, the bows and the encores, but after three years of starving in my illegal rat's nest in Hell's Kitchen, I packed my ego, pride, and prejudice into my old kit bag and tossed it in the Hudson River."

"Amazing," I said, truly bowled over by her breath control. *I'm calm. I'm calm*, I kept reminding myself. *I'm perfectly calm.*

My mantra must not have been working, because she whispered in my ear, "Are you scared? Too late!" She clapped her hands and gestured toward the doorway. A tall, lanky woman, her bushel basket of hair a shade of ruby not found in nature, had mysteriously appeared in the doorway. Draped in yards of fabrics, their clashing colors and patterns indubitably screaming for attention, fought to shine in the vibrant neon-green room. I clasped my shaking hands behind my back. *I'm done for! A dead man!*

"My mail-order groom," Christina mused, tossing a length of flocked floral scarf over her globular padded shoulder. With her diminutive waist, cinched with a puce patent belt that exaggerated her proportions, she was a cartoonish Isadora Duncan electrified in glorious technicolor.

"No time to dilly-dally," Christine said. Her eyelids hung heavy with generous helpings of aqua shadow, and the base make-up slathered over her face and neck was thick enough to scratch my initials in. "I like the period hair you did for Mrs. Ralston in *Mousetrap.*" She plopped an ash-colored wig onto a Styrofoam headblock, tapped a bank pin into the crown, and shoved it under my nose.

"Pandora's box," Regina said and giggled. "You have twenty-five minutes."

"Have you had breakfast?" Christine asked suspiciously.

"A cup of coffee and a Snickers," I blurted out.

"Well, we haven't." Regina stepped in front of me, blocking my view of Christine's contorted expression. "Miss Cadeau and I will be back shortly. Rush the wig over to the dressing room as soon as you finish."

Christine's head popped up over Regina's slumped shoulder. Up close, her face was a Monet that needed distance to be appreciated. "Pronto!" she said, her eyeliner curling like a black snake into her crow's feet. She turned and made for the door.

"Don't you want to inspect it first?"

"My sketch is right in front of you," she said without turning around. "You can follow directions, Mr. Applegate, can you not?"

My throat tightened, making it impossible for me to respond.

Miss Cadeau twisted the doorknob with her claw as if she were about to yank it out of its mechanism. "Make it now and make it perfect, and we'll make an ideal team, Mr. Applegate."

The door slammed shut, and I burst into tears. *Screwed! I'm screwed!* If I hadn't signed the lease on the apartment at the Envoy on 16th Street the day before, I would have hightailed it to the Greyhound bus station right then.

Rushing across town to Evangeline's or catching the next train headed North to Farley's new pad in New York were out of the question. *Good Lord! Running to Farley's?* At that moment, I was as desperate as he had been to find a roommate for 315 Benevolent Street. What the hell had I gotten myself into?

Through the tears, I could barely see to part the hair of the wig on the block, but somehow my hands automatically zoomed into action. I smoothed each strand of hair, sprayed it with Aqua Net, and wrapped it around my hand to create a forties rolled 'do. Using my fingers as a crimping iron, I sprayed the front into a wavy pompadour worthy of Joan Crawford. A pin here. A clip there. In ten minutes, it was complete and ready to be fitted.

"Oh my God!" Alison Geary, the lead actress in *Anything Goes*, screamed. "A masterpiece!" She looked me up and down. "You're a find. Too bad you're not four inches taller. You'd make a great leading man."

·•·

Every day I walked into the costume shop to a list longer than my arm to be completed before Ruggles returned to unlock my shackles for lunch or dinner.

At around ten, Christine would saunter in and dump a pile of wigs in front of me. "Wash and set. Dry and style," she repeated loud and clear every day to make certain I heard her over the thump and bang of the washer and dryer spinning away. With an exaggerated hand gesture, as if I was hearing impaired, she'd point to various racks and demand repairs before each performance. Then off she and Ruggles would trek to shop for such necessities as fringe and thread at G Street Fabrics or to the Library of Congress to do research for costumes for the next production she'd be designing. They'd be missing in action for the rest of the day. I was salaried, so there was no leaving until every item was checked off the list.

Thank heaven the air conditioning was cranked up or I truly would have been working in a sweat shop. Racks of clothes needed airing, mending, pressing. There was a double-decker rolling table of shoes to polish and five loads of laundry to press, fold, and store. It went on and on. My days often ended as well as they began: crappy. My scrappy Pollyanna had abandoned me, leaving me *lonely* and *depressed*, paddling backward up Shit's Creek.

· • ·

"Damn! Damn! Damn!" I screamed into the empty concrete shell behind the bolted gate of L'Enfant Plaza Metro station. Unable to leave until the last wig and costume was locked in the shop for the night, I'd missed the last train to Dupont Circle. I had been delayed in collecting the goods because Vice President Mondale and the Second Lady came backstage after the show to gush over the cast.

Trudging back up the motionless escalator, I thought of all the things I'd rather be doing with my life. I honestly didn't mind working backstage. Working alone, cranking out wigs the way Halston designed marvelous hats in the fifties and sixties at Bergdorf Goodman, gave me immense satisfaction. I suppose I'd been lucky, but I'd never suffered disrespect in theatre before. My talents and my roles had always been praised, on stage and back of house, elevated when I proved to be an asset.

Now I felt a tad like Farley the time one of the professors at Hedgerow shouted stage directions at him from the audience during rehearsals for *Man of La Mancha*, "Hey you! Yes you, the Bozo with the orange fro! Three steps to the left!"

What was it about me? What did Christine and Ruggles see in me that gave them permission to treat me like Cinderella? I delivered everything on time and with a smile. I never complained, and I even babysat Christine's loud-mouthed cat, King James. "You never should have left it lying on the floor," she said when I'd showed her where King James had urinated on my Coach bag. "It's washable. Everything's washable these days." She tossed it in the machine. My "purse," as she referred to it, never saw the light of day again. My leather-lined and -trimmed canvas bag was not washable. She thought me stupid. I thought her cruel.

• • •

I sat in the abandoned bus shelter, staring up at the Big Dipper and wondering what family members and friends were up to that night. Mama would have slathered her face with cold cream and been sound asleep for hours. Evangeline was most likely having sex with whatever partner she was captivated with at the moment. Farley would have been spinning on a bar stool at one of the many clubs near his spiffy new pad in the Village. And Pete. What would Pete be up to tonight? Cocktails with a client at the Hay Adams? Being wined and dined at Mrs. Simson's? Making love to Arabella?

A half an hour passed with no bus on the horizon. Southwest Washington was a ghost town come nightfall because it was populated mainly with government offices. Not enough cash in my pocket for a cab, I had little choice but to walk. I used the Smithsonian Castle, which was planted firmly in the center of the National Mall, as my lighthouse to direct me out of the confusing conversion of roads and alleyways.

The iconic Washington landmarks, the city's nightwatchmen, stood triumphant and humble in flooded light, calling me back to the familiarity of Northwest DC. As I passed the Castle, memories of halcyon summer days with Aunt Jessica rippled through my head. I paused before our favorite bench in the rose garden, now swathed in shadow. That precious spot afforded the ideal view of the buildings lining the Mall. Resplendent in their evening dress, every museum sat regally on their foundations rooted deep in the landscape. A backdrop to historic moments saturated with importance, they'd witnessed countless celebrations, marches, and spectacles unfolding before their grand facades. Impressed though I was by their splendor and the hordes of tourists they attracted and the buzzing beehive of activity that electrified them every day, I relished the quiet moments my aunt and I shared there; chatting about everything and nothing as we fed the insistent squirls pestering us for a bite of our lunch.

Entering the ellipse, I walked straight toward the White House. Every pane of glass in the People's House sparkled with life. Glittering chandeliers brightened every first-floor room. *Busy on a weeknight? Odd. So very odd.* Since there was no queue of limos and the vice president was at the theatre, the Carters couldn't have been hosting a state dinner.

Had something bad happened? An international incident? A late-night call from Iran? A discussion about gay liberation? His campaign for reelection floundering, perhaps a restructuring of his campaign was on the menu. I pictured President Carter plotting strategy in the red room, maps of the country and pamphlets spread over the hand-knotted cerise rug that Monsieur Baudelaire, Jacqueline Kennedy's French decorator, had suggested as the ideal option for the refurbished room.

I worried for America's future if Ronald Reagan and his conservative cronies captured the White House. They governed backward, Aunt Jessica always said. I didn't think we could move forward by living in the past. Much of the population longed for the idyllic fifties and the innocent America before Kennedy was assassinated in Dallas.

Their innocent America was ripe with prejudice. Doused in guilt; fearing for their jobs; ostracized by family, friends, and society; most gay men remained in the closet. What choice did they have? What kind of lives did they lead? I probably would have married Evangeline or some other sympathetic woman to hide behind. *I suppose. Maybe? Most likely, no. That's no way to live.*

My Black friends wouldn't have been allowed to take classes with me. The African American guys I had dated would have been . . . well, we both would have flogged and run out of town.

It was difficult to tell who was racist, homophobic, or misogynistic in a world where people said one thing and did the opposite.

No matter how many times I crossed Lafayette Park, the same historical facts blazed in my head. To my left was Blair House, where President Truman had nearly been assassinated decades before. To my right sat Dolly Madison's house. Destitute from her son's gambling debts, the widow was the first First Lady to receive a government stipend. Straight ahead lay Connecticut Avenue, where President Kennedy's funeral cortege made its way to St. Matthews' church. Glancing back at the White House, I wondered if anyone would remember we were there. Would the first gay march on Washington be recorded in the history books, or would our history be forever closeted away from the young and the uninformed searching for a reason to rise from their captivity? Only time would tell.

The problem was, now that my eyes had been pried open and I was more politically aware, I had become impatient for change. Like Dad, I considered myself a proud, forthright American. A product of Grandma Flora's tutelage, I was a Pollyanna to my core. However, there were two sides to the coin, and on the opposite side of the table, conservatives believed that the Eisenhower era of conformity best served the nation.

It had become necessary for me to reconcile the lessons of my youth and the truth of my situation. If only others could have been as supportive and accepting as my family, gay people would be acknowledged for our many contributions to life. Education was the only way out of the past.

Aware of my keen interest in history, Aunt Jessica had found new points of interest to take me to every time I came for a visit. Funny how much I knew of Northwest DC and how little I knew of its remaining three slices of the pie.

By the time I stopped for a Washington Post, Diet Pepsi, and Little Debbie crème-filled oatmeal cookie at People's Drug on Dupont Circle, it was after midnight. Except for a few homeless men swathed in blankets, curled up on the benches on the perimeter of the park, the Circle sat empty.

Heavy humidity hung in the air. After walking miles from Arena Stage to Dupont Circle, my khaki pants and once-stiffly-starched white button-down shirt clung to my body like a second skin. My beige bucks, scuffed and wet from the automatic sprinklers watering the grass in the park, bound my throbbing, sweaty feet in a suede oven, and I longed to kick them off. So, I did.

I sat on the edge of the fountain and daringly stuck my blistered feet in the cool water. Then I unwrapped my cookie and sat contently eating and soaking and glancing above at the star-studded heavens. I felt the first twang of homesickness for 315 Benevolent Street and the premiere pang of joy that DC was now my home.

•●•

Slammed with too much work for too little pay and even less leisure time, by the time autumn brushed the landscape in warm jewel tones, I was seriously considering leaving Arena Stage. Struggling to pay rent on my humble efficacy apartment and keep food on my collapsible card table seemed a hefty price to pay for a chance to become a wig stylist or costume assistant on Broadway. Although no one ever complained about my job performance and the actors and director showered me with praise for my work, I doubted that the grand and glorious Christine Cadeau would recommend me to sweep a stage floor, let alone apprentice at a Broadway costume house. Foolishly, I'd allowed her to use me.

Pacing the floor of the workshop one afternoon, cawing and warbling over some fantasy show she'd been hired to design for some theatre in Connecticut, she chipped away at Ruggles's suggestions, such as they were. Out of desperation, she turned me.

"Applegate, if you had to design a fashionable witch, how would you dress her? She must be beautiful and sexual and desirably dangerous."

Flattered that she'd addressed me as an actual person, let alone asked for my opinion, I offered a few of the million ideas running through my head. "Fifties glamor such as Gloria Swanson in *Sunset Boulevard*?"

She grimaced.

I tried again. "Sixties kitsch a la Bob Fosse's *Sweet Charity*?"

She pursed her lips.

"Marlena Dietrich!" I exclaimed. "I can see it now. A white Russian fur hat cocked dramatically to the side and secured on top of a black satin hood, fitted close to her head to highlight a stunningly made-up face. No hair exposed. Oh! But yes! The head-piece is attached to a skintight body suit; a complete one-piece that tapers down her leg and becomes a high-heeled boot. Even her arms are covered, and she wears black satin opera length gloves." I was flying. I could visualize the costume being constructed in my head as I spoke. "Over this, she'll wear a huge velvet cape with a train, embroidered with symbols and letters and snippets of incantations." I took a swig of my Fresca. "Then, the *piece de resistance*: the lining of the cape is shimmering silver, and when she spreads it open like a phoenix's wings, it becomes a screen to project flashes of color and special effects off of."

Cadeau stared at me intensely, as if she'd just been introduced to an alien. Then, she shot Ruggles a look, and they both made ugly faces.

"For Christ's sake." Ruggles stretched the words across the room as if they were Coney Island taffy.

Cadeau shook her head, sending her shoulder-duster earrings into a clinking frenzy that spelled cheap imitation gold. "So much to learn, Applegate. So much to learn."

• • •

A few days later, the director of the production who'd hired Christine was visiting Washington. He dropped in to review her renderings for the fantasy musical they were about to launch into the stratosphere.

"Applegate." Ruggles cornered me in the laundry room. "Miss Cadeau would like to thank you for your hard work." She pressed a twenty-dollar bill in my hand. "Go take a long lunch. Take a walk. Go to the Smithsonian. A treat. Enjoy!" She rushed me out onto the sidewalk and slammed the door.

My assignment list was a mile longer than the previous day. So, I took a twenty-minute break and dashed back to complete my chores.

A man's voice echoed down the hall from the workroom, followed by a few titters of laughter and a round of clapping hands. I poked my head into the back entrance of the room to see what all the fuss was about.

"Absolutely brilliant!" the buoyant fellow proclaimed.

"You're too kind," Cadeau said in mock humility worthy of a mafioso.

"A drink to celebrate," Ruggles said and gestured toward Cadeau's office.

Cadeau slithered into the office ahead of them, her beaming smile so wide it revealed her fangs glistening in the florescent light. Ruggles closed the door, and I crossed the room to take a gander at what all the fuss was about.

Standing before a rendering of my idea of a glamorous witch—satin body suit, and silver lined cape, fur hat, and all—my innocence drained from the gaping wound in my soul.

•●•

At that point, the defeatist Emily Dickenson in me had waged war on my positive Pollyanna, attempting to divide and conquer my conscience. Positive thinking had gotten me through many a harsh day with Mama and rescued me from doubt and fear. Realism, on the other hand, planted a red flag in my path I couldn't avoid bumping into.

Surviving on a box of pasta and a jar of Chef Boyardee spaghetti sauce for a week's worth of dinners and peanut butter sandwiches for lunch got old fast. I couldn't even afford my proper diet of salad topped with a generous portion of salmon. By typically nixing carbs, I had remained svelte throughout college. Being thin was a must in the gay world. The first sign of a love handle, and my gay card would be revoked at every watering hole in the city.

From sheer lack of volume, my high-carb diet added no additional pounds, but it played havoc on my psyche. I was doing the wrong things for my body, and I worried that some morning I'd wake up as large as the Yogi Bear balloon in the Macy's Thanksgiving Day Parade. I was in a quandary. *Do I walk to work from 16th Street and splurge on lean meat or purchase a Metro transport card and eat pasta?*

It came to a head one Friday morning when Mama phoned to chat, as she often did, while baking for the weekend. "I've got the most divine vanilla sponge cake in the oven. I made that orange-coconut icing you like. I used raspberry jam between the center layers. You wouldn't believe the smell. I swear, it's driving Tootie to distraction. She keeps wandering into the kitchen and asking, 'Is it done yet?' Poor thing has the IQ of a slug in a salt mine."

Surprising myself and Mama, I burst into tears.

"Mr. March? Is that you? Sounds like—are you crying, Mr. March?"

Unable to hide it, I sobbed into the receiver and confessed how overwhelmed I was by my current culinary crisis. "I'm so hungry I could eat a pizza box without sauce."

Bright and early the next day, a ginormous box, big enough to fit two six-year-olds inside, arrived at my door. "Special delivery," the man said as he held his clipboard for my signature. "Smells good, whatever's in there."

I sliced the taped seal with my pocketknife and unwrapped the plethora of goodies waiting for me. Twenty pounds of chicken and ten pounds of ground round were stored in a Styrofoam chest surrounded by dry ice. A cornucopia of fruits and vegetables were lovingly wrapped in Grandma Flora's tattered, checkered tablecloth. Boxes of Knorr soup mix and bottles of spices were stuffed in the basket I'd used to house my Lincoln Logs as a boy.

"Thank you, Mama," I said when I called home. "Thank you and Dad for everything." For a moment, I almost said *I love you*.

A long breath of silence punctured the exuberant gratitude rolling off my tongue. I had crossed Mama's invisible line of acceptance. Expressing affection outwardly had been outlawed in Mama's house. Unlike Grandma Flora, who showered us with love (though much like her father), she preferred assumption when it came to matters of the heart. Dad offered the parental mussing of our hair, pat on the back, and arm around the shoulder, but even with him, hugging and kissing was tossed out with yesterday's birthday cake.

"From now on, Mr. March, I'll send you a monthly care package. I won't have you begging on street corners."

I thanked her again, then asked, "How's Aunt Jessica?"

Silence.

When Mama finally spoke, there was an undercurrent of dread in her tone. "Oh, Mr. March. She's not well, not well at all."

"The flu swept through the theatre with a vengeance," I responded. "Everyone but me has either ended up in bed for a week or the emergency room."

"It's not the flu."

"Her work?"

"For God's sake don't tell her I told you, but she has cancer."

I stared out the window at the endless flow of traffic on 16th Street, unable to move. All sound was sucked out of the universe, and my heart plummeted to depths unexplored. My body quaked with panic.

"Breast cancer like Grandma Flora?"

"Promise me you won't tell."

"Have I ever reneged on any promise I made you, Mama?" I said, referring to her lover.

"No. I suppose you haven't." The sounds of her striking a match and puffing on a cigarette echoed in my ear. "Uterus. She has uterus cancer."

"Is that why she moved home?"

"It certainly wasn't to avoid you." She sighed, and I could feel the resignation in her voice. This was serious, and she knew it, and she was afraid. "You need to come home so she can tell you herself."

"I have Monday off. I'll gas up the old 'Stang and hit I-66 after the Sunday matinee."

CHAPTER 16

MEADOWLARK

Overwrought, exhausted, and broke, I had been steering away from discos, tea-dances, and happy hours. I had met a few guys on the train who'd given me their cards in the hope I would call them for dates, but I never had. How could I possibly have explained my hideous financial situation? Except for my shoes, which were in dire need of new soles from the amount of walking I did, I still had a decent wardrobe from college.

However, now that Mama was sending care packages on a regular basis, I had a little extra change in my pocket. So, after nearly a year of playing hermit to an empty house, I decided it was time to venture out into the wonderful world of gay. Even if the mere thought of walking through the door of any bar by myself was terrifying, a suicidal act of stupidity.

· • ·

"There you are!" I berated Evangeline for leaving me stranded, alone, at Kramerbooks & Afterwords Café for over an hour. "I read *War and Peace* twice and knocked off half of Edith Wharton's *House of Mirth* waiting for you."

"Pish-posh," she said and kissed my cheek. "We had a last-minute visitor in the showroom."

"You mean client," I corrected her. "How's it going with Pete?"

Pete had opened his own business—Pete Pace Interiors—as a passion project some years previously. He'd offered Evangeline a job not long after she moved to the city, but whenever I asked how things were, she said something about how boring it was and changed the subject.

"Fine. Dull. Do you know a guy named Danny? He said he knew you when you were jailbait."

"Danny from theatre camp?"

"The one and only." Evangeline touched up her lipstick.

"He's the nicest guy. You should have invited him along."

"Afraid he and Pete have a little thing going on."

"What about Pete's wife?" I asked. "They have a child now."

Evangeline slid her hand into the crook of my arm. "Oh Pollyanna, you've so much to learn. You can take the girl out of the country, but you can't take the country out of the girl." She guided me to the door. "Shall we?" She pointed across the street at Rascal's Bar. "The happiest happy hour in Dupont Circle."

A stiff breeze swept around the corner as we stepped onto the sidewalk, catching the slit in Evangeline's pencil skirt, exposing her skimpy black lace panties for the world to see. Two obviously straight men and a lesbian with a frosted flattop pressed their faces against the front window of the bookstore. Evangeline blew them a kiss and laughed.

"Got to enjoy it while I can," she said as we crossed Connecticut Avenue. "All too soon, I'll be riddled with cottage cheese thighs and a fat ass like my bubbe, the one you met in Miami—"

"The blind one that thinks I'm Eddie Fisher?"

"The one and only." Evangeline kicked her alligator ankle-strapped Stuart Weitzman in the air.

"People are looking," I said, somewhat shaken. I was the lamb being led to slaughter by a vixen with the longest list of paramours since Hollywood's "it girl," Ann Sheridan, had received 238 marriage proposals in one day.

I hadn't been expecting a sell-out crowd at six o'clock on a Monday evening. I felt like a meadowlark at a mockingbird convention. Evidently, happy hour at Rascal's Bar was the place to be at the beginning of a work week.

"It's the ideal spot, the honey pot for hunting hot . . . guys among the lot." Evangeline laughed heartily at her own joke.

The door bumped my bum when it closed behind me. "After you, Dr. Seuss," I said.

She took my hand and dragged me to the pulsating mass of

men, a human quilt from every walk of life. "Excuse me! Excuse me!" she sang in her best Ethel Merman impersonation. The mouth of the monster smiled broadly and sucked us into the throng.

My eyes had barely adjusted to the dungeon lighting when she tapped someone on the shoulder—a raven-haired man, tall, broad-shouldered, and beefy. He scowled until he turned around and recognized her. They embraced one another and kissed an uncomfortably long time. I gawked about, but no one batted an eyelash over their salacious salutation.

"This is Gerald Fitzgerald!" Evangeline yelled, but I still had to read her lips because the music was ear-shatteringly loud. I could have stuck my head in a tuba in the middle of Vaughn Williams's "Bass Concerto in F minor" and heard more. "He's head of interior design at Wallis & Fitch Haden Department Store!"

"Wallis & Fitch Haden?" I yelled back. "That's my aunt's favorite store!"

Evangeline cupped my ear with her hands and said, "He's a delicious bisexual I met through Pete. He wants me to come work for him."

I shook my head. "Really? You'd do that?"

"August, I presume," Gerald said, offering his meaty palm. His grip was John Wayne intense, which spelled one thing to me: he was an aggressive bottom. Whether it was at the Park Dance Club in Roanoke, the University of Virginia's monthly Gay Alliance dances, or meeting a promising stud on the Metro, every super butch cowboy I'd met in the past five years was a submissive bedroom amour.

I shook my head, and he planted a big wet one on me. Though he was sloppy and tasted a bit like Evangeline, I must admit he buckled my knees. If I hadn't been wedged between two hulking towers of masculinity keeping me upright, I would've melted onto the disgustingly sticky, liquor-soaked floor.

"For you!" the bartender barked, handing me a glass of whisky and nodding toward a gentleman at the end of the bar.

I glanced over my shoulder at a handsome man in a sporty sharkskin suit, who was planted in an overpopulated bed of pin-striped, paisley tied fossils fraternizing with tantalizing twinks clad in tight T-shirts and bum-hugging britches through whose pocket you could read the date on a quarter.

As he had a touch of gray at the temples, I surmised the stranger was somewhere in his forties. According to Aunt Tootie—who, Mama explained, had dated a long list of "bounders" in her day—dark-haired men grayed earlier than blondes or redheads. His angular face and intense stare reminded me of someone, but I couldn't place who that person was; perhaps a movie or a stage actor I'd run across at Arena or auditions in New York.

Jeremy Brett! That's it. He's a dead ringer for Jeremy Brett from My Fair Lady.

"Faster than a speeding bullet!" Evangeline yelled and laughed when I pointed him out.

"Rupert!" Gerald hollered across the bar and waved him over before turning to grin at me. "I know him. He works for the store"

That smile. Where have I seen that smile? The man swam against the current of the shape-shifting sea of bobbleheads to my side. "Hope you like scotch," he said when he reached me, then clinked his glass against mine.

"It's my favorite." I stared into his glistening Nordic-blue eyes. Every bit as intoxicatingly beautiful as the "Blue Marble" image of the Earth taken by Apollo 17 on their way to the moon, they mesmerized me. Even through his three-piece suit, which clung to and hung from all the right places, it was evident he was a compact, muscular God.

"We're going to Childe Harold for dinner if you guys want to join us," Evangeline screamed. "I'm starved!" She could, when called upon, crank the volume of her smokey, sensual speaking voice to cut through any sound barrier or squad siren.

The stranger shot me a disheartening glance that plucked my romantic heart string. "Oh . . . well." I hemmed and hawed, torn between the slightly familiar "third-wheel" gig and the "I—haven't—the—least—idea—what—to—expect" adventure.

Wrapping her arms around me, Evangeline shielded our faces with her noir charmeuse clutch and whispered, "Get laid! That's an order!" A quick kiss on the cheek, and she and Gerald bulldozed their way to the exit.

I stood speechless before this princely figure with the flawless complexion, perfectly even teeth, and sensually plump earlobes, whose name I had already managed to forget. His cock-eyed smile, genuine and endearing, calmed the turbulent storm of doubt whirling wild in my chest.

"A walk," he said in a deep bass that shivered my timbers. "I know a quiet place to talk."

We strolled down P Street, past the piano bar, Friends, which I frequented, and Mr. P's, which I'd never stepped foot in. "Not for you," Evangeline had once insisted.

Crisp and chilly, the evening was ripe with alluring twists. The man was a puzzle to me. Glaringly daring or stupendously stupid, trusting a stranger was a risk often willingly taken when searching for that special someone to fill the void. Loneliness, being alone, or being left behind was a great fear of mine. It had driven me out of my comfortable slump and into the darkest forest in the hope that the man of my dreams would be out there. Somewhere.

Far from the unwarranted saintly reputation thrust upon me by my friends, I'd put myself in harm's way on more than one occasion for the promise of passion. Perhaps not as audaciously as Evangeline, Farley, and Pete, but I had wandered off the beaten path. However sexually heightened I was during these hunts, though, I somehow stayed true to myself. Even with a one-night stand, something had to click. The guy had to have a sense of humor, be intellectually engaging, or be sincerely romantically honest. Rarely had I met a man that possessed all three.

Pete. Pete was the exception.

"Am I taking you far from home?" the man asked and smiled. His thick, dark waves were the kind I could run my fingers through for hours.

"I like to walk," I replied. "It's how I got to know the city. When I first moved here, I'd walk in a different direction on each of my days off. No matter how lost I became, I found my way home."

"An explorer," he said. "Fearless and defiant, I'd guess."

"I do what I have to and try not to complain about it. I learn along the way if need be, but I never say no to a thing before I try. Who knows, I might be good at it?"

"That's very Pollyanna of you."

I blushed. "What did Evangeline tell you about me?"

"I never met her before tonight," the man said, a strange look on his face. "Did I say something . . . ?" He brushed a piece of lint off my tweed jacket. "I didn't mean to insult you. Pollyanna; I meant it as a compliment."

I stared at him as we crossed Dumbarton Bridge, framed by the buffalos Evangeline and I loved. "Evangeline's been my best friend since we were kids," I said, pointing to a bovine. "She jokes that this will be us as elderly Washingtonians."

"She's a character." He stopped, put his hands on my shoulders, and looked me up and down. "You're an original. I've never met anyone quite like you." His hand glided down my arm. "You're— if you don't mind my saying—you're beautiful. The moment you stepped under the spotlight by the entrance of jam-packed Rascal's, I gasped. Not that anyone could hear me." Taking my hand, he asked politely, "Do you mind?"

"Not at all," I replied. My hand felt like a child's in his warm palm, soft as a kid glove. Unaccustomed to labor more intensive than lifting a Montblanc pen, his elegant fingers and perfectly buffed nails were designed to caress luxurious cashmere and rest on satin sheets.

"You were a golden pheasant in a flock of yacking geese." As we crossed the intersection of 33rd and Q Streets, he pointed to an unusual, detached house with a walled courtyard surrounding the front garden "My house," he said. An eighteenth- or early-nineteenth-century brick cottage set on a stone foundation, it was small compared to the Victorian goddesses towering over it. I fell in love with it instantly. It was handsome, compact, and sturdy like its owner. Never had I seen a house and man fit so supremely together.

"Have you ever been to La Ruche Café?"

My jaw dropped. "My favorite place in Georgetown! They have massive desserts."

"It was Jackie—"

"Kennedy's favorite lunch dive," I said, and we both laughed.

I waited on an olive leather sofa in his elegant creme-and-beige living room while he ran upstairs to change. Every inch of his home spelled class. I perused the silver-framed black-and-white photos displayed atop his baby grand: candid snaps of lovely, fashionable ladies and gentlemen through the decades, and several of him with a stunning light-haired Adonis.

"That was Markus," he said.

Startled, I snapped to attention, accidently knocking the photo I'd been inspecting to the floor. It was a picture of the two in their speedos, cavorting on the beach. "Oh my God!" Retrieving it from the blush-white carpet, I rapidly scanned it, and, finding no damage, gingerly set it back in place.

"You are the cutest thing," the man said, leaning against the piano. His ecru cashmere sweater and lightweight ivory suede pants fit like a glove and left little to the imagination. His casual crocodile loafers, sans socks, sent my heart fluttering. A man could possess fine qualities, but if he also had a penchant for beautiful shoes, I was a goner.

As if in a trance, I walked into the stranger's arms. Taking my chin in his hand, he lifted my face, and our lips met briefly; a tantalizing teaser, the sweet taste of mint on his breath. A manly flush of fragrance wafted under my nose. Grassy green spiced with cinnamon, his cologne held heavy notes of woodsy patchouli and vetiver. *Intoxicating.* He kissed my earlobe gently before lowering his attention to the nape of my neck, and my mind slipped into a sensual dream. *Oh Jesus! I'm a goner! Kiss me, for God's sake! Kiss me!*

Impatient for his taste, I took his face in my hands and planted a passionate wet one smack on his pouty lips.

• • •

I heard the alarm buzz the next morning, felt the cool breeze rushing through the open window and sun drenching the pillow, but I couldn't stir. Listening to the spritz of water hitting a glass shower door, I soon drifted back to dreamland.

A car horn blaring from the street below shocked me out of my slumber. "Hello! Hello!" I called out from my new paramour's bed, but I was greeted with a tomb of silence. The shower was no longer running. Rubbing the sleep from my peepers, I noted the time on the petite alarm clock on his side of the bed. "Eleven!" I coughed, leapt out of bed, and padded across the oak floor to the bathroom. Splashing my face with water, I grabbed a towel from the rod on the door and dashed down the stairs. "Hello! Hello!" No one answered. It being a Tuesday morning, I figured the house's owner had left for the day.

I slumped into a chrome kitchen chair and yawned. I wasn't due at the theatre until three that afternoon, so I had plenty of time to recover from the night before. The automatic coffee maker was set to brew. Once it perked to a tarty roasted bravado, I poured a cup and headed back upstairs to shower and retrieve my clothes.

The events of the previous evening unfolded in my memory as the water massaged the back of my neck. *Wow!* I hadn't been so electrocuted by a man since Pete. Total recall had me tingling from head to toe.

I remembered talking about Arena Stage and—*Oh my God! I sang for him.* He'd played the piano, and I sang the same song I sang for Pete that first day at camp, *Where Is Love?* It seemed I'd done most of the talking because I couldn't recall anything about him. Where did he work? I didn't even get his name! "Oh, that's right," I muttered to myself, "he works at Gerald's store."

It wasn't until I was making the bed that I saw the envelope with my name on it propped against the antique Louis XIV mantle clock. The fine, embossed Smythson stationary was rich to the touch, making my name, written with bold, dramatic flair, seem important.

August,

Sorry I had to dash, but I have an important meeting with the board of directors for the store, and it is imperative that I attend, or else I'd be taking you to lunch at La Ruche to make up for my failure to do so last night. Please help yourself to anything in the fridge. Enclosed is my card. I hope to hear from you soon. Wishing you a wonderful day.

Rupert

P.S. I'm walking on air.

I stared at the note for ever so long. The paper smelled like him, and I caressed my cheek with it. An explosion of joy skipped through me. I fell back into the pile of luxurious Dupioni silk pillows. "La! La! La! La!" I sang, kicking my legs in the air. I was gob-smack-smitten!

Periodically throughout the day, I studied Rupert's engraved card.

Mr. Rupert Siegal
Vice President of Advertising and Visual Merchandising
Wallis & Fitch Haden Department Store
G Street, Washington, DC 20005

Exhausted from lack of sleep, with my head in the clouds, it didn't dawn on me until intermission of the show that night why Rupert seemed so familiar. When I realized where I knew him from, I gave him a call. "Rupert," I said from the costume shop phone, "how was your day?"

He summed his day up briefly and told me what a pleasure it was to meet me. "I hope to see you again," he said, his voice deliciously deep.

"For the third time?"

He paused before responding. "The bus from Baltimore!" he said with a laugh. "So it *was* you! Unbelievable! What are the odds? When I remembered, I laughed out loud in the middle of a presentation from a New York display rep. Every head turned in my direction. I was beet red."

My heart exploded in my chest, and a smile as wide as the Mississippi stretched from ear to ear. "It took us a while, but we got there . . . here . . . oh, you know what I mean," I said.

"Had to wait for you to grow up."

"I grew as fast as I could."

CHAPTER 17

FLY, FLY AWAY

Although I had been dating Rupert for nearly six months, I avoided answering his daily proposal to move in with him. I loved his house and had fallen head over heels for the guy, but I liked my shoebox apartment and the ability to hibernate when needed. As with the playhouse Dad built for me when I was six, my tiny efficiency was a safe retreat where I could think. From my second-floor window overlooking the semicircular drive of The Envoy, I enjoyed the company of August Applegate. I liked being by myself. Long after others found me a bore, I remained completely riveted by my innermost thoughts.

"Maybe next year," I told Rupert for the umpteenth time. "Why are you in such a hurry?"

"I can't make the same mistake with you that I did with Markus. Perhaps if I'd followed my instinct, he'd still be here."

But I wouldn't. It was difficult competing with a deceased ex. By default, Markus had the upper hand because everything he'd done or said was filtered through an angelic glow. I was never comfortable wearing a cloak of jealousy, especially when it came to competition. However, romantic competition was a far field from theatre competition—or was it? From all accounts, Markus had been a beautiful, caring, and talented individual (all that I strived for but never mastered). But there it was, the elephant in the room, the major hurdle to clear if or when I decided to cohabitate with Rupert.

Markus had been Rupert's Baltimore commuter relationship for over a decade. In a freak accident, he was plowed down by a car thief speeding away from a cop on North Charles Street, near the entrance to the Peabody Institute, where he taught music. Rupert had been planning to relocate or ask Markus to move in with him when it happened, but never got the chance.

I understood. At twenty-three, my checkered romantic past was peppered with regret. However, my longest relationship had lasted nine months. Nine months. In the time it takes to grow a baby, I'd been through a roller-coaster ride of a relationship. The rest were, as Lilly Tomlin said, "like Teflon. Nothing sticks."

"If you're not ready to move in with me," Rupert said one Sunday morning, "what about coming to work for me?"

I laughed until I saw the serious expression on his face. "At Wallis & Fitch Haden? What could I do at Wallis & Fitch Haden?"

"Director of Fashion."

"I have no experience whatsoever."

"You know fashion history better than Edith Head. You predict trends better than I do, and I've been in the business for . . . well, a really long time." He blushed.

I adored him riled and red-faced. All that adrenalin pumping was a definite turn-on in more ways than one. "You're so hot," I said, loosening his bathrobe tie.

Sex with Rupert was a circus of amazing delights. A master lover, he left me longing for more, which meant he had me right where he wished. Making love was a key part of our winding down at the end of the day. However, it was Sunday mornings that afforded us the time to linger in our bliss without interruption; at least until the joy screeched to an abrupt stop at one p.m., when I had to depart our heavenly retreat and head across town to the theatre.

Tucked up in his king-sized Beauvier French cane bed, sections of the New York Times and the Washington Post littering the fawn satin spread, our dirty breakfast dishes stacked on a tray atop the ottoman, we felt that Sunday morning was our reward at the end of a long week. We would sit side by side, reading for hours while basking in glorious classical selections on 90.9 FM. Those escapes recharged me for another week of double bubble, toil, and trouble in the bowels of the theatre.

Of course, now that he'd offered me a chance at a new career, there wasn't a day that passed—okay, an hour that dragged by—in which I didn't fantasize about working at Wallis & Fitch Haden. It didn't take my Pollyanna long to convince me that I was up for the challenge.

"Rupert," I whispered into the public phone in the theatre lobby during intermission, hardly a week later, "were you serious about that job offer?"

"I never joke about jobs or lovers moving in," he said.

"I'll see you in the office next week, Mr. Siegal."

"I look forward to it, Mr. Applegate," he joked. "Pick you up in two hours."

•●•

Dad once said that the percentage of people having heart attacks on a Monday was higher than any other day of the week. As I sat in that uncomfortable chair outside Wallis & Fitch Haden's personnel department the next day, my heart pounding harder than Little Ricky from *I Love Lucy* could beat his drums, I understood how panic could do one in. I was to meet with the marketing director before interviewing with the director of visual and the head of the fashion office. I'd end my day by lunching with the director of design, who answered directly to Rupert.

"You can do this," I told my reflection in the bathroom mirror, dapperly decked out in a Harvé Bernard herringbone tweed suit and gold silk Countess Mara tie from Garfinkel's. It had been ages since I'd had an occasion to dress up, and my tapered-toe Ferragamo shoes seemed tighter than when last I'd worn them. I was fearful of gaining weight, as I'd been living and working in khakis and a white shirt, grabbing meals on the go, and running only when my schedule allowed, which wasn't often. "Wow." I dimpled my tie. "I forgot how great it feels to be wearing well-tailored clothes."

"I'd rather have one quality garment than a closet of cheap dresses," Mama often said. I totally agreed. Of course, she'd also insisted that I simply looked better dressed up. "Clothes give you a little pizzaz, Mr. March. You and April need fashion to lift your . . . your qualities." I supposed she was right. I knew she was right. I did look and feel better dressed up rather than down. Knowing I looked special heightened my confidence.

I spent the day carefully measuring my answers to the many potent questions being shot at me from experienced department heads well-versed in the language of their trade. While waiting for my final interview, I sat mystified and impressed by the machinery required to run a department store. As with theatre, it was the toiling minions behind the scenes that produced the magical backdrop that enticed audiences to suspend belief and surrender to another realm beyond their own. Visual departments designed and manufactured the atmosphere that presented products in the best possible light, one that inspired customers to shop. Jobs in both universes required a vivid imagination and calculated engineering abilities to generate a quality production.

I popped to attention the moment I heard the office door open. "Mr. Applegate," Rupert said when the last interviewer, Mr. Joseph Armstrong Jones, introduced us. "Thank you for taking time out of your busy day to meet with us." He turned to Mr. Jones and winked.

Why had he winked? Had my future at Wallis & Fitch been predetermined? Had Rupert spilled the beans about our affair to his obviously gay friend, whom I'd heard him rant and rave about in the past?

"Thanks again for your time, Mr. Applegate," said Mr. Jones, standing and collecting his paperwork. "I'm sure we'll be in touch soon."

Timid in my tweed, I shuffled through Rupert's office door and closed it behind me. It was a surreal experience standing in my boyfriend's work habitat. A million thoughts cycled through my head as I memorized the room.

I imagined his ex, Markus, refreshed from a nap on the Amtrak train from Baltimore, rushing through the door with tickets to a concert at the Kennedy Center that had been sold out for months, or off to dine at Mrs. Simpson's Restaurant on Connecticut Avenue. How many other lovers had crossed his office threshold? *Oh! Damn! Damn! Damn!* I clapped the yapping trap of envy squeezing the breath out of me.

Rupert, confident and cool, gestured to the wall of glass encapsulating the office. We stood side by side, gazing out the window. "Glowing feedback from everyone," he said and squeezed my forearm.

If I had been a marionette, I would have collapsed onto the floor.

"Wow," I exclaimed. "This is some office."

"My home away from home." Rupert walked around the enormous, tinted glass conference table to a brown velvet Chesterfield sofa. "It's yours for the taking."

"It is my talent? I mean, they do believe in me, don't they? Right?" I asked. "I mean, you believe I'm capable of handling the situation, don't you?"

He grinned and patted the sofa cushion next to him. "Do *you* believe you can? Can you handle all the work, coordinate the assignments, and deliver the campaigns on time?

"I've done it in theatre for years," I blurted out pridefully. "Sorry," I whispered and lowered my head.

"It takes a Pollyanna." Rupert looked so serious.

"What does Polly have to do with display?" I sat on the sofa beside him, a professional distance apart.

"Pollyanna," he said, sliding closer to me, "strove for the best in every situation and never gave up on herself or anyone else."

"'Some men see things as they are and say, why,'" I quoted Robert Kennedy, "'I dream things that never were and say, why not?'"

"If you can dream it, then you'll be it. That's you in a nutshell, August Applegate." A streak of sunlight streamed through the window and struck his pupils, tickling a tarantella from the twinkling depth of blue.

I'd been afraid my inner Polly, my trusting nature, had led me into a fool's trap, but I was wrong. Providence had opened the door to a new frontier for me, and I would have been a fool to bite the hand holding the golden apple before me.

Ever certain about too many things, I was sure that Rupert loved me and only wanted the best for me. It was evident in his adoring eyes. His admiration and affection gave me confidence, and I was no longer afraid to venture down a new path.

"'Two roads diverge in a yellow wood, and sorry I could not travel both and be one traveler,'" I said humbly. "Mama's favorite Frost poem. That's what I feel like at this moment." I stared out at the rooftops of the buildings surrounding Wallis & Fitch Haden and daydreamed about my future with the company. "It'll solve my financial woes. Won't have to rely on my parents to make ends meet every month."

"You can move in with me now, and—"

"No," I said firmly. "I need to do this for me."

Rupert took my hand and kissed my wrist. "You'll be great at whatever you do."

"This is huge. A huge switch in career. I never thought . . . expected to . . ."

"I trained to be an architect," Rupert said. "Life is unpredictable. One day you're here and the next—you may not be."

"I don't care to live my life worrying about the choices I've made," I said. "It's just that theatre . . . Oh, well, why complain when there's so much to gain? It won't be an easy ride. There's so much to learn and so little time to learn it. Just like Buck's County Theatre Camp."

"How so?"

"I had to learn to be the star I never thought I'd be."

"Fate led you there," Rupert said. "Fate led you to me, and I brought you here."

I sighed. "In high school and college, everything seemed to fall in my lap. Oh, I had to work hard to master and spit-shine my craft, but the rewards were bountiful. Now, after disappointing auditions and being stuck in a low paying job with little exposure . . . Don't get me wrong. Arena Stage, the administrators and actors, the ticket office, even the cleaning staff are top-notch. Polite. They're all polite and polished. I actually like the work itself, but I can't see spending my entire life doing it. Horrible as it is, I'm not built for starvation and slave wages. Am I impatient? I don't know. But I do know I detest being beholden to anyone. It's time I stand on my own two feet and not depend on my parents or my aunts or" —I gently bumped my shoulder to his— "you."

"You're young and proud and full of vim and vigor. Can you do this job, August Applegate?" said Rupert.

"Somehow, I passed the test. I pulled story-statements, clothes for windows I was shown inspirational renderings of. I unpinned a men's suit form, memorized where each pin, fold, and crease belonged. I dressed a mannequin without instruction, styled her hair, and accessorized her in less than a half an hour. I laid out a floor plan for visuals I only knew the theme of—"

"Can you do this job?" Rupert repeated, cutting me off.

I sat up straight in my three-piece suit, looked my lover in the eye, and said with cock-eyed confidence, "I can."

"If you can fly, little bird," Rupert said, "I'll teach you to soar."

CHAPTER 18

ON MY OWN

Combining the endlessly long days, meetings that dragged on for hours, and special events I was required to attend after work and on weekends, my hourly wage came to about a dollar-fifty an hour at Wallis & Fitch Haden—but I loved it. As difficult and challenging as the job was on so many levels, as demanding and ball-busting as my superiors could be, as abrasive and reluctant as my staff was to follow my orders, and as critical of and responsible for my work as Rupert made me, my first year at Wallis & Fitch Haden was one of the best years of my life.

"This is the happiest I've ever seen you!" Evangeline said one Saturday brunch at Childe Harold restaurant.

"I love my job!" I smeared a generous dollop of butter on a slice of French bread. "My Aunt Jessica used to bring me to Wallis & Fitch Haden every Christmas to see Santa when I was a boy. It was the highlight of the season for me. Well, you know what holidays were like with Mama."

"Unpredictable. I'll never forget the time she dragged a live tree, complete with twinkling lights, silver tinsel, and glass ornaments across the living room, out the front door, and heaved into a snowdrift. That was one for the Applegate history book."

"Thank God you were there. It might have been so much worse!"

We shook our heads and laughed. We needed to either laugh or cry while remembering, and I much preferred spinning the tale jolly. "Funny. We work at the same store; why is it I never see you, Mrs. Fitzgerald?"

"Mrs. Fitzgerald?! Me, marry Gerald Fitzgerald? Please! Not in this lifetime." Evangeline screwed up her face. "Or the next." She took a long drag from her Virginia Slim, then snuffed out its butt in the ashtray. "We're fine. Simply fine."

"Doesn't sound fine."

"Oh, Gerald is Gerald. We work great together. I'm simply bored sharing a house with him."

"You mean now that you're in the guest room? Sort of a de-motion."

"My idea, actually. Once he started dragging guys in for three-somes," she said, her voice wavering. "I don't know. It was exciting at first, but then the thought of it turned me off."

"Once you realize that you're basically sleeping with everyone he slept with," I pointed out.

"I'm getting a little paranoid. Maybe I'll stick with women."

"Your odds of contracting the plague would plummet by at least ninety-eight percent."

"Speaking of odds. Have you been tested?"

I pursed my lips. "No. I . . ."

"You volunteer at Whitman-Walker Clinic handing out safe sex literature, visiting the sick and soon-to-be dead, and you haven't—"

"Evangeline. I'm fine."

"Are you fucking kidding me, Pollyanna?" She dipped her fingers in her glass of water and flicked it in my face. "Wake up! You can't screw around with this shit."

She was pissing me off because I knew she was right. "What about you, girly-girl?"

Evangeline sighed and wiped her fingers with a napkin. "I'm waiting for the results." She sipped from her glass of chardonnay. "I'm getting too old for this crap."

"You're twenty-five, for heaven's sake."

She stabbed her salad with a fork. "I tried to add up all the men and women I've slept with since I was sixteen."

"I know what you mean. Rupert is my twelfth," I whispered.

"Twelve?" She smirked, removed her tortoiseshell Dior glasses, and wiped the lenses on her watch plaid skirt. "I stopped counting when I reached one hundred. I wasn't even—"

"No way!" I blurted out. "Sorry, Vange, I . . . Tourette's. I'll blame it on Tourette's."

"You don't have Tourette's, Polly. You were shocked as you should be, as I wasn't for years. Now, I'm on pins and needles waiting for my doctor to call."

I took her hand. "You can count on me."

Evangeline arched her eyebrow. "Don't make the mistake Pete made." Her cheeks suddenly glowed crimson. "Oh my God, Augie, I wasn't supposed to . . . Shit! I'm such a turd."

"Pete's positive?" We lived less than a mile from one another, but I hadn't seen him in years. It was even longer since I'd slept with him. "Pete's *positive?*"

"Oh, Augie, you can't tell a single soul until he talks to you. Promise."

"I promise." A heaviness settled on my shoulders, and I slumped in my chair. It wasn't the first I'd heard of an acquaintance or friend of mine who'd contracted the AIDS virus, but to my knowledge he was the first person I'd slept with to have been exposed. "Not Pete. Not Pete. I can't imagine him being sick. He's never had the common cold, as far as I know."

Evangeline stuck her finger in my face. "Don't go calling him out of the blue. He'll know I blabbed. Only Farley and I know," she said. "And his wife. You know, Arabella." She had a strange look on her face, and I knew it was a serious matter with Pete.

"Bad? How bad is he?"

She turned to face the window, but I could see her pained expression as the candle flame between us highlighted her anguished brow.

I flashed hot then cold. Hot then cold. My insides coursed with a nasty electrical current that jolted me into uncontrollable jitters. A deafening, high-pitched whistle shot back and forth between my ears as if someone had struck my temple with a tuning fork. "Not Pete." I searched her aqua-blue eyes for a sign of hope. "Tell me he'll survive. He will survive, won't he? Evangeline. Please!"

She looked at her bare plate. "Honestly, I can't tell you that. You know how it is, Augie. Here one day and gone the next. No one has been cured. There is no cure. They can't even control the bastard. As brilliant as Dr. Fauci is, he can't see an end to this tragedy anytime soon," she said. "Pete packed up his design firm, and his mother listed the Georgetown building she bought him the week he broke the news to her. It sold in three days, and he hasn't heard from her since except to inform him he was no longer welcome at any of their homes, cottages, or clubs." She tugged on the flaps of the bob hair framing her pensive face. "I lied to you, Augie. I was never bored working at Pete Pace Interiors. How could I be? It was a friggin' blast! But I saw the writing on the wall, and when Gerald offered me gainful employment, I jumped on the offer and the man. That's why I left Pete's so abruptly two years ago."

"Gays have become back-of-house guests," I noted. "Like Nancy Reagan's hairdresser, we're shuffled in and out the back door. Not to be seen. Not to be heard. We're the invisible zombies roaming the night. We're the makers of magic and spinners of the sublime not allowed front-of-house."

"Invisible until some redneck comes barreling out of the suburbs, guns a blazing, eager for a little 'queer action' on a Saturday night," Evangeline snorted.

"There's an article in *Women's Wear Daily* about investors pulling money from gay designers and investing in women designers," I told her. "Because they're afraid the queens will get infected and die on them. Queers are a bad investment. God knows, it's all about the almighty dollar. Our world is changing, and so few people care."

"I care," Evangeline said and peered out the window.

The restaurant having previously been a Victorian row house, we were sitting in the best spot for people-watching. Our table was tucked into the bay window and had an ideal view of Connecticut Avenue and the entrance to the Dupont Circle Metro station.

DC was a beautiful city, but it simply sparkled during the holidays. Up and down the streets, the mom-and-pop shops were decked out for Christmas. The weather could turn on a dime. Two days before, it had climbed to sixty-three degrees before plummeting below zero.

"One hundred plus. Plus!" I shook my head, remembering how we'd started on this topic. "Vange, is that really how many people you've slept with?"

Evangeline shrugged her shoulders. Her love life had been a continuous partner swap. I simply couldn't fathom having sex with that many people. I wouldn't be able to remember their names, let alone intimate details about them, and yet she often had regaled me with tales from the Black Forest.

I gestured toward a group of attractive, ostensibly gay men, perhaps a few years younger than her and me, stepping off the Metro escalator. One was talking, and the others were laughing. Joyous camaraderie. The escalator had deposited joy onto Connecticut Avenue, and I worried that it would evaporate from life altogether. "How many of those do you think have it? How many like us walk around not knowing?"

"You must get tested," Evangeline said. "It's worse not knowing."

"What will you do if you test positive?"

Evangeline took a swig of her drink and licked the excess chardonnay off her lip. "Oh, Augie. It's such a hideous way to go. I don't know. Down cyanide like the Jewish aristocracy did when Hitler's troops marched into Paris?"

She gazed down at the men cavorting on the sidewalk. One snatched a blood-red scarf from another's neck, balled it up, and tossed it in the air. The tallest one, a towering blond with a slight resemblance to Pete, reached high over his head, tugged it off the gnarled branch of a tree it had landed on, and returned it to its owner. Lovingly, the scarf's owner grabbed his hero by the collar of his wool peacoat, pulled him close, and kissed him.

I smiled at the touching scene. With the height difference, the pair could have been stand-ins for Pete and me.

Pete and me. It sounded like an echo caught in a time machine. The relationship that never got off the ground. The relationship that never had a chance from day one. "Are you certain Pete is . . ." I paused when she shot me an irritable look. "It's just that I haven't seen him forever, and . . ."

Evangeline dug in her handbag and pulled out a smart silver cigarette case and an undistinguished Bic lighter. "Except for the . . . he's still recognizable."

I touched my face with my hand. "His beautiful face."

"He's taken to wearing makeup to hide the ravages." She lit and took a drag from her Virginia Slim. The smoke curled from her nostrils and interlocked with the excess escaping from her ruby lips. Rising higher, it formed a wreath above our heads before dissipating into the draft from the customer a few tables away waving his menu in our direction.

I didn't know what excuse I would manufacture, but I knew

it was imperative that I see Pete before he got sick, really sick. "I worry about getting it, but not really," I admitted. Evangeline opened her mouth, but I cut her off. "Don't say it again. I will get tested. I can't preach the gay gospel and not follow its teachings. I know that look in your eyes, Evangeline Klein. Trust me."

"It's not that, Augie. It's Pete. I didn't say anything before because I wanted to spare you."

"Spare me!" I began to boil. Seemingly out of thin air, anger leapt on my back like a rabid mountain lion, and I couldn't shake it.

"What's the matter, Augie?" Evangeline reached for my hand.

I jerked away and crossed my arms over my chest. "After what I've seen in my lifetime; the horror of growing up in Mama's house, playing by Mama's rules. You know how it was. I lived to tell the tales, and you think I can't handle knowing about Pete?"

"I'm sorry."

"Selfish is what you are. I could have been there. Did you once stop and think that I may have needed to see him? If he had died and you hadn't told me—" I tossed my napkin on the table and exhaled. "Why do you think I gown up, mask up, glove up, and wear that oh-so-flattering plastic cap to hold babies that haven't a chance in hell to live?" Uncontrollable when I'm ticked off, my tone climbed a few octaves. However, when I noticed several diners looking at me out of the corner of my eye, I lowered the volume. "Innocent babes. Crack babies that no nurse will go near, no mother will coddle in her arms. Why do you think I do that? Why? I've done what you can't bring yourself to do. I've been to the mountaintop but saw no promised land." I must have looked terrifying, because even the prissy queens at the next table were staring at me with the same expression as Evangeline, bug-eyed with their lips pursed. I gazed at them before turning my attention to Evangeline. I leaned forward, and Evangeline sat back in her seat. "Because I care," I whispered.

"Augie," she said and put her hand on mine. "I wasn't thinking. It's just that you've been through so much for so long, and I . . . I truly wanted to spare you." She sniffled, withdrew her hand, and crossed her legs. "Stuck-up Pollyanna. You're right, of course. You're always right."

I looked out the window at the empty space on the sidewalk where the young guys had been frolicking minutes ago. "I don't understand the world, Vange. Everything is topsy-turvy, and I can't seem to find my footing."

Evangeline snuffed out the cigarette that had been burning to ash. "There's Rupert. Don't forget how lucky you are. To find someone who genuinely loves you is phenomenal. I've never found it in all the beds I've jumped into or crawled out of. You've had two great loves, and you're not even thirty."

She sat her elbows on the table, bowed her head as if she was about to pray, and stared at the candle. Her face inches away, her staccato breath fanned the flame to a flicker.

"Pete, you mean? You think Pete is one of the great loves of my life?"

She shook her head.

"Honestly, Evangeline, I don't know what love is. I certainly don't want what my parents have. They love each other, but at what cost? Of course, Mama has that dreadful affair thing on the side and . . . screw it! I'm afraid to say the words, fearful to even consider moving in with Rupert."

"That's not very Pollyanna of you. Bold and brave is my August."

"I don't want to end up like Mom and Dad, nor April and David."

"Your sister is as determined as an Ace Airman over Nagasaki to bomb the hell out of her own life," Evangeline said.

"She's a mouse with David. He sucked the life out of her just like Mama did Dad." I pressed my fingers to my forehead and closed my eyes for a second. "I love the idea of love, but I have the hardest time letting go."

"Letting go of what? The hell and damnation that was your childhood?"

"When I'm with him, I'm ten feet tall, but alone and on my own I wonder how long I could sustain it."

Evangeline made a face but parked her anger and visibly adjusted her disposition. "You've never told Rupert you love him?"

I shook my head.

"Pete? You told Pete, didn't you?"

I shook my head.

Evangeline pushed the remains of her rare hamburger away and popped a sweet potato fry in her mouth. "But you're Pollyanna Gay. You put a positive spin on the most hideous things, find that silver lining no matter how hard you have to dig. You told me in ninth grade that your mother was good training for life. No matter what curveball life tossed at your head, you've always handled it."

"Love is a curveball?"

"Honey, it's a minefield no sane person would enter, but oh well, what the hell, no one can resist tip-toing through the tulips."

"I used to be so good at it. I've tried to, but I feel over-whelmed."

"I know what lurks behind that radiant smile. You may fool most but never me. I know where the skeletons are buried. I know what gave you nightmares at ten and had you running for shelter at my house at twelve. No one knows you like I do and never will. Not Farley. Not Pete. Not even the ideal man, Rupert."

"So much being thrown at us at once, and nothing's turning out as planned, as wished for. . . . Nothing's turning out like I prayed for." I sipped my white wine and cleared my throat. "Remember when I volunteered to decorate the cathedral?"

"Yeah. Big deal. Now you're Catholic like Jackie O."

"I worked my butt off from seven a.m. on Christmas Eve morning until midnight Mass began. The other volunteers, this flock of pretty club boys more suited for dancing platforms at Badlands Disco than roping garland in the alley behind the cathedral, were too busy to perform the menial task of decorating the nave when they sought sanctuary in the backroom."

"Volunteers?"

"Friends of that hunky, weight-lifter priest from another parish. The one we saw at happy hour."

Evangeline licked her lips. "I'd go ecclesiastical for him."

"Evidently, he's dating one of the club boys."

"Go, Sister Mary-Father-Priest-Babe!"

"I asked him straight out if he believed in his vow of celiba-cy."

"Polly Purebred lights a candle under the arse of a Catholic farce."

"Know how he explained his dalliance? He had the balls to suggest that a sexual relationship was fine as long as he didn't get involved in a committed relationship."

A puzzled look on her face, Evangeline flicked her Bic to light another cigarette. "God works in mysterious ways." She dropped the Bic into her Birkin bag. "As long as he's on his knees when he shouts the Lord's name, all is well in the papist's kingdom."

"The world is changing, and I'm—"

"Your morals mean jack-shit in this day and age, Polly, my dear."

My gut twanged with tension. "In Rupert's arms, I'm content."

"You're in love."

CHAPTER 19

TONIGHT

"I'll stay," I said to Rupert. "There's little left to do. Besides, there's not enough time to make it home before I meet Evangeline."

"If you lived with me, you'd be only a few blocks away from the restaurant." Rupert glanced out his office door to see if anyone was lingering at his secretary's desk before kissing me. He closed his Louis Vuitton briefcase. "Bought you a toothbrush at the People's Drug today. Hint. Hint."

"I've always admired your subtlety, Mr. Siegel," I joked.

• • •

After adding the finishing touches to the drawings for the spring fashion windows, I glanced at the wall clock in my office. *Good.* There was enough time for me to pick up Aunt Jessica's face cream from Joyce at the Estee Lauder counter. I tossed my personals in my shoulder bag, grabbed my coat hanging on the back of my chair, and headed for the employee elevator.

My ear pressed against the elevator door, I could hear the car rising and falling, its door opening and closing, but it never ascended to the ninth floor. *Damn.* I checked my watch. *Three-twelve!* That couldn't have been right; it was supposed to be the end of the day. I shook it. *Dead. Hell, and damnation!* Impatient, I pounded down the backstairs to the ground floor.

"Sam! Sam!" I called as I approached the watch repair counter. "Took a licking and simply stopped ticking," I joked, handing him the Gucci watch Aunt Jessica had bought me for high school graduation eons ago.

Sam popped the back off. "Need to fetch a battery from the storeroom. I'll have it for you in about twenty minutes." I watched him walk across the floor toward the stockroom. Although Sam and I had never discussed it, Rupert had told me about Sam's lover passing away before Thanksgiving. They'd been together over twenty years. He'd left his wife and children in 1964 to be with the man he couldn't live without. *Brave.* His family disowned him. He lost his job with the Defense Department. It was, I supposed, better than living a lie. I couldn't image coming of age in the forties and fifties as he had.

I vaguely remembered Mama and Aunt Jessica discussing someone in the Johnson White House, a cabinet member perhaps, being arrested for soliciting a man in a public restroom. Even Dad had raised his eyebrow over that incident. He talked about two soldiers in the army he'd known were gay. "Everyone liked them, so we turned a blind eye. Good thing the colonel never caught them. They'd have been court-martialed." Although I realized that to be court-martialed in the US Army was far different from facing a firing squad in the foreign military, it was a terrible way to punish someone putting their life on the line for this country.

"Mr. Applegate," Joyce said when I plopped down on a stool at the Estee Lauder counter. "How's your aunt? I sure do miss seeing her beautiful face. Such a kind lady. Think she'll change her mind and return to DC?"

"Fingers crossed," I said, knowing damn well Aunt Jessica would never be well enough to return to the city she loved. During the last month's visit to Rockridge Hospital, I'd wondered if she'd make it through the week.

Cha . . . ding! The cash register door popped open. "Here, love," she said and handed me my receipt. "Give me a second." I kept glancing at the large, four-sided clock suspended over the center aisle. Even as a child, it reminded me of the monster from the 1957 horror movie, *The Cyclops*, which Aunt Tootie and I watched on *The Late-Late Show* when I was a boy.

6:35. Good. I had just enough time to grab my watch and hit the Metro. "Thanks," I said to Joyce, stuffing the neatly wrapped box in my bag.

"Give your aunt my best," she said. "Tell her I hope to see her soon."

"Will do!" I suppose I should have told her about Aunt Jessica's condition. Aunt Jessica had given me permission to do so, but I simply couldn't. I suppose I didn't want my memory of her shopping in her favorite store to be tainted. I was being selfish. I should have turned around and done the right thing. Heaven knows, she could've used Joyce's prayers.

I glanced back at the clock as I exited the store and checked my watch's time to it. *6:45. Perfect.* I walked around the building to the Metro entrance on the east side of the store. Passing our extravagant holiday windows, sparkling with glitter-encrusted icicles and faux frosted gardens rising from snowdrifts taller than myself, pride swelled my chest to the point of bursting. Letters from the public had been pouring in ever since I'd joined the visual team. Rupert couldn't have been more pleased, and I was thrilled by the great reviews from customers, buyers, and store personnel.

I paused at the corner window, my favorite of the twenty that wrapped around the block. The blue-black background, studded with twinkling stars, stood in sharp contrast to the white snowscape. Two massive, glass-eyed white horses, so realistic one might swear they neighed, were harnessed to a glamorous velvet-upholstered sleigh teeming with Rootstein mannequins. I'd dressed them in a frothy concoction of elegant ivory gowns, one topped with an elaborate faux silver fox fur cape and the other sporting a satin evening coat, and both stood tall with their mile-high satin pumps planted firmly in the snow. For we who created it and those who enjoyed it, it was art for art's sake, a fashion inspiration sensation, but for the business office, its purpose was for profit, a most pleasurable return on their investment.

The job had fallen into my lap and was surprisingly a perfect fit. I missed performing but loved being in a profession that allowed me to use my multiple talents, not simply a gopher for the talented professionals at Arena Stage. It had taken a few months for my seasoned coworkers to adjust to a novice manager less versed in the retail business they excelled at, but my determination and willingness to listen and learn from them soon won their respect.

What I brought was a fresh eye from a theatre perspective. Where so many would focus on a single area of a department or window, I saw the entire puzzle and how each vignette played off the others. Designing for the stage had trained me to look at the big picture, a moving, changing picture that incorporated the entirety of a story. Retail visual told a story through color, position, and form to educate its audience on the latest trends or send a message about what would best suit them as individuals.

After a fretful tug and pull between the staff and me, we adjusted to smooth sailing through countless promotions that challenged our imaginations and buoyed our work standards. We'd been thrown together in a frenzy of expectation, and it was up to me to make sure we swam and never sank. I was determined we'd not only succeed, but surprise the powers that be. Instead of dictating and threatening my staff, as I'd witnessed other managers doing, I harvested suggestions and ideas from them. I knew that if they had skin in the game, they'd fight tooth and nail to win.

So, I'd rolled up my sleeves and got down in the trenches with my soldiers. My small but mighty army marched into glory from that first promotion assigned to me. Stradling boundaries of race, language, age, social inequalities, talent, and degrees of experience, we rose to victory. The everchanging seasons rolled by, and our creations took root in the windows and in-store shops. The first several years had flown by. Being responsible for my staff, the company's reputation, and myself made me a man.

·•·

After dinner, Evangeline and I headed to Friends Piano Bar to belt out showtunes. The moment Evangeline asked the piano player if she could accompany me, I relaxed before the sweater-clad crowd gathered around the baby grand.

Standing in front of the window by an extravagantly gawdy, glitter-intensive tree backlit by the streetlamp planted in the sidewalk outside, I gripped the rim of the piano's case and stood tall. The background noise of the cash register dinging open, the rumbling mumbling of conversation, and the ice cubes clinking against the sides of glasses faded blissfully away with the first cords of the intro. It was just Evangeline, me, and the music.

The first note I sang of *My Own Morning* was soft and hesitant, but by the second line, I'd found my sea legs and sailed through the number with ease. When I finished, the voluminous applause that rattled the windows in their loose casings was a welcome sound. Its absence in my life had left a hole as big as the Grand Canyon.

Evangeline winked after the second selection, and I knew it was time for Judy Garland's *Have Yourself a Merry Little Christmas.*

"Wow, bitch." Tony, the hunky chef from Wallis & Fitch Haden's restaurant, slapped me on the back as we made our way to the bar afterward. "Not just a pretty face."

The crowd at Friends weren't the cool crowd of twenty-somethings from my generation, nor the hipster club kids bobbing around Badlands dance floor like Fagan's boys on steroids. The mostly middle-aged guys populating Friends Bar were the scarred, motley crew that had survived Cold War ethics and the Greatest Generation's pride and prejudice that confined them to second-class-citizen status. The audience, capable of appreciating my gift, had been mellowed by compromise and defeat. I was bowled over by their thunderous applause and homesick for the spotlight, not for vanity's sake, but to satisfy the performer within. I loved my job, but to share a God-given gift was gift enough for me.

A familiar voice cut through the buzz in the room. "The unsinkable Molly Brown."

"Farley Fairfield," I said when he spun around on his stool at the bar. "What are you doing in DC?"

He went to kiss my lips, but I turned, and he planted a slobbery smooch on my cheek. He was three sheets to the wind.

"Visiting Pete for the holidays."

My smile was ingenuine, and even in his intoxicated state, he knew it.

"There!" Farley pointed out the window to the bar across the street. "One more drink, a wee nightcap before slathering the cold cream on and rolling our hair."

I glanced at Evangeline, and she rolled her eyes. "One more for the road," I said. We grabbed our coats, then bopped down the front steps of Friends to the busy street. "You know Mr. P's is a biker bar."

"I've ridden a bike or two in my day." Farley stepped off the sidewalk without looking.

A car screeched to an abrupt stop beside us. A burly, bearded man in a tattered black tank top stuck his head out the window and yelled, "Fucking fag!"

I grabbed Farley by the collar of his leather bomber jacket and hoisted him back onto the sidewalk as the driver revved the engine of his decade-old gold Duster.

"Saved by my twin." Farley batted his thick black lashes and sang, "'Just two little girls from Little Rock, born on the wrong side of the tracks . . .'"

Evangeline took his arm and led him across the street. "One wee whisky, and it's off to bed with you, Wendy Darling."

Mr. P's Bar catered to a rowdy crowd of hunters hungry for action. In sharp contrast to the clubs that showtune afficionados such as myself frequented, the joint was shrouded in mystery. It pulsed with sex. My back tightened and my neck tensed as we crossed the threshold. I felt every censorious gaze investigating my "work drag," as Farley referred to it.

The pungent smells of stale beer, petiole oil, pot, and semen penetrated every inch of the beaten plank floor and rusticated paneled walls, and I crinkled my nose at first sniff. Catering to rough trade, it was the playpen for quick trick pickups or hot grinds in the backroom. So was the reputation of Mr. P's.

Haphazardly mounted on the wall behind the bar, a sparkling silver Christmas wreath fought for attention among the glowing neon signs advertising various brands of beer. Gruff-voiced, mustached, and bearded patrons slumped against the bar, refugees eager to cross into the promised land. Even through his intoxicated haze, Farley managed to size up the crowd. Lowering his voice a few octaves, he snatched my tweed newsboy cap off and stuffed it into his jacket pocket with a huff of, "Honestly, Mary."

I snatched it out of his pocket and stuffed it into the hip pocket of my gray flannel trousers. When I removed my jacket, the shocking purity of my white button-down oxford glowed amid the dirty, destressed denim in the ocean of disapproving eyes. "I hear there's a roof deck."

Evangeline held the gaze of a scruffy man who was boring holes through her. The sleeves of his shirt had been ripped off like the Incredible Hulk's, exposing his huge biceps, billboards for an extensive tattooed story featuring the cartoon characters, Rocky, Bullwinkle, and Natasha.

"Love your collection," Farley yelled in the man's ear as he tugged on the tuft of salt and pepper hair at the nape of his neck. The man slid his arm around Farley's tiny waist, hugged him close, and smooched him for what seemed like hours. Then he took Farley's hand, and they pounded up the stairs of what once was an elegant row house off Dupont Circle in his thick-soled Doc Martin boots.

The video room was a sauna. Sweaty-faced patrons glistened in the fractured light flickering from the silver screen at the far end of the room. Around fifteen feet from where I stood was a wall of French doors that opened onto a back porch, festively draped in tiny, twinkling Christmas lights. It looked like a wholesome alternative to the room, crammed as it was with hot bodies bobbing back and forth. Although it was below freezing outside, I could see a gaggle of men hanging around an outdoor bar. Jam-packed, the video room was impossible to cross without brushing against a bulge or a buttock. However, no one complained. As a matter of fact, it seemed they welcomed the intrusion.

"Augie," Evangeline said, "I think I just had threesomes with at least ten couples."

"Damn!" I said as we pushed through the jungle of wild-eyed men mesmerized by the flickering porno on the screen, "I dropped my hat." I started to turn around, but Evangeline grabbed my hand and forged ahead.

"It's a goner!" she said. "That floor is filthier than the mighty Ganges!"

Escaping through alien territory, a treacherous minefield of front-line action, we barged through the doors and bounded onto the wooden patio area. The gang of leather-clad biker-bears I'd spotted were gathered at the corner of the bar, throwing back shots and slugging beer. They paused for a second to size us up before returning to the business at hand. The tallest and broadest of the lot pulled a compact mirror from his jacket pocket and sat it on the bar. Gingerly, he cut some coke into long lines on the glassy surface and snorted a long stretch of powder before handing the mirror to the bear beside him. Their hands were in constant motion, hands on hands, hands on watches and chains, hands on hairy chests, and hands on zippers and denim encasing privates in an erotic frenzy to pander and please.

Evangeline and I crossed the complaining floorboards of the

deck and took refuge on a bench beneath a faux pine branch infested with Christmas lights.

"Christ! It's cold," she said and wrapped her arms around me.

"We have two choices," I said. "Sweatbox in there or icebox out here."

She shivered in her camel cashmere wrap coat. "I'm giving Farley ten minutes, and then I'm hailing a cab."

The intimate choreography of the bear dance was a curiosity to me. How far would they take their party under the stars? I was both repulsed and excited by their sexual bravado. I envied their boldness but wondered if their dance was true self-expression or a middle finger to middle-class morality.

"You like?" Evangeline whispered in my ear.

"Intrigued," I said.

A few minutes later, interlocked with each other like a Calder mobile, the biker-bears migrated into the video room.

Evangeline flipped the fur collar of her coat up and walked to the end of the deck, and I followed. "Gorgeous view of the Circle from here."

"I never get tired of Washington. It's beautiful from every angle." I stuffed my gloved hands in my pockets.

"Well," Evangeline said, rolling her eyes, "perhaps not Anacostia."

The clock on the turreted Rigg's Bank overlooking Dupont Circle caught my eye. 12:20. It had been a long day. It was late, and I was tired. I heard a commotion coming from the direction of P Street. I scoured the street below but couldn't see who was shouting or understand what they were saying over the bang and clank of trash cans.

"Pollyanna Gay!" a familiar voice called out from behind the dark cluster of stacked chairs by the service door.

"Pete!" Evangeline made a beeline for him, the sturdy heels of her knee-high boots thumping across the beaten planks. They embraced one another, rocking back and forth for a several moments before Pete turned his attention to me.

"Princess Pollyanna," Pete said, slurring his pronouncement. "My gay . . . princess . . . Pollyanna. My homosexual Augie Applegate. My—"

"Pete," I barked abruptly, cutting him off. I barely recognized him. Pete had traded his preppy Gucci loafers for rugged, thick-soled biker boots and his usual cashmere sweater for a skin-tight tee. His once-silky-blond hair, which in my memory fell seductively over one eye, he'd buzzed to the quick. Thin as a reed, he stood stoop-shouldered and bow-bellied before me. Where was the beautiful man I'd once known? Granted, we had all changed since college, and I hadn't laid eyes on him in years, but this gaunt, glum Don Quixote carnal vigilante shocked and appalled me. I was staring truth in the face and fighting to accept it.

He stumbled toward me, and Evangeline grabbed hold of his arm to steady him. His Bud Light slipped from his grip and hit the deck. Beer fizzed and spit as the bottle rolled under the abandoned portable bar. "I wish—I wish," he stammered.

"Wishes are free," I said. "It's the prayers that cost you." Not that he'd remember any of this in the morning when he woke up with a head tighter than a tick on the hide of a grizzly bear, but I regretted barking at him. Perplexed by my own actions, I wanted to plow through the vixens of vice in the video room, thump down all three flights to the street, run as fast as my legs could pump, and book it to the safety of home. I wanted nothing more than to jump into my own bed and pull Grandma Flora's quilt over my head.

"Let me get you a cab," Evangeline said. She guided Pete to an Adirondack chair, its wood rough and splintered by DC's abrupt weather changes.

Pete shrugged her off, clutched the arms of the chair, and leaned toward me. "A good girl like you in a place like this? Are you a mirage, Augie Applegate?" He pushed his scrawny, blue-veined hand into his leather jacket and pulled out a pack of Camel cigarettes. "Vange! Light me!"

Dutifully, Evangeline flicked her Bic, and Pete puffed the cigarette to a glowing red ember. The second suck on the Camel sent him into a coughing fit. The popping purple veins in his neck pulsed with urgency. Evangeline patted him on the back until the coughing subsided to a raspy wheezing noise. Easing him against the back of the chair, she lovingly caressed his face with her gloved hand. Divine loyalty. Evangeline expressed divine loyalty. Often, she was as much or more of a Pollyanna than me.

Pete held out his hand to me. Hesitant as a cat walking a high

TONIGHT

ledge above a dark alley, I slowly took his hand. Even through my gloves, his icy grip penetrated my resolve and weakened my reserve. "Oh, Pete," I said, wrapping my arms around him. "I've missed you."

"Augie. Oh Augie," he whispered, his liquor-soaked voice gurglingly wet.

I pressed my cheek against his, and he closed his eyes. Where was he drifting off to? Back to Buck's County Theatre Camp? Back to 315 Benevolent Street? Back to our first march on Washington? Back to the beauty of our youth?

His hand suddenly on my face, he guided my lips to his and kissed me. From the corner of my eye, I watched Evangeline open the door to the video room. Swallowed whole by the shape-shifting amoeba inside, she disappeared behind the sweaty glass panes.

I zipped Pete's jacket up and over the prominent Adam's apple of his skinny neck. Intoxicated, drugged, or displaying early signs of dementia, he stared at me as if he'd forgotten who I was. I sat on the arm of the chair, and he fell against me, pressing his face into my breast pocket.

"I volunteer at Whitman-Walker," I said and hugged him close. "You can always request me if—"

"I want," he bleated. "I want."

"You know what the real kicker is? I need them more than they need me. I need to be needed or otherwise I feel useless." I buttoned the collar of my coat against a stiff, frigid blast of wind sweeping across the deck. "We need to get you home."

Pete pushed himself up on his unsteady legs and shuffled to the railing. "Come with me. Come home with me, Augie. Stay with me. One night. Just one night."

I tugged the tremendously long scarf Tootie had crocheted for me out of my pocket and tied it around his neck. "Merry Christmas."

He gazed at me, a puzzled look on his boney face. "We'll make love in the morning . . . breakfast in bed." He pointed to the Dupont Circle fountain in the distance. "They shut the water off come winter. I always wonder why."

"Perhaps it cracks the iron or stone."

"Peter Pakington Pace!" Farley shrieked from the open French door to the video room. "As I live and breathe!" He staggered toward us, caught the toe of his cowboy boot in the uneven space between two planks, and plummeted against the bar. "Mother fucker!" he yelped, rubbing his knee. "Who built this Lincoln Log tinderbox? The Smurfs?"

Pete laughed. I nearly burst into tears seeing his face light up. For an instant, age and the ravages of the plague took a holiday. For one, brief, shining moment, Pete was beautiful.

Recovering his dignity, Farley wiggled his way between us. "I'm going two-stepping. How about it, cowboy?" He winked at Pete, then nudged my shoulder and whispered, "I'll take it from here, Princess."

My God! Is he blind? Pete could barely stand let alone do-si-do across a cowboy bar dance floor. "Come on girly-girls," I said, and taking Pete's elbow, I guided him toward the sweat-streaked French door. "And we're off like a dirty shirt!"

Downstairs, I spotted Evangeline huddled in a corner, deep in conversation with a drag queen sporting a rainbow striped mohawk. "Thank God you're still here."

Evangeline gently touched the drag queen's hand, and the queen raised her paws, spiked with six-inch nail extensions, and clawed at the air near my face. "Who, her?"

"Don't get your implants in a twist, Oxy," Evangeline joked.

I held Oxy's gaze. "Okay, sugar!" she sang. "You win. Spotlight's all yours."

"Augie's my best girlfriend." Evangeline, sitting crossed legged on a stool, leaned into me, her face against mine. "Trouble in paradise?"

The drag queen sneered and raised her sequin-studded eyebrow. "Man trouble, no doubt?" She rolled her triple-lash-framed eyes. "Don't worry, sugar. There's someone for everyone—except when there isn't." She giggled.

"Where's the dynamic duo?" Evangeline drained the last of her drink and slammed the glass on the bar.

"Farley's helping Pete in the can."

"He's an expert at that," she said snidely.

"Vange," I said and grimaced.

"Time to collect Bill Sykes and the Artful Dodger before they end up in the gutter with Fagan."

"Later, girlfriend," Oxy said and double air-kissed Evangeline.

"Let me know how it goes." She dug deep into her faux cleavage and handed me a pink-glittered card. "Here, honey." She tweaked my cheek until it throbbed. "Stop by the Rogue some night, doll-face. You'd make a damn pretty woman."

"Thanks." I squinted to read the card as she teetered toward the stairs, the crack-ice bugle beads on her tulip skirt slapping her meaty thighs. *Miss Oxy Condone, Midwife.*

"She is," Evangeline said, "truly a midwife."

Noticing Pete and Farley heading to the exit, I grabbed Evangeline by the arm and rushed her to the door. Farley was wavering on his pins, and Pete was idling like Aunt Tootie's trashed sixty-seven Chevy Impala.

Thank God! A yellow cab was conveniently parked outside the front door. Cabbies loved P Street at this hour, when the snockered queens stumbled into their back seats with cash in hand. "California Street and Connecticut Avenue," I instructed the cabbie and handed him a wad of bills. "Don't leave until they're safely inside."

Farley was wrapped around Pete so tightly they looked like an innovative, interlocking kinetic sculpture. "Good night, Sister Sledge!"

Evangeline took my arm, and we started up P Street toward Dupont Circle as the cab rolled past us. "I'm going to have a baby," she said nonchalantly.

"What?!" I stopped dead on the icy sidewalk, already shaken by the sight Pete in a state much worse than I had imagined. "Not now, Evangeline. I'm too rattled for a joke."

"I'm not joshing you."

"You're not marrying Gerald, are you?"

"Whatever for?" she said, crinkling her nose. "He's not the papa. Besides, even if he were, I wouldn't marry the fairy."

"Who's the father?" I asked, praying it wasn't one of the many whose names she'd misplaced or forgotten altogether.

"You, silly."

"Me?" *What the hell!* She'd tossed me into Dante's *Inferno*. I was spiraling through a Salvador Dali nightmare, holding tightly to the casing of a melting clock face dripping on the side of a square. Down I plunged until I landed on the back of a yak wandering the desert for entrance to Satan's palace. I bit my lip to wake myself up, but the cold wind brushing my five o'clock shadow reminded me that I was awake, wide awake, and wishing I weren't.

"Wipe that look of horror off your pretty face. I'm not going to tie you to your four-poster and have my way with you." She put her hands on her hips and smirked. "There's this wonderful little thing called a fertility clinic. A wank of the wand in a petri dish, a turkey baster and my uterus, and we're off . . . I mean, I'm off to the races."

"Don't you want to marry first?"

"No, Augie. I do not. I've had it with men . . . and women. I'm not into bestiality, but I am into being a mother. I'm twenty-seven years old. The clock is ticking, and I'm . . . I want a baby, Augie." She raised her hand in front of herself. "I don't need a man to help me raise the child, but I do need your sperm to get the ball rolling. Pun intended."

My gut churned. As bitter as the bite of the chill in the air was, a trickle of sweat tickled my backside, and I wanted to peel the layers of cashmere and tweed off my overheated body and race up 16th Street to the Envoy. *Home.* The evening had soured the moment we'd entered Mr. P's. Why hadn't I hopped in a cab when we left Friends? *Oh no! Dunce!* Faithfully, I'd followed Farley into the mouth of the volcano.

And now, Evangeline had dropped a baby bomb in my lap. *Damn her! Damn her assumption.* I wasn't prepared for fatherhood. Although I fantasized about being a dad someday, that day was not at hand, and the expectation she fostered far exceeded my duty to a friend. "Why me? Of all people, out of all those gorgeous men you've had affairs with . . ."

"I've only ever truly loved one man, and that man is you, Augie." Saturated in serenity, she glided up the sidewalk. I trembled before her audacious request.

"Only you will do, Augie," she called over her shoulder.

My heart melted before her joy, and her confession, coddled in devotion, sparked a glow inside me that I'd feared had dimmed long ago.

However, the fireworks blazed but briefly before their magic dissipated when the word "father" fizzled in my head. *Father a baby. Father a baby?* It was a vast idea too grand to comprehend at that moment.

"Evangeline!" I yelled, and she sashayed over to where I stood on the sidewalk. "Vange—" I started, then paused in mid-thought when my oxford shifted on the pavement. I felt a sticky slickness on the smooth leather soles of my shoes.

Perplexed, I stared at the pool of red liquid we were standing in. Evangeline cupped her mouth with her hand. "Oh my..."

I followed her eyes down the alleyway beside Second Story Bookstore. Reddish-brown blood decorated the cement walkway, brick façade, and toppled trash cans; a discarded plaid jacket and mismatched shoes were strung along the path to the bookstore's back door. No one else seemed to have noticed, and there were no emergency vehicles in sight. At one a.m. on a Friday night, it was strange that not one person on the well-trafficked thoroughfare had noticed the pool of blood on the sidewalk, heard any cries for help, nor witnessed any crime. *How could this be? Not one single soul has called 911?* It was impossible to wrap my Pollyanna brain around it.

Swimming against the tide, a dazed Evangeline walked back-ward into the stream of people around us making their way to last call. After crashing into a couple locked in a kiss, she stumbled into her friend Oxy. "Police!" she yelled and barreled across the street to the public phone booth.

Mesmerized by the morbid remnants of the crime, I stepped into the alleyway. Shoeless, argyle-socked feet led to splayed legs that hung over the side of a steel trashcan. Bloody blond tresses, the cracked lenses of tortoiseshell glasses dangling from his nose, his lifeless blue eyes, reminiscent of the lifeless marble ones jammed into the sockets of a merry-go-round horse—a once beautiful young man lay dead in the dumpster, his alabaster skin as smooth as Michelangelo's *Pieta*.

I felt a firm grip on my arm. "Sweetie," Oxy said in a fatherly tone. She held me tightly against her foam breast for a few mo-ments, the scent of her pungent perfume masking the rusty smell of blood emanating from the alleyway, the taste of sin succulent on my tongue.

By now, a buzzing crowd of rubberneckers had noticed and surrounded the pool of blood.

Cries of "Oh my God!" "Jesus Mary!" "What the fuck!" echoed down the strip. Screams and gasps rippled through the lake of onlookers quaking in their shoes as they realized that the dismembered victim scattered in that alley could have been any one of them. One of us. *It could have been me.*

"Back! Stand back!" a gruff, commanding voice bellowed. A bearded Moses of a policeman parted the sea of seal-eyed citizens, making way for his comrades and ambulance technicians to secure the area.

Stunned and unsure of what bodily remnants might be lifted into the light, lingering tribes of men milled about on the perimeter of the fenced off area. Grasping my sleeve, Evangeline dragged me back into the crest of the tide. Beside us, about a dozen dashing, lovely boys, maybe twenty or twenty-one, stood with their hands stuffed deep into their pockets. They were transfixed on the aftermath of murder, horrified by the sight, their mouths gaping open, their visible breath hovering in the air before them.

The seemingly endless hours of the workday, Farley's surprise appearance at Friends Bar, the searing sight of Pete's frail façade, Evangeline's entangled expectation of me, and the bombardment of horrific images now unfolding on our gay playground—I was shaken to my core. Breathless and bewildered, I wrestled with the panic pricking my raw nerves.

A speck of light above the city caught my eye; no one else seemed to notice, not even Evangeline. High above the swaying sycamores and the shifting wave of spruce trees dancing in the moonlight hung the North Star. Sparkling like a Harry Winston diamond in the night sky, its intoxicating beauty rescued me from the scene's insistent horror. The muffled voices crying for mercy, the biting chill nibbling the tips of my ungloved fingers, and the taste of death in the air were bearable in the light from above.

I can bear this. I must bear this. I took Evangeline's hand as we watched Oxy being questioned by an officer. Following my instinct, I offered my free hand to the stranger beside me. Hesitant at first, when he noticed my sincere expression, he clasped my hand firmly. One hand clutching the hand of a person clutching the hand of another spread down the lines of the onlookers. We queer folk gathered. Roped together by our fear and the rage burning beneath the surfaces of our stoic faces, we supported one another. There was strength in numbers, and we stood bold before the slain brother we would never know. That night was not like any night before, and I fretted over future nights that would be stained with the blood of the slain.

Not a word was spoken, not a sigh was heard, not a movement was felt from the crowd as we watched the bagged body of our lifeless tribe member lifted into the harsh, florescent-lit cabin of the ambulance. Stricken by the intense despair emanating from our disillusioned comrades, Evangeline and I, zombies blinded by reality, finally wandered away from the pack to the welcoming glow of Kramerbooks.

No matter how many times I scrubbed the bottom of my shoes with soap and water in Kramerbooks & Afterwords Café's restroom, I knew the soles would be permanently stained pink.

"What did Oxy say?" I asked Evangeline when I returned to the table, where she was sipping her steaming espresso.

"Oh Augie, it turned out there were three of them. She recognized one of them. All three were in their early twenties. All three had their throats slit from ear to ear."

I touched my hand to my throat. "Oh, Jesus Christ."

We looked at each other. Our chins quivered. Our teeth chattered. Tears trickled down our cheeks like rainwater from an overfull cistern.

• • •

The clock in the doorman's booth of my building read 3:25. Step by step, I trudged up the grand marble staircase to my tiny apartment on the second floor. As I struggled to unlock the door, I heard the echo of the phone ringing insistently from inside.

"Yes!" I said when I picked up, attempting to catch my breath.

There was a long pause on the other end. "Mr. March," Mama said, her voice coarse and flat, "your Aunt Jessica passed away this evening."

CHAPTER 20

SOMEWHERE

The snow squall slapped Aunt Tootie's bare legs as she stood, leaning against a noble Doric column rising from the front steps of John Quill's Funeral Home. Her arms were jammed into the tight sleeves of a toggle-buttoned coat she'd outgrown a decade before.

I wished Aunt Tootie hadn't seen me pull into the drive. I needed to collect myself before walking into Mama's nightmare. She waved, and I smiled. I desperately wanted to back out of the drive and barrel down Main Street toward 81-North and back to DC. After all that had happened the night before, I was ill prepared to face my family and do what they demanded of me.

One by one, they'd seek me out to share their misery and acknowledge their sins. I hadn't realized until I'd moved away what a central character I was in their lives. Dad was the bishop of our bawdy household and the nucleus of the family, but I was its friar, the mendicant sent to cure the crippled and calm the calamity coursing through their conscience. A humongous weight had been lifted from my shoulders when I'd moved to DC. With hundreds of miles between us, I was spared their countless confessions.

Running on less than two hours' sleep, I was at my wits' end. It was imperative that I somehow muster the strength to play the part of the dutiful son. Rest had eluded me; every time I closed my eyes, the sight of the alleyway popped into my head, and I was jolted back to that time and place, the smell, feel, and taste of which I could never erase. Now, it was my duty to march through the front doors of the funeral home and take charge as Grandma Flora would have if she were still among the living.

The funeral home at John Quill's manor house, once the center of a prosperous planation fueled by slave labor, was cheerfully adorned with boughs of holly and festive pine wreaths in every window. It was a Twelve Oaks knockoff. As a boy, I'd dreamed of living there, but now the sight of it and all it represented angered me. Now that I'd worked side by side with African Americans and understood their culture better, I could no longer delude myself with romantic fantasies about our honorable Southern past.

After our first gay march on Washington, something had broken inside me. The Southern pride we celebrated with battle reenactments and garden tours of elegant mansions recalled a gracious way of life that some still aspired to, but I'd begun to question the beauty of the past.

"Can't even light my ciggie butt in this damn wind," Aunt Tootie said and hugged me. Her tattered cotton dress reeked of fried cabbage, Kent cigarettes, and chocolate from the candy counter at Woolworth's. It was comforting to know that some things never changed. "Your mama's fit to be tied."

"What now?"

"You'll see." Tootie tossed the crumpled pack of Kents into her handbag. Its clasp was broken. "Thank God you're here, Mr. March. We've been on pins and needles. She has old man Quill so confused he doesn't know his ass from a hole in the ground."

"Thought you gave up cussing when you found Jesus?"

"I asked forgiveness in advance." Aunt Tootie swung the door open. "Welcome to hell in a handbasket."

Dad was reading the *Daily* when I walked into the reception parlor. "Augie," he said. "How was traffic?"

"Not bad after Fairfax." I removed my coat and slung it over the back of a gilded Victorian settee. "Where's Mama?"

Tootie pointed at a door across the hall. "Flying high and sinking low." I understood completely. "Just like the old days."

My heart plummeted as I joined Dad on the white sofa, whose carved wood frame boasted a plethora of cheerful cherubs frolicking with lions. Every drape and upholstered piece of furniture in the entrance hall, the front parlor, the back parlor, and probably the rest of the downstairs was snow-white faux silk acetate or poly-velvet with a sheen that spelled "cheap." Plastic runners ran down the middle of every room and crisscrossed at the intersections of the hallways. The faint sound of a string quartet's gloomy rendition of Beethoven's *La Melancholia Adagio* seeped from the speakers flanking the fireplace, which was stuffed with an explosive pale-pink-and-lavender silk flower arrangement. The overpowering smell of lilies permeated everything. Triple-hung waterfalls of lace, sheer, and damask drapes cascaded over every twelve-foot window in the room, blocking any natural view and filtering whatever sunlight managed to creep under the low roof of the wrap-around porch. My mind churned with condemnation.

Dad glanced at the viewing room door across the hallway separating Mama from the rest of the world. "Go to her, Mr. March. You're the only one she listens to."

"Mama doesn't care to hear what I have to say."

"She respects you, Augie." Dad patted my shoulder. Tired and haggard from decades of suffering Mama's verbal and physical abuse, he looked way older than his fifty-seven years.

"She and April have been at each other's throats since Jess took a turn for the worse last week," Aunt Tootie said.

"Jesus Christ," I muttered. "Why me?"

"Augie," Dad said, "since your grandmother passed, you're the only one she trusts."

I rapped lightly on the door to warn Mama of my arrival and give her time to collect herself. Seeing her in tears would have been the ultimate sin. Outrageous displays of anger she'd allow, but never tears. Tears were a sign of weakness, and heaven forbid she be perceived as weak.

I poked my head in. "Mama?"

She sat with her back to me, wiping her face with the back of her hand. The mahogany casket was open and Aunt Jessica's face, painted like a sunburned Miami tourist, came into view as I approached.

"Can you believe this, Mr. March? Look at her! She looks like a two-bit New Orleans hussy." Mama rapped her knuckles on the side of the coffin. "Look at her. Look at her. Mr. March, look at her!" She grabbed hold of my shirt cuff and shoved my hand into the coffin. It slid across the ivory satin lining, which was cold and hard.

I jerked my hand away, and Mama's finger hit the metal seal

framing the lid. She stood suddenly, knocking her petite gold bamboo chair on its side. "Fix her!" she commanded.

"Fix her? Are you insane?" I said it so casually that it felt natural. She glared at me. Nobody talked to Mama like that. Never!

She clutched the gold cross hanging from a chain around her neck and walked around the casket, scanning every inch for that one flaw she was certain was there. "Just like your father's family. 'Lock her away! She's insane! Lock her away!' Only he didn't, and they couldn't, and you won't." She untied the black silk headscarf knotted under her chin and stuffed it into the pocket of the Persian lamb coat Aunt Jessica had bought her before she left DC. "I can't bear it, Augie. I honestly can't."

"Let's just make it through the night. We're both tired, and I just drove three hours to get here."

"Always about you, Mr. March!" She poked Aunt Jessica's cheeks and chest with her finger. "This wig is atrocious. They dressed her in this Goddamn shroud Tootie picked out. Pale pink. She detested pale pink. Cerise, I told the fool! Dress her in the cerise boucle suit! How Goddamn hard is that, I ask you? Simpletons!" She slumped onto an upholstered bench, its French legs a bit wobbly from wear and tear. "Style the wig, Augie. Make them change the dress. Do it. Do it now!"

"Aunt Jessica never wanted all this," I reminded her. "She wanted to be cremated. She left instructions to be cremated."

"Oh no," Mama said, her eyes wide as double moon pies. "It's bad enough she died at forty-two. It wouldn't be fitting, Augie. Burnt like trash in some receptacle out back. Hell! These dingbats might sweep the wrong ashes into the urn. I won't have it."

"I'd rather be cremated and my ashes spread somewhere that was special to me. Someplace that meant something to me."

Mama jammed her hand into her green alligator handbag. "Where's my Goddamn Kools?" She clicked the gold case open and selected a cigarette. "Judgement day, we will rise from the dead, and she won't have a body to ascend into heaven with."

As she rarely attended church, it was strange to hear Mama talk of religious matters she knew nothing of. "It's the soul. Her soul will be taken up," I said, not certain how I felt or if I believed the whole cockamamie story myself. When I was a boy, Grandma Flora had explained that the Bible was painted in images, ideas, and parables, not to be interpreted literally. She was right. She was always right.

"Can you smoke in here?" I asked, scanning the room for an ash tray.

She grimaced, her lit cigarette dangling precariously from her lips. "I'm paying for this floorshow."

I scooted a chair up next to her and sat down. "Mama," I said, restraining any emotion that she might misconstrue as patronizing. "Go home and rest. I'll settle things here. You look tired."

Her hair hung loose and wild. Evidently, she hadn't bothered with a brush before leaving the house. A typically fastidious person, she had been careless about her appearance today, and that spelled one thing and one thing only: trouble. On the verge of an explosion, she was all sixes and sevens. Her motor idled at an uncomfortable speed I could feel through the bottom of my feet as her uncontrollable leg tremors increased. "I'm here," she stuttered. "Have to make sure my instructions are carried out."

"I simply thought—"

"Do something, Augie! Now!" she roared.

Sharp as a machete, Mama's attitude sliced my reserve of patience wide open.

"Go the fuck home, Mama! Get out of my way! You're a pain in the ass and nobody, *nobody*, wants to deal with your crazy ass!" Red-hot and sizzling, my words crackled like firewood in my ear, branding me as a tyrannical warrior.

The cigarette fell from her mouth onto the plastic runner. I swiftly stamped it out. Her shoulders drooped, her arms hung loose by her sides, and her head bobbed from her bent neck. A ragdoll, Mama sat staring at the white sculpted carpet. I'd wounded her.

"Mama," I whispered. I reached out, but my hands froze inches away from her. Like the rest of us, she was a victim of circumstance. Unwell and untreated, her predicament, whatever the correct medical term might have been, was dire and woefully unjust. However, enough was enough!

Living in DC on my own had afforded me a perspective foreign to me as a child. Mama looked different to me now. No longer a ginormous fire-breathing dragon in heels, she sat small on the gold bamboo chair next to her sister's coffin. At that moment, I could have dashed out the door, jumped in my car, and sped back to the safety of DC and Rupert. I was weary of running and sick to death of shouldering the burden of guilt. Mama needed help, professional help far above my limited knowledge of psychological traumas and their lasting effects. I was just beginning to come to Jesus about my own meteoric memories of childhood and the nightmares that plagued me.

Deflecting the gamma rays of Mama's maltreatment was second nature to me. I'd always filed her vile behavior away and tamed my pain until I achieved the ideal state of numbness. *Hear no evil. Speak no evil. See no evil. That's what a good Pollyanna does, isn't it?* Everyone assumed I was the perfect Polly Purebred, Princess Happy-Go-Lucky, the hopeful healer, and the promising Pollyanna sent to save the day. I'd become adept at dealing with challenges. I'd made so many silk purses out of sows' ears, everyone assumed I was capable of spinning straw into gold. A golden miracle was called for. It would take a gilded incantation to dispel the beastly job the Quills had performed on our Sleeping Beauty.

Miracle-worker was my role in the family and my burden to bear, but I was weary and frightened and dreaded the thought of another confrontation. I'd changed my personal narrative in DC, but returning home, as with visiting Farley, had resurrected the patterns of my youth, and I was none the better for it. It was not my job to play savior and chief, but how could I explain that to my family?

Grandma Flora had seen it. She'd warned me of the pitfalls concerning my proclivity for kindness. "You can't save people from themselves." So, she'd prayed for us. But while prayer and kind words could cleanse and stitch our gaping wounds, it was never enough to rescue us from the flames of hell scorching our hides.

Yes! I felt sorry for Mama.

I loved and adored Grandma Flora more than life itself, but a part of me had always been outraged by her passivity! Why hadn't she sought help for the daughter? The poetry they wrote together, the poems they committed to memory, quieted Mama's mind for a while, but she needed more.

Mama was beautiful but strange. She had come of age gentle as a lamb and yet fierce as a tiger. A petite, auburn-haired beauty with a tiny waist and fiery spirit, she excited lust in many a young beau that came calling, but it took my dad's calm demeanor and patient rectitude to undertake the problem called May. As he suffered a savior complex of his own, it was inevitable that they would wed. It wasn't until the bloom of spring had withered in the cold mist that Dad saw the Devil's jest. He was the captain of a sinking ship that he managed to keep afloat through the roughest sea. I respected his sacrifice, but I also detested it, because April and I had paid the price.

I was wrestling not only with Mama and our past, but with myself as well. Something had snapped in me that Friday night. Seeing Farley again, running into Pete, and stumbling onto the scene of a ruthless crime had shaken me to my core. I was rattled by unbridled terror. How could life be so cruel to those most vulnerable? Where was God's mercy when it came to Farley, the kid the stork dropped into the lap of a marauding behemoth? Why had the Lord pillaged Pete's precious assets and looted his life of hope? Where was the face of God in the scene of the three beautiful young men whose throats were slit and agile bodies tossed haphazardly into a dark alley like yesterday's trash by a redneck band of hooligans hell-bent on revenge? Revenge for what?

I couldn't believe my spiraling thoughts. Where was the positive Pollyanna everyone relied on to raise them from the dead? I no longer recognized myself in the mirror. Proportion and perception were soiled by punitive vindication. When I looked at Mama, I hated myself.

"Mama," I said. She needed hugging, but she'd be repulsed by such an action from me.

"You were a stubborn child," she muttered. "Bullheaded and vain."

I looked at the fork-tongued, two-headed monster from outer space, resentment resplendent in my retinae. "I beg your pardon?"

"I should have spanked you on a regular basis." Mama folded her arms over her chest and crossed her legs. "Too big for your britches. Always was. Always will be."

I rose and peered into the casket at Aunt Jessica's clownishly made-up face. Everything about the last forty-eight hours had been ridiculous, and my heart pined for the day before yesterday.

I wanted to retrace my missteps and erase the ugly events. Aunt Jessica had learned too late where missteps led.

"If she hadn't gone to that back-alley butcher for an abortion," Aunt Tootie had proclaimed earlier that day on the phone, "she might still be here." I wasn't certain that a botched abortion could result in a cancer diagnosis, but I understood Aunt Tootie's clutching at straws to explain the great loss in our lives. I myself was incapable of a clear thought.

I never wished to be anything like Mama, and I'd fought hard to rid any semblance of her in myself. Instead, I'd emulated Aunt Jessica: classy, calm, and collected.

A lady in her fine tailored suits and pillbox hats, Aunt Jessica had been a glamorous goddess to me. Sitting on the thick, plush carpet in her walk-in-closet as a boy, I'd marveled at the order and simplicity of her life; everything neat and tidy and sensibly housed.

"Do you remember the time I spanked you?" Mama asked, her eyes glassy and her brow furrowed. "I'll never forget the way you stared me down. You looked me square in the eye, and just as bold as red paint, told me to never do that again." She closed her twitching eyes for a moment. "What child says such a thing to their mother?" She glanced around the room as if she'd awoken to a new dawn. "You were brave, fearless, a force to reckon with." As if possessed with their own will, her fingers danced along the rim of the casket. "I read the other day that Vincent Van Gogh once said that 'Normality is a paved road: It's comfortable to walk on, but no flowers grow on it." Gently, she reached inside the casket, removed Aunt Jessica's wig, and handed it to me. Pulling a string of pearls from the pocket of her coat, she whispered, "Dear one," and threaded them around her sister's neck. She unzipped a clothing bag she'd draped over another gold bamboo chair and held up a flamingo-pink Chanel-cut suit I recognized from Aunt Jessica's closet decades before.

The light through the stained-glass skylight intensified, spotting Mama's face with Picasso-esque shapes of color. Gazing out the window, Mama and I watched the last rays of light break behind the forested horizon.

"'Keep your face always toward the sunshine,'" Mama said, her voice light as the flap of an angel's wing, "'and the shadows will fall behind you.'" She was reciting Walt Whitman. She loved Walt Whitman almost as much as she loved Robert Frost.

Mama looked small and ragtag, and not at all like the polished woman I'd grown up with. I could picture her as a little girl skipping across a flour-dusted kitchen floor. I imagined her slathering blackberry jam on a slice of pan-fried bread, dripping with freshly churned butter, and crawling into her mother's lap. Gazing into the hearth as I had on many frosty afternoons, hypnotized by the flickering flames dancing over the logs, she'd fall under Grandma Flora's intoxicating spell as she read *Little Women* aloud to her.

Had Mama once dreamed of being Jo March as I had? Had she longed to be more than a housewife and mother? Had she felt as loved and protected as I had in those monumental moments in Grandma's arms?

"Mama." I gripped the side of the casket to brace myself. She didn't look at me. She pulled a fistful of tissues out her bag and began wiping the thick layer of makeup off Aunt Jessica's face. "Mama," I repeated. A lump swelled in my throat. I was going to cry, and I didn't care. *Enough is enough!*

Short in her flats, her cheeks sunken, and her complexion shadowed gray with grief, she stood skinny in her unbelted mouse-brown housedress. Though very different beings, we were tied to one another as well. Blood is thicker than water. I hated to confess it, but people did belong to one another. I was her son. She bore me and birthed me and raised me as best she could. Our connection was an indisputable fact.

Squaring my shoulders and standing tall as she had taught me, I whispered, "Mama." I put my hand on her boney shoulder. "I love you, Mama."

Dead silence.

Focused on the work at hand, Mama didn't turn to face me nor wrap her arms around me as I had hoped. Shaking slightly, she laid her hand on top of mine. "I love you too," she said softly. Through the break in her tangled tresses, I watched a tear glide over her pale cheek.

CHAPTER 21

STORMY WEATHER

"Why doesn't it snow? This morbid weather drags me down." April pressed her palm against the frosted pane of glass, wiped it on her polyester jogging pants, and studied the imprint evaporating before her eyes. Thin as a whippet, angry as an alley cat, and as wiry as a fox, disappointment was etched into the deepening lines of her angular face. "I should go running. Shake this misery off."

"I asked you to go with me this morning," I said.

"Excuse me. Must be nice to be a Single-Go-Lucky. Some of us have responsibilities. I have a husband to get off to work and three children to pack lunches for every morning before I'm due at school."

"Not today," I reminded her. "You took the day off."

"Snow day. Remember those, Augie?" She grinned slightly, but not enough to lighten her mood. "At least snow is pretty to look at. Until the car and truck exhaust screw everything up."

April kicked one of Mama's slippers under the bed as she often had as a girl. "Mama never wanted me. Where I am, she isn't, and I'm fine with that."

"April, relationships go both ways. You've got to give a little."

"I'm just curious. Why is it you never ask about my boys or my husband?" She pulled her hair on top of her head and sneered at her reflection in the full-length mirror. "Why bother?"

"I never forget their birthdays or Christmas. I send cards." I tugged at the collar of my turtleneck. "It's hot in here."

April curled her bare arm, and her bicep danced. "Bet you can't do that." When I didn't answer, she stuck her tongue out at me.

"What are you, ten?"

"I'm glad Dad and Tootie got her out of the damn house. Moping around like it's the end of the world. If you ask me, Aunt Jessica's better off. She was a sight the last time I saw her. Scary."

"Mama adored Aunt Jessica. She's in shock."

"I don't buy it. For the past year, she's known the inevitable was creeping around the corner." She grimaced and snorted simultaneously. "I could walk out of a burning car with my head cracked open, and she'd ask, 'April, when are you going to do something with your hair?'"

"That's a bit harsh. What if it had been Mama who died?"

"She'll live forever just to spite me."

"Have you tried meditation? It works wonders for Evangeline when her panties are in a twist."

April shrugged her broad shoulders. "And everybody thinks you're the nice one." Like Mafdet, Cleopatra's serpent-eating wild cat, April circled our parents' bed, focusing on Mama's favorite peach silk duvet. As rambunctious as the kids she taught and coached at Rockridge High, she glanced at the door to the hallway before hurling herself onto the mattress.

"Weeeeee!"

The neatly tucked linens shifted under her lithe body, and the artfully arranged paisley pillows plummeted to their death on the ivory shag rug. "Mama hates me," April grumbled, grabbing hold of a bedpost to hoist herself up. Arching her back, she folded her feet onto her thighs and sat in the lotus position. "Humm! Humm! Blah! What bullshit."

Five years my senior, the mother of three tempestuous boys, and the wife of a staunch conservative City Hall bureaucrat, my sister's misery, her constant companion, was grayer than the November sky outside.

I pointed to her soiled New Balance athletic shoes. "Mama will snatch you baldheaded!"

April tugged each shoe off and hurled both at my head.

"Hey!" I shouted and batted them to the floor. "Petulant child!"

"What's eating your candy ass?"

"You're fluent in five languages, and 'candy ass' is the best you can do?"

"*Laisse moi tranquille!*"

I slumped into Dad's worn, comfy chair by the window on his side of the bed. "You're itching for a knock-down drag-out with Mama, and I refuse to referee. I swear, April, you're as bloodthirsty as a vampire bat."

April climbed out of the four-poster, plodded to Mama's dressing table, and parked her firm fanny on the pearl brocade bench. Running her curious fingers over the jars of magic potions, elixir-filled atomizers, and beauty spells Mama relied on to retain a semblance of her youthful glow, she asked, "What's all this shit do, anyway?"

I didn't answer her. I couldn't look at her. Colder than the north wind whistling though the yellow roses on Aunt Jessica's casket the day before, April's indifference to Mama's grief was downright rude, and I hated her for it.

My head against the windowpane, I gazed down at Dad's desolate garden. A month previous, it had shimmered with autumnal splendor, a three-dimensional Monet quilt of jewel tones. Barren and contorted by harsh winters, the row of ragged silver maples, drained of their crimson glory, cavorted in the frigid gusts barraging them. Their branches clicked and scratched at the picket fence, buckled and bowed under their bulging girth.

I turned at the sound of April spritzing her hair with Mama's White Rain spray. Lacking artistic instinct, she was all thumbs trying to emulate Mama's signature look. No sooner had she pinned a tuft of carrot-orange frizz atop her head, than it defiantly sprang free from the loose bobby-pin she'd stabbed into the haystack. "Hell and damnation. *Merd! Merd! Merd!*"

A sucker for a yelping animal with its paw caught in a trap, I reached for the rat-comb. "Here," I said.

April beat her drum every chance she got. Her tirades drove me insane. Kind-hearted or not, a Pollyanna can bear but so much. Mother Teresa would have galloped into a foggy Black Forest to escape listening to April's ample list of grievances.

Spritzing a tangled tendril with rose water, I gently worked the comb through the trying knots and unruly waves of her coarse hair until it felt silky between my fingers. April popped the top on a jar of rouge, which I quickly liberated from her firm grip.

"Why does Mama hate me?"

"Tell her you love her," I suggested. "She's not capable of

making the first move." April made a face, and I laid into her. "Bitch and bark all you want, but until you—Oh! Just do it, for God's sake! Be the bigger person." I curled her hair around my hand and swept it high into a French twist. "I've watched countless souls wither away from AIDS and held their hands as they went. I've seen parents, friends, lovers arrive too late . . . too late to say what they should have said a million times a hundred years ago."

"You're—you are," she stumbled, "careful, aren't you?"

"I'm still here." I was annoyed by her avoidance. "Time is fleeting." She bent a bobby-pin into a U. "Mama scarred me for life."

"No doubt about it, Mama can be scary, but sometimes . . ." I stopped when I realized April's mind was somewhere else.

She closed her eyes and shook her head as if to dislodge a blistered memory. "People don't understand why I spoil my kids or volunteer to help challenged students read, but I know what they're going through." She touched the cone of hair rising from the base of her neck. "*Tres* elegant."

Styling her hair was the first time I'd touched my sister since we were children. When we were kids and Mama's nerves had gotten the best of her, we'd hightailed it to safety. Agile as acrobats, we'd roll out our bedroom windows onto the porch roof and shimmy down the trellis faster than squirrels dodging the pounding feet of a marching band. We'd dash out, slick as seals, before the swinging doors banged shut. We were hunted gazelles sprinting through the apple orchard to the dense forest edging the Shenandoah River.

The water rushing over the falls could have broken the sound barrier, canceling our heavy breathing reverberating off the cool, damp walls of the tiny cave carved into the underbelly of a sunny overhang of rock. Far from Mama's judgmental glare, we'd held hands and prayed for forgiveness. Mama's affliction had been our fault. We'd been certain of it. However, the exact nature of our sin remained elusive. Was it the basket of Lincoln Logs I'd left on the stair? Had April's untidy room, littered with baseball gloves and muddy cleats, unraveled her?

"I'm not pretty like Mama," April said and unscrewed a lipstick. "Cerise."

"And Mama couldn't hold a candle to Aunt Jessica," I said, my positive Polly rising to the occasion. *Perhaps I can help her.* "You're built like Aunt Jessica. Tall, thin, prominent cheekbones. Lucky you.

If you'd take care of your skin, and with a little help—" I sat on the edge of the dressing table and took April's chin in my hand. "You could have been a model."

She beat the side of her legs with her fists. "I'm butch in ruffles or lace, silk or satin."

"So's Princess Anne," I mused.

April dropped her hands in her lap. "I'm not stupid. I know they called me 'Spike' in high school. I was hiding under the stairs when I heard you and Mama laugh about it." She poked her chest with her middle digit. "Got me right here."

"Oh, April," I said.

"I'm not a lesbian, Augie. I know you and Evangeline think I am, but I'm not. I swear I'm not. Why were you so cruel? Everyone thinks you're so sweet and perfect, and . . . they don't know everything."

She was right about my snooty attitude toward her in high school. I'd been as cruel and petty as the rest of her agitators in Rockridge, Virginia. Instead of standing up for my sister, I'd joined the chorus. Why? Why had I been so evil? She had stood up for me when Billy Davis called me a faggot on the school bus. She'd grabbed him by the throat and pinned him against the window. "Apologize, dickhead!" Untamable, stubborn, and conspicuous, she was often her own worst enemy.

"I'm sorry, April. Truly, I am," I whispered and stabbed the rat-comb into a matted inch of mane.

"Ouch! Ouch!" She pinched the fleshy back of my hand. "Faggot! Let go!"

I yanked hard before releasing the unruly shank. "Spike!"

The following seconds of silence weighed heavy on my shoulders. As she rubbed her head, April's eyes welled with tears. "How do I get this monkey off my back?"

"You tell me, and we'll both know." I pulled a few tissues from the box on the vanity and dabbed her face dry. Her cheeks were rosy from crying; her defensive glare and quivering lip, plump and pink, were softened by the glistening tears. For the first time in a long time, I got a good look at my sister. Except for her sunbeaten, blotchy complexion, she was a classic beauty.

April handed me Mama's compact, and I smoothed a thin coat of foundation over her sculptured face, leaving her freckles visible. I shook the tube of eyeliner, and she obediently dropped her lids. Swipe. Swipe. She furrowed her brow for a closer look. "Smile, for heaven's sake," I said and aimed the tube of Elizabeth Arden's Rose Aurora lipstick at her. "Smack your lips. Okay. Rub them together. Gently!" I handed Mama's silver-plated vanity mirror to her and stepped back to admire my painting. "A pretty face needs little more than a nudge."

April gazed at herself. "You made me lovely."

I dropped into the chintz slipper chair. "Mama never dragged you to that cockamamie cosmetic department at Hasting & Hodge's?"

April tilted her head coquettishly and smiled at her reflection. "She took no interest in me whatsoever."

"Count your lucky stars," I said.

"It was all about you. The golden boy. The talented one. The perfect, proper sissy everyone adored."

I tossed the makeup sponge on the table. "We were both there, April! Same as you, I remember every horrific detail of our agonizing childhood. Mama's nervous spells, fits, tremors, traumas, whatever the hell they were . . ." I dropped my face into my hands. Cracking like ice cubes in a glass of Glenlivet scotch, a headache speared the sclera of my eyeballs. "We were abused. Plain and simple." I'd never wanted to admit it aloud, but April and I had absolutely been abused as children, afraid of Mama's long shadow. The image of Farley's father sexually abusing him in that restroom a century ago popped into my head. "I know people who had it worse than we did."

"That's difficult to believe." She hugged her knees to her boyish chest.

"At least we had gifts, God-given gifts to get us through." I gestured to her. "You were the star athlete."

"Big whoop!" April clutched Mama's bottle of White Shoulders perfume in her hand. "Not once were my medals and awards front and center in the trophy case at school, because they were won by a girl."

I stared at her until she sat the perfume back on the table. "The theatre awards I worked my tail off for were briefly mentioned during the morning announcement, sandwiched between the weather and the lunch menu."

April bent forward and picked a wad of lint from between her toes. "You're the beauty, and I'm the brains."

I glared at her. "You have no idea."

"You do plays and cabarets and musicals," she said mockingly.

"Stop."

"Mama bragged to Lena Hoover about your New York try-out for—oh, what was it? A touring show? Chicago or something like that. Name of a city. Could be Miami, for all I know about musicals."

"That was ages ago."

"Obviously, you didn't get it, or we all would have heard about the marvelous boy tenor and—"

"I didn't get it."

"A minor setback. Like a phoenix, you'll rise again." April applied mascara to her lashes as she rattled on. "I can't believe you left Arena Stage. Who would do such an idiotic thing?"

I blushed. The tips of my ears ignited. "You want to see a fool? Look in the mirror, April." I walked to Mama's chair across the room. "What dingbat would pass up an interpreter's job at the Pentagon?" I was so irritated with her. Just when I'd thought we were connecting, she'd thrown a wrench in the works. "Someone offered you the world, and you spit in their face."

April narrowed her eyes at me and pulled several bobby-pins out of the twist. It unfolded like a jellyroll left out in the July heat.

"It was your choice to stay here," I went on. "Living five blocks from where you grew up. Ridiculous. You no sooner packed your bags then you unpacked them and sprinted down the aisle. End of the melodrama. Mrs. David Dingle Dupree lived happily ever . . . never. Cut! Wrap! Print!"

April froze, bug-eyed and her mouth gaped open, her nostrils flared like a bobcat's sniffing danger. *Jesus*. What had I done? First Mama and now April. Shame eked out of every pore of my flesh. I'd paralyzed her, clapped her trap. The sight of her sitting at Mama's dressing table, devastated, tugged at my heart. I was as hateful as Mama, as vengeful as Mama. "Oh April," I said and clasped my hands together. "I'm a nobody going nowhere. Out there . . . out in the real world, nobody wants me. Having a booming voice isn't enough. A guy has to be a triple-threat. But most of all . . . most of all, he has to be tall and strikingly handsome."

"You're pretty enough," she said, her voice wet with sniffles. "Pretty isn't handsome, and handsome is what it's all about." Her pinched expression softened. "You sing like an angel."

"But I look like a character actor." Frustrated, I screwed up my face. "Pretty fucking tragic, don't you think?"

We both laughed.

Out of seemingly nowhere, a wave of ache tightened around my ribs. "April, do you know what I miss the most? What I'd sell my soul for?" She shook her head, and I sighed. "Waiting backstage before the curtain goes up, listening to a titillating overture rising from the pit, is heavenly. Loud and brash, the trumpets spear your eardrums, but it's insanely gorgeous. The clarinets pierce your heart, and you can't breathe. The violins tickle from head to toe. I vibrate like a caterpillar on a buzz saw when the piano velocities burst wide open. The drums you feel right here," I said and patted my abdomen. "I...I..." I turned away from her and gazed out the window at a cardinal perched on the weathervane atop the kitchen. The frantic wind had ceased its howling, and the bird stopped to preen herself. Another cardinal, much larger, bolder, and more aggressive, tapped his beak on the branch, and off they flew to the roof of my ancient playhouse in the apple orchard. Tears gushed, and though I tried to fight them, I blubbered. I curled up in Mama's chair and bawled like a baby.

Unaccustomed to being comforted in my boyhood home, I winced when April rested her hand on my shoulder. "Augie," she whispered, the way we had as children hiding in the dark cave. "Can we do better than this?" Hesitantly at first, she wrapped her arms around me. When I felt her breath on my neck, I collapsed into her embrace.

Like Mama, April was a part of me. Our blood sprang from the same fountain. Mama nursed us as babies, and Dad cradled us as toddlers in his arms. I know he did. I have Kodak snapshots to prove it.

We sat there for a while, sobbing on one another's shoulders as the sun dropped behind the sable pines on the crest of the hill. Beyond words, we said nothing more, for we had ventured far around an untraveled bend in the road. Tomorrow. Tomorrow. Perhaps tomorrow we would talk some more.

CHAPTER 22

BODY AND SOUL

On the day before Christmas Eve, I was startled by a hard rap on the thick glass of the corner display window as I stripped a mannequin out of a Donna Karan dress that a customer needed desperately for an unexpected party.

Something odd embraced the public when a living being was spotted in a display window, and they often felt compelled to rap on the glass as though visiting the aquarium. *That's right! An actual homosexual in here! A fashion queen with his backup chorus of Rootstein mannequins.* There was another tap on the window, but I didn't turn around until I heard the third one.

"We're kidnapping you!" Farley yelled from the other side of the glass. As electrically charged as one of Elton John's costumes, his ensemble screamed to be noticed. Lime-green cords and red sweater topped with a cobalt double-breasted coat with two rows of glistening brass buttons. His hair had returned to its natural shade of orange. However, since "natural" was a dirty word to Farley, he'd streaked his mop with platinum stripes that, from a distance, might have been mistaken for a faux fur hat. Ditching his basic New York black either meant he was excited about the holidays, or he was in desperate need of attention.

"Now!" Evangeline mouthed with matte fuchsia lips.

Good Lord. I hadn't seen Farley since that hideous Friday night when I'd dumped him and Pete into the back of a yellow cab.

His was not the comforting shoulder on which to cry. So, I hadn't called him after Aunt Jessica's funeral. He didn't care two shakes for Aunt Jessica, and he was still pea-green with envy when it came to Pete's and my relationship.

Garfinkle's Greenbriar Tea Room had been one of my favorite treats since Aunt Jessica had first taken me there when I was five. Its grass-green floor and polished baby grand, parked on a platform in the center of the sleek, forties-designed room, added a splash of class in the middle of our busy day.

"Eye on the menu and not the piano player," Evangeline said and righted the menu in Farley's hands. "Once a ho, always a ho."

"Ho. Ho. Ha . . . happy holidays, my two lovelies!" Farley handed us each a small silver-wrapped box tied with gold ribbon. "A blast from the past."

Curiosity getting the best of her, Evangeline ripped the paper off the gift, refusing to wait until desert to unveil the petite surprise. "Oh my God!" she squealed and held up a silver-framed picture of the three of us with Pete at the Gay Rights March eons ago. She and I ogled at the picture. "Can you believe we're twenty-eight years old? Where did time go?"

Farley pointed to himself in the snapshot. "All that hair," he whined. "What I wouldn't give to do it all over again."

"No thank you," I said, studying the photo. "Attached to those shimmering sepia-toned memories is the beautiful and the bad."

We'd just been seated when Evangeline nodded toward a table on the edge of the room. "That was your aunt's favorite. You had your first eclair right over there. Remember, Augie?"

I gazed at the table. Sitting perhaps four yards from ours, it stood firmly in the past. For a fleeting moment, I was ten again, grinning with chocolate smeared over my plump, pink cheeks.

"How far we've come," Evangeline said.

"About twelve feet," I replied.

"The world is so screwed up," Farley chimed in. "If cancer doesn't get you, there's always AIDS waiting in the wings."

We ordered lunch, and since Farley claimed to have sworn off booze, we passed on a bottle of bubbly to celebrate our reunion. Though we tried desperately to avoid discussing the latest headlines, by the time lunch was served, we'd sunk a few inches into the quagmire of politics.

"Nobody cares," Evangeline said. "Our government doesn't give a whoop."

Farley scrunched up his nose. "Too many closeted Federal fags, if you ask me."

"Our own worst enemy," I interjected. "Condemning us saves their reputation while simultaneously feeding their guilt. It's a win-win for a self-loathing narcissist."

"Like your sister," Evangeline added. "Like you and Rupert."

"What?" I said, "I can't believe you're lumping me in the same category as April and Barney Frank."

Evangeline spit her bite of salmon into her napkin. "Barney's gay?"

"As a two-dollar bill," I said, allowing the snickering waiter to top my cup of coffee.

"Those in glass houses," Farley said.

I stirred a packet of Sweet'n Low into my cup. "My hands are tied."

"So, work them out, Houdini." Farley brayed at his own joke.

"If only it was that easy."

"It's as difficult as you make it." Farley popped Evangeline's cigarette case open. "May I?"

She nodded. "It is a sticky situation. I know. I've been there myself."

"With a coworker?" Farley looked puzzled. "And they call theatre perverse. Incest is best."

Flashes of his father flickered in my head, and I blushed on Farley's behalf.

He clicked the lighter. "So, April's gay?"

I shook my head. "Apparently not."

"I beg to disagree," Evangeline said and tucked the cigarette case in the velvet-edged pocket of her Ralph Lauren tweed jacket. "She's at least bi."

"Rumor and inuendo," I said, standing up for my sister as I never had in the past, even though I suspected otherwise.

"Experience." Evangeline slathered butter on a biscuit.

I cocked my head at her. "She swears she's not."

"Augie." Evangeline smeared strawberry preserves into the butter. "I slept with your sister before I slept with you."

"Next station stop: Lesbos Island!" Farley's grin spread into a Cheshire cat smile.

I was in mid-chew of my chicken and grape salad sandwich

when the news fully registered. "Wha—" I coughed and spewed chopped chicken and white grape skin across my plate. "What?" I barked a little too loud, sending a ripple of rudeness through the well-heeled crowd gawking in horror at my blatant disrespect for their holiday cheer.

"Shit happens," Evangeline whispered. "Did you really think she was giving me tennis lessons in the girl's locker room?"

• •

"Mama's not happy that I'm skipping Christmas with the family," I said as we walked down F Street. "But I've been home every weekend since Aunt Jessica passed, and I needed a break,"

Thank heaven work had slowed down. Ours was the only department in the store to look forward to December. Once the holiday decorations were installed, there was little for us to do but reorganize our mannequin and prop storage, preparing for the cruise promotion to be installed after New Year's, and take vacations. We ran on a skeleton crew throughout the month and staggered days off.

Farley adjusted his Burberry scarf against the cold gust of wind whistling past our pink ears. "I've been home once since we graduated. Mother can send all the Hallmark cards she wants, but I'm not stepping foot into enemy territory again."

"Don't blame you," I muttered to fill the dead silence.

"Don't look at me," Evangeline said. "Now that I'm openly Jewish, I can drop the whole Episcopalian-Protestant bit and hug my menorah." She paused to gaze at the pastries in Reeves Bakery. "White chocolate-coconut cake," she said dreamily.

"Ahh. The Protestant springs eternal in the Jew." I took her arm and directed her away from the enticing display on the other side of the steamy glass. "It's for your own good. You'll have plenty of time for cravings later."

Farley stopped so abruptly that he nearly knocked over a very short man carrying a very tall stack of festively wrapped boxes. "Sorry," Farley said sheepishly, catching a red foil box tied with a shimmering green satin ribbon.

The man grimaced and snatched the gift from Farley's mitted paw.

"Merry Christmas," Farley said, smiling sheepishly.

"Merry fucking Christmas," the man grumbled and stepped into the crosswalk.

"Closet case," Farley yelled.

We were halfway down the block when it dawned on him what we were alluding to about Evangeline's cravings. "You're pregnant?"

"Not yet," she said, "but soon. Hopefully very soon. I have a good feeling about the Year of the Tiger."

We walked Farley to the Metro station entrance by Woodward & Lothrop department store. "See you in a few days," he said as he descended the escalator to the jam-packed ticket arcade.

"Merry Christmas to you and Pete!" I called out.

He waved without turning around.

There was nothing left to do when we returned to the store, so Evangeline watched me wrap Rupert's gift. He'd been away in New York for the week to visit his mother and meet with several vendors. "I think he's at Rootstein Mannequin Company this afternoon. He's buying the Tina Lutz Chow collection. Anything to get those damn Joan Collins Body Gossip girls off the floor. I'm sick of looking at her wide-eyed stare."

"Do you remember the first time I came to your grandmother's house?"

"We were, like, what? Five? Six?"

"Probably," Evangeline said and handed me the scissors. "Your mother scared the bejesus out of me."

"What made you think of that?"

"I feel guilty I didn't come to your aunt's funeral." She held the ribbon down for me to knot the bow. "I should have. She has her issues, but your mother's always been nice to me, and your father's a lamb like you."

"I'm not always a lamb." I gently fed the box into my bag. "I was horrible to Mama and April the weekend after all that terrible stuff happened."

Evangeline sat on the table and wrapped her arm around my shoulder. "It was a ball-busting weekend."

"Move over." I popped up onto the worktable. "So, what did Mama do to you?"

"I wondered why my mother warned me to never get in the car with her. I learned the hard way."

"I had no choice."

"I could tell she was on edge about something by the way she revved the engine before she peeled out of the driveway." Evangeline shook her head as she relived the ancient episode I barely recalled. "We were cruising down the road fast. At least, it felt faster than my mother's insanely polite driving. Suddenly, without warning, she slammed the brakes and steered that monster Ford Country Squire off the blacktop, spraying gravel as we bobbed up and down in the back seat. Then, screeching to an abrupt stop, she sprang out of the car as if she'd been shot out of cannon, and—in high heels—she sprinted across a field and disappeared into a thicket of pines."

I rolled my eyes. "Typical. Cursed. Body and soul."

"Evidently. That wasn't the biggest shocker of the whole crazy episode. You and April didn't bat an eyelash. You sat there engrossed in your crossword puzzle, and April was glued to her book—something about Babe Ruth, I think—until your mother came back. Calm as a cucumber, she smiled, patted her hair in place, and steered away with the ease of a driving instructor." She smoothed her long circle skirt over her crossed legs. "Fucking Froot Loops. My dad was just a jackass disciplinarian who smacked me around when he'd had one too many, but you guys. Jesus. It's a miracle you two are as sane as you are."

"Are we?" I asked. "Am I sane? Was my sister sane when you slept with her? Jesus Christ, Evangeline. What in the hell were you thinking?"

"I'm thinking I'm having second thoughts about having your baby, Augie."

"Baby? Having a baby was never on the table for me," I said, sliding off the table.

"Last month it was a great idea, but now . . . Well, you know how I am. Straight one day and gay the next."

"It has nothing to do with your sexuality."

"Flighty as a bumblebee. That's little ole me."

"You never asked. You informed me I was to be a father. What the hell?"

"Perhaps I'll advertise for sperm in the *Blade*. There's got to be at least one talented, sensitive, pretty queen out there willing to sell me a bottle of his spunk."

"For Christ's sake, Evangeline. No need to be crude about it."

"Excuse me, Mrs. Schlafly."

"Drop it! Just drop the whole crazy idea!"

"Go ahead, Augie. Say it! You don't think I'm fit!"

"You just said it yourself." I inhaled deeply in an effort to hush the thunder roiling inside me. "I'm flattered, Vange. Really, I am, but I'm not ready for fatherhood," I said in measured syllables.

"For this absurd adventure, you mean!" she barked.

"I'm not a stud for hire, Evangeline."

"Bingo!"

"You fly off the handle in the snap of a pretzel, and you're ready for motherhood?"

"Was your mother ready when she got knocked up with you?"

"My point exactly."

"Don't get all prissy-sissy with me, girlfriend."

"First, you assume I'd willing jack off in a cup for you, and then you insult me by rejecting my jive juice because it's tainted." I tightened the strap of my bag and secured its belt. "You don't have to remind me I'm a looney from Toon Town. It was evident from the day I was born." I slid my arm into my coat. "My first memory . . . I swear it's true. Though experts will argue that babies cannot, no-how-no-way, remember being newborns—I do. Lying there in my bassinette in a lavender room with a single picture of an angelic blond bambino hanging in the center of the wall . . . Tootie confirmed the color *and* the picture."

"I believe you, Augie. Honestly. If you say you remember, then you do."

"I recall two sets of hands gripping the sides of my bassinette. I felt tremors in the wicker. Coral lips yapping and a Madras plaid shirt. There was this rumbling sound . . . loud and menacing and scary. Words I couldn't understand being batted across me like a sped-up tennis match." Sweat beaded on my forehead. I was burning up. I loosened my gold silk tie and pulled my coat off. It fell in a pile on the floor. "I decided right then and there that I would be the perfect baby. An ideal child, because . . . because I never wanted to rock the boat. It was up to me to stay calm." My head was spinning, and the queasiness increased to a simmer, threatening to scorch my insides. The taste of vinegar from the Salad Niçoise was bitter on my tongue, and the spicy smell of the cinnamon-scented Christmas candle on the table burned my eyes. "Augie." Evangeline rushed to my side. Yanking my pocket square out of the breast pocket of my blazer, she mopped my forehead. "I didn't mean to upset you. It's just that I always—"

"Tell me everything." I jerked the hanky from her grip. "The whole world drops their crap in my lap!" I pressed my hand to my stomach, and something kicked my gut like a baby rabbit eager to see the world. "Alka-seltzer." I pointed to the medicine cabinet above the sink.

Evangeline dug a Diet Sprite out of her oversized bag, popped the top, and broke an Alka-Seltzer into the can. "Drink this." Dropping into my desk chair, I gulped down half the can. She felt my forehead. "You're burning up." After stripping my jacket off, she tugged my tie off and tossed it on the table.

"My head," I muttered and messaged my tightening scalp with my fingers. My head pounded like an anvil being struck with an iron hammer. I cupped my hand over my mouth for fear I was about to upchuck my lunch. I dropped my head into my hands and stared at the droplets of sweat dripping on the glass desk topper.

"Augie." Evangeline slapped a wet paper towel on my forehead and eased me back into the chair. "It's all right, Augie. Vange is here. Your Vange is here."

My forearms grew heavy and fell onto the desktop, leaving my head bobbing against my chest. Before I could count to ten, Evangeline stuck the wastepaper basket under my chin and all hell broke loose. She mopped up the excess and washed my face before my head dropped onto the desk and everything faded to black.

•••

"Vange," I whispered in the dark as I raised my head off the top of the desk. "Vange."

Evangeline clicked the desk lamp on.

"How long was I out?" I asked.

"You were snoring away for nearly an hour." She pointed to the wall clock I'd recently had installed. "Time to blow this pop-stand, as we used to say in high school."

The headache was gone, and oddly enough, I felt refreshed. "Did anyone . . ."

"Don't worry. It's a ghost town on this floor. Sam the security guard poked his head in, but when he heard you snore, he winked and went on his merry way."

"What he must think of me," I said.

"Here." Evangeline held my blazer open for me to stick my arms through. "I've got enough dirt on him to sink his battleship." She retrieved my cashmere coat from the table, shook it out, and handed it to me. "A married man with a hankering for boys in bathroom stalls."

"No way!" I protested. "He's so butch. He's married with three children."

"So was Oscar Wilde."

"Oh, Vange. I don't want to end up like Mama."

She hung the strap of my newsboy bag on my shoulder. "It was food poisoning, not a manic high." She playfully shook her finger at me. "You need to take care of yourself. Tell pushy people like me to fuck off when it's too much."

"But I'm Pollyanna gay."

"And I'm Bella Abzug. Never buy into your own publicity." She kissed my cheek. "Merry Christmas, darling. I'll be at Pete's if you need me." She pushed the fringe of curls off my forehead and pulled my beret on. "Are you okay?"

I adjusted the beret to a rakish angle. "Believe it or not, I feel lighter than air."

Evangeline fish-eyed me. "Sure?"

"No." I made a funny face. "I'm completely looney-toons."

"Aren't we all, love?" She clicked out the light. "Aren't we all?"

"You know something, Vange? You were pretty motherly, I must admit."

"Even Pollyanna had to learn to accept a helping hand occasionally. Well, at least Haley Mills's Polly."

I took her arm. "How many times did Grandma Flora take us to see that movie?"

"At least five times, and don't forget the times we snuck in the back door of the Virginia Theatre."

CHAPTER 23

MY FAVORITE THINGS

Snow flurries drifted down from the darkening sky as I scurried over Buffalo Bridge. I wanted to be alone with Rupert. No phone calls. No meetings. No emergencies. Just Rupert and me together and alone in his lovely house.

Rupert was due back that evening, and I wanted to be there to welcome him home. A week before, he'd presented me with my very own set of keys to his house. It was a major milestone after four years together. He even allowed me to park my old Mustang in his garage at the rear of the garden. With its dulling army-green paint and cracked white leather interior that had seen better days, the 'Stang was a poor companion for Rupert's gleaming navy-blue BMW.

I waved to his neighbor, Mrs. Benson, as I unlocked the front door. Whatever time of day it happened to be, she never failed to peek out her hallway window whenever I arrived. *My God.* Did she sit on the stairs all day waiting for me? *Such an oddball, but who am I to judge?* Coming from my freakshow family, I was in no position to point a finger.

"Good," I muttered to myself as I peeked out the back door. The eight-foot fir tree I'd purchased at the Capitol Hill Market the previous Saturday had survived Monday's riotous windstorm. Evangeline had accompanied me to the tree lot and helped me tie the evergreen to the roof of my ancient vehicle. Everything had been hunky-dory until I'd looped around Dupont Circle en route to Rupert's house.

Inadequately secured by the frayed lengths of rope I'd knotted together, the tree had jostled forward and slid onto the hood, covering the windshield. Evangeline had screamed, rolled down the window, and grabbed hold of the tree's trunk until I managed, in a blind fury, to pull into the circular drive of the Jockey Club on Massachusetts Avenue, one of Nancy Reagan's favorite lunch haunts. Like the carved characters on a cuckoo clock, the doorman, front desk clerk, and the manager spun out the door of the restaurant and surrounded us. The doorman kept pointing to the street and whispering, "Go! Get!" as if we were scent-impaired bloodhounds at a fox hunt. The manager, afraid that a patron might happen upon the bedraggled old 'Stang, pleaded with me to remove my heap of junk immediately.

Taking matters into her own hands, Evangeline, in her corduroy micro-mini-skirt and lace tights, batted her lashes at the bellboy, the only straight man of the lot, and he immediately leapt into action. A misplaced Paul Bunyan, the strapping youth had harnessed the wounded tree to old 'Stang's roof within a few rapid minutes. Evangeline had slipped the lad her card and insisted that she treat him to a drink at the end of his shift. As soon as the doorman had swept the broken branches into his dustpan, the manager and the desk clerk paraded back inside.

"Cheapskate!" Evangeline had chided me.

"I know! I know!" I'd said, "I should have bought bungie cords."

After the tree was decorated, dinner was warming in the oven, and a toasty fire was crackling in the fireplace, I poured myself a glass of wine and sat on the fur rug before the hearth. I glanced at my watch. Sticky with tree sap, my sweater and hair sprinkled with needles and glitter from the ornaments, I needed to run into the shower before Rupert arrived, but I was too tired to move.

I'd been running since Aunt Jessica had died. I'd crammed each day with activities because I didn't want to stop. I worried that if I stopped, my mind would wander to the darkest corners. My face still ached from crying. Her death was as devastating to me as Grandma Flora's had been when I was nine. Yet, as painful as it was, I was grateful I'd bothered to hear their stories as they neared the end.

A week before she'd succumbed to cancer, Aunt Jessica,

an emaciated eighty pounds, nearly bald, and white as a painter's smock, had asked for my forgiveness.

"Whatever for?" I asked.

"I have a dreadful confession," she whispered, her voice parched and rough.

"You've been nothing but kind to me since I was a boy," I assured her.

Weak as a neonatal kitten, she took my hand in her icy fingers. "Mr. March," she said, her painted face clownishly scary, "I yelled 'fag' at a delivery guy who grazed me with his bike as he sped through Dupont Circle. I'm so sorry. Please forgive me."

There it sat, her truth in my lap. It was ugly and hurtful and evidently her automatic reaction when threatened. "Of course," I'd said. But inside, a chasm between us widened, and she seemed far away. It was disappointing to recognize this vein of hatred rooted in someone I adored, but there it was. Did all straight people, no matter how liberal (and Aunt Jessica was far left on the political spectrum), harbor hatred of some degree? Did all gay people, including myself, distrust "breeders," as Farley referred to them?

I was changing but fast. The five years I'd lived in DC had made a huge impact on me. What had started out as a temporary solution until I could relocate to the Big Apple was now my home. By accident, I'd discovered a whole new field of work I hadn't known existed. I had been jilted by lovers, passed up for casting by directors more interested in tall hunks than my singing ability, and come out in a world shattered by a plague.

Gay men were dropping like flies, and there was little I could do but march and hold the hands of the dying and encourage the living to live out loud. Death and hatred, animosity and despair threatened to destroy my world and me. Friends, lovers, and acquaintances turned to me, Pollyanna gay, as I had come to be known in Washington, in desolate times for the ray of hope they imagined the man behind the engaging smile could offer them. The burden was heavy, and I was tired. Tired of death and disappointed in God for allowing so many to wither on their family tree, I became numb in order to bear the pain. I was used to switching off, a self-taught lesson of survival I'd acquired during my formative years with Mama.

Grandma Flora had been the first of my loved ones to die. I had been an innocent pup of nine, and my curiosity about death was as keen as my heartbreak. Sneaking into her room that last day, tip-toeing across the rose-patterned carpet reeking of ammonia, necrotic tissue, and the pungent stink of antiseptic, I snuggled next to her.

Propped high on a stack of down pillows, Grandma Flora had looked like a fallen angel. Her alabaster skin was cold as a marble pastry board. Unpinned from the trademark twist of buns at the base of her skull, her waves of silver hair cascaded over the front of her ivory nightgown where her breast used to be, broke on the cliff of the rumpled ecru wool blanket, and splashed onto the snow-white eiderdown draped haphazardly over her legs. Stripped of its noonday gold, the bluish afternoon light had sliced through the part between the heavy velvet drapes, spotlighting her sparkling periwinkle eyes. The stiff March breeze teased the fine, light sheers, snapping their hems to attention as she reached toward the light. We were not alone. "They'll come for me, Mr. March," she'd warned me the week before.

I had so many questions, but Grandma Flora touched her frigid, violet-veined finger to my lips and whispered, "I'm here. I'm always here."

"She'll be fine," Aunt Tootie had said to ease my fears.

Yet I had stood in the gravel drive as they'd loaded her into the back of the ambulance, the florescent light momentarily blinding me, and I knew . . . I just knew.

My face pressed against the back window of Dad's burgundy Thunderbird, I swore I saw a star fall from the sky as the squad zipped across the stone bridge leading to the main road. It had crashed into the stream, and I'd beat the leather seat like a drummer on acid. "She's dead! She's dead!" I'd screamed.

Death knew when we were wise to him. The dying recognized that gift of wisdom. Necessity demanded that I, as a volunteer with AIDS patients, freeze my personal feelings. How many shallow breaths had I heard cease in four years? How many books had I read, how many Bible verses had I recited, how many songs had I sung to scarecrows gasping for air?

It was difficult and necessary to cut loose. Sweaty as a New Orleans dock worker, I'd bob, bounce, twirl, twist, and jive like a jackal on Badlands' impossibly packed dance floor until "Last Dance" blasted from the speakers. Sunday brunch with friends and tarrying off to Rehoboth Beach or Provincetown for the occasional fun in the sun became important rituals. To discard the joys of youth would have been a major mistake. A person only got one ride on the merry-go-round, and only a fool would spit in the face of joy. With the plague lurking outside our windows, none of us knew how many seasons we had left. No matter how careful we were, it could claim any of us at any time.

I stretched out on the rug. *Only for a minute*, I told myself.

·•·

"Augie," I heard Rupert say before he kissed me. "You are amazing." Embracing one another, we rocked back and forth. "This is a Christmas miracle."

"The oven!" I said and sat bolt upright.

"It's fine. It was on 'warm.'" Rupert plucked a few green needles out of my curls. "You made my favorite holiday treat. Sorry. I was so hungry. I nibbled on the duck. The orange sauce is unreal."

"Oh," I said, brushing glitter off the front of my sweater. "I wanted to be all spit-shined and elegant when you came home."

"You're a sight for sore eyes. You'd be beautiful in a feed sack."

"You charmer," I said and took him in my arms. "I've missed you so much."

"Me too," he replied.

"I could take you right here on the floor."

"Please do," he said and tugged on my sweater.

·•·

We watched *The Bishop's Wife* with Loretta Young and Cary Grant after dinner. It was my favorite Christmas movie. Cary Grant played an angel sent from God to rescue the bishop, David Niven, who was entangled with a widow bent on building a cathedral to honor a husband she never loved instead of investing in the city's underprivileged children's future. "Too bad we don't have real-life angels like Cary Grant," I said as the credits rolled.

"Oh, but I do," Rupert said and snuggled closer. "I have you."

"All five feet, nine inches," I joked.

"Especially with those glasses."

"It was bound to happen sooner or later. Everyone in my family wears glasses."

Rupert clicked the TV off. "Don't you think it's time? After four years . . . I don't know." Rupert was a man of action who commanded a room the moment he strutted through the door; it was disarming to see him flustered. A little boy with graying hair—that's what he looked like to me.

"You gave me keys," I said. "What more could I ask for?"

"Marriage," he said.

I looked at him over the rim of my tortoiseshell Moscots. "That's impossible. Believe me. We'll never live to see the day two men can march into city hall and get handed a marriage license."

"Just for us," he said. "An intimate affair here with a few friends."

I reached for my glass of wine. "I don't know, Rupert. It's such a big step." I was stumped. Taken completely off-guard, I struggled to keep my thoughts in order. *My God!* I'd never even told him I loved him. I hemmed and hawed around the matter. Every time he professed his love for me, I replied with a passive, "Me too." *Me too. What kind of answer is that?*

Having expressed my feelings to Mama last month, I knew the power of those three simple words and how they could change a relationship. Ever since that day, Mama couldn't say it enough. Every call or conversation ended with her saying, "I love you, Mr. March."

I wasn't certain why I hadn't told Rupert I loved him. I was crazy about the man, but admitting I loved someone would have left me vulnerable. Dad was the perfect example of a man who had been taken advantage of because he'd freely admitted how crazy he was for Mama. He'd handed her the reigns, and she tugged on them every chance she got.

Whatever April was—lesbian, bi, or straight—she was under her husband's thumb simply because she loved him. Perhaps she loved him because he'd rescued her from her true self, or maybe she truly did love the uptight twit, but she'd become his creature the moment she'd said "I do."

Rupert was not like them. My instinct had never been wrong about him, and my instinct screamed he loved me. He went out of his way to prove it. I'd once been hit by a cab while bike riding in Rock Creek Park and he'd flown back from a convention in San Francisco, where he was a guest speaker, the minute Evangeline called him to tell him.

"Scrapes and scratches!" I'd told him when he called from the airport. "A minor concussion. I'll be fit as a fiddle in a week."

He would have none of it. "I want to be there with you."

"Pollyanna Siegel," I mused. He booked the next flight home.

That was Rupert through and through. I'd never met his parents. From the pictures on the baby grand, his mother, Barb, was an Irish beauty who'd fallen for a debonaire Jewish immigrant, and they'd tied the knot a week after they met. They were a tight family, and a week never passed without Rupert phoning his parents and his brother, Sam, a sociology professor at Northwestern University.

Handsome, talented, and kind, he was the ideal lover from central casting. I knew he was top-drawer, but was I? Did I measure up? Part of the reason I'd avoided meeting his family was because I was certain they'd take one look at me and see the hayseed I truly was. Plus, although he begged to differ with my opinion, his mother always seemed a bit brisk when I answered the phone. Behind the perfect enunciation, cool demeanor, and sophisticated repartee, I was one step above Southern trash.

I had fooled myself for years, thinking no one in my hometown knew the hell boiling behind the brick façade of our two-story Cape Cod. But they did know. Evangeline had told me last year that we were the talk of the town. Even Jake the Rake, the town bum, had gossiped with folks at the local IGA Grocery about the wacky Applegates on Pleasant Hill. Pleasant Hill; I grew up on Pleasant Hill. What a joke.

"A penny for your thoughts." Rupert topped my glass of wine.

"I'm afraid," I blurted out.

"Of me?" He brushed my cheek with the back of his hand. "Few surprises at this stage of the game."

"People at work. I'm sure the Declare family wouldn't be too pleased with one of their VPs shacking up with a mid-level manager such as *moi*." The Declares were the family who owned Wallis & Fitch Haden.

"Augie," he said softly. "They're the only ones who know. I've been upfront about my sexuality from day one. It was either they accept who I was, or I wasn't accepting the job."

"Rupert," I said, "you're the amazing one."

"I know." He kicked off his slippers and stretched out on the sofa, resting his head in my lap. "I'm a catch."

We talked until the candles melted down to the wicks. Rupert's trip to New York had been a success, and his family was delighted to see him. "They're dying to meet you."

When the mantle clock struck midnight, he ran to the closet and pulled a small gift from his coat pocket. "Merry Christmas, Augie," he said, handing me the small, elegantly wrapped box.

"Wait," I said, "I bought something for you." I dashed into the kitchen and returned with my own tiny gift.

Like two children, we sat cross-legged on the floor before the hearth. I poked the log, and it broke in two, releasing the fury of the flame burning its underside. Red, yellow, and purple, the sparks ignited the center of the log, releasing a blue shoot that leapt into the dance with its kin, reaching high toward the flue.

Each checking for the other's response, we unwrapped our presents at the same time.

"Augie!" Rupert said and held the gold cufflinks close to the flame.

"They're made from a chunk of malachite left over from the renovation of the main floor. Galt Jewelers cut them and mounted them for me. There's an inscription. Read both."

Rupert unhooked them from their box and rolled one over in his hand, reading. "'The sun . . .'" He rolled over and inspected the second. "'. . . the moon & stars.'"

"That's what you are to me. It's from *Peter Pan*."

"I know, Augie. I know," he said and kissed them. A tear trickled down his unshaven cheek, and he pressed my hand against it.

"One of my favorite stories," I said as I popped the top of the Tiffany's box. "Rupert!" I slid the emerald pinky ring on and marveled at its facets sparkling as I turned it toward the light. "A perfect fit."

"I wanted it to be a wedding band, but I wasn't going to press my luck." Rupert kissed me. "A touch of Oz wherever you go, my pretty Pollyanna." He pushed himself up and offered his hand.

I took his hand and looked up at him. "I have one more gift for you," I whispered, and he pulled me to my feet. Then, taking his head in my hands, I said boldly, "I love you."

He wrapped his arms round my waist, dropped his head on my shoulder, and cried.

CHAPTER 24

YOU'VE GOT TO GIVE A LITTLE

"Heavens," I said as I slid behind the reception desk at Whitman Walker Clinic on 14th Street. "All these people."

"Test results," whispered Chancy, the African American beauty, whose mesmerizing green eyes shimmered like the waters of Destin Beach on the Gulf of Mexico. "It's all yours, girl. 'This joint is jumpin'. It's really jumpin'," he sang.

"My results are due back today, but I had the test at Dr. George's office."

"Same here, sugar. In case it was bad news, I figured his office is closer to the Potomac. I'd have to take a cab to the harbor from here."

"You wouldn't actually . . . you know?"

"Please, honey! I'm going to squeeze every last drop out of this life before I surrender." He shook his head. "I've seen sights I never hoped to see in my glamorous lifetime. But sugar, AIDS ain't so choosy. Doesn't care if the bitch has a Harvard degree or flunked out of night school. Appetite of a lumberjack." He stuck a ballpoint pen in his pumped-up pompadour. "Always losing these bitches when I need them most."

A middle-aged man in cowboy boots and a fisherman's sweater stepped up to the counter, and Chancy turned his attention to him. "What can I do for you, sugar?"

I enjoyed the volunteers but loathed traveling to and from the clinic. It was surrounded by abandoned store fronts, crack houses, and homeless alcoholics and drug abusers rifling through alley trashcans for any morsel of uneaten food. I worried I was tempting fate every time I crossed 15th Street and into the zone of trouble. Evangeline and I attempted to coordinate our schedules so we could walk together, but that day it hadn't been possible. She'd had to switch shifts with Chancy because she had an appointment with Dr. George to discuss her plans to have a baby.

My first week of volunteering, three years before, I had been accosted on the corner of 14th and S Streets by a rowdy gang. Most likely my Armani trench coat caught their attention as I'd passed by. I'd ignored their catcalls and derogatory name calling, but when one of the guys rushed across the street and grabbed me by the collar, for an instant, I'd frozen. Inside, I was a leaf in a cyclone, but outside I was the picture of composure.

His hands on my throat, he'd slammed me against the crumbling stucco wall. "Fucking fag," he'd mumbled as he searched my pockets. He released his grip when he discovered my wallet. "Five fucking dollars, man? You're going to die for five fucking dollars." He looked at my shoes and felt the fabric of my coat. "Off with it, faggot," he grumbled, tugging on my coat sleeve. As much as I'd loved parading through the employee entrance in my chic new coat (which made me feel like Mary Richards from *The Mary Tyler Moore Show*), and as frigging freezing it had been on that shadowy block with its shot-out streetlamp, I'd quickly handed over my treasure in exchange for my life.

"Listen, faggot," he'd whispered as he took hold of my shoulders. "Run when I kick you." I glanced at his eyes, as intensely black as the Chinese checker marbles I'd had as a boy, and realized he was afraid. A strong and aggressive man, tall and brawny, I abruptly recognized him. Not long before, I had walked a sickly patient to the check-cashing store a few blocks away. At the time, this guy had been behind the glass window.

The next second, he'd punched me in the face, knocked me to the pavement, and kicked me in the ribs. *Mother fucker! That hurt!* From that day on, if Evangeline couldn't make it, I called for a replacement volunteer. I wasn't convinced that lightning wouldn't strike twice.

"August Applegate?" a faint but familiar voice said.

I hung up the phone and stared at the gaunt fellow whose face and neck were peppered with purple lesions. "Do I know you, sir?"

"You haven't changed a bit." The man grinned, the thin, translucent flesh like a taught plastic mattress cover, stretched over his prominent cheek bones. Evidently, he'd changed quite a bit. "Danny from Buck's County Theatre Camp."

Well, you could have knocked me over with a feather. "Danny? Danny?" I stammered to collect myself. One of my assets was my gift to resist ogling at a patient. Other volunteers marveled at my control. "Look them straight in the eye," I often advised. Now, I was doing everything but following the fine example I'd set.

Frightfully thin and bent back, Danny leaned over the counter and hugged me. "Damn, Augie. You're prettier than ever."

It would have been insulting to pretend he was anything other than the scarecrow he was. "It's been ages," I said. "I often think of you and those halcyon days of our youth."

Danny shuffled around the counter and eased himself into a chair. His breathing was labored. He was bandy-legged, his arms were willow-thin, and his bloated stomach was shelved atop his thick belt, fastened in an extra hole he must have punched into its leather. I searched for the gorgeous dancer he had been a decade before. *How could God do this to him?* I glanced around the waiting room as Danny reminisced about our golden age of theatre. He had been right when he'd told me at camp, "We come in all shapes and sizes." It was true. Unlike my 99-percent Caucasian hometown, DC had exposed me to people from all walks of life. My friends, neighbors, and workmates included all races, educational levels, and varying political viewpoints.

"You were an amazing George M.," Danny said. "I've never seen anything like you on any stage in any theatre I've had the pleasure to visit. You are an original . . . Polly." His eyes brightened. "Pollyanna! That's what we called you!"

"Danny!" I hushed him. "I'm attempting to be a professional here." I checked for his name on the schedule. "Who are you seeing today?"

"Mr. Kavanaugh." Danny peered at the appointment book.

"We don't have a Mr. Kavanaugh, Danny."

"Kaiden Kavanaugh. He's my therapist. He just started volunteering here on Monday."

Kaiden Kavanaugh. Kaiden Kavanaugh. Where have I heard that name before? I found the name on the schedule. "Oh, there you are." I checked my watch. "He must be running a tad late."

"Normal with him. He always runs over."

That's when it hit me. I knew the name had sounded familiar—but it couldn't be him. The Kaiden Kavanaugh I'd known as a child was a jock.

"Here he is now." Danny planted his cane against the desk surround to push himself up. "Hey, Mr. Kavanaugh, this is—"

"August Applegate," Kaiden said.

I jerked around so fast I knocked the appointment book on the floor. Still as handsome as the day was long, my former swim coach (now with a sexy brush of gray at his temples), stood before me. Both our smiles stretched from ear to ear. "Kaiden Kavanaugh from Virginia?"

"The one and only." He dived in for a hug. "My little August Applegate." With his arm around my shoulder, he said to Danny. "I taught him how to swim when he was . . ." He looked me up and down. "What, fourteen or fifteen?"

"Small world," Danny chimed in. "We did theatre together when he was sixteen."

"What are the odds?" I said, my head flipping through an index file of memories.

Kaiden gripped Danny's arm, so thin his fingers nearly fully circled it. "Don't leave until we have a chance to talk," he said to me before he led Danny down the hall to a private room.

I watched them as they made their way to the office at the end of the corridor. Danny was stiff and frail and looked way older than Dad, especially walking next to Kaiden, a perfectly preserved specimen of manly virtues. Flashes of him in his speedo danced in my head. He had been my first crush. The smell of chlorine and the touch of his hand on my stomach when he taught me the breaststroke would remain etched on my mind for eternity.

Stop daydreaming! I pinched myself. He was real and here in Whitman Walker, and I was . . . Oh heavens! I was just as clumsy and tongue-tied as the first day I'd met him. What must he think of me?

The phone rang, and I jumped. "Hello," I said into the receiver. "Whitman Walker Clinic. How may I help you?"

"Hello, Mr. Applegate?" It was the receptionist from Dr. George's office. I stammered an affirmative. "We have your test results ready. Is now a convenient time?"

"You mean I don't have to come in?" I asked nervously.

"Not when it's good news," he assured me. "You're negative."

"Thank you," I made myself say, trying not to let my voice show how worried I'd truly been. "Thanks a lot."

I hung up and sighed. The week I'd spent waiting for my HIV test results had been the longest of my life, each day dragging along, delivering extra buckets of tension. But now, I wanted to zip across town to Rupert's and celebrate. His test results were due back the same day, and since we'd been faithful to each other for nearly four years, I had nothing to worry about.

Chancy, who'd snuck out the back door for a smoke and a snort of his laced tobacco, returned glassy-eyed and a touch loopy. "You look like the feline that gobbled the canary."

"Just got my results," I whispered. "I'm free!"

"To be you and me, sugar. To be you and me." He batted his long lashes. "My second test this year. So far so good."

I was in the restroom only a couple of minutes later when I heard the ambulance siren blaring. Opening the door to the corridor, I nearly smacked into Danny being rolled out on a gurney by EMTs. Danny pressed his hand against his chest and puckered his lips as if he was braving pain. Shielding his red-ringed eyes from the harsh glare of the fluorescent lights with the back of his hand, he mustered up the slightest grin when he saw my face.

"Danny," I called out, but he was out the door before I had a chance to talk to him—if he even could talk. His head was bobbing from side to side when the burly attendants lifted him into the back of the ambulance. Please, God. Please be kind to him. I prayed the Grim Reaper had taken a holiday and would spare him a while longer, but I knew with lesions as dark and pronounced as his, it was simply a matter of time. Christ! I hated to think about it, but it was second nature to me at that point. I could visualize his funeral service in my head.

"Old gal has had a rough ride of it," Chancy said. "I almost pray he goes sooner than later."

"As much as I hate to admit it, I'm with you."

"He looks miserable. Today, when he was talking to you, was the first time I've seen him smile in a year. For a minute, sugar, I thought you'd conjured up a miracle." He paused thoughtfully, hands hovering over a stack of paperwork. "Odd seeing him today. Monday's his usual day." He made a face. "By the way, why are you here on a Thursday and not at your magnifique, chic department store?

"It was either take the day off or lose a personal day this quarter."

"Nice work if you can get it. Unfortunately, I work weekends. Not all of us have a rich sugar daddy like you, honey." Chancy tucked his floral shirt into his tapered jeans. "Funny. His friend Pete usually accompanies him. They live together in a fancy pad on California Street." He made a face. "A far cry from my hovel on the wrong side of Rhode Island Avenue."

"I'm with you, sister. I was born on the wrong side of the tracks."

"But look at you now, sugar! A lady in a fine house, married to a sexy, classy Jew . . ."

"We're not married, and it's not my house. I don't live there."

"Yet." Chancy dusted some cracker crumbs off the counter, muttering, "Dirty. Nasty. Nasty. Dirty. Filthy bitches could clean after their nasty selves." He leaned closer. "The breeders are the worst. No offense, sugar, but the whiter their skin, the worse their attitude. They pull up to the front door in a taxi and don't leave until another one arrives to chauffeur their boney ass back to the high-toned part of town. They have no idea the hell we go through. It makes them feel good and gives them something to talk about at cocktail hour. Do they understand the odds against my people? Sometimes, I want to look them square in the eye and say, 'Bitch, try being a double minority like yours truly.'" He spritzed Windex on the counter, then wiped it with a wad of paper towel. "And the bitches on the street are ten times worse. Sugar, most of them would step over our corpse if they found us dead in the gutter."

I glanced down the hallway, but there was still no sight of Kaiden. "How well I know."

"Thank God for you, or my friend Thelma would have been unceremoniously dumped in a landfill."

Oh, how I wished he hadn't brought up the incident on that blustery afternoon a few weeks before. The thought of it taunted me in the gentle moments before dawn signaled the sparrows to sing. Safe in Rupert's arms as he pleasantly snored away, my tears had for weeks flowed freely at the thought of Thelma clutching her chest as we waited at the 14th Street stop for the 54 bus.

"You're top-drawer for sure," Chancy went on.

"I did what I could."

"Unlike our valiant men in uniform?"

I shook my head, but the image of Thelma keeling over on the sidewalk looped in my head.

Chancy snorted. "Coppers."

I flushed hot as I recalled dashing across the street that day, dodging traffic in both directions. Pounding on the windshield of the police car, I'd yelled at the top of my lungs, "Help! Emergency!"

Once the policemen had spotted Thelma writhing on the ground, they'd sprung out of the car so fast, I'd had to hold on to the rearview mirror to keep from being knocked to the blacktop.

"Help her! Help her!" I'd shouted, shattering the conversation of the heroin addicts scouring for the lunch scraps in a nearby trash bin.

The burly, mustachioed cop had called for the squad as his beefy buddy in blue had ripped Thelma's silk blouse open, the buttons popping off like beads on a gyrating cooch dancer. Inhaling deeply, he had been inches away from performing mouth-to-mouth when the burly partner had pointed to Thelma's chest, flatter than Gomer Pile's. As Thelma had lain there, gasping for her life, they'd doubled over laughing. "Sister freak!" one had bleated.

"Mother fucker!" I'd roared, pushed through the tangle of uniformed limbs and knelt over Thelma. For a split second, I'd hesitated. She'd tested positive for the AIDS virus, and the sight of her slobbering turned my stomach. So, I'd hesitated. *Good God!* Had my hesitation cost Thelma her life? I still wondered.

Sucking in air, I'd planted my lips on hers and blown. Nothing. Her chest hadn't risen. So, I'd repeated it again and again until one of the policemen had pulled me off her.

I'd sat there on the icy sidewalk, the toxic taste of her mouth on my tongue, as the ambulance screeched around the corner.

Their faces suddenly serious, the artful dodgers of duty had rushed to assist the emergency attendants.

"Nothing we could do," one had bemoaned.

"God knows we tried," the other had proclaimed.

I'd glanced at the addicts, who had snapped to attention when the siren screamed. Wild eyed and as jittery as a posse of feral cats, they'd stared dumbfounded at the blatant liars brazenly passing the buck. There had been no mystery to solve. It had been an open-and-shut case of neglect.

Chancy touched up his lip liner. "Poor old bitch was this close to those implants she'd been dreaming of since puberty."

My insides knotted at the thought of Thelma, half naked and rejected, her dignity stripped bare in the frigid frost of winter. Was the periwinkle sky she had stared at in those moments permanently etched into her dead gray eyes? A tragedy. The thought that someone's death could be made more tragic by the negligence of law enforcement was mind-bending. *They laughed. They laughed.* I'd barely known Thelma, and she hadn't been the nicest person I'd ever met, but she'd been a human being—a vulnerable human being. "What in the hell is wrong with people?"

"Except for Pollyannas such as yourself, the world is a cruel and nasty place. That's modern life." Chancy flipped through the pages of the *Blade* newspaper. "Sugar, I know what you've been going through. You've been hairy-scary since your auntie passed."

"I can't get over it. Cops left someone to die on the street because they weren't the right type of person to save?"

"Sugar, we have a president who refuses to even mention AIDS in any speech or press conference from the Oval Office. Gay men are plagued by an uncurable disease that few care to hear about because it could never happen to them. It all makes my blood boil."

"Until that afternoon at the bus stop, I thought the world was on our side," I said. "But between Thelma and the slaughter of those three innocent gay boys in that P Street alley, I've been made keenly aware of the hatred festering in the world. Why isn't the world more appalled by this abhorrent behavior?"

Chancy made a face. "No better than the ancestors of slaveholders who deny their kin was anything but kind and fair to the people they'd purchased on auction blocks."

"I had no idea there were so many prejudiced people in the world."

Every fiber of my Pollyanna being was wrestling with the rebel rattling my ribcage. Rupert had cautioned me to keep a level head when it came to the battlefield for gay rights. He was right, of course. I, one tiny speck of the human race, couldn't challenge global prejudice no matter how loud I protested, but I could fight one battle at a time. "Slow and steady wins the race," he advised.

"Excuse me, Chancy." I picked up the phone and dialed a number dear to me. "Rupert," I whispered into the receiver. "Meet me at Childe Harold. I need to celebrate something, and us testing negative is the best news I've had all day."

"No problem darling," he said, the rich, warm tone of his voice caressing my ears and softening the hard ache thumping inside me. "I'll nab the table in the window if I get there before you do."

"I love you," I said and dropped the phone into its cradle.

"Sugar," Chancy said, "I didn't mean to upset you."

"Oh Chancy, it's not you. It's the world and me. Everywhere I look, there's injustice."

"That's because you're a Pollyanna. My heroine in Armani."

"I don't feel like a hero."

"True heroes never do." Chancy held a compact mirror up and plucked a hair from his brow with tweezers. "I swear, these hairs grow faster than my ex, Roland's, pickle on a nude beach." He opened his bag, a Clinique gift-with-purchase, tossed the mirror and tweezers into it, and zipped it closed. "Your gift is greatly needed here, sugar."

• ● •

I waved from the street when I saw Rupert sitting at our favorite table. Damn was I lucky. If I had nothing else in the world, I had an honest man who honestly loved me.

Rupert handed me a glass of scotch before I claimed my chair. "To us," I said and clinked my glass to his. "To testing negative! Yeah!" I took a hearty swig of my drink. "Oh, that burns so good," I joked. "So, how was your meeting with the head honchos?"

"Great!" Rupert said. "They're rewarding me with a grand bonus. Nothing like I was expecting. I should take you to Paris for Easter."

"Now that's a gift-with-purchase," I jested. The street below was bustling with gay and straight couples heading out to dinner or a bar to let off steam on a Thursday night. What did they care if they woke up a little worse for wear? If they could plow through their eight-hour Friday, they'd be free for an entire weekend of indulgence.

"It was major test result day at Whitman Walker. As dismal as it can be at NIH, I'd rather be there talking to guys or reading to them. It's fine at the clinic, but you know what I mean."

Rupert grinned and shook his head.

"Oh!" I said, remembering. "I ran into an old friend from my hometown today. Well, his family had a country house there. He taught me how to swim. A regular John-John Kennedy in a speedo."

"How many times did you nearly drown?" Rupert mused.

"Nothing like that," I said and crinkled my nose. "He's straight. He's a therapist now."

"So, how did he end up at Whitman Walker?"

"Not sure. There was a problem with a patient—actually, my friend Danny from theatre camp. Oh my God! I *didn't* recognize him. He used to be so beautiful. Magnificent dancer's body and model-striking face. He had it all. But now—I nearly cried when I was talking to him." I softly smacked my palm against my forehead. "Jesus! It just hit me what Chancy was saying. Duh. I'm a bit slow on the pickup." I took a quick sip of my drink. "Get this: Danny must live with Pete. Chancy said that Pete usually comes in with him, but for whatever reason, he didn't today. Anyway, he has the same address."

"Some men do share a residence," Rupert said, squeezing my leg under the table.

I held the ring he gave me up to the candle to admire the emerald. "This is amazing. Every time it sparkles, I think of you." I touched his hand. "I love you."

"Took you long enough, Augie."

"Yeah, but you were the first to know."

We ordered dinner and talked about our days and our plans for the weekend. However, my mind kept drifting back to the clinic, and Chancy, and Danny and Kaiden and Pete, and Thelma's senseless death. No matter how I tried to separate my personal life from work and from my volunteer projects, I smeared the dividing lines, and one bled into the other.

"I realized something today," I said, setting my coffee cup on its saucer. "When I was a boy and Mama would fly into a rage, I escaped by drawing a beautiful world of beautiful people dressed in beautiful clothes and painting them in cheery colors. . . . Or I'd sing happy ditties and dance around my playhouse. I could breathe. I could function. It gave me balance. I discovered sex in college . . . well, then sex became my drug of choice. I was, as Elizabeth Taylor said of herself, a serial monogamist. Tense about an audition, opening night, a final project . . . I'd have sex. It would always break the curse. Calm was restored. But now, the problems in the world we face as gay men, as a minority . . . we're second-class citizens. The problems are gargantuan. What was once a disagreement has blossomed into a war."

"Augie," Rupert said, his expression suddenly sad, "you can't save the world."

"Oh Rupert, I have a silly prayer I repeat to myself every night before I fall asleep."

"So Southern. So cute."

I crossed my eyes and made a funny face. "Real cute."

"You help more people than you give yourself credit for."

"It never feels like enough."

"It has to be," Rupert insisted. "When you get older, you'll see that a balanced life is the only way."

"Way to what?" I asked.

"Way to live." He added a healthy tip for the waiter and signed the credit card receipt. "Shall we?"

"At one point a few years ago, I couldn't afford a cup of coffee."

"I remember something about you walking from 16th Street to Arena Stage?"

"I did what I had to do. I did what my father taught me to do. I took care of the situation."

Rupert smiled. "So is the way with a Pollyanna gay."

I tucked my scarf under my coat collar as we stood in the vestibule of the restaurant. "'Baby, it's cold outside.'"

"I hear they're going to cancel the outdoor part of Reagan's Inaugural festivities on Monday," Rupert said. "A simple swearing-in in the Capitol rotunda."

"No Nancy swathed in fur?"

A frigid blast smacked our exposed faces as we descended the front steps of Childe Harold. I stuffed a gloved hand in Rupert's pocket, and we walked to the corner in hopes of hailing a cab. Plenty of cabs whizzed by, but every single one was occupied.

Frustrated after five occupied cabs drove past, Rupert stamped his foot on the sidewalk. "Hell! Hell! Fucking hell!"

How odd. Rupert wasn't a swearer. He was typically measured and polite, so his outburst seemed completely out of character.

"Rupert," I said and took his hand. "Let's go in Kramerbooks to get out the cold."

He jerked his hand away and stormed off down the sidewalk. The warmth created by our joined body heat dissipated the moment he stepped away, and the cold, an invisible ghost, rushed me head on.

"Rupert." I followed him a few yards down the block. "Rupert!" What the hell! Gawking at him, I stood stunned on the sidewalk as he headed toward the Q Street Metro station. His coat flapping in the unrelenting ocean of wind rushing down the avenue, he held on to the chest-high wall surrounding the Metro entrance escalators, his back to me.

"Are you alright?" I asked. "Was it the onions or the tomato sauce?" I suspected his acid reflux was playing havoc with his esophagus. I put my hand on his shoulder, but he pushed away.

"Don't touch me!" He scurried into the shadowy area and away from the glaring streetlamp. Blurred by the dark, his contorted face looked like a Japanese Noh mask of sadness as he paced back and forth in the whistling wind.

I didn't care if he had swung at me; I wasn't going to watch my tormented lover without trying to help. "Enough!" I said firmly and gripped his shoulders.

The elevator door dinged, and a herd of people poured out onto the street, separating us. The group flowed into the sea of people exiting the escalators before dispersing in all directions, leaving us standing several feet from one another.

"Rupert, please don't do this. I finally tell you how I feel and now you pull away? What did I do?"

"I lied, Augie. I'm a liar."

Frozen in mid-step, I was suddenly one with the frigid Mother Nature. Fearing that the wind would rip my beret off and carry it away, I snatched it off my head and stuffed into my coat pocket.

A mighty gust swept through my mass of curls, separating the snapping tendrils until they felt like a circus of snakes dancing to differing tunes. "What are you talking about? Rupert, what do you mean? Don't you love me anymore?"

Holding his chin high, he marched to me and stood inches from my face. Exasperated, I took his arm and guided him to the Rigg's Bank automatic teller booth. Swiping my card at its entrance, I opened the door and pulled him inside. The door clicked closed behind us. Exposed to the world in our glass aquarium, my body stiffened even as my flesh thawed. I removed my fogged glasses and swiped a tear away.

"Oh Augie," Rupert said and kissed my cheek. "How could you even think such a thing?"

"I'm so lost and confused," I said, my voice cracking. "What did I do?"

"It was me. It's what I did."

A spear of jealousy pierced my heart, and I braced myself for the worst. "Don't tell me who. I don't want to know."

He pressed his eyes closed. "I'm positive."

The silence in the booth was deafening, and the heat blowing in my face rendered me breathless. My bag weighed heavy on my shoulders. I wanted to run, but my legs refused to obey my commands. "Rupert. Rupert," I repeated. I couldn't make myself say anything else.

"I'm going to lose you," Rupert muttered so softly I strained to hear him.

Just then, a cab pulled up to the curb. Two passengers leapt out the back doors and bounded down the Metro escalator. I grabbed the door of the booth and shouted, "Taxi! Taxi!" Squeezing Rupert's hand, I dragged him to the idling cab. "Home! We're going home."

We didn't speak on the short ride to his Georgetown house. He stared out the window and bolted out of the cab right as it rolled to a stop. I settled with the cabbie and ran into the house. He'd left the door open.

"Rupert." I clicked on the living room light, and he collapsed into a heap on the overstuffed chesterfield sofa. "Rupert." I tossed my coat into a bucket chair and wrapped my arms around him, but he squirmed out of my embrace.

"Don't touch me, Augie. I'm filthy and disgusting and—"

"Are you certain of the test results?"

"They only have you come in if it's bad news."

Rupert was right. I knew he was right, but I was in shock. Outwardly, I was calm, but inside, Camille Saint-Saens' "Danse Macabre" streamed through every fiber of my being. I felt that the need to talk him down was imperative. "Let's not assume anything until you speak with Dr. George." I removed his coat and tossed it on top of mine. "A nice, steamy bath. You need a nice hot bath."

A short while later, as I sat on the edge of the tub, sponging Rupert's back as he sipped his snifter of brandy, I scanned his naked body for any tell-tell signs of lesions. Not even razor rash or a papercut was visible.

Try though I might to repel them, a band of banshees bombarded my head. Images of deathbeds, weeping widows, coffins, and graves taunted me, and I bit my lip to keep my emotions in check. I would not—could not—upset Rupert by panicking over the paranoid propaganda punching pinpricks in my common sense. How could I have tested negative while he'd tested positive? I dabbed at my perspiring temple. I wanted to run, dash out naked into the cold, let the bitter frost nip at my exposed bits. *Please, God. Please. Let this all be a bad dream we'll soon wake from.*

Tension imbued my soul, swelling in volume and velocity. What would Polly have done in my situation? Or Jo March? Or Florence Nightingale? Or Grandma Flora?

Heroically, Dad's first thought was of Mama whenever she slipped from grace. I needed to follow his example and take charge. No matter what his domestic crime may have been, no matter if he'd cheated with another guy or contracted it from his ex-lover long before me, the responsibility to comfort him sat on my shoulders.

"Here." I handed him his prescription Clonazepam as I dried his wet hair with a towel. Dr. George had prescribed it for those stressful periods Rupert often faced at work or when sleep eluded him. Without resistance, he popped the pill into his mouth and washed it down with the last of the warm brandy. Crawling under the covers beside him, I held him in my arms.

Egotistically, I relished being in charge for a change. Within the span of a first date, the roles of two gay men are determined, and Rupert had definitely taken charge when we first went out together. Twenty years older and comfortable with himself, he was a man of means, and that generally lent itself to dominance in any relationship. Of course, there were countless combinations of dominance, but in our case, Rupert was an alpha male who automatically rose in stature around me. Call it a daddy complex, but although I had mostly dated men who were my contemporaries or younger, I welcomed Rupert's direction. His doting and spoiling me made me feel special in a way I'd never experienced. And no matter how long we'd be together, I'd always be his bright, young thing.

"We'll not jump to conclusions," I said resolutely as I pulled the comforter up to his chin. "We'll know better after your appointment tomorrow."

Drowsy-eyed, he looked up at me and grinned that cock-eyed grin that got me right here every time. "It's not like we're due at Reagan's swearing-in ceremony," he quipped.

A million questions circled in my head, but not wishing to exacerbate the situation, I swallowed my pride. From his earlier reaction, I surmised he had not been as faithful as I had assumed. Perhaps I wasn't prepared to discuss his possible infidelity, but at that moment I wished for another of my favorite things: a night of cuddling under the covers with the man I loved while Old Man Winter waged war on Mother Nature outside the frozen, ice-edged windowpanes. His frigid exhale promiscuously pummeled the hairless branches of the black birch, which in turn clawed frantically at its invisible torturer.

As the night inched toward midnight, I sat still in the last stretch of that awful day. Rupert's rhythmic breathing against my chest was a lullaby sweeter than anything penned by Brahms. The day, ripe with machinations abundantly perplexing, would require processing that, in that moment, I hadn't the spirit to face. Slumping into the down-filled pillows, I let them engulf me and surrendered to sleep.

CHAPTER 25

FOR SENTIMENTAL REASONS

If yesterday had been a time of tribulation, then the day that followed dawned with ample trepidation as we attempted to proceed as usual. However, the usual could not be sustained while Rupert waited for the firing squad to riddle him with the truth. Buried in his test results was the past I knew little of, a period in his life that was hunting him down. No matter how deep into the forest we ran, there was no escaping the burden weighing heavy on our hearts.

Rupert's playground in the seventies had been New York's gay underground, resplendent with bawdy back-alley bars, the extravagant Studio 54, and a plethora of other nightclubs where anything and everything was on the menu. Early on in our relationship, he'd admitted that he hadn't been a saint, but neither had I. However, he had laughed off my confession of sleeping with twelve men.

My heart fluttered when the taxi beeped for him. "I wish I could be there for you."

"No. It's something I need to face alone." Rupert was like that. I knew he felt that he was shielding me from the worst part of a tragedy, but his pride perpetuated my fear, which was already scaling the charts.

"If only you didn't have that breakfast meeting at the Ritz," I complained.

"But I do, Augie. I do."

His doctor's appointment wasn't until three, which meant we'd have to wait a dismal, drawn-out eight hours for any news.

I kissed the back of his neck when he reached for the door-knob.

"I love you, August Applegate. More than life itself."

My tears flowed freely as I watched the cab pull away.

I said nothing to Evangeline when we met in the Oak Room for lunch.

Evangeline played with the salt and pepper shaker on the table. "Certainly Dr. George has your test results by now?"

I never lied to her. She was my best friend and confidant. We shared everything. "I'm fine."

"Thank God!" Cocking her head, she puckered her mouth. "I'm thrilled about your revelation, but there's something else you're keeping from me. Something's rotten in the state of Denmark."

"That's the tuna casserole at table five you smell."

"Ha. Ha. You can't fool me, August Applegate."

"It's nothing. Don't dig a hole next to a dry well. There's nothing there. Nothing. I just realized I forgot to fill out a requisition form for the props I ordered from Bernhard. You know how Midge Mudge is about requisitions."

"Midge Mudge, my patootie. You're not worried about Rupert's bookkeeper. She'd take a bullet for you."

"Crime has increased in downtown."

She patted my hand, her tennis bracelet tickling my wrist. "You can tell me anything." A shadow passed through her eyes, and her smile drifted south as she studied my face as intensely as she had Singer Sargent's "Lady in Black" in the National Gallery the last time we went. "Rupert?" she ventured. "What did he do?"

I jerked my hand free and pushed my vegetable plate between us. "You don't know what you don't know, and you know squat. So don't assume you're the expert on everything."

"Jesus Christ, Augie!" Evangeline scooted her chair out and stood. Her hands gripping the table, she bent near and whispered. "Fuck you!" Then she grabbed her Kelly bag off the table and marched out of the restaurant.

I stared at the chair she'd vacated, the trace of her Chanel N°5 circling the table, and my chest tightened. I was the keeper of secrets, stuck between my loyalty to a friend and my allegiance to my lover. Rupert's truth was not mine to tell.

In a daze, I returned to my semi-private sanctuary at work and closed the glass door behind me. Unable to focus on the paperwork stacked on my desk, I grabbed my coat and dashed down the back corridor to avoid any probing eyes from the glass-fronted offices lining the main hall.

My footsteps echoed down the dank, dark, dingy back stairwell that reeked of piss and semen as I descended the nine stories to the street.

I pushed the door open and smacked face-first into the wall of cold. Instantly, the chill nibbled on my hands, but I didn't bother with gloves. I wanted to feel something, the harsher the better. Blinded by my tears, I walked down F Street, toward the blazing sunlight. Past Woodward & Lothrop department store, past Garfinkle's department store I hustled, quickening my step with each block I covered. Defying Rupert's request that I not accompany him to his appointment, I headed toward Dr. George's office.

Fool! Fool! You little fool! Rupert had been a Godsend when I needed him most. No fuss. No bother. Just love. He'd offered a love that I'd never known existed. I hadn't trusted it at first. Where was the acrimony I'd witnessed in my parent's marriage? Pete's expectations—and my unwillingness to meet them—had saturated me in his disappointment, disrupting the natural pull of our planetary orbits. Without dabbling in difficulty, could love exist? No pain, no gain?

I was jolted back to the present when I entered Lafayette Square Park. *Damn.* Reagan's second inauguration had completely slipped my mind. Because they had canceled the outside events due to the unbearable cold, the bleachers constructed for the parade sat abandoned. Washington was put on hold, a ghost town on Inauguration weekend.

On the sidewalk, several hundred bundled revelers had braved the weather to prove their support for their commander-in-chief. Red-faced and hoarse, they shouted "Prouder! Stronger! Better! America's back! Making America Great Again."

In Lafayette Park, Democratic supporters waved signs spelling out the horrors of reality. "President Straw Man!" "Social Injustice Kills!" "A Harvest of Shame!" and "Silence = Death!" were held high on banners as the protesters sang their slogans loud and clear, their words hanging frozen in the air.

Injustice, Shame, and *Silence = Death* looped like a newsreel in my head as the Democratic group began marching around the square. Though I longed to, I didn't follow. I checked my watch as I shuffled past Decatur House. A quarter to three. Dr. George's office was two blocks away. *Fuck it!* I didn't care if Rupert ripped me limb from limb, I was not going to let him face this alone. He'd been there for me countless times. I owed it to him to be there whether he wanted me there or not. No one truly walks alone in a relationship.

Rupert's cologne hung in the air as I entered the waiting room. The receptionist was on the phone, but he winked at me and nodded to Rupert at the far end of the room.

"Augie," he said when he spotted me. "I didn't want you here."

I dropped into the seat next to him. "Yes, you do. You're just too pig-headed to admit it." I took his hand.

"You're cold as ice," he said and rubbed my hand between his hands.

"Cold hands, warm heart." I wrapped my arm around his shoulder, and he leaned his head against mine.

"Rupert Seigel," Dr. George's beefcake nurse called from the doorway.

Rupert and I stared at each other before he broke away and stood.

"Oh no, buddy," I said as I followed him through the door to the office. "We're in this together."

"Dr. George's running a tad behind," the nurse, Franco, informed us as he recorded Rupert's vitals. "Can I get you a magazine to pass the time?" We both shook our heads, and he sidestepped out the door, his non-regulation snakeskin cowboy boots thumping against the sterile, white-tiled floor.

"Puss in boots," I jested when I heard his footsteps fade away down the hall.

Rupert, perched on the exam table, his eyes wide and his cheeks blushed rose, laughed heartily at my lame joke. "Thanks. I needed that."

"You're so adorable when you blush." I gripped his ankle. "It should be against the law to be as handsome as my man."

Rupert grinned. "'My man,'" he sang, "'I love him so.'"

I made a face and laughed.

"I know. I'm not ready for prime time."

I took his hand and squeezed it tenderly. "Whatever we hear, I'm here to stay, Rupert Seigel. No if, ands, or buts. You're mine and . . . Oh, Rupert why did it take this situation to make me come to my senses?"

He looked at me, perplexed.

"You are the love of my life."

He took my face in his hands and kissed me passionately.

"I can come back if this isn't a convenient time," Dr. George said from the doorway.

"Dr. George," I sputtered. "We didn't hear you . . . see you . . ."

"August Applegate," the doctor said, patting me on the back. "I wish more of my patients had your zest for life."

The door clicked closed behind him, sealing us off from the rest of the world. Rattling above our heads, a heating grate I hadn't noticed hummed to life and flapped in my ear. I wanted to rip it off its loose screws and toss it out the window. The day of reckoning was at hand, leaving me light-headed and queasy. I couldn't breathe.

Rupert, the consummate professional, adjusted his noncommittal mask to brace himself for the big reveal.

Dr. George sat behind his desk, engrossed in the papers on the clipboard. "John called you yesterday. I hope he didn't upset you, but—"

"But what?" I blurted out.

"Augie," Rupert said and squeezed my hand.

"Sorry. So sorry." I slumped back into my chair, pink and petrified by my behavior.

"Rupert," Dr. George said, smoothing the papers against the clipboard. "John was so busy making appointments yesterday, he forgot to give you your test results."

Oh Jesus Christ! What is this? A torture chamber?

Rupert sat tall on the exam table, his legs dangling limp and motionless. That's when the revelation struck me. "John delivers good news over the phone," I whispered in the airless room.

"You mean I . . . ?" Rupert stumbled, a smile spreading across his face. "I'm not?"

Dr. George shook his head. "You are not positive for the

AIDS virus, I am happy to say, but . . ." The conjunction that had rolled out of the doctor's mouth echoed in my head. *But? But? But what?*

Rupert's smile flattened, and deep, long furrows stretched across his brow. "What is it, Dr. George? Why all the drama if I'm not positive? I can handle anything, but AIDS . . . who would stand a chance against that mass murderer?"

"I'm sending you to Dr. Bart at Georgetown; he's a neurologist from the Mayo Clinic with an excellent reputation. We're lucky to get him."

"Whatever for?" Rupert looked worried, and if my cool, collected man looked worried, then he must have been terrified.

"His partner, Dr. Milton, is a top-notch neuroradiologist. You couldn't be in better hands. As long as we keep close tabs on the suspected aneurysm . . ."

"Aneurism!" Rupert spit the word out like moonshine.

"Yes—apologies, the results of your scan came back. There's a spot on the left side of your brain. It's small and manageable."

I stood and slid my hand around his waist. "Oh Rupert," I whispered in his ear. "Everything will be fine."

"My headaches have subsided," Rupert said meekly.

"August is right, Rupert. It's only a suspicion of a problem at this point."

· • ·

The elevator stopped on every other floor on its descent from the twelfth. In the mirrored doors, I was able to peek at Rupert's stoic face. His chin was held high, his posture was perfect, and his flawless complexion was radiant. It seemed inconceivable that he could be sick. He appeared the picture of health. *It's nothing. A shadow on an X-ray means squat.* Once they'd run the proper tests and discovered nothing, we'd celebrate. We could take that Mediterranean cruise he'd been obsessively talking about, or Venice, perhaps. Wherever he wished to go, I was game for.

"What did I tell you, Rupert! It's not the end of the world after all." I said as we crossed the grand lobby of the medical building. "We'll simply play it safe until we know more."

"Play it safe!" he growled, pushing hard on the carousel

door—and wedging me in the frame in the process. "Augie! Augie!" he yelped, scampering to right the wrong.

"Hey, mister!" a bison of a woman yelled when the door finally spun free and rapped her rear. "What the hell!" She rubbed her tush as she hobbled away.

"Oh, Augie," Rupert said, pulling me free from the revolving pie slice. "I panicked. I panicked, and I took it out on you."

"I'm an easy target." I adjusted my beret and walked ahead.

"Augie!" I heard the click of his leather heels quicken before I felt his hand on my shoulder. "Augie! Stop! Please."

I didn't stop until I reached the intersection crossing Farragut Square. Rupert gripped my arm, but I jerked it away and stepped into the crosswalk when the light changed. When he tugged on my sleeve, I planted my feet on the angled sidewalk. "Rupert," I said sternly. "Don't ever, ever feel that you have the right to take your bullshit out on me. I love you, but you've been an absolute—"

"Asshole, Augie. I'm an asshole." He slumped onto a bench as the throngs of office workers, released from their cubbies at the end of a long week, scurried by, eager to catch a train, bus, or cab to whisk them away to warmth. A cold blast of wind rushed me from the front, and I realized I hadn't bothered to button my coat. "Let me," Rupert said, his voice dry and sheepish. "I'm a damn fool." He fastened the toggle buttons of my knee-length cashmere and touched his gloved hand to my face. Soft and mellow and rich with the scent of him, the supple leather of his glove enticed my forgiving nature to the surface. "I've never been sick a day in my life."

"Now you'll know what we mere mortals suffer," I said, my teeth chattering. Hooking my arm into the crux of his, I pleaded, "Can we discuss this at home?"

"Home. You called it home."

Rupert tapped the window of a cab parked on the curb. "Cafe La Ruche," he instructed as we climbed into the back.

• • •

"Dr. George scheduled Rupert's exam with the specialists this Thursday," I told Evangeline over lunch the following Monday. "I'm so sorry about the other day, but I . . ."

"You could have said something," she complained. "I would never have mentioned it to Rupert."

I toyed with a wedge of tomato on my plate. "Right."

"Pollyannas can be such bitches."

I tittered. "Loose lips . . ."

"Okay! You win, but in this case I truly wouldn't have."

"You're so cute when you're riled. Just as defensive as you were in elementary school."

"A lifetime ago." She wiped a dribble of mayo off her chin. "I'm thrilled you guys are both negative, but damn. What a shocker about Rupert. Who would've thunk it?"

"Did you ever once think we'd end up here, in DC? Working at Wallis & Fitch Haden?"

She shook her head and dusted the potato chip crumbs off the top of her BLT. "Oh, I forgot to tell you. Kaiden wants to get together soon. He's anxious to catch up on the last twenty years."

"Except for the whisps of gray at his temples, he looks the same."

"Hot," she sighed. "So hot."

"I hadn't noticed."

"Sure, August Applegate. And I'm Mother Teresa."

•●•

Buzz! Buzz! Buzz! I hit the "off" button on the alarm. Rupert had surprised me with tickets to *Out of Africa* the night before, and it being a lengthy epic, we hadn't gotten home till after midnight. "Oh. Oh." I massaged my stiff neck. Since it was one of the "must see" movies of the year, the eight o'clock show had been jammed, and we'd ended up in the first row, craning our necks to watch another extraordinary performance by Meryl Streep.

The rushing water in the shower stopped abruptly, and Rupert's off-key bass reverberated off the tiled bath. "'You've got to give a little . . . take a little and sometimes sing the blues a little,'" he sang. "'That's the story of, that's the glory of love, love, love. That's the story of, that's the glory of love.'"

I loved watching Rupert dress. For someone who had never lifted a barbell or run a block, he had a wonderful, taut body. His muscular legs, bulging thighs, rounded buttocks, bulbous chest, and tiny waist defied his forty-seven years. Talk about good genes! It was especially delightful when he'd walk around the bedroom in the buff, horn-rimmed glasses perched on his nose, reading the newspaper. His particular combination of brains, brawn, and talent was the ultimate aphrodisiac for me.

"I could come to the doctor with you, but we're installing the first set of spring windows today," I said. "What time is your appointment?"

Rupert mussed my hair and kissed my neck as I lathered my face in preparation for my morning shave. "I'll be back in time for the eleven o'clock meeting."

"Everyone's raving about the store's first-floor reno. Can't wait until the final phase is behind us."

He pinched my naked rump, and I jumped. "Hey!"

"You mentioned a behind," he said, and snickered at his own joke as he left the room.

Rupert was on his second cup of coffee by the time I thumped down the backstairs to the kitchen. "What's this?" I said, amazed by the lovely breakfast he'd prepared for us. "We're going to be late."

"Well, I'll handle that Simon Legree of a VP of yours. I'll give him what's what."

I took his hand, and he pulled me onto his lap.

"Someone's up early today," I mused.

Rupert stuck his hand in my robe, and I was a goner.

Over breakfast, I daydreamed about the day before and the windows I was anxious for Rupert to see. He'd given me cart blanche to do whatever I wished with the spring windows. Using the store's campaign "Busting Out All Over," my staff and I had created a salute to English Gardens. From topiary boxwood that stretched through five windows, to the vine-draped, Greek-columned follies in the windows flanking the main entrance, to a trickling fountain I had built in the corner window, every inch of the props and background was saturated in spring flowers and lush greenery. I was thrilled with the results of our exquisite work and couldn't wait to open them for Rupert's preview.

"What are you doing?" I said, looking up from my reheated bacon and Gruyere cheese omelet as Rupert shuffled around my chair, reaching for the radio. He turned up the volume, and no sooner did I recognize the song—Stephanie Mills's nineteen-eighty hit, "Never Knew Love Like This Before"—than he'd pulled me to my feet. It had been the song playing on the pop station the first night we'd made love.

Rupert let go briefly and lit the candles, just as he'd done that first night, and taking me in his arms again, we danced around the living room until we bumped into the glass coffee table, toppling the candelabrum. Both of us laughing over our lilting lunacy, we rushed to catch the candles before they hit the carpet. I handed one to Rupert, its flame unhindered by its fall from grace, and he righted the rest in their holders. "An eternal flame."

"Excuse me," I said, feigning being insulted. "What did you call me?"

··•··

I had no sooner hung my coat up in my office than I was dashing down to the bank of fashion windows. Every detail had to be checked and rechecked. Nothing less than perfection would do, because I wanted Rupert to be proud of me, my team, and the job we'd done. "Hand me the glue gun and hold the back of the wig," I instructed Maggie, one of my assistants.

We were packing up our tools when I heard someone clomping through the access corridor to the window. "Mr. Seigel?" I called out, hoping to slow him down before our excess was neatly tucked away.

"Augie! Augie!" Evangeline yelled. There was a pitch of panic in her voice that sent a rippling wave of melancholy through me, and I shivered.

"Evangeline?"

She gripped the side of a flat and poked her head in. "Augie," she said, tears streaming down her face.

"Oh no. Pete."

With the same intensity, she looked at Maggie. No words were exchanged between them, but Maggie understood and shimmed past a mannequin grouping and out of the window. When she heard the stockroom door click shut, Evangeline took my hand and led me to the entrance of the anteroom. "Augie," she said, "I don't know how to tell you this."

"I wanted to be there for Pete, but I didn't know he was . . ."

Evangeline gently pressed her fingers to my lips. "It's not Pete."

She sat on a crate and tugged on my sleeve for me to join her, but I resisted and broke away. "You're scaring me."

"Rupert." She brushed a tear from her cheek and cleared her throat. "Rupert . . . Oh, Augie, I don't know how to tell you this, but Rupert . . ."

"Rupert?"

Her laser-focused stare, too penetrating, too fearfully intense, rattled me to my core. I stepped back, bumping into the raised window platform. Immediately, she jumped up and took hold of my jacket lapels. "For Christ's sake, Augie, this is hard enough as it is."

"Get off me, Vange." I gripped her wrists, but she held tight.

"Augie."

Rupert's face flashed in my head, and my soul jiggled like gelatin on a bumpy rolling cart. "No. I don't want to know."

Releasing me, she stood over me, a compassionate expression on her face. "It happened so fast. There was nothing anyone could do."

"It's so hot in here," I said and loosened my tie.

"Augie, look at me," she pleaded, but I couldn't look her in the eye. "He's gone, Augie. Rupert is gone."

The word "gone" smacked me square between the eyes. My skull vibrated like a struck bell.

"He's dead."

I pressed my eyes closed. My chin quivered. My teeth chattered. I pulled my jacket snugly around myself. Cold and hot. I was hot and cold at the same time.

A distant, muffled sound, someone mumbled, "He's dead," and the frigid phrase, thorny and prickly, scratched the message into my cranium. A dissident note scraped across my scalp, and a taut violin string screeched between my ears. I covered them with my palms. However, the sound was inside my head, not outside, and the futile act only amplified the volume.

From the balls of my feet to the tip of my head, a heavy numbness settled in, forcing me down. I tried to stand, but my legs buckled, and I fell to my knees. Kneeling before me, Evangeline wrapped her arms around my shoulders. Her wet face against mine, her breath puffed warm against my throbbing neck.

"I need to see him. I need to be with him," I said, but she didn't budge. "Did you talk to him? Did you see him? How did he look? Where did they take him? Where did it happen?" Violently, my hands began to shake. "Vange! Vange!" I gasped for air. Inches from her nose, I could smell the dull floral fragrance of her foundation. As exaggerated as Maleficent, her rubbery red lips and magnified mascara-ringed eyes terrified me. I pushed out of her embrace. "No! You're lying, and I hate liars!"

Evangeline shook me, but when I couldn't stop mumbling, she slapped my face, and I burst into tears. "Augie. Augie, I'm so sorry." She hugged me tightly again, and I couldn't breathe. "Rupert had an aneurism. It ruptured in the ambulance on the way to GW Hospital."

"Stop! Stop! Stop lying!" I shouted. The room went fuzzy, and the florescent light broke into fragmented, blurry-edged shapes of color. Lightheaded and giddy, I swayed back and forth on the heels of my shoes before stumbling into the window. "I must finish this before Rupert sees it." Each step I took was hard labor, as if my legs weighed five hundred pounds each. I heard a *snap* and a mannequin toppled over, cracking her head on an iron urn. Another step. Another *snap*, and a second mannequin crashed against a trellis and landed face-first in the trickling fountain.

Startled by a hand on my shoulder, I spun around, accidently slapping Evangeline against the wall. A sharp pain, no bigger than a pinprick, electrified every vein in my body, like the Rockefeller Christmas tree when the switch is flicked. The magnified sound of the water gossiping in my ear was not invitingly serene, as it had been moments ago, but instead rumbled louder than Niagara Falls.

"Augie!" Evangeline yelled.

Blinded by a bright spotlight, I squinted to get a better view of her, but the glare was punishing, and I retreated to the anteroom. "Oh!" I clasped my neck. Like wriggling, writhing worms in a hot skillet, the veins in my neck pulsed. My scalp tightened. Rivulets of tears dripped off the tip of my nose, their salty residue an unwelcome sting to my parched lips.

Brushing fake cherry blossoms off her wool skirt, Evangeline marched to the stockroom door, but as soon as she swung it open, I shot past. I heard the thump of her body bouncing off the wall as I barreled through the stockroom and out the employee's entrance.

The moment my feet hit the sidewalk, I was flying. Pumping my legs higher and higher, I ran down G Street. Sprinting past Farragut Square and Dupont Circle, I headed for Q Street and the Buffalo Bridge.

The air was icy against my face, the cold flooding my lungs painful. My curls bounced higher and higher, slapping my sweaty brow. There she stood waiting for me. Home. Our house's windows sparkled like Cinderella's Castle at Disneyland in the brilliant sunshine, and I pounded my wingtips harder against the cement, skittering over ice patches but by some miracle remaining upright.

"Fuck!" I yelled when I searched my pockets for the key I'd left in the office. After peeping into the living room and dining room windows, I remembered the one hidden under a brick in the garden. Pawing through five inches of snow, I shoved at the brick until it loosened.

The key shook in my hands as I stabbed at the keyhole several times before successfully unlocking the door. The kitchen, still warm from our morning fry-up, sat still as a tomb. "Rupert!" I didn't find him reading the *New Yorker* in his favorite chair in the living room. He was not in the master suite or his study on the third floor. Not in the wine cellar. Not in the garage or the mother-in-law apartment out back.

Dead. The word danced in my head as I climbed the stairs to our bedroom. Turning down the comforter, I slid, damp and fully dressed, under the covers. I rolled my head into Rupert's pillow and buried my face in its puffy down. His pillowcase smelled like him, just as it always had. "Rupert. Rupert." His lingering scent was exceptionally rich and sweet that day. Pulling the covers over my head, alone in the dark, I clutched his pillow and wept until my face throbbed and sleep whisked me away to Never-Never Land.

CHAPTER 26

MY OWN MORNING

Except for the luminescent streak from the nightlight cutting through the crack in the bathroom door, I woke to a darkened room. Silhouetted against the chalky shadow, a blackened figure sat slumped forward in the slipper chair by the cold marble fireplace.

"Rupert," I whispered, but he didn't budge. Uncomfortably aligned, his head bobbed from side to side. A book he'd evidently been reading lay open next to his shoe. "Rupert," I said with authority.

He stirred slightly, sending the long flap of his bangs swinging gently before his face. I adored the gentle sweep of Rupert's hair curling around his ears. The visible streaks of gray at his temples were a comforting sight.

"Rupert!"

He tugged on his earlobe and yawned. "August," he said, his voice thick with sleep. "You're awake."

Why does he sound so strange? "Why didn't you come to bed?"

The figure's face moved into the light, and I saw that it was not my Rupert. "Kaiden." The nightmare ensnaring me in its lasso was real and not simply the bad dream I'd prayed for it to be. My head buzzed, and I dry-heaved over the side of the bed. Kaiden snatched the leather wastebasket from beside the nightstand and shoved it under my chin.

"August," Kaiden said, setting the wastebasket aside as he studied my face as intensely as Evangeline had, making me terribly self-conscious in my own skin. "I'm so very sorry for your loss."

"Where's Evangeline?" I wrapped the comforter around me. "It's freezing in here."

"She ran home to change for work. She called me at Whitman-Walker yesterday, and I came as soon as I could. I'm here to help. When you're ready, we'll talk."

"Where's Rupert?" I asked, my sharp tone spearing his friendly smile.

"He's gone." Kaiden sounded sincere and looked concerned, but I wanted to be alone. "Evangeline broke the news to you. Do you remember?" he asked.

It's true? It's true? I shook my head, hoping to shake the doom and gloom engulfing me like a London fog.

"She's worried about you. Everyone's worried about you. *I'm* worried about you, Augie."

I leaned back into the shadows and rubbed my burning eyes. My mouth was Sahara-dry, and my mood was darkening by the moment. Kaiden kept jabbering on, talking bullshit. Talking death and dying and asking me if I understood the crap he was spewing. I did and I didn't; I cared, and I didn't give a flying fuck, and my insides were scorched, and my head was pounding, and I just wanted him to shut up and leave me alone.

"You're talking rubbish." I shot him a withering look. "I'm tired. I want to sleep." Rambunctious as an unbridled stallion, my scattered recollections bucked against their harnessed confinement. I couldn't focus. On him. On the room. On the Goddamn voices yelling in my head. "Where's Rupert?"

I felt the plush shag beneath my feet and realized I must have stepped out of bed.

"August," Kaiden whispered, the same way Dad did when Mama was climbing out of a well she'd tumbled into. "I'm here. Lean on me."

I pressed my palms over my ears. "Stop!" *Fly.* I wanted to fly. I wanted to smash the ice-encrusted window and fly away. I wanted to migrate to the warmth of the Key West or South Beach. To meet Rupert at the Fountain Bleu Hotel and order champagne and watch the sun set. "The sunset. The sunset!" I reached for the lamp, my fingers dancing under its shade, feeling for the switch. "It's so dark, and I can't find him."

Grabbing my shoulders, Kaiden eased me down onto the

bed and ran his fingers through my matted ginger mop. I opened my mouth to speak, but not a word surfaced. Strange animalistic sounds escaped from my gullet, and I heaved again, certain I'd toss my cookies, but no evidence of sick emerged.

"Let it go," he instructed. "Let it go." My ear pressed against his chest, as warm as a hot water bottle, I closed my eyes and moaned. "I've got you . . ." His voice was a hot toddy of a manly timbre, as smooth as shantung silk and as soothing as a dip in his family's heated pool on the days when temperatures had plummeted below zero.

I laid powerless on the silk duvet stained with tears. It felt like shards of glass were piercing the back of my eyeballs, so I pressed my fingers into their sockets until that pain was more unbearably intense than the throbbing of bleeding corneas. The heavens rumbled, a searing streak of lightning electrified the crescent moon, and my body shook uncontrollably.

The faint complaint from the seams of Kaiden's starched white shirt cut through the silence when I grasped his collar tightly. Holding on to him for dear life, I watched in horror as the ceiling cracked down the middle and the floorboards separated beneath the bed. I think I even screamed.

"Augie," Kaiden whispered as the room tilted askew.

"I . . . I . . ." I stammered. "I don't know . . . I can't . . ."

His face came into focus, and I was fifteen again, holding my breath under water.

"You're safe with me, August. I taught you how to swim. You trusted me then. Please trust me now."

Both bright and dim, shimmering silver to dull iron black, the seconds crammed into my head, tighter than the surprises stuffed into a piñata, were a jumbled mess of imagined secrets and harsh facts. *Recollections? Hallucinations?* Had I crossed the line of sanity?

Evangeline's face popped into my head, the phrase, "He's gone" sliding over her matte red lips.

Kaiden's embrace was firm but gentle. My hand had fit ideally into his palm when I was fifteen. He'd cupped the back of my hands, and together we'd pantomimed various strokes until I was fluent in each. *Funny.* He smelled of a familiar patchouli-laced cologne. No matter what cologne he wore, powder, or hair gel, nothing could erase the remembered smell of a chlorinated pool from his hide. He had been my sunshine on many a grim day. He'd rescued me from a fear Mama had paralyzed me with and introduced me to one of the great loves of my life. Swimming was an escape to an aquatic paradise, and I needed an escape. Gliding through liquid salvation would surely strip away the stain of suffering searing my skin.

To mourn is to suffer, and to suffer is to die by a million minuscule cuts. Slowly. Methodically. And so, to keep from drowning in my grief, I needed an equally mechanized schedule. The Potomac River. The Chesapeake Bay. Rehoboth Beach. Water. I needed a body of water. "The Y has an indoor pool," I said aloud.

"Of course," Kaiden chuckled softly. "As soon as you're able."

Tucked under his arm, secure that he wouldn't let me fall, I loosened the strap on my heart an inch at a time, fearful of the demons I'd barricaded in the nave. One sniff of freedom, and the multi-headed creatures stirred. Digging, dragging, and stabbing, they clawed their way up from the depths. The agony was severe, and the rupture was acute, and I wept long and hard into Kaiden's sweater-vest.

•••

The night before the funeral, I drifted in and out of sleep. It was an endless night of waiting for a dawn I was reluctant to face. Blindfolded, I walked the plank of uncertainty. When I did drift into a state resembling sleep, I was plagued by phantoms prancing about in the dark. Shapeshifting shadows sailed around my bed, some sweeping over or through me, all ugly, nagging apparitions. Beelzebub had wrung beauty from my life, and I was angry that the almighty had permitted such a vengeful act of violence.

Only one dream slithered through the slash of a second. Only one dream offered relief from the rack of mourning. Though it left me heartbroken and lonely, there was only one dream that delivered solace.

"Augie," Rupert whispered in my ear, so low I could barely hear him. "Augie." He laid his head on the pillow next to mine, and I thawed when he took my face in his hands. Kissing the tip of my ear, he murmured again, "Augie."

I rolled into his arms, and he held me for a while as I faded in and out of rooms we'd crossed together long ago. "Think of me, and I'll be here. I am always near," he assured me.

Then, slick as a porpoise, he popped out of bed. *How odd*. In the four years I'd known him, I'd never once seen Rupert in tennis whites. He sat on the edge of the bed and laughed at my expression. "I know," he said. "We wear a lot of this up there."

•●•

"What do you need, Mr. March?" Mama asked the next morning. Perfectly coifed and as steady as a sedated circus lion, she appeared her level-headed best. The family had hit the road before dawn to be there when I awoke alone in Rupert's house. Unexpectedly, Rupert's brother, Asher, and his sister-in-law—whom I'd never laid eyes on before and had only briefly made small talk with on the phone when Rupert insisted I say hello—had surprised me with an unannounced visit soon after my own family's arrival.

Eva, Asher's wife, was no bullshitter; she shot straight from the hip. "I'm sorry, August, but Rupert made no provisions nor legacy for you in his will, and unfortunately . . ."

"So," Asher interjected, "we need to close the house and ready it for the market. Spring is right around the corner."

"Cold as a tin brasier in Alaska," Aunt Tootie commented after they'd left for the synagogue.

"It's not mine. It was almost mine, but . . ."

"Oh, Augie." Aunt Tootie slid a plate of her pumpkin-spiced flapjacks under my nose. In her world, there was no problem, tiny or tremendous, that couldn't be eased with a good helping of comfort food. "Be thankful for what you had. Four glorious years is better than the four pretty good months I had with . . . well, you didn't know him, anyway."

"For you, Augie." April, in the caring manner she typically reserved for the underprivileged children she devoted countless hours of her volunteer time to, handed me an omelet the size of Ohio.

I looked at my family sitting in Rupert's bedroom. "I don't know what to say. Thanks, you, guys. This means the world to me."

Dad lowered the shade to cut the blinding light pouring through the east set of windows. "Better?"

"It's a shame. This is a beautiful house." Mama sat down beside me on the bed, and her scent wafted under my nose. YSL's Opium perfume was the fragrance she chose when even-keeled and confident. The cadence of her voice was unmistakably gentle, as soft as the patter of a ladybug crossing a spring twig.

An illogical mishmash of minutes and hours, time sat beside me, a bedraggled beast I needed to make peace with. There was no past or future, only a state of perpetual perdition. With all eyes on me, I was as exposed as a plucked chicken on a conveyor belt headed for a steam bath. Unless I was on stage and in control of my every gesture, unwanted attention embarrassed me. I rarely displayed my vulnerability to my family, and the thought of them seeing me defeated and down was nearly impossible to bear. They knew and expected the strong and willful Pollyanna. I was comfortable being their Pollyanna gay. The beaten boy of a man before them I feared was a baffling sight.

"Unless you truly need me to be there, I'd rather not attend the service," Mama said. "I'd be uncomfortable and out of place." It wasn't clear what she was fretting over most: being the rock to lean on or being the clumsy Episcopalian amongst a plethora of Jews. I'd never heard her speak ill of any Jewish person. She adored Bella Abzug, Betty Freidan, and Gloria Steinem. Perhaps her pride got in the way. To stumble over unaccustomed rituals might have been devastating for Mama, who always preferred to be in control. *Heavens!* It seemed we had more in common than I wished.

How could I argue with such a gift of love? None in my family would attend the service, but they wanted to be there for me. They did what they knew to be right. As with accepting my being gay, they didn't ask for permission to visit, they simply packed up the car at four a.m. and headed north to DC. Together, we decided that I would meet Evangeline outside the temple with the rest of the Wallis & Fitch Haden employees.

"We couldn't let you wake up alone," Aunt Tootie explained. "No one should face a day like this alone."

"Tomorrow I'll wake up in my own morning . . . alone."

They'd met Rupert only three times, but as with everyone who'd had the privilege, they'd fallen under his spell before the introductions were complete. That was how special he was. He was a rare breed of mortal. He was as faithful as Lassie and as right as rain. His being taken was unforgivable, and I doubted I'd ever trust God again. I couldn't bring myself to attempt Pollyanna's Glad Game. What was there to be glad about?

"Once you've had the best . . ." Mama said, trailing off. The rest of the pack had carried my few belongings from Rupert's house to the trunk of my old, faithful 'Stang. She stood before the hall mirror, tidying her hair. "Now we both have a taste of the misery your gay friends go through when they lose their special someone to the plague."

"Rupert and I were petrified he was going to be positive. Little did we know . . ."

"You never know, Mr. March. Anything can happen. The worst often happens when you least expect it." Her face was drawn and boney. "Do you remember my special friend, Augie?" I didn't reply because I couldn't bear the thought of them together. "He went like that." She snapped her fingers. "Massive heart attack on a train in Switzerland. Have no idea why the fool was in Switzerland. Come to think of it, he had longed to go back to visit the places he never got a chance to see when he was stationed on the border during the war."

I gazed out the window at Dad and April arranging my belongings in the trunk. *Does he know about Mama?*

"His wife called to tell me. Figured I was a friend of his from high school or something." She paused for a moment, waiting for me to respond. "We have a lot in common, Mr. March. Neither one of us got to say goodbye."

April opened the door and poked her head inside, the rush of frigid air rustling the stack of Rupert's unread *New York Times* piled high in their basket.

• • •

"Come on, Augie," April said. "I'll drop you at the synagogue while they scrub all traces of you from Rupert's house."

I held on to the dash as she backed out of the drive. Our house—his house, their house—diminished in size with every roll of the tires. I watched it shrink to a dollhouse through the side mirror of April's aged Pacer, and my heart skipped a beat.

Awkward as April may have been, she patted my leg, and I touched her hand. We were trying. I'd planted a Pollyanna seed in her that had evidently taken root and prayed it would bear fruit. *Prayer.* Old habits die hard. Since God had forsaken me, I would need to search elsewhere for solace. "You and Mama aren't at each other's throats today."

"It's not perfect," she said, referring to hers and Mama's relationship. "When I told her I loved her, as you suggested, it did open doors. I mean . . . Well, to be honest, I was a little disappointed. I thought she'd hug me, shower me with apologies, and smother me with kisses, like I do with my children. My expectations were in the stratosphere. I don't even know if I mean it when I say it. Not certain she does either. But like Louise Hay, I figure if we keep repeating it, eventually we'll believe it."

"It's a start, April," I said. "I'm proud of you."

"You need to be brave when you return to work, Augie. It's going to be . . . well, I can't imagine."

"To walk into his office, to sit at his conference table, to . . ." I swallowed the knot in my throat. "God deliver me." *God.* I glanced quickly at a gentleman on the street; at first glance, he was the spitting image of Rupert, but upon closer inspection, the resemblance faded quickly. "I was so different with Rupert. Another person."

"I can relate to that," she said, "Away from the family, I'm a totally different person. Myself."

"It strikes me as demonic that he could be here one moment, vital and alive, and the next . . . gone. All his knowledge, his talent, his kindness, his love. Where does it all go? Does the universe suck it up and spit it back into the atmosphere to be dispensed among the newborns? Will he become a butterfly come spring? A budding cherry tree? Is he part of the great heavenly hive of souls waiting, reviewing their past, and contemplating their future post-human? Will he walk with me? Whisper in my ear? Is he here now?"

April kept her eyes on the road and waited a good minute before she responded. "I met your fella only but a few times, but I liked him. You definitely chose better than me."

"That was my Rupert. He was the best part of me."

"Evangeline was supposedly in the room when it happened."

"I know. I know." *Jesus Christ! I knew her transformation was too good to last. Don't go there. Please! Don't go there, April.* But of course she did.

"She said that he was conducting a meeting when he clutched his head and excused himself." *Holy hell! That's April.* Accidently salting the wound when she's attempting to comfort someone is her gift that just keeps giving. I was expecting as much from her as she was from Mama. "She said he walked into the ambulance and collapsed. Discreet to the end."

My eyes welled up, and I sniffled. "Sorry. So sorry."

April popped the glove compartment door. "Kleenex."

I yanked a handful out and dabbed my face. "I wish we'd had more time. I wish I could have said goodbye."

"Goodbyes are never enough. You torture yourself over what you should have said but didn't, or what you did say but shouldn't have."

"To think that I was nine floors below in the window when it happened." I blew my nose. "To think he died in the ambulance around the corner from where I was working. It's . . . ungodly." Tears were dripping off my chin at this point. "My face throbs from crying. I think I'm all cried out, and then I think of him, and I'm . . ."

"Why worry? No need to apologize. Aren't all gays emotional? Breakdowns are expected of women and gays."

I made a face.

"Well," she said and raised an eyebrow. "What do want from a basketball coach?"

• • •

"This is it." Dad dropped a box of books on the kitchen counter of my compact studio apartment in the Envoy. Glancing down the hall to make certain we were alone, he asked sincerely, "Have I been a good father?"

I stared into his searching brown eyes, framed by his graying brows, and nearly burst into tears as I recalled the wonderful playhouse he'd built me, the way he'd searched high and low to find Kaiden, the perfect swim coach, and the million times he'd taken the blows and insults from Mama to spare April and me. He deserved a Nobel Peace Prize.

I wrapped my arms around him and kissed his stubbled cheek. "The best. You're the best father a boy could have."

I had been born into a circus of misfits. I had sailed with a ship of fools into the future and harbored on the bank of the Potomac River. Occasionally, I'd grabbed the brass ring and succeeded where destiny led me. I knew that someday, when I was eighty or ninety years old, blind and bald and bewildered by age, I would look back on my days with Rupert as some of the happiest days of my life. I was in love with a man who'd loved me just as I was, warts and all. "The love of my life," I wrote on the back of my favorite photo of him before I sealed the back of the silver frame.

CHAPTER 27

OPEN A NEW WINDOW

"I envied your life," I admitted to Kaiden during one of our afternoon coffees. "Everyone in Rockridge wanted to be you, live in your house, swim in your pool."

"Your dad was one of the few locals to actually talk to me."

"Can't believe he had the guts to ask you to teach me how to swim."

"Even we knew about your mother. Our housekeeper shared all the town gossip whether we wanted to hear it or not."

"Your housekeeper was scary. When she opened the door that first day Dad dropped me off, she looked at me as if I was trailer trash."

"She should know," Kaiden grinned. "Mother let her park her double-wide in a clearing in our woods."

"Your woods," I said without thinking. "Odd that someone can own a wood."

"With our very own witch hazel," he said, laughing.

We always ordered the same things. He was mad for hot chocolate and oatmeal raisin cookies. I'd never met a caramel latte or Scottish shortbread I could resist.

"What's it like, being you?" I asked.

In mid-slurp, Kaiden coughed and spewed the hot brew over himself.

"Sorry," I said and handed him my napkin. "Are you okay?"

His eyes watering, he smiled to assure me he was fine. It was that lovely smile that roped me into his confidence. Except for confessing he was the first guy I'd ever masturbated over, I'd shared nearly every detail of my personal life with him—and yet he remained a mystery to me.

Evangeline had warned me about therapists. "They can be the most fucked up people in the world. Easier to solve someone else's problems. Far simpler to rescue than reveal."

He dipped the napkin into his glass of water and dabbed it at the brown stains on his beige cashmere cardigan. "I grew up in a life of privilege. But on the flip side of the coin, I do know what it is to struggle."

He was a professional listener. I supposed I should have been thrilled with the free sessions. I was thankful; truly, I was. But . . . *Oh, hell.* I was fooling myself in thinking I really knew him because he rarely shared anything too deep or too personal about himself. We talked about real-life things but dodged subjects neither of us cared to discuss. I never asked who he was dating or what his marriage had been like, and he never volunteered any details that might have exposed the depth of the man he was.

Only occasionally did he share fragments of his past. His stories about his year in Liberia serving with the Peace Corps were most intriguing. I hung on every word, hoping to discover more about the man I knew so little of. "Most Americans have no idea of Liberians' everyday struggle to survive and educate themselves. But the students," he'd said excitedly, "so polite. I taught them English, and they opened my eyes to love. Beauty is everywhere for the taking. It can bloom in Central Park or a hut in Monrovia. My eyes have been opened, and I can never see America the same way again."

I sat there at the corner table of Kramerbooks & Afterwords Café, spellbound by the man who'd so patiently taught me the backstroke. Now, step by step, one coffee date at a time, he waltzed me through the world's languishing landscape, down the corridor of clemency, and onto the ridge of reliance.

"Mama said your son goes to the Haverford School in Pennsylvania."

"He does," Kaiden responded. "My ex-wife moved there with her husband."

"Pete's son goes there as well," I added.

"They're in the same year. Small world." Kaiden gazed out the window at the still December dark. The old, bare trees lining the

street stood like naughty children, their arms raised high to intim-
idate the competition from the small fruit trees on the opposite
side of the block. "There's no escaping comparison," he muttered.

"You must miss your little boy."

"Every second of every day," he said.

"Do you know his stepfather?"

"He's my cousin from Newport. We summered together."

"Oh," I said, "I didn't know."

He fiddled with the plaid wool scarf draped over the empty
chair between us. "He's better off there. Really. He has a good
home and two parents who love him."

"And, I'm certain, a wonderful father who spoils him rotten."

Kaiden smiled. I liked when he smiled. Not at all as carefree
and bright as in his youth, his handsome face, when at rest, soaked
up the shadows, painting his portrait in a somber hue. However,
when he smiled, he was a young man again, ready to take on the
world.

"It was a matter of honesty," he said. "I couldn't commit to
her as I should, and she knew it. I was the only one capable of
saving us from myself."

I touched his arm. "You're the therapist, but I'm a good listener if you need to bend an ear."

Kaiden cocked his head and stared at me. "Augie, you're one
in a million." He grinned and played with his napkin. Although his
waist wasn't as trim as it had been when I was sixteen, he looked
very much the same. Oh, he had a little paunch, ever so tiny, like
his father, whom I'd seen pictures of. Actually, I found it rather appealing in a "daddy" sort of way. It made him more approachable,
more human, and less godlike. At twenty-nine, I myself was but a
few steps away from inheriting my own dad's paunch.

The nine months since Rupert's death had dragged on like a
decade. It felt extremely odd to have sexual thoughts about anyone, let alone a friend who had helped me through the most difficult period of my life. Our off-the-record therapy sessions had
bloomed into a friendship neither of us had expected. We had
more in common than I would have guessed.

Kaiden loved musical theatre, so on Friday nights, we'd meet
Evangeline at Friends Piano Bar and belt out showtunes till they
bolted the door. We ran together on Saturday mornings and met

at the Y on Wednesday evenings to swim. His paunch, I noticed, was the only visible addition to his otherwise stellar physique. He was even a Merchant-Ivory fan. I'd be embarrassed to share how many times we'd rented *A Room with a View*.

•●•

"Kaiden likes you. He really likes you," Evangeline claimed.

"He doesn't like me that way," I replied. "He's straight, for God's sake. Besides, it's too soon to date anyone." I shook the notion out of my head. "I'm not ready."

"It's been over a year, Augie," she said. "Christ! Farley didn't wait a month to hook up with Walter after Simon succumbed."

"That's Farley." I looked away from her. She'd climbed on her high horse and was swinging her lasso in my direction, determined to tame my fear. "I'd feel like I was cheating on Rupert."

"Being alone is the last thing Rupert would have wanted for you. He loved you—ridiculously. Good God! Augie, you know he disliked being put on a pedestal, and that's precisely what you're doing. He was an amazing person none of us will ever forget. But Augie—"

"I don't want to hear it!" I snapped.

"You're scared," Evangeline said, crossing her arms over her chest. "Chicken-shit, Augie. Chicken-shit."

"You don't understand."

"You're right. I don't."

"It's hard when . . . when . . ."

"When you've had the best, I know. But you're still young. Even Jackie Kennedy hung up her widow's weeds and joined the human race again."

"I'm done with romance. I . . . I . . . ." I gripped the edge of the table. "I want to . . . Do you know how many times a day I talk myself off the ledge? More than I care to admit. I have a dreadful track record with men. Look at Pete."

"You certainly can't blame yourself for that."

"If he hadn't met me—"

"It would have been someone else. You're not that special. You're not the angel of death."

"I'm such a coward," I whispered, my voice tight with emotion. "I should have moved in . . . should have told Rupert I loved him sooner. I was cruel. I'm a cruel person."

Evangeline brushed a tear from my chin. "Cruel people do not worry about being cruel."

CHAPTER 28

GOODNIGHT MY SOMEONE

Every Sunday after Mass, I'd hop on the Red Line to NIH. It was a two-fold exercise. It got me out of the house, where otherwise I'd toss and turn in bed, my linens moist with tears recalling those idyllic Sundays with Rupert. Plus, it allotted me time with Pete that we both dearly needed.

"This isn't penance for whatever you think you did to Rupert, is it?" Pete asked flat-out once. "I refuse to play second fiddle to God."

"I want to spend time with you," I replied sincerely. "It's better to give than receive. Truly, it is."

Pete's hard stare softened, and he touched my face. "Oh Polly, my Polly, my Pollyanna gay. You'll never change."

"None of that talk, Mr. Pace." I opened the copy of *Great Expectations* on his nightstand. "Shall I pick up where I left Pip and Estella last week?"

"Pip just noticed Estella meeting that cad, Bentley." Pete rearranged the bundle of tubes he'd accidently sat on when I adjusted his pillows. "Funny, I never met your hubby. Farley told me he was quite the catch."

"'Catch'?" That phrase made my blood boil. "You make it sound like I dressed in safari khakis and headed for the jungle." I was angry and short-tempered and couldn't understand why. "Funny, I've never met your wife." He shot me a look. I'd crossed the line and knew it. "Sorry. I'm a bit worse for wear today."

"Get over it, Polly. Perfection is highly overrated."

I forced a grin. "How does your son like Haverford? Did you know Kaiden's son is in the same class?"

There was a beep, and Pete flipped the switch on a portable machine whose function I wasn't certain of. The lights on its front panel flickered and dimmed before settling into its normal pattern. "I barely know my boy. My parents made sure of that. I pray he's not gay, because they'll repeat the hellish cycle of torment they imposed on me."

"They haven't mellowed with age?"

"If anything, they've hardened." Pete opened the drawer of the nightstand and withdrew a small, framed picture of a young boy with a woman I assumed was his mother. "My son," he said and handed me the picture.

"Wow! The spitting image of you!" I tapped on the glass over the woman. "Arabella?"

Pete nodded. "She's their captive. Actually, I feel sorry for her. Being a psychoanalyst, I thought she'd outsmart them. 'Money. Money. Money.' As the old song goes."

"She's beautiful."

"That she is." He had a faraway look in his eyes. "In my way, I loved her."

I set the photo on the window ledge where he could see it. "This okay?"

He nodded. "It's admirable the way you help out with the guys in this ward. Roland adores you. You know he's one of NIH's top infectious disease nurses? Every time he sees me, he raves, 'He's one in a million.'"

I didn't feel like one in a million. I felt like one of the millions of loved ones whose prayers had been scattered to the wind, buried with a lover, or burned in a crematorium alongside a friend. No matter how brilliantly the sun shone, it couldn't strip the murky gray veil draped over the city. A smidge of melancholia stained every smile, and a pang of guilt accompanied every laugh. Where was God? Over and over I cursed the heavens, only to be stricken with remorse five minutes later. Loneliness crippled me and hopelessness dragged me down to the darkest part of myself, where anger resided. Already unable to cope with my own loss, I found that the AIDS epidemic only multiplied my pain and resentment.

There was no escaping the plague. It subverted the toughest men and feasted on the vulnerable. Doom trailed one victim to the next. Death, quiet as a bobcat's paw on granite, waited in stairways and corridors, eager to pounce. In less than a month, Pete had gone from having a home-care nurse checking on him daily to residing in NIH's infectious disease ward.

"I volunteered to be a guinea pig for the latest protocol available," Pete said. "It's the best possible care. The best available, Augie."

He was riddled with sores and bruises, marked with scars, his puncture wounds from PICC lines patched over. He was probably as uncomfortable as he looked. Bent-backed and stoop-shouldered, his withered six-four frame and remaining ounces of flesh weighed a measly one-forty.

Evangeline and Farley struggled to look at him when they came to visit.

"He's thirty-two and looks like a ninety-year-old man," Evangeline would murmur whenever Pete dozed off.

"Simon committed suicide when he knew the end was near," Farley often reminded us, referring to his lover who'd passed, "and he was nowhere near this bad."

"But he's still here," I would say. "As long as he has breath in his body, I will visit and pretend he's still the most beautiful man I've ever seen. I owe him that much." Whenever I looked at Pete, I focused on his stunning eyes. Like Grandma Flora's mischievous orbs that defied the decay they were encased in, Pete's eyes flashed with excitement upon hearing a familiar voice or seeing a dear friend cross the threshold of his room.

It was a blessing that the NIH staff handled his care with proficiency and unbiased urgency. Under their roof, he would never be left to die on the street like Chancy's friend, Thelma.

• • •

"August," Roland, the nurse, called from the front desk as I entered the ward several days after Pete's birthday. "Pete fell asleep on his glasses and snapped an arm off the frame."

"I can drop them by the optical department for him," I said. "What floor is it on?"

"August, we have no optical department."

"What?" I exclaimed. "You can't be serious. NIH is a city unto itself. It has everything."

"Except an optical department." Roland lowered his voice. "He's actually well enough to go out today."

"It's a crazy world we live in. One day the Grim Reaper is pacing the hallway, and the next everything is hunky-dory."

"Well." Roland gathered his stethoscope. "Not quite hunky-dory. Never hunky-dory again."

I went into Pete's room to help him get dressed for our outing.

"Thanks, Augie," he said as I struggled to belt his suede leather Gucci pants without snagging a PICC line or crushing a tube. "Tighter."

"I'll need to punch a new hole," I said. "We're at the end of the line."

While Pete's glasses were being repaired at Mazza Gallerie's optical store, I walked Pete to Neiman Marcus to buy underwear.

"I can do this," Pete yapped. "Don't fawn over me. It's bad enough as it is."

"Fine," I said and let go of his arm. "I'm behind you if you need me." Why on Earth he cared what the snooty sales-queens thought of him was beyond me—especially since he'd slept with most of them.

Like a bodyguard, I walked a few paces behind him. My heart jumped when he paused at the La Prairie counter to button his baggy silk blazer that only a few years before had clung to his muscular physique like a second skin.

Two over-coifed women, their hair piled high and their jeweled choker necklaces advantageously positioned to mask their aging necks, had the nerve to grimace when they noticed Pete's made-up face.

No matter how hard Pete tried to mask his battle scars, he wound up resembling a beardless Abe Lincoln during the final year of the Civil War. So, with his herringbone cap tilted at a rakish angle to hide his major bald spots, and his mile-long Quintin Crisp-esque Burberry scarf tossed casually over his shoulder, he held his head high and shuffled toward the men's department. Two of the three salesmen, who used to smother Rupert with attention, wound their way around the fixtures like pythons late for dinner upon recognizing Pete and slithered into the stockroom.

"Excuse me," I said, nabbing the last man standing. "My friend has a few purchases to make. I'm sure you'd be more than delighted to assist." I shot him a withering look that, if he'd been nude, would have castrated him.

Pete dozed off in the passenger's seat of his silver-cloud Maserati on the drive back to NIH's campus. I had never been comfortable driving his nor Rupert's expensive cars, but circumstance trumped my apprehension. Since I no longer had access to Rupert's garage, and Mama and Dad were visiting me more often, I had put the 'Stang out to pasture for the time being.

Passing through NIH's front gates, I slowed to glance at the meticulously manicured grounds, the sprawling lawn and rolling vistas that formed the backdrop for most of mine and Pete's Sunday outings. "Our bench," I muttered, noting our favorite spot under the shaggy weeping willow, which was sporting early lime-green buds. The decorative cabbages and petunias had been cleared to make room for a huge beds of tulip fingers bursting through the mulch and bobble-headed daffodils, their intense yellow commanding the attention of the many windblown visitors eager to shed their winter wraps.

Pete's head bobbed forward, his glasses sitting precariously on his nostrils. He was seconds away from taking the plunge before I righted him in his seat.

"Au-au-gee," he muttered, a string of slobber connecting his lips to the spittle soaking into the lapel of his jacket.

Though I'd never wish to trade places with him, there were aspects of Pete's life I envied. Having seen so little of the world, I was more than a tad jealous of his privileged lifestyle. He had traveled extensively, much as Evangeline had, and was far more sophisticated than I was. He'd walked the avenues and streets of cities I'd only read about. He'd partied in Paris and Madrid. He'd enjoyed ravenous affairs in Rome and Venice and swam naked in Switzerland's Lake Lucerne. Pete had climbed Mount Olympus in Greece and gambled his way through Monte Carlo.

I'd crossed the pond twice with Farley. We had always planned to see more of the historic sights, but both times had barely made it out of London's West End.

"Who needs ancient ruins," Farley would say, "or spas, or monumental palaces when we can see the world from our comfy seats in the third row?"

Inside, Roland wheeled Pete back to his room. Together, we

undressed him and helped him onto the bed. When the nurse was called away for an emergency, I filled a plastic tub with warm water, soaped a cloth, and gently washed Pete's wrinkled hide, careful not to disturb the tubes and splints Roland had secured to whatever apparatus was sustaining him. There wasn't an inch of him not stained by medical equipment. He was a conduit for chemicals. The body I cleansed was no longer the breathtaking beauty that excited a mass of men willing to surrender to his carnal charms. His naked splendor had been savagely pummeled into a decaying slab of meat.

His Italian flannel pajamas hung like a caftan from his scrawny shoulders. As numb as I had become to the depredations of the plague, to wash, to touch, to smell the corrosion of Pete's once smooth, supple, sun-kissed skin that tasted sweet as butter—it haunted me day and night. If Rupert had had to go, I was thankful that it had been quick and nothing like the dragged-out horror the cursed men of the infectious disease ward suffered through.

"Stay until I fall asleep, Augie," Pete said in a raspy voice that broke into a coughing fit. For nearly a half an hour, I sat holding his hand. Except for the orchestra of machines, gasping, cawing, beeping, and buzzing, the room was eerily still. I watched his chest rise and fall, then hesitate. I was always relieved when it rose and fell again. I wiped the drool that dripped from his chin onto the white sheets, and an immense weight settled on my shoulders. It was difficult to breathe in that sterile environment.

A chamber of horror, the room had become a nightmare that was impossible to shake. I closed my eyes, hoping to vanquish the evil overpowering my Pete. But when I opened them, nothing had changed. The curse raged on victoriously, eating away at my friend, my champion, my first great love. *Please God! Please.* I pleaded for him to spare my Pete. I offered years from my life in exchange. His suffering was pure madness. I was willing to believe, if only God would produce one miracle.

Wake up! Pete, wake up! Please! I wanted him to rise like Sleeping Beauty from her years of captive slumber and return to the living, as exquisite as the day before he fell under that sinister spell. I would have settled for a fraction of the man I once knew. But there was no bargaining with God. There was no market of exchange in heaven, only acceptance and truth-bearing that drained every ounce of hope from my humble prayers. What were prayers for if not salvation? Evidently God had abandoned the act of repentance in the Dark Ages. *Jesus Christ! We are living in an age of darkness!*

"Polly. My Polly," Pete said, his eyes flickering open and rolling back in his head.

I slid my arm under his neck and stretched out on the bed beside him. "I'm here. Your Polly is here." I could hear Kaiden's voice in my head saying the same thing, that night I was twisted by agony and grief.

Pete's head sank into the pillow, and his forehead tapped against mine. "We could be so happy."

"Oh, Pete," I whispered, unable to muster more than that inadequate response.

He laid his icy palm on my cheek. "Do you love me?" His thin, gnarled fingers searched my face for any sign of emotion. "I love you. I love you, August Applegate. You are the only one."

I held him close and caressed his head. Lumpy, balding, and damp, it felt like a stone after an early spring rain. I kissed that rock and kissed that rock until we both dozed off to sleep.

• • •

"August," Roland said as he gently shook me awake. "He's out for the night."

In a daze, I extracted myself from Pete's hospital bed and headed toward the exit. I stood in the elevator well, still as a morgue. The sound of the cables pulling and dropping the cars from floor to floor broke the oppressive quiet momentarily. As I waited, I glanced out the darkening window at a grove of elms embedded on the slope of a grassy ravine. Unprotected from the elements, their knobbly black branches stood strong against Mother Nature, silhouetted in front of the blood-orange horizon. Their century-old roots, reaching to the center of the earth for nourishment, adjusted to the tug and pull of nature, bowing to her emphatic whims, and surviving to bud again. Where was God in all this? Was he the breath of life that I needed to bow to?

The elevator door dinged open, and I stepped into the car.

"Which floor?" a perky young intern asked.

I stared at the man, whose lovely face beamed with hope. "Sorry," I said. Robotically, I stepped back onto the landing. I felt a *whoosh* of cold air when the elevator doors closed behind me. As if in a trance, I walked back to the infectious disease ward and past the nurses' station.

Pete was standing outside his door. I walked into his open arms and hugged him tightly.

"I love you," I whispered in his ear.

We stood embracing one another for several minutes. We spoke not another word. There was nothing left to say.

Be there. Just be there for them, my team leader from Whitman-Walker had advised. The writing was on the wall. After all the marches and meetings; all the newspaper articles; the many petitions to Congress; and letters to the White House from parents who had just buried their only son, partners who'd lost the love of their lives, and friends who no longer had a best friend to call—after all that, the federal government had still taken no action. There would be no tax-funded research or presidential address to the nation from the Oval Office. *Justice is fucking blind!*

I jumped into the shower as soon as I got home to scrub the putrid smell of the hospital off me.

The telephone rang as I was getting out of the tub, but I knew it was either Farley or Evangeline checking in. I was too tired to talk, so I let it ring.

•●•

The next morning, the phone and the alarm clock exploded simultaneously. I threw the covers off and hit the clock button before answering the phone.

"Hello," Farley said in a Lauren Bacall bass. "He's gone. Pete's gone."

I dropped the phone and clutched the windowsill.

"August!" Farley yelled from the receiver banging against the nightstand. "August!"

Unlatching the window, I did what the reverent Danish do when a loved one passes. Although it was only symbolic since I wasn't in his actual room, I opened the window to allow Pete's soul to pass through. Outside, bright and insistent, sunshine washed over the lime-green grass of the Malcom X Park across the street. The lilting swish of the sycamores whispered to the bold bark of the giant oak on the verge of budding. A gentle breeze tickled the flapping leaves of the hydrangea bush drinking in the light.

I heard the click of the phone and realized that Farley had hung up. I'd call him back later. At that moment, I needed to be alone with Pete. He was ever-present in the beauty of the day, and I wished to wallow a while longer in his arms.

Nestled in branches of a dogwood, a bluebird had returned to her nest with a beak full of nourishment for her excited chicks. One by one, she poked her long beak into her babes' open mouths. Feeding her offspring struck me as the greatest gift she could possibly give them. The sight reduced me to tears.

Pete had given me hope when I'd doubted its existence. He'd offered encouragement when I'd needed it most. He'd introduced me to the joy of sensual pleasure, and he'd loved me. He'd changed my life for the better. His branding me a Pollyanna had not reduced me to the joke Farley took joy in but had instead opened the door to the man I was. Where was God on that morning bursting with spring marvels? He was everywhere.

CHAPTER 29

STOP THE WORLD

Not wishing to draw attention to the fact that their one and only son had passed from the dreaded "gay plague," Pete's parents had decided to forgo any service or memorial. He was immediately cremated, and his ashes were flown to his uncle's house on the Mediterranean to be scattered in a garden that had meant zilch to him.

The day Pete had entered the hospital, his mother had zipped down to DC to liquidate his assets. Pete had said little about either of his parents. No family photos had sat on his baby grand. No oil portraits of the Pakingtons or the Paces had greeted visitors in his entrance hall. Except for the occasional joke at his "old man's" expense, it was his mother, Adela Alexandra, who'd received the bulk of his abhorrence. "Mother is a Goddamn Phyllis Schlafly supporter! Need I say more?"

Although we had no body to bury or ashes to toss into the wind, Farley, Evangeline, and I dined at Pete's favorite restaurant in DC, Le Maison Blanche. Pete had prearranged our evening. The maître d' recognized Evangeline from the many times she'd dined there with Pete. "I'm so sorry for your loss, ma cher. Monsieur Pete was a lovely man, outside and in."

Farley, who'd been packing on the pounds since his ultra-thin days in college, had filled out and then out again. Ringed in mascara to accentuate his aqua-blue lenses, he batted his lashes at the mesmerizingly handsome Monsieur Jacque, who fished-eyed him with displeasure as he walked away.

"Sorry, sister," Evangeline whispered in his ear. "He bats for my team."

"Whatever in the hell that means," Farley fired back. "One week you're the sapphic-sister-woman-thing deluxe, and the following week you've ditched your inner diesel dyke and emerged from your lair as a singular, sensational, Mary-Tyler-Moore-esque career woman extraordinaire pining for motherhood and the ideal Mr. Grant."

Evangeline immediately launched her battleship into choppy seas. "So tell me, oh drag impresario de la Fairfield Follies, who are you pretending to be this week in that melon-colored mock turtleneck and crimson velvet peplum jack? Little Eddie from Grey Gardens or Lilly Pulitzer on acid?"

"Please, darling," Farley said as he slid into the black leather banket, "whichever 'she' I choose to be will rate top billing."

"On way-way-way-off-off Broadway," she teased, "otherwise known as Staten Island."

Farley had taken to wearing bracelets again, only this time it wasn't a stack of horse bits, but three elegant David Yurman pieces. "All I have to do is snap my fingers." He snapped his fingers, and his two smaller bracelets dinged against the impressive gold cuff. Ding. Ding.

"And what?" Evangeline asked. "The three men of the apocalypse appear?" She adjusted the clip in her hair. "With your appetite for orgies, three sturdy studs may come in handy."

"Funny," the waiter said and handed a menu to Evangeline. "A comedy act, non?"

"Non," I said and opened a menu.

Farley folded his menu and handed it to a waiter. "I'll have a bucket of ice," he said, pointing to Evangeline, "on her head."

Evangeline whipped her lighter out of her handbag and clicked it in Farley's face. "A little fire, scarecrow?"

"Enough!" I whispered. "Have you two lost your marbles?"

Evangeline stuffed her lighter back into her Judith Lieber clutch, which was shaped like a Buddha, and held it up. "See how much I love you, Farley dear? I carry you everywhere I go."

"Ha! Ha! Ha!" he brayed. "As with fashion designers, no one invests in a skinny drag queen these days. 'Oh, look at her,' they say. 'I'll bet that skinny bitch has it.' So the latest fad is hardcore weightlifting. My coach at the Y—"

"You have a coach, and you look like that?" Scanning him from head to toe, she sneered.

Farley looked her up and down in return. "You're getting a bit broad across the beam yourself, dear."

"Wait a minute!" I raised my hand. "This paranoia is crazy. Male designers have ruled the runway ever since Worth invented couture."

Evangeline scrunched up her nose as if she'd just gotten a whiff of something rotten. "After Willy Smith and Perry Ellis kicked the bucket from AIDS, the asshole money men who've made millions off clever queens for decades now invest primarily in women designers."

"How did this happen?"

"How?" Farley polished his silver cuff with his napkin. "I'm surprised you can see anything through that thick widow's veil you sport."

"Crass jackass," Evangeline said to Farley and turned to me as she fished a powder-blue envelope from her bag and tossed it on the table. "Surprise. Surprise."

Scrawled across the front of it in Pete's flamboyant cursive was my name. "What's this?"

"You'll see." She stirred the ice cubes in her glass of water with her finger. "Best save it for the privacy of your own home. Wouldn't want you blubbering on the beef bourguignon."

"Fine." I slipped it into my jacket pocket.

She glared at me. "'Fine'? You're not curious?"

"I'll open mine if you two open yours."

"Too late. I was way too curious to wait." She grinned mischievously.

Farley held out his hand.

"Sorry, Miss Good N. Plenty," said Evangeline, "the cupboard was bare."

"What do you mean?" he snarled.

"Pete gave these to me eons ago with strict instructions to not open them until he was gone."

Farley stared at Evangeline. "I get passed over when he passes on? What kind of sick joke is that? Pete screwed me over when he was alive, and now he's fucked me over from the grave."

"Surely he left a blue envelope for Farley," I protested.

She shook her head. "Sorry. Don't blame me. I'm the messenger."

"Well, ain't that grand." Farley was seething. When he unbuttoned his cinch-waisted jacket, his tummy settled over his belt. The moment I turned my attention to Evangeline, he lunged across the table at me and snatched the envelope from my suit pocket.

"Hey!" I snatched it back from his greedy fingers. "That's personal."

"So's the insult he flipped in my face."

I snapped a starched damask napkin, draped it over my lap, and changed the subject. "Rupert brought me here for my twenty-seventh birthday. The food is divine."

"Yeah?" Farley slathered butter onto a wedge of French bread. "I wouldn't know."

Evangeline tapped her ring against her glass. "Actions speak louder than any words he might have penned."

"I take it you're referring to his gesture of friendship," Farley said, unbridled anger seeping out of his every pore.

"Nice ring," I said, taking Evangeline's hand and moving it closer to the candle. "Is that a real sapphire?"

"From my blue envelope. Pete was a lot of things but cheap he wasn't."

"No. Never. Our darling Pete, cheap?" Farley swiped butter off his chin. "Never! He was generous to everyone," he said, then muttered, "except me."

"Oh, Farley Fairfield," I said.

"Oh, Princess Pollyanna." He crossed his arms over his chest and pouted. "I shall hate him till the day I kick the bucket."

"Not that I'm pointing fingers," Evangeline said as she pointed her finger directly at him, "But bitter, bitchy, and vindictive, that's who you are."

Damn. They were spoiling everything with their bickering. Evangeline was determined to rub salt in Farley's wound, and Farley was acting worse than Mama when she'd been slighted. Understandably, he was crushed by Pete's gesture. God knows, I would have been.

"What's your favorite on the menu?" I asked Evangeline, hoping again to steer the conversation into safe waters.

"I hear 'skewered *ami*' is highly recommended by certain clientele."

Evangeline stared at the empty fourth chair at our table. "How is it he's not here?"

A hush sat in the middle of the table, and our personal thoughts divided momentarily. That is, until Farley fractured the tranquility. "Perhaps he would be if a certain princess had spread her legs and not her sainted wings." Farley brushed crumbs off the front of his jacket. "Murderer." Then, resting his elbows on the table, he clasped his hands. "Oh, but she didn't miss the eleven o'clock number. In Pollyanna rushed for the big finish."

Evangeline's lovely face could turn ugly on a dime when she was angry. "Where were you, Fairfield?"

He nodded toward me. "Where was Princess Polly for years?"

Someone nearby was wearing atrociously overbearing Giorgio Beverly Hills perfume that walloped even the putrid crap smell of the blood sausage from a neighboring table. The intense mix of jasmine, gardenia, and orchid topped with patchouli oil never failed to strike a blinding headache behind my eyes. And now, with two of my oldest friends squabbling like fishwives, my empty stomach roiled with contempt for my disrespectful cohorts. "I apologized to him. I had waited too long, and I regret it. However, he forgave me. If he could, certainly you can. Besides, Farley Fairfield, you haven't an inkling of what transpired between us. You weren't there!"

I suppose our voices drifted above the acceptable level of conversational speech, because the maître d' shot me a look of consternation. I smiled politely to deflect his repressed wrath.

"How was it that you were there that last day?" Farley demanded of me.

Evangeline shrugged the padded shoulders of her black Norma Kamali dress that made her look like a linebacker for the Chicago Bears.

"We had a standing date every Sunday," I said. "Wait." I massaged my temples, my head tightening with each waft of Giorgio that bombarded my sinus cavities. "Why am I defending myself to you? You hadn't bothered to visit for three months."

Farley screwed up his face. "I couldn't get away. The show must go on, and when—"

"You're afraid to stare the truth in the face."

"Grifter," he whispered.

"Excuse me?"

"You heard me."

Evangeline leaned into him. "If anyone grifted Pete," she said, sitting up tall, "it was an orange-haired viper from Greenwich Village."

Farley's nostrils flared. "I never—"

"Never paid him back?" I took a sip of water as he struggled to regain his composure. "Hit a nerve . . . darling?"

"He was an investor in my theatre!"

"Sure," I said and rolled my eyes. "Keep telling yourself that, and maybe you'll start believing it . . . like we don't."

The candle burning inches beneath Farley's face highlighted the sharp angles of his pointy chin and peaked nose. His beady eyes had sunk in their sockets, and his menacing plucked eyebrows arched higher than a Gothic cathedral window.

"You whined, kicked, and screamed," I went on, "played the victim until Pete shelled out the cash. Strike while the iron is hot, and your prey's life is in disarray. Right, Farley? People babble a lot when they're overmedicated, and Pete was fueled by more foreign fluids than an oil tanker." I tossed my napkin on the table. "You had no intention of paying him back. You simply ran the clock out." I detested this side of me, but I'd had it up to *here* with Farley's bullshit.

"I was there," Evangeline stepped up to the plate. "I was there when he returned from Dr. George's. I held his hand and mopped his brow when he was too frightened to ask for help, to frightened tell anyone he was sick."

"I called you that last weekend, Farley, because Pete wanted to talk to you," I said, though I'd told him as much when I'd left a voicemail. "Had you bothered to return my call, perhaps you'd have gotten a blue envelope too."

"It was you," Farley snarled. "It was always you. Since the first day he met you. It was all about Augie Applegate. His Pollyanna. The love of his life."

"Jesus Christ. Jealous. You're still jealous after all these years."

"I tried to tell him."

"Tell him what?"

Farley hemmed and hawed. "You . . . you led him on."

Frustration clasped the back of my neck. "If I had pursued

a relationship with Pete, you'd have ripped yourself in two like Rumpelstiltskin." I pushed back from the table and looked Farley square in the eye. "Goodnight, farewell, and God damn you." I could have banged his pointed head against the banket for ruining the evening. "Thanks for destroying Pete's gift."

I started to stand, but he dug his nails into the top of my hand to stop me.

"Go ahead," I said. "Draw blood if it makes you happy. Nothing you can do or say could hurt any worse than your betrayal."

He jerked his hand away, but I didn't rub my pulsing paw. I preferred the pain. I welcomed the pain. It counterbalanced my aching heart.

"Fly away, Peter Pan." Farley ran his forked tongue over his lips. "That's what you always do when it gets a little heated in the kitchen."

"The last time we rumbled in a kitchen was at 315 Benevolent Street. Remember?"

"I remember smearing Crisco on your sour puss."

"It was butter, butthead," I corrected him.

"So imperial."

"That's rich coming from you, Countess."

"Baroness!" he yelped, sending the maître d' scampering around the corner. Farley made a funny face as if he'd accidently farted, and the poor man skittered back to his desk.

"Please." Evangeline patted my hand. "The evening's young."

I gestured toward Farley. "And his nasty attitude is old."

"But you're ageless, dear," Farley growled. "Pollyanna never grows old, and she never grows up, and you, August Applegate, always land in a sugar daddy's lap."

My blood simmering to a boil, I couldn't look at him. "Give me one good reason why I should dine with the demon barber of Fleet Street," I told Evangeline.

Farley was the speared bull in the ring. "Because you owe it to me, Pollyanna."

I leaned back into my chair. The waiter, his eyes darting left and right, cautiously slid a basket of bread onto the table and side-stepped behind the screened bussing station. "I've been around you for five minutes, and I'm as crabby, vulgar, petty, and spiteful as you, you spoiled, arrogant, narcissistic, pessimistic bully." I held my balled fist under the table for fear it might plow uncontrollably into his kisser. "You couldn't face the sight of him during those last months. That's why you never came. You didn't have the stomach for it."

"Augie." Her face fierce with anger, Evangeline started in on me, but I raised my hand, and she dropped whatever fevered missive she had stored in her cannon.

"No! Enough."

In dealing with Mama's many moods, I'd learned at a young age to go calm when her rage escalated. Perhaps it was Dad's steadiness under fire or Grandma Flora's civility during a crisis—or, as I preferred to think, my instinct to fly high when another swung low—that typically inspired me to float cool in a heated situation.

But I needed, for my own sake, to ease out of the detrimental situation dragging me under. I could hear Pollyanna's voice in my head (or rather, the voice of Haley Mills, who'd played her in the Disney adaptation): "Just breathing isn't living." However, I had a monkey on my back I couldn't shake, and I was gasping for air.

"I wanted to die when Rupert passed. Liquor, drugs, shopping . . . nothing worked. No substance on earth could have dulled the pain. It was unbearable." I inhaled deeply in an attempt to pacify the rising rage wrangling for revenge. "There was no reprieve from the life sentence I'd been handed. I was nothing. A table without legs. A Pollyanna without God. Without hope. Without a purpose. But . . . something happened when you called, Farley, to tell me Pete had passed. The two-ton weight I'd been dragging behind me since Rupert died crumbled to gravel, and I was lighter than air. I was thankful when he went." I sipped from my cool glass of water. "I was sick to death of death. Dying is an ugly affair. Figuratively and literally, it stinks. Mopping his brow. Changing his diaper. Wringing the piss out of his pajama bottoms." I held the glass against my hot cheek. "You were there when Rupert vanished from my life. I couldn't have asked for better friends." I turned to Evangeline. "Your shoulder to cry on was the ultimate gift when I needed it most." Farley's face softened when I held his gaze. "Your calls meant more to me than you'll ever know, because . . . you were genuinely concerned. You were the brother I never had." Resting my chin in my hand, I stared into the flickering candle. "I figured the three of us would be here for one another now. Well, I figured wrong. Do you know how long it took me to get here?" I looked each of them in the eye. "It felt like an eternity. I missed saying goodbye to my aunt. I was robbed of the farewell I should have had with Rupert." I paused for a moment to collect myself. "I hated the world. I detested life. I wanted to dash into the China Department at Wallis & Fitch Haden and smash every frigging porcelain plate, cup, and saucer I could get my hands on. Fuck the world. Fuck you."

Farley raised his head and stared down his nose at me. "Polly . . ."

"It takes a Pollyanna to stand strong against people like you, Farley Fairfield. You consider Pollyanna to be a punchline of a joke. A paper doll. Two-dimensional. A cartoon." My head was throbbing, and the tips of my ears burned. "I had to learn the hard way. I bashed my head against the wall until it sank into my thick skull, but I learned. I learned that my unabashed Pollyanna was a tower of strength. I refuse to wallow in self-loathing and self-pity, as you so grandly do. I learned it was a narcissistic luxury I couldn't afford. You connive to eviscerate anyone you conceive as competition. What you don't get—what you've never gotten—is that we're not running in the same race."

"Pete was mine," Farley announced. "I met him first."

Evangeline grimaced. "No one belongs to another person."

"We do," I said and studied her stunned face. "The four of us, each damaged by our families, each a survivor of a treacherous childhood, were drawn to each other because we saw in one another what we felt in ourselves." I glanced at Farley, but he quickly turned away. "I loved Pete," I began, "but . . . we're all given choices, and he made his. He made his bed . . ."

"So he had to lie in it?" Evangeline was cautious and guarded.

"I don't think Pete and I stopped loving one another. If anything, we loved each other too much. There was no way we could have simply been friends. One would have destroyed the other."

Farley cleared his throat. "I would have walked through fire for him."

"He was well aware of your obsession," I assured him.

"Why you?" Farley sneered. "What's so special about you?"

"Don't know. You tell me."

If they had been lasers, Farley's eyes would have burned a hole through me. "Nothing! There's nothing . . . nothing I couldn't have given him."

"You can't force someone to love you, Farley." Evangeline's anger broke the surface of her silence. "Certainly, you know that. Look how you've treated your exes. Perhaps if you had dropped the impossible dream about Pete, you might have let yourself love someone else. You might have been happy. Simon, God rest his soul—he loved you, Farley Fairfield."

The waiter poked his head around the banket, his pen ready to take our order, but Evangeline waved him away. "For Christ's sake, Farley, nothing was ever going to happen with you and Pete," she blurted out like a drunken sailor with Tourette's. "You're delusional."

Farley narrowed his beady eyes on her. "Delusional? Who's more delusional than a fag-hag hot for a fag?"

"I never—"

"Right." Farley laughed. "But I knew. Nobody fools me for long. First your merry fairy dandy Augie Applegate, and then Peter Pakington Pace . . . you fall for fags. The fatal flaw with your feline infatuation."

"I need a drink," Evangeline said, the tension draining from her face.

Farley removed his glasses and wiped them with his napkin. "Booze. A second fatal flaw."

Evangeline fiddled with the ring on her finger. "We're some sick fucks."

"No matter how many times we whack each other on the head, we can't bring him back," I said.

"He's irreplaceable. A tie that binds," Evangeline said. "He hated fighting. Couldn't stand conflict."

"He was a lover, not a hater." I rubbed my weary eyes.

Evangeline dropped her head, and though her Louise Brooks bob shielded the sides of her face, I noticed her wet cheeks glistening in the candlelight. "What's happened to the world? I understand nothing. Why would I have even wanted to bring a baby into this? Look at the people in this room."

Scanning the buzzing crowd from our table, I realized I was sitting in a purgatory I'd never wished for myself. Except for the time Rupert had taken me to Maison Blanche for my birthday, I'd never wandered into this part of Pete's universe.

The restaurant was a mixed bag of tragedy and triumph for its patrons, who walked between the lines of decency and debauchery. These people—society mavens accompanied by questionably young escorts, doddering old men with wandering toupees glued to the tops of their bald heads, sidled so close to their overcompensating mistresses that they risked an orgasm— represented the cream of society. This had been the world Pete was born into. He complained about them, despised his own kind, joked at their expense, and from all accounts, had flaunted his sexuality in a way that was both alluring and revolting to all assembled.

Farley looked around the room. "Why this place?"

"The very thing I envied about Pete's life was this," Evangeline replied. "But now, seeing it without him, it's terribly lackluster. It was his sparkle, his elegance that made it glamorous."

Her napkin slid off her lap, so I reached down to retrieve it for her. "I'm so sick and tired of losing people. Have any of these people been touched by the fickle finger of fate? They must know someone plagued. I just want to prick my finger like Sleeping Beauty and wake up in another century."

"Unlike Sleeping Beauty, I'd wake up looking like I hadn't slept in a hundred years," Farley said. "I've lost over half the guys in my act and a third of my regulars at the club. His watery eyes glistened in the yellow glow of the flame. "I miss Pete."

"He could be an utter bitch when riled, but oh." Evangeline smiled to suppress her rising emotion. "He was kind-hearted. So gentle and loving with Little Pete. So . . ."

"He was there when I needed him most," Farley confessed. "He marched into my father's house one Christmas Eve and let him have it. After what he did . . . I couldn't stay there; not a minute more." He inhaled deeply and sighed. "He crippled the old bastard. Threatened to call the police if he ever touched me again. He took me under his wing. He saved me."

"Believe it or not," Evangeline said, "he was an excellent listener. And wise . . . gave the best advice."

"Not that he ever followed it himself," Farley added.

"Everyone took him for a narcissist," I added, "but he was the last person he thought of. I was mad about the boy."

Evangeline's chin quivered. "I was proud to be his friend."

"He was ours," I said, unable to suppress the tears. "For one brief, shining moment . . ."

"He'd parade through those doors to his table, this table, number five," she whispered as if she was reciting a prayer. "As captivating as Cary Grant, everyone basked in his beauty, and he adored it."

My thoughts were flooded with memories of brighter celebrations. "Rupert was the love of my life, but Pete was my first love."

"Mine too," Farley said. "You never get over your first love. Perhaps because it's the most painful."

I grinned at him. "That's why they call it a crush."

Grandma Flora had believed that as long as there was one person left who remembered you after you passed, you lived on.

A chill tickled my backside when I looked at the empty chair opposite me. I sensed Pete was nearby. As long as I remembered him, he'd be with me always, loving me as I loved him.

Right then and there, I promised God and the universe that I would forever utter their names. I would whisper Rupert, Pete, and Aunt Jessica's names to the wind whistling past my ear as I biked along the Potomac to Mount Vernon. I'd shout their names over the crashing waves at Rehoboth Beach and mouth their names in silent prayer on my knees at St. Matthews's. I would keep them alive.

The people I loved recognized something in me that they'd discovered in themselves. Through our acts and deeds and devotion to honesty, we were all Pollyanna.

.

CHAPTER 30

TWO PEAS IN A POD

The blue envelope sat on my kitchen counter for nearly a week before I opened it. I needed time to prepare myself for whatever Pete's last words would be. I was spurred into opening it when I played back a perplexing message left on my answering machine from the law firm of Rhinehart, Rhinehart, and Shaffer. "Please call us at your earliest convenience," Mr. Reynolds Rhinehart, Esq., said.

So I opened the letter and read its contents.

"Evangeline." I spoke slowly into the receiver, measuring every syllable. The deliberate speech was more for me than her, because it was I who needed convincing that the miracle I held in my hand was true. "Pete left me his co-op on California Street."

I could hear her sucking a drag from her cigarette. "Your co-op, August Applegate. I'm thrilled for you."

"Except for my playhouse, I never had a home of my own."

The image of myself as a lonely lad lounging on the rag rug that covered the floor of my Mediterranean-blue playhouse washed me with melancholy for what I'd never dared dream of: a place to call home.

• • •

"An amazing view," Farley said, leaning over the balustrade. "I never tired of this view." He turned to me and sat cross-legged on the floor. "Nice gift." He was trying not to be a pain in the ass, and I appreciated the gesture. After all, it was the dawn of a new day.

"I can barely afford the co-op fees," I said. "What was he thinking?"

Evangeline sat down beside me and offered me a drag from her joint. "You'd disappoint him if you sold it."

"My few sticks of furniture will never furnish this joint." I ran my hand over the polished parquet floor. Smooth and cool, it was a nice respite from the climbing humidity of June in Washington. "It feels lonely."

Evangeline stretched her shapely legs before her and rested her back against the wall. "Now that his good ol' mama sold Arabella's apartment, it's not too big, Augie."

"With the door removed and the wall plastered, you'd never know the two units were once one apartment," I said. "How symbolic. They were separated from the beginning."

"One apartment for each of the influential women in his life," Farley mused.

Evangeline nudged me with her shoulder. "What was that Robert Frost poem your grandmother read to us after my grandfather passed?"

"'Spoils of the Dead,'" I said and recited a few lines. "'Two fairies it was / On a still summer day / Came forth in the woods / With flowers to play . . .'"

"'Flowers-guided it was,'" Evangeline recited, "'That they came as they ran / On something that lay / In the shape of a man.'"

"'When you came on death,'" I continued, "'Did you not come flower-guided / Like the elves in the wood? / I remember that I did. / But I recognize death / With sorrow and dread / And I hated and hate / The spoils of the dead.'"

• • •

I was cleaning my compact studio one Saturday morning when a bright idea popped into my head. Silly though it had seemed to Mama when she'd called, I decided it was a necessary rite of passage for me.

"Ashes in a box?" Mama asked. "What kind of box?"

"A carved wooden box he gave me eons ago."

"But it's not his ashes. I don't understand, Mr. March."

"It's symbolic," Dad piped in from the extension upstairs.

"Should have been buried in the ground instead of like some ancient Roman," Mama said. "What is this obsession with cremation, anyway?"

"If anything happens to me, you'd best send me to the ovens."

I could hear Mama's nail lightly tapping the receiver. "Over my dead body."

"My wish, Mama."

"Oh," Mama piped up. "Your friend from high school, the one who tried to drown you in the pool."

"Chester Chad?" My heart skipped a beat.

"Saw him in the IGA last Saturday," Mama said. "I think he's got it. All skinny and pale. I'm sure his wife is struck pink over the whole embarrassing affair."

"She ran off with Selena Loggins's boy two years ago," Dad said. "Woman, get your gossip straight."

"Straight." Mama snickered. "That's funny, old man."

What Chester Chad must have gone through. All the sympathy in the world couldn't save him from the prejudice in our one-horse hometown. No matter how much he'd bullied me, no one deserved the plague.

·•·

The air was unseasonably crisp and cool when I tucked the box of ashes in my backpack and mounted my seven-speed Schwinn. Early mornings in Rock Creek Park had been so joyful for me and Pete before his illness ravaged his body beyond repair. He'd hop on his sleek black carbon Bianchi, and away we'd fly, two cowboys speeding down the trail to Mount Vernon. On the ride back to the city, we'd stop at Lady Bird Johnson Park on the George Washington Parkway. Lying on the grass of the undulating lawn stretching along the western bank of the Potomac, surrounded by deciduous and evergreen trees that framed postcard picture views of DC, we'd gaze across the wide span of water, and I'd imagine a life where nothing bad could touch us.

I leaned my bike against an elm and kneeled beneath a cherry tree, its frilly skirt of verdant green lace fluttering in the breeze sweeping off the Potomac. I uncovered the intricately carved pencil box Pete had gifted me long ago at 315 Benevolent Street and clicked the verdigris latch. I held it close among whatever wildlife was hiding in the carpet of dewy centipede grass and bushy fountain grasses along the riverbank. The rustling foliage of the pignut hickory and American chestnut branches swaying convinced me Pete was nearby. "I'm still here," I said aloud, "aching for your laughter, your touch."

Holding the box to my chest, I recited Emily Dickinson: "'Because I could not stop for Death / He kindly stopped for me; / The carriage held but just ourselves / And Immortality.'"

I waited for the wind to intensify, and when it tickled my ears, I popped the lid of the box. Swirling and curling like an army of bees returning to their hive, the ashes rode the gust and disappeared into the blur of the rushing water.

CHAPTER 31

AND THE WORLD GOES ROUND

Washington's downtown streets on Independence Day 1987 were asphalt-melting hot. Trickles of weeping tar puddled in the recently patched blacktop. The department store awnings hung heavy with humidity, and the flags mounted over their entrances sank morbidly in the breathless evening heat.

I had been hoping for a break in the weather, but the temperature soared as the day progressed. It remained a scorcher at 6:45 p.m. I arrived early, and Kaiden was late. I spent nearly an hour waiting, drenched with perspiration outside the Woodward & Lothrop's F Street Metro entrance.

I tried calling Kaiden from the phone booth across the street, but no one picked up. "I'm at Metro Center. I hope you get this message. I've been . . ."

BEEP! His message machine signaled before clicking off.

I'd already had mixed feelings about Kaiden joining us for a picnic on the Capitol lawn. He knew Evangeline. They got on like a house on fire. It was Farley I worried about. He'd gone all bandy-legged when I'd introduced them at the Whitman-Walker Clinic Gala he'd performed in. I'd never heard such bracelet clanking in my life.

"Oh honey, if you don't want him," Farley said, "leave him to this showgirl who has a way with men." He shimmied. "I got hot and bothered when he was all big and before me."

It was easy to imagine Farley going on and on with his captivating stories of Wig Stock and the magnificent responses to his performances. Oh hell, even if Farley controlled himself, which I doubted was possible, I wasn't certain I was doing the right thing. Plus, since Kaiden was straight, Farley would surely blame me for his failure to woo the wicked out of a straight man he didn't stand a tinker's damn of a chance of bedding. I'd never been territorial, but Lord have mercy, Kaiden was *my* straight man friend, and I was tired of sharing.

It was bad enough that Farley and Mama wrote to one another. What did they have in common but me? I supposed it was egotistical of me to think that way, but—*Oh!* At least it was only annual or biannual correspondence at the most. Still, it was a thorn in my side. I cared but didn't care, much the way Jo March felt in *Little Women* when her sister, Amy, married Lauri, who'd proposed to Jo first.

Except for the occasional holiday and birthday cards, I received zilch in the mail from Mama; and the notion of penning a letter to her son would have completely baffled and befuddled her.

"Any man can be had in the right situation," Farley liked to brag.

Jesus! He was relentless, a double-edged sword capable of shaving your face and slicing your head off.

The bottom had dropped out of my world when Rupert had died. I'd just been getting my life in order when Pete kicked the bucket. I felt like a ninety-five-year-old expecting word that another friend in the nursing home had bit the dust. AIDS threatened every aspect of gay life.

I tried to believe that the future held promise beyond the pale. There was bound to be a cure someday. Right?

It had been several months since I'd last seen Kaiden. I had butterflies, which felt absolutely ridiculous. "Oh, Rupert," I muttered under my breath. "What should I do?" I purposefully busied myself at work. When I got home, I'd spend hours painting a wall or rearranging a closet until I passed out exhausted. It was a race to oblivion.

Now that I had grown accustomed to my inherited co-op, I was beginning to enjoy owning something. Except for the 'Stang, I'd never owned anything—and besides, I had inherited the 'Stang from April, so it was a hand-me-down. Of course, so was the co-op. Was that to be my lot in life?

Pete's mother had even attempted pulling a fast one. She'd sent her burly bully of a K Street lawyer to put the fear of God in me, or at least the fear of the wealthy. However, my lawyer—Beauford Bixby, Evangeline's ex—had assured me that Pete's will was iron-clad. "Jesus!" I'd told Evangeline, "Like she doesn't own enough already. Greed. Is there no satisfying its monstrous appetite?"

After Kaiden's parents had sold their modern glass mansion jutting out from the side of the Blueridge, I'd heard very little sec-ondhand gossip about the family.

"His parents split," Tootie had informed me when asked. "Two psychiatrists under one roof . . . I'm surprised they lasted as long as they did."

"He's a good boy," Dad said. "A gentleman through and through."

"The world is going to hell in a handbasket, and Oscar's search-ing for that silver lining," Tootie retorted. "Your father's just like you, Augie: an eternal optimist." I didn't have the guts to tell her the truth: that I'd lost my eternal optimism on the battlefield.

"I must admit," Mama had said, referring to Kaiden, "although rumor has it that he abandoned his wife and child, he is a 'fine young man.'"

"He's not gay," I'd protested, not wishing for her to get her hopes up about any future between Mr. Kavanaugh and me.

"You're so optimistic," Chancey from Whitman-Walker would say whenever we volunteered together.

Heavens. I felt anything but optimistic. I stayed upbeat for my AIDS buddies and the suicide call-ins at the clinic, and of course my staff at the store, but at home, I hung my Pollyanna mask on the hook by the door.

"The golden age of the department store is coming to an end," Evangeline had taken to grumbling. "People don't care for glamor-ous and extravagant displays when they can get a bargain at Syms' Discount and Filene's Basement."

I'd been praying she was wrong, but signs everywhere pointed in that direction. Displays were being streamlined and staffs cut to save money. Top executives were stuffing the forty percent they'd once reinvested into the business into their own pockets. Shop-ping centers and strip malls, like bunnies in a cabbage patch, were popping up everywhere there was a new subdivision or empty plot of land. Flagship stores like ours were no longer the jewels in the crown. With the decrease in foot traffic at Wallis & Fitch Haden, as with its neighbors, much-needed renovations were being put on hold. Every time I passed by Rupert's old office or sat at the glass conference table, I wondered what he'd think of this latest trend. It was amazing how the world had changed so much in a few short years.

"Augie," Kaiden yelled, snapping me out of my thoughts. He smiled, waving from the bottom of the Metro escalator, and my sweaty anger puddled on the hot concrete. "Sorry," he said. "The trains were running on holiday schedule, and when they did arrive, they were jam-packed."

"Oh Kaiden, I'd hug you, but I'm kinda gross."

He wrapped his arms around me and hugged me close. He was dry and his T-shirt cool from the air-conditioned train. He smelled of fresh lavender soap and a citrusy cologne I didn't recognize. "What's a little perspiration between friends?"

"I know it's a walk from here, but the Capitol South and Union Station exits would have been a nightmare. Worse than this," I said as we sauntered down the sidewalk on the edge of the crowd.

Roberta Flack was into her second number by the time we secured a tiny patch of green on the Capitol lawn. Relegated to the less desirable angle to the left of the stage, we had an ideal view of the guest conductor and Ms. Flack's back. To no avail, I scanned the crowd for Evangeline and Farley. Farley's bangles weren't even sounding an alarm.

"I'll treat you to dinner later," Kaiden said. "It's the least I can do."

I was famished. I'd skipped lunch to prepare for the picnic feast I knew Evangeline had packed. Southern fare for a hot July evening. Cold honey-fried chicken, potato salad with white grapes, hummingbird cake so sweet it would make me cringe—but that wouldn't stop me from a second helping.

Oh dear. My belly grumbled, and I was as disappointed as Aunt Tootie when the candy-apple stand closed up shop early at the state fair. "Thanks," I replied to Kaiden, knowing damn well we'd never find a restaurant open, and that if, miracle of miracles, we did happen upon such a rare animal, it was unlikely an empty table would be available.

The audience jumped to their feet when Roberta burst into "The Star-Spangled Banner," and when the ocean of people crushed into me, I was smashed against the trunk of a buckeye tree. Kaiden, in his grass-stained white tennis shorts and soaked navy polo, reached into the human wave and yanked me into the clearing. Deluged by the restless herd, we were swept into the densely populated plasmodium spreading rapidly toward the Ulysses S. Grant Memorial across the street.

Fireworks shot upward from stations along the banks of the Potomac and burst into a magnificent multi-colored display. Fiery red, blue-magenta, silver-white, and glimmering gold, the colors fizzled, crackled, and sparked bright, so intense in their splendor that I could practically taste them popping on my tongue. With each exploding combination, the fountains of glittering majesty, shimmering tinsel, and star-spurting brilliance, the delighted crowd cheered louder.

By the time we reached the Grant Memorial fountain, the crowd had tightened, weaving in and around us. A man hoisted his ebullient little boy up onto his shoulders, and the lad reached for the sky as if he might grab the tail of a shooting star.

We maneuvered to the front of the granite platform and climbed up onto the lip of the pedestal. Freed from the ocean of people flooding the National Mall, Kaiden looped his fingers into the belt loops of my seersucker shorts to keep me from slipping off the ledge and rested his chin on my shoulder. The scent of Kaiden's sweat-wet hair against my cheek was sweet, a tad mellow, with a permanent hint of chlorine. It renewed my youthful crush on the hunk from the hill. That smell had infused every sweater and jacket I'd worn to Kaiden's parents' house eons ago. I'd resisted laundering the items until Mama had threatened to throw them on a bonfire if I didn't toss them in the Maytag. "Now!"

The fantastic firework display climaxed with a spectacular shower of glittering brilliance as bright as the noon sun before tapering into a spittle of sparks, revealing the man in the moon as the mile-wide cloud of smoke dissipated over the Potomac.

"Come on." Kaiden whispered in my ear, so close it felt like a kiss. He took my hand, and we swam against the tide of thousands toward Constitution Avenue.

When we reached the Willard Hotel, we made a beeline for

Pennsylvania Avenue to Farragut North Park. "Have you ever abandoned, absolutely abandoned, your insecurities?" Kaiden smiled, and his cheekbones rose to aristocratic heights. With the exuberance of a child, he danced around the people-free park. He attempted a shuffle-step but tripped over his size-twelve shoes and hit the grass with a splat.

"Kaiden!" I knelt beside him.

"I'm such a klutz," he said. "That's what I get for trying to impress you."

I found it odd that he was attempting to impress me. *Whatever for? Please! He's impressive standing still.* I started to help him to his feet, but he slid on the grass and brought me down with him. We burst into infectious laughter.

"Okay," I said once we were back on our feet, "right foot first." I taught him how to shuffle, and we danced up Connecticut Avenue to Dupont Circle.

"Oh no! Childe Harold's closed!" Kaiden complained when we noticed the sign in the window. It was a ghost town.

"I know a Chinese carry-out on 17th Street," I said, and his eyes brightened.

•●•

I spread a plaid picnic blanket over my living room carpet and arranged the containers while Kaiden showered. He changed into my terry bath robe while his clothes spun in the dryer.

"I feel human again," he said as he rubbed his hair dry with a towel.

"My turn!" I padded across the nearly empty apartment to the bathroom.

We chatted while we ate, catching up on the time that had passed between our outings.

"It's depressing out there," he said, stretching his legs across the blanket. The robe parted for a split second before he pulled the flap back over his privates, and I blushed when he caught me staring at his impressive family jewels, but he was kind enough not to mention it. "How are you really, Augie?"

I selected a fortune cookie from the bag and handed it to him. "One day at a time."

"The gay world is difficult at best," he said with authority, "but you know what drives me absolutely bonkers?"

I arched an eyebrow.

"Pigeonholing."

"'Pigeonholing'?" I took a swig of wine.

"Men, gay or straight, are comfortable with black and white. It's the many shades of light that disorient us."

"How do you mean?"

"A definitive," he said. "An absolute. Like Farley is fabulous."

I laughed. "Camp sounds hysterical coming from you."

He topped my glass. "Hey! Give the old man a break."

"Stereotyping."

"Exactly!" He ran his fingers through his wet locks, his muscular forearms exposed when the sleeve of the robe slid into the crux of his arm. Surprisingly modest, he quickly pulled it down again. *Christ!* I was enjoying the view. With his powerful legs and large, flipper-like feet, he reminded me of the Olympic swimming champion Mark Spitz. "As if a guy should either be a butch or a nelly? Top or bottom?"

I grinned and shook my head. "Yuck."

I found Kaiden sweet. It was obvious that he was going out of his way to be respectful of the fact that I was gay. Actually, it was quite touching. If more straight men were as supportive and understanding as him, the world would have been a far greater place.

"Why is it we can't celebrate our differences?" I asked. "It's kinda creepy for Aryans to prefer Aryans when the world is spiced with a wide range of delights. Way too Nazi *pour moi.*"

He scrunched up his aquiline nose. "Makes me absolutely contrite."

Kaiden fished in the bag and tossed me another fortune cookie. "Even as a child, you knew who you were. I envied that."

I reclined on my side, careful not to accidently touch any part of his sensuous hide. "I suppose. It was the rest of the world that confused me. I was the oddball, the misfit, the . . . I don't know. Freak?"

Kaiden tossed his napkin at me. "Original. You were a ginger-haired original in that hick town." He tossed his plastic fork in the bag and pushed the container of shrimp fried rice away from himself. "No self-control when it comes to Chinese carry-out."

His long, dark bangs drifted over his eye, and he hooked them behind his ear. "Washington is crawling with guys looking to find themselves, to discover who they truly are. It's a city of redefinition because few people are who they pretend to be. Keeps me in business."

"They migrate here, like peasants to ancient Rome, to be near the powerful and the great. Hoping to rub elbows with the right people who know the best people who can mold them into the absolute top-drawer super beings envied by the world. These interlopers sell their souls to the highest bidder, thinking they'll never need them again."

Kaiden let his foot fall against my leg. The jolt of electricity that shot through my loins was powerful enough to make me shiver. "You're a rare bird, Augie."

"A Pollyanna gay. Pete hung that label around my neck."

"Sounds like a movement to me." Kaiden sat up. "Pollyanna gay is sweeping the nation. Do you have one? Are you a Pollyanna gay?" he jested. "Where can I buy one? I must have one! You're nobody without a Pollyanna gay. Every home should have one."

I sat up and applauded. "You should play Harold Hill in *The Music Man*. You nearly convinced me I'm the latest, greatest fad."

"I heard you sing at Friends Bar one night before I ran into you at Whitman-Walker," he said. "You should've gone to New York. Truly."

"I did audition in New York, but nothing came of it. I'm not what they're looking for."

"What are they looking for? Attila the Hun?"

"Evidently, I'm 'Not leading man material.'"

"*Merde*," he said, and we both laughed. "Do you have a scrapbook?" he asked.

"What actor doesn't?" A bit tipsy, I headed to the bedroom to fetch it. "Back in a sec."

He didn't wait for me to return. He picked up our glasses and followed close behind. He sat on the bed as I searched for the scrapbook. "Here it is!" I handed him my catalogued past.

He took it and opened to the first page, then paused, looking thoughtful, and rolled the sleeve of the robe up to show me his wrist. His flawless tan was tattooed with a raised, white line. "Five years ago."

Gently, I ran my finger over the scar. "Did it hurt?"

"Like a motherfucker," he said.

I kissed the scar. I don't know why. I supposed it was his honesty. His willingness to share his pain meant a lot to me. He was my friend, and I cared deeply about him. "I've grown fond of you, Mr. Kavanaugh." I chided myself for being judgmental of him without proper proof. Evidently, it had been my insecurities about being born on the wrong side of the tracks that had teased my prejudice to the surface. Just as Farley and Evangeline had pigeonholed me into being the Pollyanna of their description, I stood guilty of the same crime with Kaiden. "You've always held a special place in my heart." *Lordy. Lordy. Good God!* Now I'd done it, crossed the line, opened my big trap before thinking.

"I'm special because I taught you how to swim?" He looked into my eyes for an uncomfortably long time, but I held his steady gaze. After a long moment, he looked down at the scrapbook.

At 2:35 a.m., I closed the book he'd perused for an hour, asking endless questions about each picture. "I'm sorry, Kaiden. I can't hold my eyes open. You can sleep on the sofa or here. Wherever you like, but . . ." I slid under the covers and was out like a light.

I'm not certain how long I slept, but I awoke when Kaiden kissed me. "Augie," he whispered. I shook my head, opened and closed my eyes, but I couldn't dispel the dream. My hands slid across his naked back, and he kissed me again. Spiced with garlic, the taste of his tongue cupping mine was mellowed by the alcoholic lift of chardonnay. *Oh my God! This is real!* The whites of his eyes in the dark glowed bright as twin Venuses in the solar system. His tongue in my ear, in the nape of my neck, on my nipple, over my belly, and on my thigh charged my electrical wattage a thousand-fold. *Good Lord! Kaiden Kavanaugh is making love to me!*

"Wait!" I said as he tugged at my boxers.

"What?"

"Your status?"

"Oh, Augie." Kaiden caressed my cheek. "I've been tested so many times I've got track marks like a junkie. Negative. And you?"

"Negative." I took hold of his large ears, pulled him close, and planted a passionate, wet one on his delicious lips.

Rupert's poetic passion had seduced me with a cinematic sensuality that sizzled to a shuddering climax. Pete's lovemaking had coaxed my inner coy coquette into his salacious circus of chemical explosions. However, it was Kaiden, a spirited species gifted with athletic aplomb, that released the darshan eagle I was meant to be.

When he pressed his hairy chest against my smooth skin, a titillating tangle of impulses poked at the snoring stimulation I'd shuttered tightly in the sacred sanctuary sealed by Rupert's demise. It wasn't the first tryst that had tempted me into action since his passing, but it was the first episode to unshackle me from my devotion to his death.

No inch of flesh was left untouched, and we moaned and groaned with pleasure, rolling under the covers of my four-poster bed.

Around ten a.m., the sun cutting across my eyes stirred me awake. Lying beside me, his arm over my chest, Kaiden was pleasantly snoring away, so I eased out of the bed and tip-toed to the bathroom.

Splashing water on my face, I stared at my refection in the mirror. *Oh my God!* What had I done? I had crossed the line of friendship. When he woke up and realized . . . *Damn! Damn!* He'd never forgive me.

I patted my face dry with a hand towel and opened the bathroom door. There, leaning against the bedroom doorway, Kaiden stood, tanned and stark naked. He raised his bowed head when I stepped closer. With those sad, pensive eyes framed by a set of luxurious lashes, Kaiden said, "I love you, August Applegate. I always have."

I didn't answer him. I couldn't. Stunned by the confession and his lack of decorum, I shuffled past him to my walk-in closet. Although I'd just showered, I changed into my jogging shorts and running shoes.

"Want to grab a bite?" He stepped into his tennis shorts.

I tied a bandana over my wet mop of curls and selected a tee from the chest of drawers. "I need to run. I can't think right now."

Kaiden sat on the bed, his broad shoulders slumped, and stared at me like a wounded deer. "But we made love, Augie."

"Oh, Kaiden. That only complicates things."

"You can't go until we talk."

"I can't even think straight."

He took my hand and kissed it. It was thrilling and chilling simultaneously. The sexual electricity short-circuited my wiring, and I wanted nothing more than to jump his bones again, right then and there. However, the chilling reality of the situation was a cold slap in the face. "Don't look at me that way. Oh Kaiden, I'm so screwed up, and you're . . ."

"I'm far from perfect," he said. "As a matter of fact, I find most people to be a frigging mess."

I took a step from him, but he tugged on my shorts, and I acquiesced to sit by his side. I could run but never hide. Pollyanna, a therapist's therapist.

"Honestly," he said, his jutting jaw rigid. "I've spent years being a bastard and a bully to my family and friends because I couldn't face who I was."

"Your parents were psychoanalysts, for heaven's sake."

"That only made it worse."

I leaned against the headboard, and he scooted closer to me, his hand on my ankle. *RUN! RUN, August Applegate!* But I couldn't budge. Wouldn't budge. Didn't care to run with his breath against my bare neck.

"They knew," he went on. "I never fooled them, but . . . foolishly, I rebelled against them. I was going to prove them wrong because they knew everything about everyone, and I hated them for it. My God, I wasn't even reprimanded for masturbating. As a matter of fact, they encouraged it."

"It *is* a natural phenomenon."

"I know that now, but not at fourteen. What the hell did I know?" He squeezed my ankle. "You're so damn cute. I love the way you look at me with those inquisitive green eyes."

"You're mind-bending. This situation. For God's sake, Kaiden! I thought you were straight. However, after last night . . ."

"Which was pretty spectacular." He smiled confidently.

"True," I said and grinned. "Just don't let it go to your head."

He wrapped his arms around my bent legs and rested his chin on my knees. "Too late."

I ran my fingers through his matted hair. "It's so soon after Rupert. It almost feels like I'm cheating."

"Augie," Kaiden said, his smile sliding sideways. "Not that there's a timeline with these matters, but it's been well over a year now." He kissed my kneecap. "Part of you will always love Rupert. There's nothing wrong with that. But you can love more than one person. Everyone you connect with ignites a different flame in you." Tenderly, he massaged my calves. "I don't want to replace Rupert, wipe his memory from your life. It's important to remember those we've loved and were loved by."

I couldn't figure out how to answer, so I changed the subject. "I wasn't your first . . . man, was I?"

"Honestly," Kaiden said, his hand on my cheek, "now who's full of himself?"

"I wasn't certain, that's all. I mean, you definitely knew what you were doing last night."

He blushed, and I was touched.

"You're quite the tiger, Mr. Kavanaugh."

"I've been around. Not that I'm proud of my promiscuity— or cheating on my wife—but I learned a few things out there, how to survive in the jungle."

"Did you love your wife?"

"We were best friends. Sort of like you and Evangeline." His eyes glazed over. "It was one of the most God-awful times in my life, and it was all my fault. I take full responsibility."

"You definitely take charge. You're quite comfortable being the aggressor."

"Augie," Kaiden said and gazed out the window. "I lied to you. I lied about working yesterday."

A pang of panic pinged inside me. "I don't understand."

He stuffed a pillow behind himself and sat tall. "Sorry, I'm sinking into your feather bed."

"Birds of a feather."

"So bad." He kissed my cheek. "I need to be upfront with you."

Another pang tinged in my tummy.

"I was late on purpose."

This wasn't what I'd been expecting to hear, so I automatically winced. "Whatever for?"

"To have you all to myself. No Farley and his endless chatter. No Evangeline adding her two cents' worth. Just you and me and . . ."

"A few thousand others on the Capitol lawn."

"I'd waited so long, Augie. You know something?"

"Nothing. I feel I know nothing."

"I felt a connection with you since that first day. When you descended the stairs to the pool, I had goosebumps."

"God knows I wanted you too."

"I wasn't certain as to what it might be, but I wanted more from you than tricking in my parents' house. Which I'm sure they wouldn't have minded one iota." Kaiden rested his head on my shoulder, and his hand drifted over my chest and downward toward my nether region, but I pushed it away. "I've had too many wives of friends," he said, "slept with too many husbands, experimented with too many substances, spent a fortune on pleasure."

"I can't save you, Kaiden."

"Don't want you to. I can't save you, either. What I can be is upfront and honest with you." He took me in his arms and kissed me passionately, a lengthy spell; if I had been standing, it would have buckled my knees.

Surfacing for air, I muttered, "I should go running. Clear my head."

But there was no arguing with the man. He knew what he liked, and what he liked was me. Who was I to deny him another plunge into the deep end of pleasure, especially now that my engine was fired up?

CHAPTER 32

I AM WHAT I AM

"Faster than a lesbian," Evangeline said as we sat, sunning our tanned faces, on the roof of Wallis & Fitch Haden. "Only lesbians move this fast into a relationship."

I stuck my tongue out at her and took a sip from my can of Diet Pepsi. "I'm tired of hesitating. Besides, it was your playing matchmaker that pushed me over the edge."

"I invited him to the picnic. It's his fault you never showed. Farley was pissed. He *so* had his sights set on Kaiden Kavanaugh."

"Last night, Kaiden confessed he was late on purpose. He knew if we were late, we'd never find you in the crowd."

Evangeline pushed her Fendi sunglasses onto the bridge of her nose. "Sounds a bit controlling." She looked at me, but I couldn't see her eyes through the dark glass. "Are you sure you're doing the right thing?"

"Are you sure you're not more than a bit jealous?" I pushed out of the chair and walked to the edge of the terrace that was once an outdoor café. After the restaurant closed in the seventies, the space had been transformed into a second display workshop, where props could be built or painted. In the summer months, the visual staff often sunbathed during our lunch breaks. We only tanned our faces and legs, though. Stripping completely down would have been totally inappropriate at work. That was why I kept a pair of swim trunks in my office for just such occasions.

I was wearing them now. Earlier, Evangeline had accidently spilled her Diet Coke on my white linen pants, so I'd washed the spot out in the shop sink and hung them on an old clothesline we used to suspend items for spray-painting. I wandered toward them to test their dampness.

"Are they dry?" she asked.

I shook my head.

"Augie." Evangeline clicked across the paint-splattered tile in her Chanel slingbacks. "Don't get all pouty-faced. I'm simply worried about you. You're such a Pollyanna about men." I snatched her glasses off, and she shielded her face against the glaring sun. "What the hell, Augie? You need me. You know I have your best interests at heart."

"Look at me," I said softly.

"Give me my glasses, for Christ's sake!" She grabbed them from my hand.

"Where have you been, Evangeline Kline?" I sat on the wall behind the huge Bella Epoque friezes topping the façade of Wallis & Fitch Haden. "Didn't you hear a cock-a-mamie thing I said at Le Maison Blanche? I've been to hell, thumbed my nose at the view, and survived. I'm different. Certainly, you've noticed I'm not the innocent you seduced in high school."

She jammed the glasses onto her nose. "You should be grateful I bothered."

"You loved me. It was a precious, unselfish act of love, and I am eternally grateful."

She flopped onto a chaise and raised her skirt to mid-thigh to tan her pale legs. "I've supported you every step of the way."

"You've bullied and badgered me, cajoled and coddled me, but respecting me to do the right thing? On my own? Well, that's another story." I raised my hand before she cut me off. "No. You did, but I now understand why. You saw what I couldn't. Perspective is a blessing. Let's face it: you're way more sophisticated and world-wise than I am. I've leaned on you most of my life. Too often, I've wandered the wrong way down a one-way street, chosen the wrong exit, turned too soon or too late. The extrovert in me barreled bravely into the fray, but the introvert in me, the biggest part of me, hid behind your moxie. We've spent our entire lives playing dress-up. Playing with our Barbies. Trying this or that hat on. But you must remember . . . realize . . . we played it together."

"Through thick and thin."

"Through hell and high water."

325

"The good and the bad," she said as she shooed an insistent fly away.

"You've known me longer than any other friend in my life. You're irreplaceable. A rock. My therapist. The mother I never had and the sister I always wanted. My God! Where would I be without you?" I took a swig of my drink. "I've had great love. Heaven knows, I passed up many years of possible happiness with Pete because of my cock-eyed morality. Thinking being pure was being right, being a proper Pollyanna. I realize now what Pete meant when he nicknamed me Pollyanna. It had nothing to do with being perfect, pure, monogamous. You can sleep with a hundred men—"

"I have," Evangeline said, "and another hundred for good measure."

"It's all about honesty, and if I am anything, I have tried to be honest." I snapped the sunglass lenses on top of my glass's frame. I loved Pete, and he, one of the most beautiful men on the planet, loved plain, ginger-headed me. Who else but a lucky fool happens onto someone like Rupert? Handsome, talented, brilliant, and dependable. So what if I missed the bar-hopping ecstasy that Farley chided me for passing up for my 'daddy'? God, was he wrong and my instinct so . . . so right. You see, I have chosen the right path at times."

She smiled as she turned her face to the sun.

"I wouldn't have passed up my gorgeous, quiet life with Rupert for anything. Not even theatre, because he was unbelievably ideal for me. Our life together was too short, but it was grand. Truly grand. I only regret not telling him I loved him sooner. If I had shuffled the cards, I may have been with Pete and would never have met Rupert. That would have been a mistake. We loved each other, but Pete and I were not a good fit."

"Well," Evangeline snorted, "in some ways you were ideal. And I'm not just talking sex."

"Fate, I suppose, guides us to where we need to be. It wasn't until I told Mama I loved her that I saw the power those three amazing words have. Three simple words can change a life forever. It didn't wipe away the hurt or erase the sweaty nightmares, but it did open new doors."

Although hot, the breeze sweeping across the rooftop made

our conversation bearable, pleasantly therapeutic. "You've called me Pollyanna as if it was a bad thing. It wasn't until after Pete passed that I understood and accepted, wholeheartedly, the compliment he paid me when he called me his gay Pollyanna. Rupert knew. He understood what Pete meant. Pollyanna . . . being a Pollyanna isn't being afraid or naïve or stupid, though I've been guilty of all three. Mama was right. I am like Dad. Always searching for the silver lining. Yes, that's true. I do. But what I've learned from the dying and the dead, from the hard knocks, failures, and triumphs, is that they're all mine, and they are fine. F-I-N-E. Fine. And if finding the silver lining is impossible, I'll make my own. That determination makes me a Pollyanna."

"A Pollyanna can be a pain in the ass," she interjected.

"Because we never give up. We *are* strong. We plow away and plod along until we finish the job. I put my heart and soul into everything I do. I give it my all—and if I fall, I fall—but by God, I try. I gazed into Grandma Flora's eyes when death was knocking. Surprisingly, I saw beauty. Bodies change and change and change as life drains away. Pale. Pale. Cold. White. Blue. Green, gray. Sunken. Gone. The dancing sparks deep in her corneas, the lingering light of childhood was the last to depart. Like Grandma Flora, Kaiden told me I have always known who I am. You know something, Vange? He's right. I wasted so much time trying to facilitate the ones who could never see the glory of me. Plain and pure, I never thought anyone would want me. I shouldn't have bought Mama's propaganda."

"You were a kid, Augie."

"What does a child know?" I asked. "Mama failed to cripple me. She wanted to because she was terrified of being left behind. I never made it to Broadway. Never sang on a national tour or dined at Kitty Carlyle Hart's dinner table, but I feasted with friends and gorged myself on passion." A gust of wind blew my hair into my eyes, and I tucked my long fringe behind an ear. "Last year, I wanted to die. I wanted to lay down and die. I missed Rupert. I missed Aunt Jessica, and I was afraid for Pete. I tried, but life got in the way. A mountain of guilt sat heavy on my shoulders. I was still here while others were dropping like flies. I convinced myself that if I sacrificed love and pleasure, I would level the playing field, even the score. I didn't want to feel superior in any way to the people suffering the wrath of the plague. I got down on my knees and prayed, 'Take me God. Take me!' Anything to spare Pete. I knew I was stronger. I could bear the pain. 'Take me, dear Lord, instead of Pete.' He loved life so much. He gobbled it up with both hands full."

"Augie . . ." Evangeline said.

I scooted my chair closer to hers. "You have to believe what I'm about to tell you." I gripped the arms of her chair and looked her straight in the eyes. "I love Kaiden. I love him. I have been in love with him since I was fifteen."

"Augie—"

"He's moving in with me, and that's that. Life is short, and I refuse to waste one more day feeling guilty because someone loves me. He may leave tomorrow. I may kick him out next Thursday. I may be hit by a bus next Monday. I can't stop living to save the dying. All I can . . . all I have to offer to AIDS patients, work, friends, family, and Kaiden is me. Imperfect *moi*. I don't know why these marvelous men love me. Kaiden does, and I am grateful, and to reject it would be giving the middle finger to the universe. Never say 'No thanks' when someone drops a blessing in your lap."

"Augie," Evangeline said. "May I speak now?"

I kissed her cheek. "What is it?"

She pointed to the clothesline. "Augie, your damn pants just blew off the roof."

• • •

The phone was ringing insistently when I stepped out of the shower. Slipping my robe on over my sopping wet self, I shot into my bedroom to put the poor answering machine out of its misery. "Hello."

"Mr. Applegate, this is Raymond, the doorman. There's a Mr. Fairfield here to see you."

I froze for a moment.

"Mr. Applegate, should I send him up?"

"I . . . I . . ." I stuttered as I fiddled with the belt of my robe. "Sure. Sure. Thank you, Raymond." I dropped the receiver into its cradle and stood there dripping on the parquets for a moment. *Farley Fairfield. What in hell is he doing in my lobby?*

Flummoxed, I dashed into the closet, yanked a pair of khakis off a hanger, and snatched a long-sleeved silk tee off the shelf. I dressed quickly, without properly drying myself.

I deliberately hadn't seen Farley in months. Every time he called, I let it go to voicemail. I never returned his calls nor answered any of the letters or responded to the cards he'd sent. His letters, as usual, ran on and on about every minute detail of his life, and quite frankly, they bored me to tears. When correspondences and phone messages didn't pan out in his desperation to contact me, he'd resorted to cards, those noncommittal affairs blank of verse and absent of purpose. His cards often featured crude stick figure drawings of us. At first, they'd been pleasant scenes of us out on the town or performing together, but lately, he'd been depicting me in various states of agony. The latest had been a picture of Farley laughing as I, bound and gagged, was being lowered into a raging fire.

I didn't rush to the door when his knock echoed through my home. At that point I wasn't certain I wanted to be alone with him. He could have had a knife up his sleeve, a pistol in his pocket, or even a vial of poison to stir into the jug of orange juice in my fridge. *Damn!* There was no time to call Kaiden. He was volunteering at Whitman-Walker and most likely tied up with a patient. *Tied up!* That's how I feared I'd be found days from now, hogtied in the kitchen cupboard.

"August," he sang sweetly from the other side of the door.

I checked myself in the mirror and muttered to myself, "So long, gorgeous."

Inhaling deeply, I closed my eyes, called on Polly, and unlatched the door. "Farley Fairfield, as I live and breathe, what brings you down to my neck of the woods?"

The bloodshot whites of his eyes surrounding his aqua lenses all but vibrated with vexation, betraying the plastered smile on his face.

"I was worried sick about you, darling." He swept into the hall, his tea-length trench flapping like a sail as he spun through the living room arch. In a single swirl, he slipped out of his coat and slung it over the back of the ancient wing chair that once sat beside the hearth at 315 Benevolent Street. "Chilly for September *n'est-ce pas?*"

My hair, a flopping mop of wet tendrils, slapped my forehead as I rushed to push back the drapes and open the window. If I was going to die, I wanted it to be in the bright light of the sun blasted day. *Woosh! Woosh!* Sunlight washed the room in the pure white light breaking though the Chinese elms in the courtyard.

"How many mornings did I wake up here with Pete?" he said, checking my reaction.

I gave him nothing. As with Mama, I believed it would be better to starve the beast rather than tossing a crumb into its mouth, unhinged with the potential to swallow a person whole.

"Too many! Too many mornings exhausted from endless nights of dancing and debauchery. You don't know what you missed Princess."

He reeked of debauchery indeed. At ten a.m., the livid lush was lounging on my living room sofa, the overpowering smell of booze oozing from every pore of his bloated body. Evidently, he'd been on a bender.

Farley patted the sofa aggressively. "Come, Princess. Sit with your dear old friend, the Baroness."

I sat on the window seat ten feet away instead. Never too close to the mouth of a volcano.

"Have any scotch?" As brazenly as a Molly House madam, he crossed to the bar. "Jesus, Polly. Some host you are. Not even a dribble of Drambuie. Mother fuck!" He slammed the cabinet door closed and held his hand to his mouth. "Did I say that out loud?"

"What is you want, Farley? Kaiden is expecting me at the clinic," I lied. *God forgive me.*

"Such a busy girl. Such a busy life. Such a busy sow for her hunk of ham. My. My. My. I'd envy you. Honestly, I would if your situation wasn't so tragic."

Farley could be a pain in the patootie and a petulant pig at times, but I had never been afraid to be alone with him. But no matter how hard I tried, I couldn't shake the memory of those stick drawings.

Flapping his arms like the dying swan in *Swan Lake*, Farley danced across the bare floor to the fireplace. "Now." He grinned and ran his hand over Aphrodite, the Grecian goddess of love, sex, and passion, who was carved into the leg of the mantle. Somewhere along her tunic was a trick lever I hadn't known existed before, and when Farley touched it, Aphrodite sprang open to reveal a hidden chamber stocked with a silver flask, a packed bong, and a bag of weed. "Salvation!" He unscrewed the flask's cap, pressed it to his lips, and threw his head back to drink.

Without hesitation, I shot across the room to the front door. Dashing into the main corridor, I made a beeline for the elevator.

"Hey!" Farley yelled. I kept hitting the button, but the car was a slow riser.

Damn! There was no making a break for the staircase because Farley was already blocking my path. *Damn! Damn!*

"Polly!" he yelped and started toward me.

That's when I spotted the door to the roof deck. I swung the creaky metal fire door wide open and dashed up the stairs to the roof.

Unfortunately for me, Farley was a speedy sot, and he was hot on my trail. "Polly!"

I ducked behind an ivy-wrapped column of the trellised pergola. His footsteps softened, and with the wind whistling through the boxwood topiary and the dying wisteria branches tapping the colonnade, it was difficult to decipher exactly where he was.

The boards squawked a few feet away from me, and I stepped back onto the raised platform of the tanning deck. Exposed in the open air, the stiff wind swept the terrace, my hair slapping my face ridiculously and obstructing my view.

"Polly!"

I continued to back up until I felt the railing against my derriere. Quickly, I scanned the depth and breadth of the courtyard below. I gripped the railing and planted my feet firmly on the cedar planks.

"God damn, Polly!" Farley screamed into the wind beating his face. His orange hair defied its sprayed confinement, flapping, waving, snapping like a sail in a category-five hurricane. He squinted and, defying Mother Nature, lunged toward me.

Whether he'd misjudged the height of the platform or been wrapped too tightly in regal revenge to focus properly, he miscalculated. The rubber toe of his Doc Martin caught on a loose plank, and he plowed into a seven-foot topiary. The furry-bristled top of the tree snapped off in his hands when he grabbed its trunk to steady himself. Over an iron chair Farley tumbled, smacking his head on the edge of a tempered-glass coffee table. He squealed like a stuck pig as he writhed on the platform.

I leapt to his side and knelt. The door banged open, and out rushed Raymond, the doorman.

"Mr. Applegate! I saw you on the security camera. You okay?" Raymond pushed past the jack-knifed topiary. "Should I call 911?"

I shook my head. "Yes!" Raymond dashed off to perform his duty.

"Farley!" I hollered inches from his face. "Farley!"

He stopped rocking back and forth, and the hand he held to his head slid down his bloody cheek like a wounded seal.

"Farley!"

• • •

It was nearly eight p.m. before I was allowed to see him.

"A visitor, Mr. Fairfield," announced the studly Black nurse, gowned and covered from head to toe, with shoulders as broad and squared as the grill of a Rolls Royce. "He's spruced up and ready to party."

I extended my hand, and the man shook it. "Mr. Applegate, I presume." He squeezed my hand and winked. "Stubborn as the mule he rode in on." The nurse opened the door and kicked its stopper into place. "Call me if you need me." Leaning in close to Farley, he spoke in a low, deliberate tone. "I'll make the arrangements for Saint Vincent's, as you wish."

A flutter of dread flittered in my heart when he mentioned Saint Vincent's Hospital in Manhattan, because that meant one thing and one thing only. Saint Vincent's was the numero-uno hospital for HIV patients in NYC. If that was the next stop on Farley's medical train, then Farley had tested positive.

Slipping into the corridor, the nurse nodded toward the front desk, "I'll be at the nurse's station right over there if you need me." Whispering in my ear, he added, "You're cute." I blushed as he walked away. Although terribly unprofessional, I was thrilled that I could still poke the flames of desire now and again.

"Jesus Christ," Farley said, a cushioned bandage the size of Texas plastered above his right eye. "You need to bottle your pheromones and sell it at Wallis & Fitch Haden. There'd be a line around the block."

"So, what did they say?"

"How long have you been here?"

I looked at my watch. "Around . . . ten hours and fifteen minutes."

"Why?"

"I couldn't leave you alone. What if you called for me?"

Farley lay in his sterilized gown, staring at the ceiling, mesmerized by ghostly visions imperceptible by me. The foundation had been washed from his face, the eyeliner and mascara sponged off, and his hair slicked off his forehead. Farley's exposed complexion was one with the white sheets he was wrapped in.

"I . . . I came here . . . I was going to . . ." He choked on the words drowning in the spittle sputtering from between his lips like baby gibberish. Unhinged, his mouth dropped open as if he were about to scream, but only silence blasted from him. The veins in his neck pulsed and his body tensed as a flood of tears gushed from his puffy eyes, which were unaccustomed to waterworks.

In a split second, something snapped inside me, and I cried too.

I dragged a chair next to the bed, sat down, and took Farley's hand. "It's what Pollyannas do. A Pollyanna is me," I said, "and . . . a Pollyanna I am happy to be."

CHAPTER 33

NEVER WALK ALONE

The events of autumn 1987 would forever be etched into my mind. It was a time of personal farewells, public mourning, and change. Good, bad, or indifferent, change was sweeping the country. Change was difficult in the best of times, but in an era where people were sharply divided along religious, political, and scientific lines, there was little to unite the passionate contributors, waving their flags from opposite sides of the avenue. Hate and hope marched side by side. It was easy to stumble onto an unmarked battlefield, peppered with imperceptible landmines.

Death was the great equalizer. No one escaped death: not the rich and entitled, not the famous and infamous, not the devoted and devout, not the haters and destroyers, not the lovers and forgivers. Everyone had an end, a final curtain.

Major transformation sneaked in on tip-toe through the garden gate, hitching a ride on the back of a spring breeze. AIDS snuck under the door and took everyone by surprise. It was a catalyst of change few could ignore. It was not a discriminating plague, as some would have the world believe. It struck who it damn well pleased. It divided to conquer. However, it also brought throngs of people together, people who otherwise would never have found their way into the same room fighting the fight of their lives, often *for* their lives.

The day the AIDS Quilt was spread across the rolling acreage of the National Mall, oppressive grief blanketed the city. Contained within a meandering fence, the National Guard had arranged to protect the memorial. Patches, each representing a life, were laid side by side to honor the dead. Through the jack-fence corral, people from every walk of life, color, and creed were herded into the sacred space.

I worked early that day as one of many foot soldiers to put the finishing touches on the quilt. Once assembled, it stood as a tremendous memorial to a lost generation the world would never see the likes of again. Ours may not have been history's greatest generation, but it was *my* greatest generation.

As still and silent as a Vatican vault, melancholy mourners roamed the gently rolling hills of the Mall, searching desperately for the grave-sized panel that represented their loved one. Mothers, fathers, lovers, friends, and rivals fell to their knees that windswept October day. Tears streamed down their faces and spotted the panels bearing the names of sacrificial lambs who'd succumbed to a formidable foe.

"Where do we begin?" Aunt Tootie asked as we approached the first row of colorful panels.

Tootie's friend, Bev Richards, took her hand and led her to her husband's patch, stitched with shaky hands. "It's emerald-green," she said, "his favorite color."

"Poor thing," Tootie said.

"I'm not the best quilter in the world," Bev said, "but I tried to include mementos of Robert's life he'd be proud of."

Mama slid her hand into Bev's bent arm. "He was the finest minister in Rockridge. You should be proud."

Dad knelt next to his brother's patch and bowed his head. He had kept Edgar's secret for decades, protecting him from ridicule. AIDS was the one thing he could not protect his brother from.

In the distance, Farley was hand-stitching the finishing touches on Pete's rectangle. Evangeline and I broke away from Aunt Tootie and Bev to join him. Ivory silk lilies-of-the-valley on an indigo velvet panel, Evangeline and I dutifully sewed for our friend.

"This is Arabella," Farley said as we approached, and gestured to the beautiful ginger-haired woman sitting beside him in tears.

"Oh, August." Arabella hugged me. "I've so longed to meet you." Beside her, a stunning seven-year-old blond boy handed Farley a spray of ivory lilies. "This is my son," she said, dabbing her wet cheek with a linen hanky. I saw Pete's monogram stitched on the edge. "This is Peter August Pakington Pace."

I stood speechless, stunned by the tribute from my friend, teacher, and the first love of my life. Our names and our history were woven together in the name of Pete's little love and Arabella's beautiful boy, who'd march our combined legacy into the future. He wasn't the spitting image of his father as I had expected. His features were fine and delicate like his mother's. Unlike Pete, he would likely never sprout to six-foot-four. However, his stance, those piercing, perceptive peepers, and a smile that could charm the heat out of the Bayou—those were all pure Pete.

Peter extended his hand, as good gentlemen do, and I shook it gently, his warm palm pressed into mine. "A pleasure to meet you, Mr. Applegate," he said.

"The pleasure's all mine."

I wasn't certain why I did what I did next, except that I was running on instinct and not logic. I took Arabella's hand, and she squeezed mine as if she was holding on for dear life. Farley held my other hand, and Evangeline connected Peter to his mother. The wind swept through the crowd, sweetly singing silence, and the clouds parted momentarily to bathe the panels in gracious clarity. No one moved. No one breathed. No one spoke. We wept.

Linked together, Farley, Evangeline, Arabella, and me wept as Peter knelt on his father's rectangle and fed the last spray of lilies into the boutonniere.

After a few long minutes, I had to take a walk. I wandered around, looking at the colorful patches of life on the quilt, wondering about the people they'd been made to honor. Eventually, my family found me again.

Mama had never been one for tears, but that day, she was a dripping spicket. "Oh, Augie," she said, her voice as flat and lifeless as when she'd called to tell me that Aunt Jessica had passed away. "We're walking through purgatory." She hugged me tightly, and I leaned my head against hers.

Tootie tapped me on the shoulder and nodded toward a woman I recognized after a moment as one of my childhood bullies. My knees nearly buckled at the sight of Mrs. Fry, who had tried her damnedest to not sell me my first Barbie in her dilapidated toy store in Rockridge. Weeping and wailing, she fell onto her son's patch.

"She suffered mighty hard," Tootie whispered in my ear. "She loved her boy more than anything in the world. Folks thought our little town was safe from a city disease." She cleared her throat. "There's still rest stops on the interstate."

When Mrs. Fry saw me, she wrapped her arms around me. "Oh, August, my boy . . . my boy . . . he's gone."

"He was Chester Chad's lover," Mama said as Mr. Fry escorted her into the mass lingering in limbo. "They say it's just a matter of time for him now."

"You know, Dad," I said as we walked a step behind the others, "it was the dead who helped me live again."

"Bravery is tested in dire times," Dad said. "This is your war, Augie." Tears trickled down his cheeks, and I embraced him.

"I wonder how many fathers built how many playhouses for their sons," I said.

The conversion of the crowd ballooned as mourners filed through the security line into the sacred area. Dad raised his hand slightly when he saw Kaiden approaching.

"Mr. Applegate." Kaiden shook Dad's hand.

"Nice of you to volunteer as a guide for so many bereaved loved ones." Dad stepped aside when Kaiden took my hand. As small a gesture as it might have seemed to a passing stranger, my holding hands with a man before anyone in my family was a momentous moment for me. Dad smiled, disarming my last ounce of reserve.

In the distance, in plain view, the White House sat empty, its occupants having escaped to the pleasurable view afforded by Camp David in Maryland. No half-mast flag flapped from the pole atop the People's House.

As I crossed the puzzle of patches, holding Kaiden's hand, I thought of Pete. Though Rupert and Aunt Jessica hadn't died from an AIDS-related disease, I wished they were represented there among so many celebrated souls.

"I wish I'd known them all," I said to Kaiden. He was crying.

There was a reception at the Willard Hotel following the unveiling of the quilt. The director of the Whitman-Walker Clinic rushed over to ask me to say a few words about my time in the volunteer program. I hadn't planned a speech because I had been asked at the last minute to fill in for Chancy, who'd been rushed to GW's ER in the middle of the night when he struggled to breathe.

Of course, he also had HIV now. I wished I'd had time to write something, but that was life. Stand and deliver I did.

Evangeline introduced me. "Allow me to introduce you to Mr. August Applegate, a proud member of the silenced minority of people marching for our beliefs."

I stood on the small stage of the ballroom. The room was packed with political agitators and mourners from all over the country, some from the far reaches of the world.

As I stood before the bereaved audience, the front-line minorities struggling to be heard above the pandemonium of objection that had drowned out our voices too many times before, it dawned on me that it was time now to raise my voice. I took a deep breath and stepped to the microphone.

"I didn't stop to think if we were making history," I started. "Inspired by events around me, I rolled up my sleeves and carried on. Together, we fought the good fight. Why? To be noticed. We longed for our place at the table. We craved acceptance. No longer content to be 'the other ones,' we shouted loud and clear at marches in New York and DC, 'We are here, and we are queer!'

"What was running through my mind every time we unfurled the rainbow flag? I had a job to do. We matter greatly to one another. There is strength in numbers, and we gathered by the thousands, the millions, from every nook and cranny of our country . . . *our* country!

"As one of many volunteers, I reverently smoothed out patches of the AIDS Quilt over the rolling acreage of the National Mall today. This prayer, overwhelmingly visible from the White House and the Capitol, has been overlooked by many.

"Just beyond the White House fence today, I saw inconsolable parents, lovers, and friends fall to their knees with tears streaming down their cheeks. Mr. Reagan! Please! Walk this quilt with the mother who just buried her twenty-five-year-old son. Have you not the time to console a broken-hearted partner who lost the love of his life and his best friend? These patches are gestures of love, stitched with trembling hands, in remembrance of those taken too soon . . . gobbled up by unimaginable ugliness. Will Mr. Reagan offer kind words of sympathy, a speck of hope, an empathetic ear? The president is never home when we come knocking.

"There was little time to think of history as I rushed from work to volunteer at the Whitman-Walker Aids Clinic on 14th Street. Someone needed me. I needed to be needed.

"At Capitol Hill Hospital, gray, convulsing crack babies are left to die in isolated incubators. Even nurses are afraid 'it' is contagious," I said, making air quotes with my fingers, "and refuse to touch the infants. So, we gay men, covered from head to toe, volunteer to hold them. Yes. Death is inevitable, but doesn't every living, breathing creature deserve to feel the tender human touch of another before they die?

"We raised our voices against the haters of our generation, the anti-gay, self-righteous Anita Bryants and Jerry Falwells preaching homophobic rhetoric from the pulpit. This plague was sent from the Almighty himself! We were getting what we deserved. It's difficult to find God in the holy houses they walk in.

"We risk being beaten, arrested. I know people beaten beyond repair. I stood in a pool of blood on P Street, the aftermath of a knifing. Three beautiful young men had their throats slit by rednecks hell-bent on revenge. Revenge for what?

"We are the countless agitators marching, waging war on prejudice and bigotry. We yelled and will continue to yell until we're too hoarse to be heard. We've marched our boot heels flat. We've never asked for marble monuments to honor our victories, minute and great. We've sung too many funeral hymns, cried too many tears to ever turn back to our life before . . . before our enlightenment. We long for the same remarkable unremarkable life promised to all citizens of the United States of America.

"Harry Truman said that when one sits behind the president's desk, that person has the obligation to set aside his personal prejudice and rise to the occasion as a leader to all. Abraham Lincoln was quoted as saying, 'You cannot escape the responsibility of tomorrow by evading it today.' Why is this lesson so difficult to learn and retain? We never asked for special privileges. However, we demand the equal rights promised in our Constitution.

"Without our bullhorns, our banners, our flags, where would we be? Our struggle is worth the pain. Please don't forget the ones who are no longer here. Some of us are still standing. By the thousands, by the millions, from across the globe, we rallied, marched, and cried out for freedom. Guard our victories and never, never, never allow your victories to die at the hands of tyrants. We warriors are tired. Look at our scars. Read our tombstones. Study your history. Our time is now. We must be brave. Listen, learn, march, and remember our loved ones gone too soon."

I bowed my head and wept as the audience rose to their feet. Everyone stood quietly for a few minutes. The silence, salted with sniffles and snuffles, soon broke into applause, not for me, but for the loved ones lost, our sacred specters serenading us from the starry sky.

•●•

That night, we gathered at my place. We used sawhorses and an old door as a table, which we set up in the living room by a crackling fire. It was a potluck, so each of us brought a favorite dish of ours or a deceased loved one.

"You are a marvel," Kaiden said as we gathered silverware to set the table. "I'm the luckiest man in the world."

I wrapped my arm around him and studied his sparkling eyes. He was eager to live, perhaps for the first time in his life. That spark was contagious, and I willingly leapt into the flame with him. He wasn't Rupert. He wasn't Pete. He was far from perfect, but he was real, an organic, evolving being shaking the shackles of the past off and diving into the deep end with me. "I—" I kissed him. "I love you."

The dining room door's drapes parted. "Mommy sent me to help," Peter said, his silky, blond shock of hair dangling over one eye. I went to hand him the slatted wooden box that housed Mama's best silverware. "Wow," he said noticing my cufflinks. "They're beautiful."

I set the box down and popped one off to show him the back. "See? The inscription says, 'You are the sun.'"

"'And the moon and the stars,'" he finished. "Like Peter Pan."

"Here." I held out the box of silverware. "Can you set the table please?"

Smiling, he accepted the box and headed for the dining room. I followed with a stack of Grandma Flora's friendly village plates.

Gathered around that makeshift table draped in one of Aunt Tootie's hand-sewn quilted tablecloths, we joked, we laughed, and we wept uncontrollably, remembering the finest and gravest epi-sodes of our shared past.

Farley poked his head into the kitchen as I was arranging a tray of sweets for dessert. On the verge of tears, he asked softly, "Can you ever forgive me?"

I stared into his watery eyes and froze. A sharp pain speared the melancholia as the many episodes of our life together flashed in my head. Flawed and often fretful, our lives were linked. There was no denying the turmoil he'd unleashed on me over the years, but I needed to forgive him. I wished to start again. I wanted to love him. "Oh Farley, I was about to walk away from you, never phone you again—but then you did what you've always done."

He winced.

"You wrangled the devil out of me."

"I was awful."

"Awful? Absolutely. But . . . well." I added a few choco-late-dipped strawberries to the display, then popped one in Farley's mouth. "Without you, I'd never truly appreciate the Pollyanna I am."

"Damn. These are good." Farley swallowed the remainder of the strawberry. "I've got the plague. Oh Polly . . ."

"And I'm here for you."

He laid his head atop mine, and I felt the warm, wet droplets of his tears drip onto my ear. We stood that way for just another moment before we finally broke apart and returned to the meal, dessert in hand.

"August," Arabella said from the far end of the table. "Won't you sing? Pete said you have the most beautiful voice."

"Not today," I said. I'd been through more than enough for one day, and I wasn't sure I could hold a note without my voice cracking. "Some other time."

"There is no better time. All of us here in his old home. I feel him here. Sing one last time for Pete." She took her son's hand, and they sat together where his father had sat so many times before, on the piano bench. Although I didn't play piano, I was grateful that Pete had specified in his will that it was a gift to me.

I'd sat there often, soaking up the magic he'd once filled the silence with as his long fingers effortlessly danced across the keys. His soul was imprinted in the piano's lacquer and his heart in its mechanics, and as long as it sat in my living room, he'd always be with me.

"Do you know 'Where Is Love' from *Oliver*?" Peter asked.

"I do." I crossed to the piano, wondering if Arabella knew that was the very first song I'd sung to our Pete as he tickled the ivories. She struck the intro chord, and Peter joined her.

"'Where is love? Does it fall from skies above?'" I sang. "'Is it underneath the willow tree that I've been dreaming of? Where is love?'"

THE END

ACKNOWLEDMENTS FOR *POLLYANNA GAY*

Though not always aware of my blessings, I am grateful for the many and the few, the old and the new, the inspirational and the challenging characters who have touched, brushed past, and lingered in my life, splashing splendor on an otherwise dull routine.

For his love and encouragement, I thank my husband, Eddy, whose gentle prodding lit a literary fire in my belly.

The support I received from Lori Mirabelli (who encouraged my short story scratches) and Susan Hankla (who freed the caged poet tangled in my uncertainty) are gifts I forever treasure.

Baring my truth at Valley Haggard's sacred table at Life in Ten Minutes ushered in a revolutionary realignment to my passion for writing. Her nurturing hugs were life-support on steroids.

Amy Ritchie Johnson opened my mind to possibilities unimaginable to me. I am appreciative for the courage she instilled in this reluctant soldier to dream beyond the short story. In her class, August Applegate, who started as a line drawing in my sketchbook, blossomed into a fully formed being.

I bow humbly before the sensational seven (Mary Jo McLaughlin, Gary Durnan, Cathy Smith, Rosie Messer, Maddy McCoy, Bronwyn Hughes, and Heather Rutherford) who weathered the stormy seas of storytelling with me. Faithfully, they read each chapter, born weekly, of my manuscript. Their sincere suggestions and crucial inquiries kept me on my toes. Their loyalty I shall cherish always. A rare and beautiful contribution, their support rescued me from debilitating doubt.

Lastly, I want to thank Haley Simpkiss and Christina Kann of Brandylane Publishers/Belle Isle Books for their invaluable knowledge and expert advice concerning this piece of historical fiction. Pushing from behind, these literary mechanics helped me fine-tune the music in my head into an anthem of promise.

ABOUT THE AUTHOR

Jer Long is a devoted worshiper of the written word. Comforted by his grandmother's soothing baritone as she recited verse and fairytales to him, he became obsessed with "story time" as a boy. As a young man, the intriguing dialogue of famous playwrights and the inspiring lyrics of clever songwriters lured him onto the stage as a performer. Backstage captured his artistic imagination as well, and ultimately led him to rewarding experiences as a costume designer, a makeup artist, and a hair stylist.

Later in life, having suffered from loss of speech while battling Lyme Disease, he struggled to complete a coherent sentence until he bucked up the courage to enroll in a writing class. Forcing himself to read aloud the words he had written finally lifted the curse. Smitten with the art of language, he now writes daily.

Retired from a lengthy career as a visual director in upscale retail, Jer currently resides in Pennsylvania with his husband, Ed, and their dog, Lucy Honeychurch.

"Keep your face always toward the sunshine and
the shadows will fall behind."
—Walt Whitman

Milton Keynes UK
Ingram Content Group UK Ltd.
UKHW012044071223
433957UK00004B/210